WALK WITH PERIL

WALK
WITH PERIL

D. V. S. JACKSON

G. P. PUTNAM'S SONS
NEW YORK

To

VERNON LOGGINS

Who Read It First Of All

WALK WITH PERIL

Chapter 1

THE BOWMAN hissed a warning, and the merchant Lewis Chapelle swung sharply around to the danger, hand to sword, squinting against the driving rain.

The bowman said, "One horse, Your Worship."

Chapelle listened to the suck of hooves in mud around the bend of the road. One rider, but it could be a trap to reassure them, with others lurking behind. The roads were infested with robbers this June of 1415, and here his party was dismounted and in trouble with broken horse gear. The merchant set his heavy jaw, and his black beard jutted forward over the magnificent belly and wet purple gown. There was but him, the bowman, Paul the stableboy, and his daughter. That was the worry now. His daughter, standing in the green weeds holding her restive gray barbary studhorse.

Now came a whistling from the unseen rider. A carefree knave. The merchant nodded to the bowman, who put a shaft to his ready bow. Paul straightened from where he worked at a strap under a horse belly. The merchant glared, and Paul bent again, to hurry his repair.

The merchant watched the place where the road bent in a forest of dripping bushes.

A horse head in sight. A horse breast. And a rider now, muffled in a sodden green cloak. The rider saw them. His hand snapped first to his sword; then he pulled up his horse. All poised together in the moment of discovery. Chapelle felt the rider's eyes flick over them from the shadow of the enveloping mantle hood. Then the ominous, muffled figure relaxed. The hand came from the sword to saddlebow.

9

The horse moved slowly forward. The hand went up to push away the hood.

He was young and he was handsome, with blue eyes that looked everywhere for ambush, under a fringe of blond hair plastered to his forehead by the rain. He halted again, in the road, by them.

"Sir," he said, addressing the merchant in English that sang of Wales, "I would have of you only the way to London."

"Begone," Chapelle said.

"Ah, Father," came his daughter's voice. Chapelle did not have to turn to know how she would look to a stranger. Her hair was black, her eyes were brown, and her tones all honied gold. "It is not lack of manners that makes us hostile, sir," she was saying, "but rather lack of escort. We missed our party and my father fears for me with but two bowmen by."

"I will not have you speak with strangers, Constance," the merchant said.

"He's no thief, Father, unless it be of hearts! Look at his blue eyes! There's honesty."

"I do not look at eyes," the merchant said, "but at a sword hilt mightily worn, while I think that no man rides these roads alone."

"I do," the blond stranger said.

"Then you are a fool, a knave or a very brave man."

"As to the way for London," Constance said hastily, "that is our way. Would you join us?"

"Constance!" her father said.

"This is my father," she said, turning winsome, "the great wool merchant Lewis Chapelle, an Alderman of London."

"Robert Fairfield," the stranger said, bowing from the saddle, and gracefully too, for all he was encased in wet green wool below the neck. "My father is a vassal of the king."

"We are surfeit with sons of vassals of the king," the merchant said. "They make the roads unsafe with robbing. Yet . . ." His glance swept from tight yellow-and-green striped hose showing below the mantle hem, to the fringe of flaxen hair above. He thought of the muddy bog of a road again, and considered the robbers all the way. "Yet, if you will travel with us, welcome. If you will not, get you gone! Constance, on your horse, or the flat of my hand will send you there.

Paul? Fixed at last? You had time enough to build a church. Into the road, ride ahead. Arthur, to the rear, behind us."

The girl clambered on her palfrey, under her father's glare, but took time enough to fuss prettily over the drape of her scarlet skirts, for she rode cross saddle in the good English style, nor aped the new foreign custom of riding all on one side like an ill-roped pack on a sumpter horse.

The merchant mounted his own horse, impatient at this play, and as his daughter passed gave her gray stallion a whack on the rump that sent the animal squealing with rage to the road, splashing mud high on her gown, so that Constance squealed in tune with her horse. Then demurely, she took her place in the middle beside the stranger, with her eyes downcast in maiden modesty, while the merchant came to her other side and closed the circle around her.

They rode in silence for a while, till the merchant's anger evaporated in the rain and discomfort. The maid was flirtatious as yet, but she'd be safely married soon. Ah well, he thought, turning tolerant, she was his only child, and all in the world that he valued, though he had ships and houses, land and gold piled by. This was but for an afternoon, and a fourth man added strength. He noted narrowly how this Robert watched before and behind and to both sides, alert enough for ten. Such a man had learned to be so, for he must.

At length Robert Fairfield looked his way and their eyes met.

"Is there news of the war?" Robert asked politely.

"Another target for the French king's lances?" the merchant inquired.

"I'm a squire who would be a knight," Robert said. "Yet if I would wear gold spurs, I must earn them in France."

"Fight the Lombards instead, if it's loot you're after," the merchant advised. "They undersell me on the continent, and it were a work of mercy to destroy them. I would King Hal let my French markets be!"

Robert Fairfield turned his face away to watch some bushes, and what he thought could not be guessed. Unless, of course, he was only a handsome fool, and there was nothing to be shown.

"You must admit," the merchant said, trying to draw him out, "that a Saxon face with a Welsh accent is strange enough to meet on any road."

"My mother was Welsh," Robert said, "and I was raised in Wales by her cousin."

"A choice background," the merchant said. "Nourished among rocks, rebellion and heresy."

Constance cut in swiftly. "My father dotes on teasing, sir."

"I've had much of it," Robert said, unexpectedly.

A difficult man to provoke, the merchant decided, for he always tried to heat a man's temper to let the truth steam out.

"You have the bluest eyes I ever saw on any man," Constance said. "Tell me, do they name you for them?"

"I was called Blue-Eyed Rob," he admitted.

"By your mother?"

"My mother died when I was born."

"A sadness," she said, with honest sympathy. "My mother is also dead. Your wife. Of course. It's your wife who calls you so."

"I have no wife," he said.

"Ah," she said.

The merchant interrupted now.

"The sun out at last," he announced, "and the world growing hotter." He pulled at the close neck of his paltock.

"I agree," Robert Fairfield said, and unfastened his wet mantle. From a corner of his eye, the merchant saw green slide back to his nag's rump, but his daughter was between them, and he could see no more. But he heard a tinkling sound.

"Bells!" his daughter exclaimed. "Look, Father, look! Folly bells! How glad they sound at freedom!"

The merchant leaned forward to stare at the Welshman's waist. He wore a leather belt. There were tiny gold chains dangling from it, each entangling a multitude of small gold bells that jingled to his horse's jog, free of the clogging mantle.

"Before God!" the merchant exclaimed. "In my day a sword was ornament enough for any man!"

"I take jesting at them ill," the Welshman said, and his tone was suddenly cold. And dangerous.

The merchant studied his face, but saw nothing. Only the tone gave a warning.

"So your sword hilt's smooth," he guessed.

"The Welshmen would not leave off laughing."

"And you would not leave off your bells." The merchant nodded, satisfied. "So was I when I was young. No man could force me."

Silence again, as the horses struggled through the mud. The merchant watched Robert, and watching, saw his daughter's head turn too often that way also.

He began to talk to distract her. They discussed sheep in pastures, cargoes for ships, taxes, and the countinghouse in Calais, for he was training her in his business, having no other child. They talked so often, and in such moments were close-knit, like two sides of a coin, so the one must go with the other, though both were different too.

Yet even when he grew choleric over the cost of canvas for packing fells, he remembered to glance at the stranger. He was rewarded only once by a glimpse of a fleeting expression, gone the instant that he saw it.

It puzzled the merchant greatly. This Robert seemed a man who liked to ride alone and needed no one. Could it be possible he was otherwise? Could it be possible that he was lonely?

Chapter 2

CONSTANCE watched him covertly all that afternoon, stealing glances while her father talked of business. He was handsome and that pleased her, which was strange, for she'd distrusted the handsome before this. He was blond, and that pleased; though she had never liked pale hair. She had scoffed at dandies in tight clothes and gauds; but his tight green-and-yellow striped hose were gay. His green wool cote-hardie could not be shorter; it was scarce to his hips, and strained to contain his chest and shoulders. The fur that rimmed the low neck and long flowing sleeves was cony. *Rabbit,* she thought, and was touched by its plainness. This Robert liked to be fashionable then, but lacked money to follow the frisky path.

And those folly bells, in Wales. Well enough in a great city, where young nobles fancied them, but in Wales! She could guess the sly grins and dainty gestures with which they had provoked him. But he'd not retired in confusion, or flung curses. He'd fought. One by one, he'd fought till they ceased laughing. Boldness set well on a man. It made her breathe faster, and falter in replies to her father.

The bells were pure gold. She knew true metal when she saw it. His clothes were common wool, his sword hilt plain; his nag a poor thing, but the useless folly bells were gold. He was all paradox, a fighter who wore bells!

He had a gentle mouth. It smiled at birds and chirruped to a squirrel that scolded from a branch. But he did not seek to talk to her, as the other young men did, so it pleased her to toss her head and talk of fortune seekers. What would his kisses be like?

And not married? He'd be almost twenty, surely, if he sought knighthood now. Why not married, then? Any girl would overlook his poverty for the sake of the smile he had thrown to a doe with a fawn that crossed their path. She thought of the gross old husbands of her girlhood friends and almost shuddered. Let her die before such a one touched her! But this Robert, there was another matter. He had fine hands, and wore one ring, a seal, on the thumb of his left hand.

She thought she could judge a man quickly. She had handled the household since she was fourteen. Three years of dealing with kitchen boys, cooks, stablehands and the sailors from her father's ships. It was often enough she went off to the sheriff to get these last released in time to make the tide when the *Jesu* sailed for Calais. She knew she was a legend in Thames Street for the times she had paraded down it with sheepish lurching sailors staggering after her like goslings after their dam.

But this man was different. Always before, men talked of their prowess and boasted to impress her. This one watched the road, as if she was not there. Who called him Blue-Eyed Rob?

Why must she marry the old man? She'd heard of old men's habits from her friends, married too tender to ancients; touching and pinching and prying, and not much else. She would marry the old man with repugnance, yet it was her father's will, and the match was long since made. She consoled herself daily with the thought that old men die; and it would not be forever till she was a widow.

Did this Robert Fairfield truly not notice her at all? They said that blond men had no fire. They made good priests, listening to hot confessions with icy disapproval and no more.

Why must she marry the old man? Suddenly she was angry with it, though she'd consented and knew she must. She tossed her head abruptly, and announced in the middle of her father's sentence that she was tired and would not ride another step today.

Her father looked at her, astonished, seeing no reason for this gust of temper. "Females!" he exclaimed, and raised his eyes to heaven.

But he sent Paul galloping instantly forward to make arrangements for dinner and a place to sleep.

The landlord led them up a flight of stairs to a room strewn all over with straw.

"The stairs squeak," she complained, determined to plague her father.

"Well enough," Robert Fairfield said. "They'll cry out if a strange foot touch them."

Always watchful, she thought, resentful he thought of all but her. What a barbarous country, this Wales, if a man must look to his life every moment.

The landlord hung the lantern on a hook in the wall and departed. The bowmen dropped like tired animals and were asleep in one moment and snoring in another. Her father set about kicking together a soft pile of straw. Robert Fairfield put down his saddlebags between a window and the stairhead and set his shield against a wall. It was the first time she saw it well. It was green in tincture, giving the appearance of a green field, a fair field, a Fairfield. A red chief with three gold molets differenced it to identify a son of the house, but under this was emblazoned a golden lion, sleeping, yet armed with bloody claws to show he had not always slept. Beneath the beast was a motto on a painted scroll; Wake me no man, it proclaimed.

The merchant blew out the lantern with a huff and left them all in darkness. But a jingle of bells told Constance that Robert had gone to the window, and she saw he had pushed the covering hide away, for there was starlight and the angle of his shoulder as he looked out.

"Is there someone below?" she inquired.

"I'll watch a while," he said.

"No one will steal the horses. My King-at-Arms is high-tempered. He'd rouse the county."

"I'll watch a while," he said.

Stubborn, she thought. Could a woman rule him? She moved a little closer, almost fearful. "Those men below, by the fire," she said softly. "They spoke of you when we supped. One pointed you out, and called you Robert Heartless."

"It's a name I was called," he said. His silhouette against the starlight never moved.

"It is such a name," she said, "as is given to a murderous man."

"I've fought enough, my lady," he said, "but fairly."

"Have you considered, Constance," came her father's voice from darkness, "that this could have another meaning? Have you considered he grew tall and blond in a land of short, dark men, and the maids would look twice over?"

"Then," she ventured, "you'd cast true love aside?"

"Sir," the merchant said, "you must forgive her. She asks too many questions. Constance, get to sleep!"

In the same moment, Robert dropped the hide before the window, and nothing could be seen. She sat down in the straw, back to the wall, to think. The bowmen snored lustily, and from below came the sounds of reveling, drunken men. It was noisy enough but she heard the jingle of small gold bells. He was sleeping by the window, to hear if horses fussed in the night, or anyone came up the stair.

"If the Welshmen called you Robert Heartless," she said, "who called you Blue-Eyed Rob?"

"Enough!" her father shouted.

Blue-Eyed Rob. A woman, who thought so lightly of him as to let him wander off. He might be killed in France. Some French slut robbing the dead would find him, and weep for his bonnie face. Tears came to her own eyes.

"Robert Fairfield," she said, in a pitiful voice, "I did not mean to anger you with prying."

Her father burst out in a rage. "In the name of the Most Holy Saints!" he bellowed. "Will you let us sleep?" He thrashed in the straw, and snorted anger.

The bowmen snored on. The drunken men shouted below. An owl hooted in the woods. Then, across the room, the small bells jingled.

Her voice was like a conspirator's. "Robert Fairfield? I am very fearful on these dangerous roads. Would you come with us all the way?"

"If you wish it, my lady," he said.

Her father breathed heavily. She dared not goad him further. And besides, she had won her point. If Robert made the trip to London, then her father must invite him to stay in their home. It was common courtesy, expected of all. Hospitality must be offered; and when offered, it must be accepted.

She had never tricked her father so before; and she did not know why she did it now. This Robin was a wanderer, not for her. But thinking of him made her wakeful. Being wakeful, she caught one glimpse behind the mask he wore by daylight. Robin Fairfield tossed and turned all night; his bells proclaimed it. He murmured, too.

He was a dreamer, and his dreams were bad.

Chapter 3

ROBERT emerged from his chamber on the gallery and looked over the rail to the merchant's great hall below. Deep shadows hid the most part, but where the marble fireplace crackled in the forepart, light reached around the outlines of a gross man who watched the flames. Beside him was another shadow, slim as an eel, a white greyhound sitting on delicate haunches.

It was a splendid house, Robert thought, admiring the arched and pointed windows that ran down the left side of the hall, before him now, to fling pointed moonlight over the pale parquet through panes of expensive glass. The room was paneled in oak, and hung with tapestries where possible. Opposite the windows were the stairs to the upper story, with the gallery where Robert stood. There was yet another flight of stairs at the end of this, leading to a third story. Robert wondered, even now, what lay above.

They seemed well enough here, and yet he was very restless. It was more than being hemmed in by forty thousand people in this congested metropolis. There was danger here. He felt it like a chill.

And so he had looked about every step he took, seeking exits and boltholes and where a lone man might make a stand, for so he had remained alive in Wales. He'd learned to trust the sense that had neither eyes, nor ears, nor nose.

He watched a while, and memorized the house. Chambers at the foot of this stair, and that the door to the street, set one step up from the cobbles so they'd not run with mud when it rained. More doors at the back, to kitchens.

Then, very quietly, for he'd left his gold bells behind on the bed, he went down the wooden stairs on the soft leather soles of his fresh-changed hose.

It was the dog who heard him. She turned her slim white head. The merchant saw her action and revolved, pulling up his dark blue gown so his hairy legs showed as he took warmth behind.

"God's blood!" he exclaimed, as Robert came into the firelight, wearing tawny and brown counterchanged.

The merchant gave careful attention to the orange-clad leg, and then to the brown leg; to the low neck cut to show the high white collar of his linen paltock beneath his cote-hardie; to the brown sleeve and the orange sleeve, each sweeping the floor and slit from wrist to elbow so the white linen paltock sleeves showed, tight down his fore-arm and fastened with myriad buttons.

"Every hen in this household," the merchant pronounced, "will cackle after this rooster. Blaunchette, you've a rival for their petting."

The hound stood languidly as her name was spoken. She wore a collar of red silk, with a white pearl dangling. Robert made a coaxing sound. The hound wagged gravely to acknowledge him, no more.

"She has but one master," came Constance's voice from another part of the shadowy hall. "She is a true member of her sex."

The merchant laughed coarsely.

Constance came into the half-circle of red-and-amber firelight, tossing her head. She wore an azure gown now, of silk, with fleur-de-lis worked on it in gold so each floweret sparkled as she bent to pet the dog. Her hair was loose, floating like black silk. Robert intertwined his fingers behind his back, to keep from touching it. He knew his face would not betray him when he did not wish it to.

"And what is there to eat?" the merchant asked.

"Venison, eels, black pudding, a pastry, beer. It's meager, but remember, we were not expected. Save for Robin, we could not have ridden so late with robbers thicker than fleas."

"With the eels?" the merchant inquired.

"A pungent sauce, such as you love." Constance clapped her hands smartly. "Johannis!"

And instantly, there was turbulence. Kitchen boys came racing from a door at the rear of the hall, laden with planks and trestles. They set up a table by the fireplace with wild activity, falling over one another in their haste, while Robert made a silent note that this house was strongly built, with such thick walls it could hide the presence of many. Maids came next, skirts flying, to fling three thicknesses of fine linen over the boards, to set gleaming silver spoons and cups, and candelabra burning beeswax candles. Constance lit these prettily, and the smell of warm wax was added to burning wood, an odor of hospitality.

Now came boys with round truncheons of bread, sliced in two through the middle to form plates. These were set at each place, crust side down, so the sauces might drip on the soft part and be eaten later as a sop if it pleased the diner to do so. Chairs were dragged up triumphantly. And all was ready.

Four chairs? The answer came with the puzzle. Another woman from the kitchen, red-faced with overseeing a cook angered by haste and unexpected diners, leading a parade of boys with silver serving plates.

"Dame Margaret," Constance said with affection and started to her, to take the woman by the hand and lead her forward. "Aunt, this is our Robert of the road."

The woman was small, fat and homely, with a faint mustache clear across her upper lip; but there was a twinkle in her eye. She'd looked after the young men in her day, Robert thought. With sudden mischief, he swept her an extravagant bow.

"Ha!" Dame Margaret boomed. "A lady-pleaser!"

She shook her finger in mock disapproval, and spoiled it all by laughing and stating she would lock up the maids after supping.

They sat down to table, and in silence did justice to the full repast. At the end, the merchant wiped his greasy mouth on the end of the linen cloth topmost, and sighed, replete.

"Your husband will bless you for the meals you'll serve," he said to his daughter, "and I will miss you sore."

"I will not wed him," Constance said.

The merchant put his hand lazily to his beard; then stopped, astonished, as he realized what she had said.

"And why not?" he inquired.

"I will not," she said, and put out her chin, determined.

"You were obedient enough when the match was made," her father said.

"I will not have a grandsire to husband," she told him.

"He'll die the sooner," her father said, to reassure her.

"He has hairs in his nose," she objected.

The merchant put both hands on the table, annoyed at this nonsense.

"You are seventeen years old," he stated bluntly for any to hear. "It's time you were married, well past it. All your friends have bounced two babies on their knees."

"And buried them also," she reminded.

"An old man will give you all your way," he coaxed, turning wily. "Ha! Do you?"

He scowled. "I am your father, and when I command, it's not for you to question me. We jumped for a word when I was a boy, or got a beating, and all the better for it!"

Dame Margaret squirmed warningly in her chair, and Constance turned the subject abruptly.

"We had a letter from Calais," she said. "Wat brought it to me in the kitchen, and I thought to wait till you had fed. *Holy Mary* was chased of a pirate and is fled into Ostend."

"Her cargo!" the merchant demanded, diverted.

"Overboard," Constance said.

The merchant slammed both fists down so hard on the table that the beer overleaped the cups and stained the cloth.

"Where's my cargo list?" he yelled.

Constance called out, "Wat!"

Out of the darkness near the kitchen came a man, thick-chested, thick-thighed, and built for strength but never beauty. His black hair was unkempt and greasy. Three days' beard was on his chin. His eyes were black glints, set deep and close together on either side of a high hooked nose. His face was narrow and cruel and alert as well. His leather jacket was all food-stained. His leather hose hung in wrinkles down his legs, and his heavy boots were marked with dung. He smelt of low taverns and the stable, and did not belong in an honest house. Yet Constance took papers from his very hand; though her father snatched them from her instantly, pulled candles closer and pored over his losses with exclamations and curses. The dog Blaunchette leaped lightly to the table and walked the length of it, sampling daintily at dishes with her clean pink tongue.

Robert watched the knave called Wat fade again into a shadow. He had not come from the kitchen, nor had he gone to it; but a corner. He had been watching them all the while.

"We have a countinghouse in Calais," Constance was saying to Robert, as his attention returned to her. "Our ships go between that port and this on a schedule. The channel's full of pirates and it seems they wait for the Calais trade. That cargo is a sore loss."

Robert knew vaguely that Calais was a seaport in France; that it belonged to England by conquest, and that the French slavered to seize it back.

"It will be different," he consoled her, "when King Henry holds all France. There'll be no ports in the north for French pirates then."

The merchant looked up, staring under Blaunchette's tucked-up belly.

"King Henry will never hold all France," he said, "though he fight a dozen wars."

And that was treason. Were they spies here?

A door clicked somewhere. Robert had his back to the chamber doors, but he was sure the noise had come from there. Also, the merchant had glanced up and away. Robert sipped languidly at his beer, lounging. He'd been schooled in Wales, where betrayal supped at every table while men laughed together, and no one knew what his neighbor planned.

Now the merchant flung down his list, yawned and stood.

"To bed for all!" he announced. "Clean sleeping and soft. We'll not be stabled on straw in my house! Johannis!"

Robert set the candle on a chest in his chamber. The fire yet burned in his grate, warming the damp creeping in from the river and reflecting on the red hangings of the great carved bed. A chamber for one man alone. Here's luxury. They'd slept in twenties in the castle.

Oh, this was a great, expensive house, but it seethed! Robert moved to one of the windows and looked through real glass panes to the court. Two torches wavered there, in brackets, one below by the kitchen, the other at the stone lintel of the stable across the yard. The feeble light showed the inner part of the wall that kept their court-yard closed from Thames Street, the face of the stable with a dove-cote on it, and a cote for pigeons also. Pigeons for swift messages. The third part to bound the yard was at the far left, stone steps shrouded with darkness, leading to the water of the river Thames. A thin fog was drifting in. Then a motion below caught Robert's eyes. He waited, patiently, and finally out of a deeper shadow walked a ponderous mastiff, sniffing the air. It was to be expected. Such wealth as was displayed so openly here must be protected. Yet Robert felt suddenly pent. Then he shrugged. If he would go out from any place, neither man nor beast could hold him. He turned from the window, got his candle again, and picked up the nightgown laid at the foot of the bed. It was of red silk, broidered at hem and sleeves, soft to the touch. He'd lie down in it gladly.

He went out onto the gallery again with its carved rail, glancing over it to the empty hall below as he made his way to the stewroom. He saw no one the length of the gallery. He glanced again, by habit, without turning his head, up the flight of narrow enclosed stairs that led like a silent black tunnel to the floor above. He did not hesitate a step, to show his interest, for there was an alarm in him like a trumpet, announcing a reason for caution. The hall below was empty, but he knew that he was watched.

The stewroom was warm, with fine beeswax candles burning mer-rily and expensively, reflecting on the silver washing basins. Robert noted that these could be tipped to fling dirty water down a drain. There was another thing, a convenience he studied with amazement and delight. He had heard of such as curiosities for kings. Lesser men went out of doors for this, and a chilly business it was when snow was on the ground! At the Welsh castle there had been a great stone staircase with generous space beneath where it was conveniently dim.

He finished by cleaning his teeth with a wash of vinegar, myrrh and honey set out for him, then padded back barefoot to his chamber in the nightgown, with his cote-hardie, paltock and trunk hose in a bundle under his arm, his drawers wrapped in the middle. Somewhere below, behind closed doors, the merchant bawled for "Wat! Wat!"

Robert closed his chamber door behind him, satisfied he was not likely to be disturbed. From his saddlebags he took a leather pouch, and out of this, a bundle wrapped in leather, tied with a thong. Within was a pile of unbound pages. With these he settled crosslegged on the bed by the candle, facing the door, with his red silk gown billowing out around him. His sword lay naked on the coverlet beside him. For he was risking his life now.

He thought again, with amusement, of the merchant's chance remark on *rocks, rebellion and heresy.* Bred among rocks, nurtured on rebellion—and he was a heretic besides. The years in Wales had made a Lollard of him. He had listened to the barefoot ragged priests preaching in rocky fields. They had taught him no man had dominion over him in the attainment of heaven; that confession was vain and pilgrimage useless; that the authority of the scriptures was over all. These things Robert believed, and it was his death if any could prove it. Every day of his life he walked with peril, for the papers he held here were the most part of a Wyclif Bible, in English, uncovered and unsewed, but death at the stake by burning if discovered in his possession.

He had, with infinite labor, also inscribed his name on the topmost page.

But he smiled as he read slowly, a forefinger moving under the words, as he pronounced them in his mind, syllable by syllable. He meant to read all these pages, a monumental task. Meanwhile, for this purpose, and to please heaven too, he carried the Bible wherever he went.

When he was finished, he wrapped all the pages again, tying them with a knot that none could retie without his knowledge, and placed it safe under the coverlet, together with his sword, his silver comb, and the belt of gold bells, all his treasures together. Then he blew out the candle and settled for the night. The bed was clean and comfortable, and in a few moments he was sure it was free of fleas. He sighed with utter delight. And waited for sleep that came hard to him always, as if his senses feared to abandon his body unconscious to the risky chance of night.

. . . the fog. He thought of the fog, gathering outside. Whenever he saw mist, he remembered gaunt Wales with an aching. Let men call it a savage land. For him it had been refuge.

Six years old, a motherless, servant-cuffed child, foisted off gladly on a cousin of his mother because it was the custom that a man's child be educated by another. It had been a long trip and a hard one, and a windy sharp day when he was shoved ahead of some lout into the Welsh castle. He was thrust forward in little pushes, until he came by a chair at the roaring fire, with a woman in it, and a man standing by, staring at him with distaste. It was the count, his mother's cousin, looking down.

"He's pale and weakly," the count pronounced. "That cough will take him before spring. It racks his bones!" He stood back further, judging. "He's his father's son."

The woman in the chair said, "I care not whose he was, if now he's mine."

"You've six sons already," the count said.

"Not mine, though I bred them," she said, and turned to Robert. "Come to the fire, child. Your nose is blue with cold." She reached out and drew him nearer. "You need a good wool shirt, not this patched thing. Your hands are bits of ice. Ah!" she exclaimed, seeing him now in the good light. "You're handsome!"

"Girlish," the count contradicted, peering too. Six dark-faced boys behind him crowded closer, looking wolfish. Robert turned his face away. They'd pounce on him soon enough, he knew.

"Handsome," the countess said again. "Even in tatters. He'll break hearts."

"But never lances," the count said. "These handsome boys make weaklings."

The countess put her fingers under Robert's chin and raised his head. "What do they call you?" she asked, very soft.

"Robert, madam," he whispered.

"Another Robert?" the count said. "We've five in the castle already. We'll call you by another name."

"I'm *Robert*," he said distinctly, for it was all he owned.

The countess chuckled. "He'll back for no bidding," she said, as if it pleased her fiercely. "You are Robert and we will call you so."

"Robert the Simple," the count suggested.

"Robert the Fearful," shouted one of his boys.

The countess held Robert at arm's length, thinking. "I'll call you for your blue eyes," she declared. "In this house you are Blue-Eyed Rob."

24

"Call him what you will," the count said. "Spoil him if you will, but from this moment, leave my sons to me!"

"Gladly," the countess said. "I've made exchange. Bear witness! Your six for this one, and I've the best of the bargain!"

The count stamped out, with his boys after him.

"Stupid as a bull," the countess said, "and his sons like their sire. Come, sit on my lap, Blue-Eyed Rob."

Hesitantly he moved closer, like a wild thing. She put her arms around him. Her ladies watched. Robert resisted though he did not want to. She tugged. And then, even before the women, he let her pull him to her lap and hug him tight. Suddenly he ached with loving. She lowered her voice to a whisper, her mouth almost at his ear.

"I'm a Frenchwoman," she said softly. "Do you know what that is?"

He shook his head.

"That means I'm a stranger here. No matter, so are you. We shall speak French together, Rob. I'll teach you that, and more, and confound this castle full of wild men. My sons are animals and unteachable, but we will show them that manners do not make a man the less."

She cuddled him a moment, then a fit of coughing seized him, and she held him till the spasm passed.

"You'll be a swordsman," she said, as if the matter were concluded. "I'll send to my brother and have his fencing master, that he may teach you properly. Rob, we are two strangers in a strange land. No one loves us, so we must love each other."

She kissed him suddenly. A log crashed in the fireplace and startled them both. Sparks soared up and the wind roared in the chimney.

"See," the countess said. "She's contending with me now. Your mother was a Welshwoman, and they're jealous. She knows I'll seize you from her if I can. Hear her screaming in the wind?"

They listened to it, while Robert shivered, and ever after heard his mother in high winds.

"I do not fear her, poor thing," the countess said. "Rob, will you have me for mother now?"

She was warm and comforting; and the other only a sound. Her arms were around him, who had had no love from any creature.

Let the wind roar and the fire soar. He placed both of his arms

25

around her as far as they would go, and buried his cold face in her neck.

He served as her page thereafter, and learned all she could teach, even to writing, though a sword came easier to his hand as she predicted—a fortunate thing in that wild, embattled house, where brother turned on brother. When he was fourteen, the countess gave him a silver comb, with fine teeth on the one side and coarse teeth on the other. The center between was polished, and set with blue stones the color of his eyes. This was to signify he had done with lady's teachings and was given over to learning the serious business of men. Which was fighting. Thereafter Robert followed the count wherever he went, was ready at every call, polished armor, and fought in the border wars.

In time, the ladies greatly favored Blue-Eyed Rob. Yet if the countess frowned on a maid, Robert tossed the girl aside; so that they called him Robert Heartless, saying he would never love any lady, but was ensnared by the Frenchwoman.

Yet now in this house, a girl had reached past his guard. This Constance was more than an hour's sport while he waited for the countess to get ready for a hunt. *Ah well*, he thought, *I'll forget her fast enough*.

The fire died slowly to glowing ashes, but yet he could not sleep. The house was still alive, and he could not rest while others moved about. Finally he flung the cover back and set his bare feet squarely on the chilled stone floor. He went to the door quietly, opened it, and put an eye to the crack. The upper hall was dark, but against a faint glow from below Robert could see the silhouette of a thick-shouldered man sitting on the top step by the rail, stretching and yawning with loud aspirates, like one set to guard and warned to stay awake. The watcher turned his head. Robert glimpsed a hooked nose and unkempt hair, and knew him instantly. The man called Wat.

There was a murmuring from below. A drone, impossible to decipher. Only once did choler betray the merchant's presence.

"In the name of Mary!" he swore, "the king shall never . . ."

He was immediately interrupted, as if reminded of a stranger in the house. The drone resumed. There seemed to be three voices and it had a sound of plotting. Then the watcher on the stair stood up. Robert had on the instant a sense of danger, and closed the door and stood behind it. A moment, and he heard breathing outside, as

Wat listened there. Then the breathing stopped, and Wat was gone.

What could a rich merchant not do, with ships plying constantly to France and back. Men turned their coats for little enough, and a merchant could make great gain. A half-mad king tried to rule France; a young king called Usurper for his father's act tried to rule in England. Three popes of Holy Church quarreled like snapping curs over who was true pope and held the Keys of Heaven. Which way did a man face in wild times like these? Some men spun like weathervanes in search of safety. Some sold themselves for present gain, and did not look to the hereafter. But Robert had turned to King Henry in this world, and to the Lollards and their belief for the next.

Oil and water, his friends had said. *You'll walk with peril, Robin.* For King Henry sent Lollards to the stake.

The mastiff in the garden barked, and was instantly hushed. Robert crossed to a window to see why the dog cried alarum. Two men had come out below. The dog ran with them to the river steps. The tall man must have rowed away, for he did not reappear. It was Wat who came out of the fog. The mastiff galloped heavily around him, fawning awkwardly, till he was thrust back as Wat went into the stable. The dog stood by the door a while, then gave up hope and prowled away.

All seemed quiet. But just as Robert turned again to his bed, he heard feet pass along the gallery. A glow of light appeared under his door, and vanished. Robert waited. There were stealthy creaks from the floor above, as if they walked up there. Yet a while, and they came down again. The glow appeared and vanished.

And Robert identified the heavy tread of the merchant, the scuff of a girl's slippers, and the click of a greyhound's claws.

Chapter 4

THE FOG was still thick as Wat Strongbow came scowling from the stables in the morning, to snuff at the smell of the river and guess at the weather of the day. After which he took the four horses the other boys had saddled and led them through the fog to the kitchen door with a hollow clattering of hooves. He had not long to wait; he heard them come, heralded by the jingle of gold bells. All mounted in silence, and Wat led the way into Thames Street on his nag, while Paul closed the gate behind them.

"Wat . . . Wat!" my lady said. "Turn the other way. Not St. Olave's this morning. St. Paul's!"

So he had to swing to the other direction. Their church was not good enough. No, they must ride half across London to the great cruciform cathedral that all travelers should see! Then, inside the three of them: my lady, Dame Margaret and the Welshman, to stare at the high altar, and the seventy-odd chantries, blazing with candles and gold, lighting the dim interior. While he was left to hold horses in the damp.

It was endless, impatient waiting for him, surrounded by lawyers quarreling in the mist with half-seen clients, for this was the accustomed place for such to meet.

And inside, no doubt, my lady had the relics out. Both arms of St. Mellitus, hair of Mary Magdalene, blood of St. Paul, the very milk from the breasts of the Virgin, a hand of St. John, the skull of St. Thomas of Canterbury. She was wealthy, and they hoped for money from her father. Every saint they had would be unearthed from his casket!

Some gallant brushed by, going into church proudly with his spurs on so the choristers would besiege him shouting for their spur-money, as was their right, and draw all eyes to his entry. Wat swore after the dandy, even now picking over coins in his palm, to pay for his loud greeting.

And finally, with the saints back in their boxes, came the three from his household.

They rode back through what seemed a different city; for the fog was dispelled and London had come alive and bustling. Vendors shouted, cart drivers swore from their rattling vehicles, industry clanked, and smoke streamed up to the sky. Wat snuffed in a great breath of London's diverse odors: mud, horses, strange cargoes, tide, tanners, tar and sewage, garlic, foreigners, breweries, slaughterhouses, dried fish, flowers and manure.

When they entered the house they met the merchant yawning from his chamber with Blaunchette a step behind, her thin tongue curling pink as she stretched her length and prepared for the day.

Now Wat was ill at ease. He always felt apologetic in the house, though he acted more uncouth to hide it. Still, he felt like a lump of dirt the housemaids would sweep out. The wenches hated him, and he despised them in return. A good, fat, greasy tavern wench was more to his liking. These skinny, whey-faced wenches gave him naught but a high nose, and said he never washed. Why should he?

Anger boiled in Wat like bubbling, bursting mud, seeing those same housemaids looking after the Welshman. They were not even covert about it; they all but invited themselves to his chamber. Because he was tall and had a clean, tanned skin? What did that prove of a man? He bathed, ay, he bathed. Wat had carried the water up himself, steaming hot, wishing the Welshman would boil himself raw.

". . . hot water," the Welshman was saying.

Before God, Wat thought with horror. *Would he wash* AGAIN?

"Wherefore?" Constance asked, struck with the same thought.

"I would like to wash my hair," he said, "if it would not trouble you."

Wat sneered. Dainty as a wench before her wedding.

But my lady did not laugh. "I'll wash it for you," she declared.

"Do not trouble," the Welshman said. "I would be a guest, and not a nuisance."

He had a way, no mistaking it. Envy seethed in Wat.

"We'll bring the tub into the garden," my lady was saying. "Wat! Get the tub! Wat! Put it on a stool. And bring rosewater. Wat! Call Mary. See to hot water. Wat! Be sure the mastiff's tied!"

Wat do this, Wat do that, Wat do the other and hurry!

Wrathfully he strode out, snatched up a tub from the kitchen, ordered kitchen boys to bring hot water, stools, a towel, soap, fetch rosewater and send Mary; then out into the court to shout to Paul to tie the dog. Paul shouted back he could do that himself. Wat stamped across the yard in a temper, seized the mastiff where he stood snuffing at the crack below the street gate, dragged the brute to an iron ring set in the wall and tied him there. Promptly Murdach began to leap and bark, and his iron ring clanged up and down.

"Wat?" yelled a kitchen boy. "Is the dog tied?"

"Use your ears," he bawled in return.

The kitchen boys came out to set a tub upon a stool, and put a smaller stool before it with a pillow. Wat meant to fling into the stables and sulk there, but somehow, he had to stay. With hatred and resentment, yet he had to stay.

Paul came over then. "You're not prettier for the expression on your face," he said.

"You'll be no prettier if I put this fist in yours!"

Anger flashed in Paul's expression, for they had never liked each other, but a quarrel could not be started here. Paul moved away, and left Wat to stand alone.

Now the Welshman appeared, with my lady, and three maids all giggling, and it seemed a signal for a hubbub to begin. Heads were peering out of windows across the street, where the upper stories oversaw their wall; their own household crowded out, and neighbors crowded in. All London would stop for sport of any kind. The mastiff Murdach roared from his wall at strangers on his property and his iron ring clashed incessantly.

The Welshman knelt on the smaller stool with the pillow, bells jingling, while a maid stood behind to hold his sleeves from the wet. My lady dunked his head herself and soaped it.

"The best castile," she proclaimed, above the splash and laughter. "Fresh-purchased from the apothecary."

The Welshman spat out soapsuds. "Still," he replied, "not the best for eating."

A sally of laughter from all and a deeper dunking from my lady repaid him for being saucy. He came up choking and proclaiming he had never learned to swim. Onlookers yelled comment, and were answered smartly by Mary, who held a bowl of fresh water on her hip, spilling it down her skirts as she laughed and jumped.

Anger boiled in Wat. What did that one have but a handsome face and garments so tight he'd split his hose if he dared sit low. He'd break every point that laced his hose to his paltock! Yet, unconsciously, Wat's hands pulled at his own leather hose. He wore separate stockings in the old-fashioned way, while the Welshman followed new fashion and wore them like hose and drawers together in one garment, lacing at the waist to the bottom of his undershirt hem. His upper garment, the long-sleeved cote-hardie, was only long enough to hide that joining.

The Welshman began to straighten, his face running soapy water, and Mary suddenly drenched him with clear, startling him straight up completely. Constance flung a great cloth over his head and shouted the tub must be dumped in the Thames. The Welshman was guided to sit on the stool, for he was blinded by the towel. He squatted very cautiously, while Wat hoped to hear a point snap, but he got safely down. The Welshman's hand was out like a blind man's, offering a silver comb to the air. My lady snatched it from him.

"A beauty!" she exclaimed.

Wat stretched to see. A silver comb with fine teeth on one side and coarse on the other, with the center polished and set with stones.

"See the work on it," Constance exclaimed. "This is a very fair comb and never another like it in the world." She paused, significantly. "I would cherish such a comb."

"I will try to get one for you," answered the Welshman, muffled in the towel, "but as for this, my lady, it was given me for a remembrance."

And my lady did not like that at all.

"Oh, do not trouble," she said, with a toss of her head. "I can send a servant and buy its like."

Whereupon she snatched the towel off his face, and with much pulling, combed his hair. That called Wat's attention to how the stranger carried his dagger, at the back of his neck between his shoulders, from a silver collar that fitted below the fur on his cote-hardie. Rabbit! In this household, mink was hardly good enough.

And when would my lady finish with him? There was not much to comb. The Welshman wore his hair in the common style, as if a bowl had been placed on his head, and all below the tops of his ears shaved off. A good thick pad under a helm, they said of this style. But no armor had come with him. Only his lance with its green ribbon, a shield, and saddlebags he carried himself, nor trusted to a knave. Himself. There was a thought. If he sought to guard them, what was within? Could he carry something valuable? Wat's fingers itched. It might be worth the stealing.

My lady backed away, as if to admire her work, but she held on to the comb. She was determined to have the bauble. Wat grinned at the acquisitiveness of the sex. To get something of a man and keep it was a little triumph, whether given willingly or tricked away. As a man desired victories by the sword, so they collected trifles. And the Welshman knew this also, for he had turned swiftly around on his stool, and as my lady hiked up her overskirt to idly thrust the comb in a pocket beneath, whence no man would see it come again, the Welshman reached out.

"It's a keepsake," he said, smiling, "and very dear to me. I'll match it for you, my lady, but I'll not part with this."

My lady saw with stupefaction that he would take it from her if he must. Perforce, she returned the bauble, but a storm was brewing in her look.

"Take the old man for husband," her father advised her joyously from the sidelines, "he'll give you all you want!"

She ignored the provocation, though her brown eyes snapped.

"Who was the lady?" she asked, head atilt.

"A Frenchwoman," the stranger said.

"A Frenchwoman! I've heard tales of Frenchwomen! Dark of hair?"

"Light," he answered. He would not say *graying*.

That vexed her.

"Blond women are wraiths," she stated bluntly. "They all look drowned to me. Could you kiss a drowned woman?"

"I have never seen one," he answered. "Have you?"

"Many," she declared, with a flourish of the hand she'd kept from childhood when she told lies and swore that they were true. "They float by, there, on the river. They drown themselves for love, the fools!"

Her father guffawed. "Thou liar!" he declared.

"Wat!" she shrieked. "Loose the dog!"

The neighbor women squealed and fled, and slammed the street gate hard. The kitchen boys dove for their kitchen. Wat watched, with hands on hips, pleased to see the scattering.

My lady yelled, "Wat!" and flung the soap at him.

"A poor shot, Mistress Constance," he said, to show the Welshman he could talk free with my lady. Then he strolled in his own time to loose the dog, while the merchant and his daughter and their guest went back into the kitchen. Wat hurried then, let Murdach go free, and rushed after them to see what happened. He almost crashed into my lady, who had stopped at the top of the three steps down inside. His Worship was halted at the bottom, and the Welshman was on the step between.

"See," the merchant was saying indulgently, "see the hussy? The cook would fetch her a clout if he dared."

It was Blaunchette, the brazen one, with her forepaws on the table, engaged in nosing some meat. The cook watched balefully, while kitchen boys tending a goose on the spit had their heads turned almost backwards.

"Now, Blaunchette," the merchant said. "Let it be!"

But when, perverse, she dragged it down, he only shook his head.

"Naughty!" he said, as she settled down to toy with it.

But Wat's attention had gone to my lady, who was stroking at the Welshman's head. *He did not even seem to notice. There's a man used to women, disdaining their attention by reason of having too much.* Envy was strong in Wat again. They treated him as they treated Murdach, with fear, and stayed beyond his reach. He'd heard of men who were fools for women, forever some wench's victim. He'd be such a one and gladly, if they would only pursue him. But he was ugly, his tones were rough and his words came out harsh. His legs were short, his nose was hooked, his hair all greasy cowlicks. Why should a man made as he was trouble to keep his body clean, or his chin shaven, or his hair cut? Should he wear tight hose to show off misshapen legs?

"It's fine and silky now," my lady was saying, to make the Welshman notice her. "The journey's dust is in the Thames."

Her father heard her speak, and turned to see her arrange a lock not set to her liking.

"Be done with that!" he roared.

Instantly, Blaunchette seized up her prize and fled to the great hall.

"I was but seeing if the wash had dried," Constance answered impudently.

"You'll be wed this August, and that's not soon enough!"

"I'll not wed this August or any August to that grandsire," she declared. "I'll get to a convent first!"

"You'll go to no convent! I'll have grandsons of you, mistress!"

"Ha! You'll get none from that old man," she said.

"Will I not? With his fourth wife dead of her seventh child last year?"

33

"I'll poison him first," she shrieked in a gust of temper.

"Mortal sin!" he bawled, and they were merrily off on a battle with the Welshman standing quietly between them, blank-faced, though Wat's heart went to beating faster.

No, no, he pleaded silently. *If you will not have the old man, I'll kill him, but do not provoke your father.*

He could do nothing now to aid her, and the Welshman did not care, but put his back to the wall and a foot across the stair between them, lounging. That was the way of gentry, to make sport of everything.

A dark mood rushed on Wat as he remembered another quarrel in another kitchen; a smoke-blackened greasy hole in a thieves' inn, where his mother was cook, and more when a man had the money. He was twelve, or thereabouts, and they told him a real gentleman had come by, driven in by the snow. He rushed to tell his mother this exciting news and found the gentleman himself, with his mother.

"Is this your whelp?" the gentleman had asked, furious at interruption. "This . . . this . . . you'd best drown it, woman!"

His mother flung the nearest missile at her child, then pursued him as he leaped and crouched away. She was black-toothed and dirty, but he had so unreasoning loved her. . . .

A pot caught him a blow on the head as he sought to reach the door. It sent him reeling, too dazed to think or move. He staggered into a wall and went to his knees, and his mother came at him with a chunk of firewood snatched up.

When he was conscious again, the gentleman was gone and she was snoring in a corner. Always before he'd gone back to her after a beating, to the only human to whom he belonged, but he heard the gentleman laughing, or some such sound in his head. He did not go near her but crawled away instead, to the door, and rested there, then crawled again along the frozen ruts that were like mountains stabbing his belly. He dragged himself across a snowy meadow, leaving a trail like a snake, red-spotted, until he reached a fence where he pulled himself to his feet, leaned to rest, then staggered on.

The inescapable memory choked him now, years after, while the quarrel cracked on and the Welshman studied his fingers. As if he knew he was watched, the Welshman's head turned and caught his glance. Wat dropped his eyes.

"I'll have my way!" my lady shrieked.

The merchant's neck swelled over his collar and his face was like raw meat. In a moment he would strike her. But the Welshman moved first. He seemed to sway forward and stand upright facing the merchant. He said nothing more. Did nothing more. But it almost numbed Wat's brain. Whom should he aid? The Welshman, his enemy, who would protect my lady? Or His Worship, who might strike her, but was master of the house?

The moment of panic was resolved by an accident. The kitchen boy at the spit, intent on the battle, now pulled something wrong and the goose crashed into the fire. The cook shouted and sprang. The merchant swung around with a bellow. The cook dragged the bird out with a poker, rolled it clear on the floor, flapped a cloth over it, and threw the red-hot dinner on a table, where he anxiously stripped off the fat that wrapped the bird. A fragrance surrounded them all, rising with the steam, to bring Blaunchette's slim presence inquiring to the door. The cook was smiling over his undamaged bird when he saw her appear. His face changed and he reached again for his poker. Merchant or no merchant, he meant to defend this bird, though His Worship stood right there.

But the red had faded from the merchant's face.

My lady turned sweet-toned.

"Cooked with the fat of swine," she said, seeing His Worship admire it, "and stuffed with apples and honey. We'll brown it with butter and baste it with wine . . ."

". . . and devour it the instant it is done!" the merchant finished. "Now, we'll leave the kitchen to those who need it, and settle family matters another time. Blaunchette, not a tooth will you put in that goose." He seized her by her cloth-of-gold collar, half lifted her from the floor, and dragged her into the great hall. "Robin?" he inquired mildly. "A game of chess before dinner?"

Wat was horrified instantly. *Robin!* Pet names, now.

". . . and take that sword off," came the merchant's voice. "It's only fit for tripping women in this house."

Wat looked through the door. The Welshman was taking off his sword, but very slowly, though the merchant had already flung his clattering on a chest.

"I had thought to go out on business," His Worship said, "but it will wait until we make bones of the goose. And so will your trip to Westminster Palace, Robin, to sign your indenture to fight in France. This afternoon will be time enough, and I'll send Paul to guide you!"

Paul! Wat was angry at this preferment. But it would be as well, he thought with disdain. Paul could keep nothing to himself, and he'd tell all that passed.

"Wat! The chess pieces," the merchant yelled across. "We'll sit here in this sunny window. Wat! Bring chairs!"

The Welshman got his own, and hung his sword on the back of it, easy to his hand.

Chapter 5

LIKE most official documents, the Indenture was in French, which Robert read laboriously, while the bored clerk watched with superiority.

This Indenture, made between the Kynge our Sovereign Lorde of the One Part, and Robert de Fayrfyeld, Esquire, of the other parte: Witnesseth, that the sayde Robett is bound to our sayd Lorde the Kynge, to serve him for a wholl yere in a voiage whyche our Lorde the Kynge in his owne person will make, if it pleaseth God . . . commencing with the month of Juli next comyng, if hee then bee redy to make the sayd muster. And that the sayd Robit shalle hav with him . . .

Here Robert drew in a deep breath, for God alone knew how this next could be managed by a penniless squire.

. . . three horse archers; the sayd Robertt takynge for wages for hymself two shillings a dai . . . and for each of the saide archers twenty marks for the said hole yere.

Three men, with horses. Where could he get them? Horses! As well require pearls!

And the sayde Robete shalle bee bound to bee ready at the see, with hys sayd peple well mounted, armed and equiptt, suitably to

Bradford Bachrach

D. V. S. Jackson was born at Sheepshead Bay and has been a racing fan ever since. She went to Columbia University and now lives on Long Island. She has written many short stories and two teen-age novels. This is her first book of adult fiction.

*thyr condition, for hys muster on the fourth dai of Juli next comyng,
and from the tyme of there arryval at the playce above sayd, the sayde
Robet is bound to musster thee peopell of hys retinue befor such
person or personnes as it mai plese our sayde Lorde the Kynge to
assygn, as often as hee shalle resonably requyre.*

*And the sayd Robert shal hav as usualle at the charge of our said
Lorde the Kinge, shippynge for hym and hys retinu, ther horses, har-
nesse and provisions and also reshyppynge as others of his condition
in thee saide voiage.*

Details of how his loot must be shared with the king, what prisoners
he might keep for ransom, and those that must go to the crown. With
luck, he'd have enough to pay for a knighting, and only as a knight
would he return to Wales.

In Witnesse of whyche thynges, the Indenture concluded, *the
aforsayde Robbert has put his seel, Given at Westminster this xxviii
day of June.* . . .

The bored clerk dripped sealing wax upon the document. Robert
set his seal ring firmly into the red blob. When he raised it, he was
the king's man, signed and sealed and sworn; his loyalty belonged
wholly now to King Henry the Fifth, three years on his shaky throne.

Robert strode out into the noisy street, exalted and magnified. Paul
brought the horses, and he mounted, still borne up by the signing.
He followed Paul, scarcely noticing the hundreds of women around
of all hues and nations, shouting their wares in diverse tongues. This
was the worst stew of the city, at the southern end of London Bridge.
Vaguely he heard the babble of nations, but he neither knew nor
cared these stews were famous. Whatever any man wanted, no matter
how strange, he would find it here.

But Robert looked to his horse; for now the beast was skittish, un-
used to these screeching crowds. The stream of traffic on London
Bridge was a mad thing; jostling and shouting and faces all about,
struggling in and out of shops that lined the outer parts of the bridge.
Robert would have liked to stop at the chapel in the very middle, to
pray and give thanks for the signing, but Paul hurried on and never
turned, and Robert knew he would lose himself in this sweltering press
if he stopped.

Paul pointed upwards, as they came off the north end of the bridge. Severed heads aloft on pikes. Traitors' heads, displayed. One was bearded with the eyes turned upward, clotted blood still fresh on the stem of the neck. Robert fancied he had seen that face when it possessed a body, but Paul forced his way steadily through the crowd and there was no time to linger and think on it.

And so they forged their way back to the merchant's house, the great stone building topped by a tiled roof with a winch fastened there to the back. All lower windows facing the street were stoutly barred, with stained-glass panes, and a motto spelled out: I THANK THEE LORDE AND EVER SHAL, IT IS THE SHEEP HATH PAYED FOR ALLE. It was a great, expensive house, decorated with a gilt band of carved lambs gamboling among hawthorn, straight across the front at the height above the door, continuing along the top of the long stone wall that shut the courtyard away from the street. In this gilt band, above the house door that opened a step above the street, was inset a plain shield bearing the device of a cross inside a circle, the merchant's mark of Lewis Chapelle of London, known wherever ships took trade. A man did not need to know how to read to understand a thing was his.

They stopped at the courtyard gate, and Wat Strongbow opened it to Paul's shout. He had a surly look, like the mastiff chained to the wall. Robert dismounted inside and flung him the reins as Constance came skipping out to meet him.

"Here's one home at least," she said, "and my father should come any moment. Sit in the great hall, Robin, and I'll be with you soon. I have to watch the cook or he'll have the sauce too mild."

She sent him out of the kitchen, and he walked to the row of arched windows and stared out at the side garden of roses, still borne up by the signing of the Indenture. It was the end of a long affair.

Twelve years training in Wales, and Count Llewellyn had decreed that Robert must go home, for the last step was his knighting, and this a matter for his sire. Therefore, in the fall Robert rode back to the place where he was born, a stone manor set in a neglected wood, with barren fields around, for the serfs had long since run off to the cities. The house was somber, brooding, streaked with wet and unremembered. It seemed small and mean after the castle. Stones had fallen from the tower and lay mossy green among the weeds all around. The silence was broken only by the harsh cries of the ravens.

The old man did not remember Robert. He had thought little enough of his only child, got in old age of a wife who died in gesine. He thought even less of Robert's reappearance, for a knight was a great expense. With resentment the old man said it could not be afforded; he was already in heavy debt.

All that winter Robert strode restlessly around the snowed-in ruin, while the old man sat in his oak chair before the fire, snoring or drinking, having long since forgotten youth and its ambitions. He looked only into the flames and what he saw was over long ago. What was to come he did not care, for death was his companion.

Spring came at last, with green things bursting up through muddied snow. The roads were open, to horses if not to carts, and rumors of impending war came with wandering merchants. Henry the Fifth, by the Grace of God, King of England, was pressing for war with France. A young king for a new war, the merchants said, and disapproved. But Robert had known no other ruler in his life; it had been Prince Henry governing Wales, and now it was King Henry governing England. If he wanted France also, it was natural. In Wales everyone wanted his neighbor's lands. And Robert was ambitious also. Yet he waited still, riding out over the unplowed fields every day to think where his duty lay, in the home manor with the old man who did not want him, or with the king who needed loyalty but hated Lollards now, though he'd had enough for friends when he was prince. Robert returned from such a ride in early summer to find his father in the great oak chair as if he had never moved. Except that this time he swung his head around.

"The king's messenger came by the woods' road," he stated dully. "King Henry is asking all his vassals to contribute. I said I had no money and nothing to sell."

God! to grow so old all things were alike! Let me die young, still eager, regretting bitterly the years I'll lose!

"And," the old man finished, "I must list what men I have who can bear arms for defense of the realm when the king is out of it."

"A home guard? Not for me," Robert said. "I'm for the fighting in France."

"As you will," his father said, without interest. "As you will. You'll get no gold spurs of me." . . .

39

"La!" Constance said. "You dreamer! You'll move from that place, or we'll set the table atop you! Johannis!" She guided him out of the way. "My father is not yet home," Constance shouted over the din and clatter of planks. "I cannot think what keeps him."

"He started later than he planned," Robert reminded her. "No doubt he'll return that much later."

"Dame Margaret argues the same," Constance said.

So they dined with one place empty, and as the daylight faded, Robert saw that she grew worried.

"This is a handsome goblet," he said to distract her, fingering chased silver.

"My father had it from the coronation feast," she said, but her eyes were on the street door that did not open. "He sat with the Aldermen of London, near enough to the king to see him well."

"How does the king look?" Robert asked. "I've never seen him."

"Brown-haired," Constance said, reciting without interest. "Hazel-eyed. A cleft in the chin. A high color. A scar, here." She indicated a place by her left eye. "From an arrow wound at Shrewsbury that nearly killed him."

She had little thought for this, her manner said, but all for the lateness of the merchant.

"Tall?" Robert asked.

"Tall?" she inquired vaguely.

"The king," Dame Margaret prompted her.

"Oh, the king. Nay. To your nose. No higher."

"Merry?"

"My father said at the feast you'd think he was buried, not crowned. He sat alone in a marble chair on a dais with a gold canopy, and ate nothing, nor drank anything, but brooded. My father said no doubt he wished the party all in hell, for the king could not leave till the guests had done, and the feast went on forever. The servants were on horseback, and the nags so skittish with crowding, my father said, they were like to spill all on the diners' heads; but the king never noticed nor smiled. That was a night I worried about my father also. Drunk and coming through the streets by night, and the snow . . . oh, the snow! I thought I'd be an orphan, with a frozen man for a sire. I *would* he were home now!"

She looked up as Wat came to the table with the hangdog air he had in the house. He wiped the back of his hand across his mouth, and muttered something about *Jesu. Jesu* just tied up at the quay.

"*Jesu* in?" Dame Margaret asked from the end of the table.

"But my father is not," Constance said. "Let me look in the street."

She went swiftly, with Dame Margaret clucking behind her. Opening doors at night was not a woman's business, so Robert followed them. There was no one outside. Constance came slowly back to the table.

"Now," Dame Margaret said, "he started late and will return so."

"He would not be late tonight if he could avoid it," Constance said. "*Jesu*'s in from Calais." Her voice turned fretful. "He carries money too often, and too many know it. Wat, you should have gone with him!"

She spoke across the room. Robert glanced and saw a lumpier shadow, darker than the rest. The monstrously ill-favored knave had not left. How quietly he moved and stood! It was a fact to be remembered. Robert was glad he'd flung his saddlebags over his horse that morning when he'd ridden to the palace. A varlet that silent was bound to be a thief, and God forbid he find a Bible!

Dame Margaret was saying, "You fret like your King-at-Arms. There's no cause yet for worry. We'll make a time and you'll be calm till then. We will not worry until the moon reaches around that window and touches the foot of his chair. Then indeed he would be too late."

Robert identified the chair she meant, a large one, carved, marked with a cross and circle in a shield, set in a shadow with a long streak of moonlight by it on the floor.

"So the king has forsworn smiling?" Robert asked, resuming as if the conversation had never been interrupted.

"It seems so," she said, trying to play the hostess. "But they're seeking him a wife and that may make him merry."

"He wants no wife," Dame Margaret contradicted flatly. "They've tossed brides enough at his head, and he's tossed them all back swifter."

"He may yet wed Catherine of France," Constance said, with her eyes on the door.

"Her father's mad and she's worse than emptyheaded," Dame

41

Margaret said, shocked. "God defend England from such a queen, to get mad sons for the realm."

"She's but twelve years old," Constance said, still trying valiantly. "She'll grow wiser as she grows older."

"Let her grow older in France," Dame Margaret said. "A Portuguese princess is what we need. *That* would be good for trade."

Constance did not answer, and silence fell over them.

"Though a king cannot choose his wife as he will," Dame Margaret said, to make a sound in the huge, still room. "They'll force him to marry, and I fear it will be Catherine in the end, and so does he. No wonder he brooded at his coronation feast."

Dame Margaret poured more wine and it gurgled. Robert looked at the moonlight creeping nearer the chair.

"His throne's shaky besides," Dame Margaret said. "Too many say Henry should have gone to the Church and his brother Thomas to the throne."

"In Wales," Robert said, "they favor the Earl of March."

"And well he knows it," Dame Margaret said. "He's no fool. He had old enemies at the coronation feast to show he would not carry grudges. He'll have peace in England to go to war the faster, thrusting aside the prophecy."

"What prophecy?" Robert asked.

"Why, there was a two-day blizzard when he was crowned. It snowed so hard and deep, men froze in the street, and many lords never reached Westminster at all to swear their loyalty. Therefore, it was prophesied that King Henry's reign would be as the snow, full of violence and short besides, for the snow was gone in a week."

"He's but twenty-seven," Robert protested.

"Yet he pardons men who try to murder him," Dame Margaret said, "and he goes abroad alone. This is not the description of a long-lived man. Constance! Not to the door again? Your father will be in a temper when he finds you opened it at night. The streets are dangerous now."

"I am thinking just that," Constance said from the doorway, "and that my father is out among them."

The moonlight touched the leg of the merchant's chair. They were not all they seemed in this house, and something was afoot tonight to which the merchant should have hurried. Robert was full of suspicion, but he was a guest and a man and the girl was worried. He pushed back his chair and rose.

"All excuse is at an end," he said. "Therefore, tell me the way he would take and I will find him."

Chapter 6

ROBERT FAIRFIELD was no coward, but he'd not have Wat Strongbow behind him in a pitch-black street, so he sent the knave ahead to show the way. He followed close, for they carried no light. The stableboy had a cudgel as thick as a wrist in one hand, and with the other he held the mastiff Murdach on a thick rope doubled through his collar, so loosing one end would free the beast to run.

The streets were black tunnels hereabouts. The houses were tall and slammed tight together, and since each story overlapped the lower the top floors almost bridged the streets. Robert could not see where he put his feet. Night dampness crawled along the slimy cobbles with the smell of dirt and fish and tide.

"Where's the watch?" he asked once.

"Against a door with a wench, every man," Wat replied. "Here's Candlewick Street. It's wider."

A little moonlight forced its way down to illumine their way and keep them from falling into the sewage ditch. They were in an area of old houses and buildings used for storage. Wat halted before an unlit bulk looming into the night sky.

"Our warehouse," Wat said. "His Worship was to oversee delivery of arrows from the north today."

Robert drew his sword with a soft hiss of steel.

"Stay here," he said, "and see if any run out."

He walked warily into an alley beside it, after trying the door. All was silent and deserted. He made a complete circuit, overleaping a fence at the back, and returned.

"Nothing," he said to the waiting man and dog. "Is there another place the Worshipful Alderman might stop?"

"The Pope's Head Tavern in Lombard Street," Wat hazarded. "He knows the landlord well, and often stops there when he's late."

Robert gestured, and Wat took the lead again. No light showed anywhere, for all fires must be covered when the curfew rang. A forgotten fire could mean a conflagration among the wooden tenements, and a slum burned down by morning. They passed dark churches with spires high against the stars; cemeteries that were pools of thick darkness, and only the holy saints knew what lay within besides the silent dead. Once two men slunk across their path, but Murdach snarled, and when they came to where the men had been, there was nothing but a cough heard in some alley.

They turned into Lombard Street.

And in the center lay a fallen torch, still burning. Wat went to it.

"I know the mark," he said. "It's one of ours."

"Loose the dog," Robert told him. "Tell him to find his master."

Murdach stood a moment, hard-chested and belligerent, with a long line of slobber dangling from his jaw. Then he leaped away, heavy and slow and exceedingly dangerous, searching shadows and on the hunt.

"He has no nose for trailing," Wat said, "nor Blaunchette's speed in a fight, but he's diligent and will attack whatever appears."

Murdach paused on the very words, to stare into an alley. Suddenly he leaped, and the night burst into snarling bedlam. Wat and Robert ran after him instantly, and were as instantly beset. Robert had no time to pick opponents, but fought whatever stood before him. The first knave fled when the sword but pricked him, and was a swift shadow illumined at the end of the alley and a sound of running feet. Another rascal came from nowhere. Robert tripped him, and stuck him on the ground. Then against the light at the end of their battleground he saw Wat engaged, and a third man coming up behind him. He stepped lightly forward and struck hard. He heard a sharp intake of breath, smelled onions on it. Wat and his man went crashing down, and Wat bestrode the other and burst his skull against the cobbles, while Robert's ruffian staggered back and back, still spitted, dragging sword and swordsman to the alley's mouth, where Robert heaved back on the weapon. It snapped, set hard in bone. The knave fell backwards into Lombard Street. Robert flung down the useless hilt, jumped backwards into darkness, and drew his dagger from its scabbard at his back.

A great bulk was outlined now against the light from Lombard Street. Robert almost struck it until he realized it was the merchant, so he stabbed the other, who screamed and fled. One more yell and the last of them fled after the screaming man, with Murdach bellowing after.

Wat yelled, "Murdach!" then pounded in pursuit.

"Who's that?" the merchant's voice demanded. "Paul?"

"Robin Fairfield."

"I thought that too bold for Paul," the merchant said, and came to the light, where he turned his back. "Cut those thongs, if you will, Robin."

Robert cut them and sheathed his dagger again, while the merchant rubbed his sore wrists. "Where's the dog?"

"Wat's after him."

The merchant kicked thoughtfully at the body of the man Robert had killed. The ruffian lay on his back in a welter of spreading blood, with the broken sword protruding from his chest. The dead hands clutched it yet, as if to tug it out. There was a gleam on one of the fingers. Robert picked up the warm, limp, bloody hand. In Wales one did not waste good loot on dead men. He pried the jewel off. Then, bending again, he picked up the varlet's sword.

"Nicked like a saw," he said, "and balanced like a rock. An ax were a better weapon." He flung it with a clatter to the alley, disappointed.

"I will match yours for you, and more," the merchant said. "That's but justice. Here's Wat, returning. Did you run all over London," he inquired, "to take so long?"

Wat made no answer but scuffled to hold Murdach, who reared up and struggled and would return to a fight.

Robert picked up the torch, still burning in Lombard Street, and they walked on by its ill light, for though they had come in darkness, now the Alderman was with them, and it was the law that honest men abroad after curfew on emergencies must carry torches to prove they were not prowlers.

All London lay inert and silent, dark except for the stars, the moon, the beacon fire in the spire of St. Mary-le-Bow, and the pinpoint of their torch. The furious battle brought no investigation. If the householders heard the uproar, they remained prudently in bed behind their shutters and bolts. As for the watch, it never came at all.

"Welladay," the merchant said, before his own door, "at least they got no money of me. As for my gelding, it ran off and will come home when it is pleased to do so. Wat, there were seven of them in the alley. This is a fighting man, for all his pretty bells."

"Seven men in a small space," Robert said, honestly, "and more disposed to run than fight."

"Modesty, modesty," the merchant said, and knocked upon the door.

It opened too promptly to suit him, and he shouted at his daughter for flinging doors wide when no men fit to wield swords were in the house. As for Constance, she did not listen but bolted the door and came running after them into the great hall and the candlelight. There she yelped at their gory looks.

"Be quiet!" the merchant commanded. "It's only a little blood and none of it ours. Wat, is that dog injured sorely? No, well throw him in the river and cleanse him, he's tracking blood on the floor. Constance, be useful. Tell the cook I'm hungry. Dame Margaret, see to our nightgowns and menservants to attend us."

Dame Margaret hustled off, but Constance stood staring at Robert anxiously.

He backed away, protesting she would stain her gown.

"But your hand is hurt," she said. "You hold it closed and it's bloody."

"The blood is a robber's, and as for the fist, it holds a bauble for a lady."

Her eyes glowed. "For me?"

Then she pounced at him, and pried his fingers open.

"Ah," she cried out, greedy. "A ring. A balas?" She caught up the expensive silk of her skirt to wipe it clean. "A balas! Taken of a thief by moonlight. I will cherish this pale ruby, Robin. Jesu, I would I had seen the fight that took it!"

Dame Margaret came up behind her, frowning at this behavior.

"Your Worship," she said, "the menservants are coming, and I've . . ." here she looked hard at Constance, who'd been derelict in this assigned duty, ". . . roused the cook also."

"Then get to bed," the merchant said, and when his daughter would only stand trying on her ring to see which finger it suited, he raised his voice to a shout. "Constance! Must we strip naked before you?"

Constance dallied off then, trailing behind her aunt, looking at her balas, though it did not capture all her attention, for she turned to grin like an imp at Robert as she closed her chamber door.

"Never a thought to *my* welfare," the merchant proclaimed piteously. "I could have been killed in the streets. She did not inquire if *I* was wounded." He subsided into grumbles, and at length began to laugh.

They stood upon footcloths before the fire and were washed by menservants, who put the nightgowns on them; black silk for the merchant and garnet silk for the guest, trimmed with ermine dyed the color of a salmon's flesh.

By then the table had been put up by sleepy kitchen boys, and candles brought in profusion. Wine was poured. Wat came in and whispered in the merchant's ear, and walked away with a glance for Robert that slid off guiltily. A yawning kitchen boy came with honied breads, cold mutton and a crock of pickled lampreys, and a basket of strange tawny-colored fruit.

"Oranges," the merchant said, seeing Robert look with interest. "*St. Joseph* brought them to Calais, and transhipped to *Jesu*, for we like them in this house. Wat! Did the searchers see them?"

Wat said hoarsely that no man had set foot on the ship, and the customs searchers would only come in the morning.

It seemed to Robert that more was meant than stated, but he paid no attention outwardly. But this time he had seated himself with his back to the fireplace, facing the hall and the merchant with his black beetling brows, black beard, and long hair following the fashion of an older day. The man was masked in hair.

The merchant suddenly snapped his fingers. "I am reminded. A sword to replace that broken in my behalf."

He rose instantly and stalked off to his chamber with a candle. Robert heard him fumbling in some chest within. Then he returned across the room to fling a scabbarded sword on the table, in the midst of the many candles, and all the flames bowed abruptly.

An omen! Robert caught in his breath. His Welsh blood saw the sign!

"Take it, use it," the merchant said, "but bring it back when the fighting's done. It is not yet mine and I must answer for its safety till it is."

The sword was not ordinary. The hilt was wrought by the goldsmith's art into the form of three ostrich feathers, unique, beautiful, strange. Robert had never seen a real ostrich feather, only stiff drawings on shields, but now he knew how one should look, and yet, it would fit the hand. The goldsmith who had created this hilt had used a model; every shaft of every soft feather was here in precious metal.

The artist was long-gone dead or blind; for those who followed the goldsmith's trade lost their sight early from the smoke of quicksilver, or turned madmen, as all knew. But this man had left remembrance of his great gift behind. He had left this sword. Robert reached for it; then dropped his hand to the linen cloth and left the jewel untouched.

"I have it on security for a loan," the merchant said, biting into cold mutton with relish. He saw only its value in crowns and marks and that was great enough. "If it is not redeemed in a year and a day and a month, I will give it to you utterly, in exchange for my life this night."

He could not touch it. Something cold ran in his blood.

"Take it," the merchant said, impatient with this dawdling. "Take it!"

With a sharp motion, Robert picked it up. He drew the blade, and it hissed free. What was the message it spoke; the portent; the meaning? He held the sword out. Balanced finely, the best steel. The firelight glittered red as blood along the blade.

That was the omen! Blood! He would pay for this gem among swords with his blood! He knew it, and he did not care.

The merchant threw down the bone of the mutton and reached for a honied bun.

"It was King Henry's jewel," he said, "when he was Prince of Wales."

Chapter 7

ROBERT sat on the bench against the wall that shut out Thames Street. From there he could oversee the courtyard and the quay where *Jesu* was unloading. Bales sailed upward into the capacious third story of the house, swung by the squeaking winch on the roof through double doors that opened into air.

The merchant basked in a sunny place, his presence the peace-keeper, for otherwise sailors and stableboys fought. Constance was sewing with her maids, and Dame Margaret was watching the washing of clothes at the stairs to the river.

It was peaceful enough; diligent pursuit of profit and cleanliness in a kindly household. So it seemed by day. But by night they were like owls, awake and flying after prey.

There had been a visitor last night. It was a strange, shy visitor who had not appeared until Robert was long abed, and given much time to sleep.

Wat sat on the stairhead guarding when Robert risked opening the door a crack, sensing someone below. He heard a murmuring. The voices were not clear, but in one the intonation was distinctive. It was good northern French. A Frenchman below, and the two countries on the edge of war. He deciphered talk of a hundred thousand gold crowns. They were setting a price, and that the price of betrayal in high places. Who'd give it? The French were frugal, and might think it cheaper to murder a king than fight a war.

Wat on the stair grew restless. Robert closed the door. Nor opened it again that night, for reason of Wat's settling outside against the very panel.

A hundred thousand gold crowns. That went far beyond the price of poor Wat Strongbow's murderous service.

Robert's eyes drifted speculatively to where butts had been set up near the stable, and some neighbor lads were shooting a match with the stableboys to decide the better archers. The garden was full of the sound of huzzing arrows, mingled with screams from the winch, the cursing of sailors, yells from men within the ship, and the gentle cooing of the white doves that strutted softly at his feet. Robert fed them idly with bits of bread he crumpled in his fingers. All the soft white company attended him, though great Murdach was dangerously near, tied fast to his iron ring. The birds fluttered and flew with flashing wings to Robert's hand, feathers aglare in the sun as they balanced on his fingers and pecked crumbs from his palm.

Constance glanced over frequently, but there was another watcher too, and not so pretty as she. Wat Strongbow paid little attention to his archery. As often as Robert withdrew his attention from *Jesu* and the soaring bales, or the red-legged doves clinging with beating wings to his tanned fingers, so often did he catch Wat looking hastily away. Had the merchant set the knave to spying? Lewis Chapelle had no look of trickery now, for all he plotted with Frenchmen while Englishmen slept. He sat on his chair in the sun with Blaunchette half off and half on his lap by reason of his great belly and her great length. They were playing at her being a lap-dog, and the merchant made much of her, petting and patting and promising if St. *Joseph* came safely home from this venture to Venetia, there would surely be a collar of pretty stones for her.

Robert chanced to glance at Murdach when a dove strayed too near the beast. But Murdach saw no dove to be snapped up, nor anything but the merchant with his Blaunchette. The mastiff stood square at the end of his rope, and queerly, sadly, unexpectedly, out of his ugliness, beyond the torn ears and scarred hide and raw wounds from the night before, from some deep, unsuspected softness and pitiful need, came a low, longing whine, a small crying wrenched from a fierce heart that could be loyally loving, if any could but see it.

"Now pretty, now hussy," the merchant said, and teased Blaunchette by pulling her ears.

Murdach cried, and Robert was all compassion.

"Here, Murdach," he called softly. "Will you take second best with me?"

And he tossed a bit of the sweet bread over. Murdach snarled and showed his fangs. The merchant heard that quick enough and hitched round in his chair on the instant.

"Snarling?" he inquired. "At guests? Down, you brute! Or I'll take a rope and teach you manners!"

Murdach flattened to the ground, abject at having sinned, his shy attempt at affection crushed. The merchant grunted, and faced front again. Blaunchette licked his face and had him back in humor soon, laughing at her. She threw back her lovely, graceful head, as if she laughed too, while very quietly, great Murdach crouched on his belly and cried in his throat.

Sadly, Robert resumed feeding the clustering doves, until abruptly aware he was watched again. He snapped his head up this time, and caught Wat Strongbow barefaced. There was no masking it. The knave was staring. Wat did not drop his eyes this time. Robert's mouth tightened. Perhaps it was the ugly face, the look, Robert never knew.

But he remembered luckless Murdach, not as evil as he seemed. Tentatively, Robert smiled. Wat Strongbow grimaced shyly, and Robert guessed it was meant for a smile.

"That looks to be a fine bow," he called, for want of something to say.

Wat came to him hesitantly, proffering the weapon.

Robert showed his surprise at the stoutness of the bow, almost shocked by the abnormal strength it would demand.

Wat wiped his hand nervously across his mouth. "I've shot at the mark all my life, sir."

"You have a Welsh look," Robert said. "Do you come from there?"

"From under a stone for all I know, sir," Wat said. "I was got of a tavern wench by a passing stranger. In the year of the plague I came here and they took me in. My breeding, sir, is a ban-dog's—unguessed at." He looked down at his toes. "It was my life you saved last night, sir, as well as . . ." He gestured with his chin, and Robert realized suddenly there was no love lost there. "Only I cannot discharge my debt with such as . . ." He jerked his chin again, to indicate King Henry's sword.

"I'd have had a knife in my back," Robert said, "if you had not been there."

Wat stood, without words.

A shouting made them both look up. It was Wat's turn to shoot again. He ducked in a clumsy bow and stepped up to the mark. Immediately Constance left her women and came to sit by Robert with her embroidery needle still in her hand, trailing a long gold thread.

"You were speaking with Wat," she said. "Did he offend you that you called him?"

"I admired his bow," Robert said.

She seemed relieved. "He's ugly and he's forward, and he stared at you, I know, yet he but watched admiring."

"Admiring?"

"Have you not noticed he's lost his shaggy look? He's close-shaven today, instead of bristling. He's pulled his hose tight, and cut his hair, and this morning he swam in the river. I screamed at him for years and never accomplished improvement, yet one street fight and you're the hero. He has need of one. He's not liked in the household. You heard them jeer just now when he missed the mark? I never knew him to miss before; but this morning he cares nothing for the match. Before, he had to best all comers. He's found his hero and lost his aim! Robin, he has a crafty look, but his face is his misfortune and turns away trust. Therefore, let me speak for him, since he cannot and there is no other who will. He's tired of the household and would go adventuring. He'd die for me, but hates a woman to order him. Robin, when you go to France, you must take three followers to go as a gentleman. My father, I think, will offer men from our household. If he does, and you choose, I beg you, choose Wat Strongbow first of all if you would please me."

Her face seemed full of concern for Wat, but Robert did not trust it altogether. With plotting he had come to manhood amid great treachery that had often as fair a face. Yet he inclined his head, though warily.

"Sometimes your face cannot be read," Constance said. "What are you thinking?"

"Of nothing, mistress," he said, "and therefore nothing appears."

"I would not have you for an enemy, Robert Heartless," she said. Her face turned impish. "Therefore . . . let us be great friends!"

Then she leaped to her feet, alarmed by her own words, and skipped hastily back to her handmaids. She glanced once to Wat as she sat, and Wat glanced at her and away. No word was spoken, but the message was given and received. Wat knew he was going to France.

His aim improved. The last of the arrows were shot; the match concluded. The neighbor lads drifted out of the garden with shouts of retribution due another day. The stableboys crowded into the stables, yelling of thirst and victory. No doubt they'd go out the other side into a small dirt court which they frequented as their private yard. They'd drink beer, reshoot the match, and brag. Wat might boast of going adventuring abroad. A sentence here, another added, while they thought themselves unheard. A man could read much from a little. Robert got up casually and walked idly to the river to some swans floating there, going double with their reflections. He spoke briefly with Dame Margaret at her washing, flung the last of his sweet bread to the great white birds, and wandered along the steps toward a grape arbor that stood on the far side of the yard at the top of the steps, backed by thick lilac bushes, behind which was the stableyard for the lads who lived there. Under the arbor was a stone bench. Robert sat, elbows on knees, as if looking over the water; being quiet to keep his bells from telling of his presence. Behind the lilac bushes a jangle of voices shouted of triumph.

Then a shadow fell over him. He raised his eyes. Constance stood there, bright-eyed. He smiled welcome and rose politely.

"It's a forest overhead," she said. "Leaves. Few grapes and those sour, but it makes a pleasant place to sit apart."

She slapped idly at a spray of leafy vine that trailed down into her face. She moved toward him at the same time, her foot seemed to catch on some flagging, she stumbled and fell forward. He caught her. She was soft and warm and he did not think and kissed her. She moved her head back a little, surveyed him with a wise look.

"Sir Knave," she said, "you've had much practice at this sport."

"And you, Mistress Constance?"

"Was it the lady of the silver comb?" she inquired.

"Was it the apothecary's son, who dawdled in the garden before and gave me marvelous black looks?"

"A man with a quick tongue is a man who's been much around ladies."

"There was little to do in our country castle," he said, "but play chess or flirt."

"Chess," she said. "You've lost three times to my father, and he's indifferent at the game." She disentangled herself firmly and sat at the far end of the bench, almost but not quite laughing.

Ah, he liked her, despite her imperious nature. She was warmhearted and loving, and her kisses, judged by the one she'd tossed him, would drive no man away. Yet he feared her, also, for he thought on her too often and sought to excuse her nightwalking, when he knew well enough she did what she did with a will. It was as well the Indenture was signed and he could not stay.

Abruptly Constance moved closer and put her arm confidingly through his. "I do not want that grandsire to wed," she whispered, like a naughty child with secrets. "Robin, I have a better dowry," she said, very slowly, "than a nobleman's daughter."

He was sorry it had come to this. But she was headstrong and indulged. She would reach for what she wanted.

"You know nothing of me," he pointed out.

"I know all that I desire. You befriended Wat. You are kindhearted then, the greatest virtue of all in a husband. You are merry, too, which makes a happy house. Also you are bold, to make a safe one." She raised her hand and touched his face, so gently. "That you are handsome is the will of God, added to the rest."

"Mistress Constance," he said, "I thank you and will remember what you have said, but I cannot stay."

She dropped her hand from his face and her dark eyes flashed. "So it's the lady of the silver comb who's bewitched you! And how many men has she been with since you left?"

"None," he said. He dismissed explaining what she so gravely misunderstood.

"How do you know what she does, so far away in Wales?"

"She's not in Wales," he said, "for she left the castle when I did, and fled back to her brother in France."

"France?" she said. "France? It seems to me that's where you're going."

"With King Henry," he reminded.

"Ha!" she said, and tossed her head. "You may go with King Henry, but will you stay with him?"

She pulled her arm from under his and flounced back to the far end of the bench. "Robert Heartless. They knew how to call you in Wales. I'll marry my old man and when I'm a widow I'll find another husband, black-haired as Satan. These flaxen-heads are light of hair and head, and fickle as a wind and cold as winter!" Her anger was hot with jealousy, and she tried to burn. She and her father quarreled readily, and she had never learned to hold her tongue.

Robert said nothing. Should he explain she had no rival, and so encourage her to defy her father by refusing to marry the old man?

Constance wet her lips with her tongue, almost spoke again, then restrained herself with an effort, a new thing for her. She moved uneasily, disconcerted by his failure to answer her bitter taunt. Her face grew anxious. She feared she'd gone too far. She would make amends, but did not know how. She squirmed and twisted her fingers and glanced sideways at him.

The sounds in the garden seemed to swell. The stableboys behind the lilac bushes were pushing one another about and gossiping. Wat's voice rose above them all, exultant.

". . . but I would not be King Henry for such a price! A crown's no

54

payment!" Roars of knowing laughter from the others. "Here's Paul.
Paul! The beer's gone. Drink water and die of fever!"

"There's beer or better be," Paul said roughly. "I've been working
while you've been swilling, and if you've had it all I'll cut your throat
and drink your blood!"

"Sweet Paul," Wat said, with false solicitude, "we did but wonder
if you'd be king."

"I never trust you or your questions," Paul said bluntly. "Move over
and give me room to sit."

"Chance an answer, Paul," Wat urged. "Chance it! Would you be
king and change places with our Henry?"

"Willingly, you clod," Paul said. "I'd never lift a finger again."

Screams of raucous laughter, as the stable lads took their own meaning, and Paul saw he was the fool.

"I'll take this rock to your head, Wat," he said, "if you mock me."

"It's a joke, Paul, a joke."

"I see no joke," Paul said, growing furious. "If it's my accent, I'll
strangle you with your own bowstring, dwarf! You reek of the gutter,
but do not stand so high!"

There was instant scuffling. A peacemaker intervened hastily.

"Soft! Soft! Will you have His Worship back here, and beatings all
around?"

"I'll kill him," Paul said.

Another scuffle, wilder now, and cries as they were separated.

"Irishman!" Wat spat. "Your people run naked in your land!"

"At least I know my father!" Paul snarled back.

"Your mother brought you to see him hung!" Wat yelled.

Peacemakers again, redoubling their efforts. It was hastily explained
as only a joke and no cause for affray.

"Name me that joke," Paul demanded. "Make me laugh!"

"The joke was only this," someone explained. "The king sleeps
alone, and when you said—"

"Go to the devil, you liar," Paul said.

"It's true!" Wat was defending his gossip. "I had it of John the
Brewer, and he had it of a guard for Bishop Courtenay, King Henry's
friend. The bishop swears the king has been continent since he took
the crown. Two years . . . more! Dear God! Tie a stone about my
neck and drown me in the river first!"

Did knaves dare talk so of the king, poking scurrilous fun at a man who had no defender here! Did they dare! Henry had been a gallant prince and was an honest sovereign, and this cruel jesting was not his due; to be a butt for stableboys.

Constance caught at Robert's wrist, distracting him, as if she guessed at Welsh blood brewing a storm despite the Saxon heritage.

"It's only gossip," she was assuring him. "No harm is meant."

Robert jerked his wrist free.

". . . and the night before his coronation," Wat said avidly, "he called in a priest and made confession, and needed all the dark hours for remembering his sins. Now he lives like a monk, and why should any man want a crown if he can have no joy of it?"

"You've made that up!" Paul swore.

"Never! King Hal leaves it to stout lads like us to make more soldiers." He guffawed.

Robert lunged straight through the lilacs. A stableboy fell off the end of a bench with fright, and Wat swung around with a jerk.

"If any man will malign my sovereign," Robert said distinctly, "let him dare it to my face."

Wat's smile vanished, and he looked evil.

"It was Bishop Courtenay who said it, sir."

"What the king does is not for your amusement."

"And what the king does *not?*"

Robert slapped him sharply across the face.

Then Constance shoved between them.

"Wat, move back. Robert, my father is in the courtyard, and if he comes here, it will turn I'm to blame for all. Paul, if you sneak to my father with this tale, you'll have my displeasure. Robin, please. I cannot order you, but will you hear my plea?"

She tugged at his arm. And so he went, for it was her household and he her guest, and he had lunged into this unseemly situation without consideration. He had never flared up so before to lose his head. But he could not bear to hear the king maligned so roughly. It had stirred his wild Welsh blood, and the calmer Saxon strain lost ground.

"I'll have Wat beaten," Constance said, after they had passed her father's chair.

"Nay," he said bitterly. "I was the fool and know it. No man should suffer for that but myself."

Chapter 8

AS THEY supped that night Robert announced from a deep silence that he must be in Southampton by the fifth day of July, that he was grateful for their hospitality but must leave on the morrow. Constance gave a squeak. Dame Margaret gasped. The merchant looked between them.

"Did you think he would stay forever?" he inquired. "Now, Robin, we can't have you setting out like a beggar. You'll go from this house as a gentleman with a retinue. Have you thought on this matter?"

"I'll find three men in Southampton," Robert said, very stiffly.

"You'll find three men in *London*," the merchant amended. "You'll pick three lads from this house, and I'll supply the horses."

"Your Worship, I cannot accept it," Robert said.

"Pride fills no stomach," the merchant said. "I hold my life valuable and will make due return."

"I have the sword, for which I am grateful," Robert said.

"Loaned," the merchant reminded him. "You'll take three lads or I'll hold it as an insult. Do you think my life worth nothing? Before God," he roared, "I'll teach you better!"

Constance said hastily, "Robin, choose the men!"

The merchant took another tack. "Robin, I have no son, I'm too old for fighting now and I would send someone from this house."

Robert hesitated. The merchant had his own reasons, he was sure. It might be as well to learn them.

"John," he said.

"Gladly," the merchant said. "For the second?"

Constance looked at Robert, and tried to signal.

"Walter," he said.

Constance frowned, reminding of the promise to choose Wat. But could the knave be trusted now? Was he forgiving?

"For the third?" the merchant asked.

"I had not thought."

"Take Paul," the merchant suggested. "He speaks French."

"Wat speaks it better," Constance said. "He's been in France, besides."

Her father frowned this time.

"And he does not carry tales," she added.

"No, but he carries a knife," her father said. "I doubt he can be trusted, his feelings are too tender and he's proud above his station. John then, and Walter, and Paul."

A kitchen boy serving them slammed down a goblet and streaked for the door.

"Off to the stables," the merchant said, looking after him. "To tell who's going to France. They've talked of nothing but that since I said that three might go if you'd have them."

Had Wat bragged that he was chosen, since his mistress had assured him? Paul would drive that home.

"Now," the merchant said, turning businesslike, "I give nothing for nothing. With the retinue go letters I must have delivered in France."

"What do they deal in?" Robert asked.

"Merchandise," the merchant said. "My business must go on despite a war."

"It will not come to war," Constance insisted. "The French king's mad, his Dauphin spits blood, and their lords are like wolves at each other. They must have peace."

"While King Hal lives," the merchant said, "he'll pursue the war. His policy demands it, and his parliament backs him. Meanwhile, I must get a cargo for *Holy Mary*, lying empty at Ostend wasting money by the bag as she sits anchored."

"King Henry will give her a cargo fast enough," Robert suggested.

"Transporting soldiers? You're tangled in loyalty and expediency, two things that seldom agree. I am not so troubled. I'll not dirty my ship with soldiers. They'd fight with my sailors, and there's a man killed and my ship confiscated by the crown, for the ship is blamed if a man dies on her. Nay, Robin, I've done my duty, lending money."

He had grace enough to grin in his beard.

". . . against good security, of course. Constance, a sulky look does not improve you. When you are married, I hope you will be meeker. Your future husband's eager. I'll set a date within the week."

"I tell you," she said, "I will not marry him."

"And I tell you that you will. No more argument! Robin's off to a war, and you to a churching."

She stood up at her chair. "I will not marry him!"

The merchant did not move.

"I am master in this house," he said. "You must obey me and you will. I am determined on this marriage."

Constance burst into tears and ran for her chamber. Dame Margaret rose in a flurry of skirts and went off clucking after her.

The merchant sighed and leaned back in his chair.

"And weeping cannot change it," he said, with pity and regret.

Though the quarrel was a bitter one, the merchant and his daughter patched the breach, for late in the night they passed by Robert's chamber. He sat up in bed as he heard them go.

He had opened the letters given him to bear to France, to find they were all in Latin. He dared not take them to a priest to read, for fear of what they might contain. If treason were within, and his belongings searched, the Bible would prove him a Lollard and hang him. What then must he do next? He would not deliver what he could not understand, and there was little chance of translation.

He reached beneath the covers where he kept King Henry's sword. Moonlight came through the window to illuminate its hilt. It made a weird brightness, a glow, a misty . . . Robert went suddenly cold. It seemed as if a damp mist spread to surround him and he could see mistily within. . . .

His mother was Welsh. The race had magical powers. She had stared, they told him, at things that were not there. She stood, when she was young in Wales, and listened. He had his mother's nature, they said; she had bequeathed much of herself. And tonight, now, he felt this strangeness stirring in this seeming mist that obliterated this room, this house, this London, and carried him far away. He clasped the hilt of the sword, and it seemed he was near to the king.

The night is full of betrayal. The waning moon is the ill portent. Tonight one walks to meet another who travels by her dying light. Someone near the king. His price is reached. The money's paid. And King Henry is betrayed!

He saw no more, he knew no more. The mist seemed to float back and away, and left him sitting there, breathing as if he had fought.

King Henry had a trick, they said, of ever looking backwards. He liked no man behind him, and well might he be wary, for there had been assassins enough but none with the courage to face him. Ambush from behind was the king's lot, or poison in a cup.

Wherever he is tonight, God grant him a true man to guard him.

Robert waited tensely until at last the departing glow of the night-walkers in this house showed beneath his door. Let them go down. Let them sleep. Tonight he would be abroad the last of all. If a Frenchman lay above, they'd find him a body by morning. Robert flung back the covers and reached for his sword.

Then he waited, with the weapon buckled over the cold silk of his gown, waited with the patience learned in Wales. At last, he stepped out into the corridor. Black quiet was over all, yet it seemed as if the house itself was wakeful yet. The baleful light of the treacherous moon shone through the tall and pointed windows, marking their patterns aslant on the floor of the empty hall. All seemed clear.

He went back and lit his candle from a last ember in the bed of the fireplace, and emerged again to listen and then to climb upward in the stairway like a tunnel. The little candle he carried wavered like an unsteady pinnacle of light, stretching long and crouching short; the smell of wax was warm in his nostrils. He thought he heard a small sound! He flattened himself to the wall, but his own candle blinded him to all below, so he went on.

The upper corridor was plain and narrow, with rough doors on either side shutting away rooms that were compartments to store bales, until there was a door of oak with an iron lock. It would take a battering ram to force it. Robert tried the room on one side, but the common wall was perfect. He tried the room on the other side, and as he moved among the bales with his candle high toward the barrier he saw a loose plank. He set down his candle, hooked his fingers in the broken place and heaved backwards with all his weight. The board ripped away with a tortured squall. He stopped, appalled at the noise, and listened, but nothing stirred. They were, after all, two floors below. So he resumed. There was a piece of tall furniture blocking the other side, ample reason they had not discovered the flaw from there. He set his shoulder against it, and flung his strength toward it. The great chest squealed and shifted, and he eeled through the opening he made, thrusting the candle before. There were no windows; and no hidden Frenchmen. There was a table, two chairs, some half-used candles, and a cloth such as a dog might bed on. The only other furniture was the heavy cupboard. Robert opened it, puzzled.

There were a few books within. Two in Latin. The third in English, the vulgar tongue, and that he deciphered slowly. *The Lan-tern of Light*. Holy Mary! He seized another book below. A Bible! Forbidden! Contraband! There was enough in here to send all the household to the stake for heresy! Before God! They were *Lollards* in this house! He grinned with pure delight. He had suspected assassins and found fellow heretics. He had so carefully concealed his Bible, and they had so carefully hid theirs! He pushed their splendid book back and closed the cupboard doors. At the same moment, he heard a lock grate, and jumped to extinguish his candle. He was too late, the oaken door flung inward. Filling it was the merchant, with death in his eyes and a sword in his hand. Behind him stood Wat Strongbow, holding gleaming candles and an ax.

"I had liked you well," the merchant said, reproachful.

"You have nothing to fear from me," Robert said. "I'm as Lollard as you. They'd burn me at the same stake and save fuel."

The merchant moved in, but Robert did not back.

"Send Wat," he said. "Let him look beneath my pillow, and bring the Bible I've hid there in a leather skin. It is not so elegant as yours, but twice as perilous. My name's writ in."

The merchant paused, as a bull before it charges.

"Wat. Go down."

The knave went.

"If you think to fight," the merchant said, "I stand before you. If you think to flee, Blaunchette holds your bolthole."

Robert glanced back and glimpsed the white hound by the cupboard. Her eyes glittered, and the hairs rose on his neck.

"She'll rip out your throat for a snap of my fingers," the merchant said, quite pleasantly. "So do not move, Welshman. I'll take no chance with my daughter's life."

Robert stood very still. The merchant also. They listened to their own breathing until Wat came again, panting up the steps with a bundle of pages he thrust at the merchant.

He'd come back. He could have said the Bible was not there and had revenge for his slap. Yet he had returned. Robert stared at him, but Wat would not look up. Chapelle riffled through the pages awkwardly, by reason of holding his sword.

"God have mercy!" he exclaimed, and "By all the Holy Angels! St. George be my witness, he speaks the truth. And his name writ in besides! Wat, he carries his death warrant with him, and he King Henry's man. Did ever anyone make trouble for himself like this? King Henry's man and Lollard too? Let me look at this strange being. Has he two heads to hold two loyalties? Robin, either you are the one or the other. You may never be both."

"Nevertheless," Robert said, "that is how I stand."

"You'll not stand long then," the merchant said grimly. "One hint to the king, and you're dead. He let them sentence Oldcastle to the stake and Oldcastle was his dearest friend. He's pious!"

"But Oldcastle escaped, for all that," Robert reminded him. "I know he's running free in Wales right now."

"An outlaw," the merchant pointed out, "with a price on his head, and the stake waiting when he's captured."

The merchant walked in further, to survey the hole in the wall.

"You've torn my house apart," he declared. "What did you seek?"

"Assassins. Frenchmen. Spies. I've heard you come up here by night and I know you've had strangers in after dark."

"You've the ears of a fox, and sleep like a sinner, lightly. We came to read our Bible, and as for night callers, Lollards hang together, and merchants smuggle. When it comes to French, I have naught to do with them, save take my profits."

"A hundred thousand golden crowns?" Robert inquired.

"You heard that also? If you know that much, I'll tell a little more. I bought a French duke for my king, to keep him in his duchy when his own king calls him. Merchants may go where heralds may not. Come, I'll lock my door again and fix the wall tomorrow. Softly down the stairs. Constance sleeps like the dead but is perverse. She'd never rouse for twenty men fighting to the death in her chamber, but she might come inquiring as we go down on tiptoe."

The merchant led the way with the candles. Robert followed, and Wat came last of all. Halfway down the tunneled stair, Robert paused and Wat was forced to stop.

"Wat? I wondered if you'd return with the Bible, or say it never was and take revenge."

Wat's eyes glittered in the candlelight as the merchant turned to listen.

"I am sorry for the blow I dealt you," Robert said. "I was angry for Henry's sake." He held out his hand impulsively.

Hesitantly, Wat took it. Then abruptly bent and kissed it. Robert pulled his hand away, surprised.

Wat said hoarsely, "I have beaten Murdach often, but when I call he comes, ears flat, tail tight and all apology. I have no tail, and my ears stand out, but if you call, I'll follow."

The merchant looked between them. "It's a useless knave," he said, "brawling and wenching when there's work to be done. But take him if you will, or he'll kill Paul for jealousy. Now, who's to tell Paul he'll not go?"

Wat's face was savage.

"Your Worship," he said, "I told Paul hours since and put a hole in his head in the telling, to be sure the words went in."

They sat in the great hall near the kitchen, and Wat fetched two cups made of half-coconuts bound with silver. The merchant gestured from his chair to slanting shafts of moonlight beyond the glow of their candles.

"Once I filled that hall with my children," he said. "Arnulph was the eldest, and I think on him when I look at you. You favor him, though Arnulph's hair was black and yours is pale. His build was more stout, as I think on it. Also, his nose was larger and his mouth more wide. His eyes were dark. Nay, you are not alike at all. I do not understand it, but every time you pass I see my Arnulph. Yet he was never gay like you, but a serious lad worried for all England."

"I am worried enough for England," Robert said.

"Wherefore?"

"I had a dream, a dream of ill portent. I saw King Henry betrayed."

"By whom?"

"A cloaked man, holding out his hand for gold. I saw his fist close on it."

"So you searched my attic for him! You're forthright. That's the Saxon blood. But the dreaming, that's Welsh. They're a queer, dark,

brooding people. They see in the night and talk with spirits. I knew a
Welshman well. A ship of mine sailed, and he said he saw her breaking up on rocks in wild surf."

"Did she?"

"I do not know. She never came again to any port." The merchant
stared hard at Robert. "Some people scorn dreams, but I am not so
foolish. I'll ask about, cautiously. I'll listen if I can hear of any plots
against the king. Whatever crows in Southampton must hatch in London first. Ah, God, if but one of my sons were alive!"

He sighed.

"I had ten to begin; eight boys, two girls. Arnulph was the eldest.
Well, babies die, it's the will of God and not to be gainsaid, but I
was luckier than most and seven lived. Five boys, two girls. Fine children, obedient, except for Constance who was ever a spitfire and small
besides, the last of all the litter."

He sighed again.

"I see now the gentle ones took after my wife, God rest her well,
but as for Constance, that acorn fell under the oak tree. What I would,
that she would not. What I would not, that she would. My wife was
helpless with her, and I away too much. I said at last she must go to
the nuns at St. Anne's."

He tossed down wine against his painful memories.

"The last time, I was two months on a journey. When I returned,
I rode through the Aldgate unchallenged, not a man on guard. Here's
slackness, I bethought me, I'll set aright. Then I saw there were none
abroad in the streets, and this full daylight."

He crossed himself, and the candles flickered with the motion.

"Next came a cart rumbling down the street with a little bell sounding, piled with dead thrown in like wood. I thought I had the nightmare. In this nightmare I spoke to the driver. *Is the city taken?* I
asked. He said, *Yes, of the angel of death. The plague is upon us,
and more die than can be buried.*

"I galloped home. The street door there was open and blowing in
a wind. There was no one in this house or garden or stables. All vanished. I ran across the way and pounded at their door and it opened
of itself. They were all dead within. I ran down the street, shouting
and beating at doors, begging that they tell me where my wife was,
my wife and all my children. At length a man looked down from an

upper room and said, *Dead and carried to Pardon Churchyard, buried with a hundred others in a common grave.* I stood out in the street and wept. I think I meant to kill myself. My hand was on my dagger. Then I remembered. I had one child who was not in the house when the plague passed through.

"It was well no man sought to stop me. I galloped all the way. I smote the gate of St. Anne's convent, and frightened the poor nuns inside. I swore if no one answered, I'd burn all down, for if God took this last child, then I would as soon send the smoke of a convent to Him and serve the Devil the rest of my days!

"I know not what I did in my wrath, but one nun, God give her blessing, said I fetched straw from a field and piled it against the gate to begin my burning, until she came and spoke to me gently and opened, and praise to St. Anne, my daughter was left me. I built them new kitchens and gave them land and gold. To this day, they may ask of me what they will and I give it."

The merchant held out his cup and Wat stepped from a shadow and filled it.

"So it may be that you understand what this child means to me. She is spoiled, I acknowledge it. But what man can forbear to give his only child her way in all she desires? Now she desires you, and this I cannot grant. You know us for Lollards, others suspect it. I am surrounded by my enemies. I have lived hard and will die hard. I ask no quarter in this, but I must provide for my daughter when I am not here to protect her. Nay! I know you'd do what you could, but you have not dealt with enemies like mine, who lurk aside and use whispers for weapons. You have no friends in high places, the only bulwark against them. Therefore, she must marry the old man. I have thought much on it. She must! He's wily and his family's powerful, and once they're wed he must defend her or fall himself. Yet it is a pity, for she has a marvelous fond heart."

He gestured at Wat to refill Robert's cup.

"She brought this knave into the house, the winter after the plague. The snow was deep, the wind bitter. They died in the streets. One day there was a whimpering at our courtyard gate. Constance cried out that someone starved there, and would give me no peace until I had opened. Wat was lying there, ragged and beaten, with blood frozen on him and streaked down our gate where he fell. He would not tell us whence he came, or could not, for he had been much struck about the head and was a little foolish. I would have turned him away, for he had a dangerous crazed eye, and though he was starved, the muscles stood out on his arms. He was a dirty, bloody animal and maddened, but Constance seized him, and I could not drag her back without him."

The merchant turned his head slightly as Wat moved away.

"Therefore," he said, "he will do anything for her, but as for me, he remembers I did not want him."

Wat did not move in his shadow, and the merchant sighed and set down his cup.

"When must you be in Southampton?"

"The fifth day after St. Peter and St. Paul."

"You can reach Southampton in five days' time," the merchant said. "Therefore, stay one more day with us. St. Peter and St. Paul is a great holiday in London, and Constance has made such plans. Let her have this celebration. She'll be married and sober soon enough. She had Arnulph's clothes from the press yesterday before you woke, to choose a garment for you to wear for holiday array. The maids have worked in secret to shorten the cote-hardie to the fashion that you favor. It's fine dress, Robin, brown velvet trimmed with sable, embroidered in gold with oak leaves. My wife did the orphrey work. Arnulph swore he would not wear it else, the garment was too plain. I remember my wife sitting there by the fire and the gold thread flashing while Arnulph leaned on her chair, overseeing every stitch."

"How can I take what was your son's?"

"Because I wish it for my daughter's sake. She is yet alive, and the boy's long dead. Will you stay another day?"

He should not. He knew he should not, for a premonition of ill-chance was on him. But he dismissed it. They had been kind to him here, and he had grown fond of them all.

"I'll stay till tomorrow," he said.

Chapter 9

THERE were huge bonfires in every square, each circled by singing and dancing maids and men. London blazed, kissed strangers, picked pockets and went mad. Every door was garnished with green birch and long fennel, and flowers, and lighted by lamps of glass with oil burning in them.

Up and down the lighted streets more lights went marching with the marching watch, while noise crashed all around: singing, bellowing, shouting, neighing, barking. Armor clanked, trumpeters trumpeted, and drummers and fifers banged and squealed. The mayor marched, and his footmen and henchmen and torchmen. The sheriff marched, and the guilds of the City marched too. Archers marched, pushing back the mobs with their ranks, dressed in coats of white fustian with the arms of the City on breast and back, their bows bent in their hands. Pikemen marched in glittering corselets; and morris dancers bounced at the tail of every procession.

It was worse than a battle. Robert had to spur his horse against a wall of screaming humans swaying in one mass in the streets.

Wat shouted, "The French can be no worse than this!" and laid about him with a whip to clear more space for his horse. Bearded sailors off *Jesu* rode behind Wat and Robert with Constance and her aunt between them, and last came Walter and John and Paul, waving torches that spewed sparks on the heads of everyone.

They reached their destination after a bitter struggle to the alley at the back of the Pope's Head Tavern. Here in this favorite ambush of thieves the crowd shied off for a brighter path while they jumped in with a rush and clattered down the long dark way to a mean court at the back. They left their horses there, with a boy who swore he'd stay by them.

"Though God have mercy on any man who thinks to steal my King-at-Arms," Constance said. "He's all in a passion from the crowds. They get rougher every year."

67

The smell of roasting flesh reached to them as they entered, and a blast of heat from the kitchen.

One of the sailors inquired if the ale was good. This was a tavern above a poor man's purse, he said apologetically, and so he did not know.

"You'll find soon enough how it is," Robert said. "And His Worship bid me tell you this. He will pay for all!"

There was a delightful, shocked pause for a moment, as they realized what Robert said.

Then the men all shouted alike and stampeded for the front to seize room at a table by the empty fireplace, while the landlord himself escorted Robert and the women to the place he had saved for them.

"This is not choice," Constance declared, with a scowl that was a sweeter miniature of her father's.

"But I like it very well," Robert said. It had a handy exit and was near the horses.

She shrugged and sat down without argument and looked around at the noisy crowd, while a sweating serving wench fought her way through to them, laying about lustily with a wet towel to beat down hands that reached for her, until at length she stood by Robert.

Dame Margaret wanted beer and so did Constance. Robert thought of all the wine he'd already drunk this day and ordered more, to avoid a sickness in his middle. It seemed to him as if all the merchants in London had put tables of dainties at their door, serving out food and drink all afternoon. Since the Worshipful Alderman was known all over London, they had been able to pass scarcely a single house without a horsebridle seized and demands made that they drink up or forfeit forever the regards of the master there. Constance was mannerly and whatever was offered went down at the homes of her father's friends: salt fish and ham, birds, puddings, pickled fruits, lampreys, pasties, honey cakes, figs, and God alone knew what some things were she devoured.

Now she looked about restlessly with bright, excited eyes. Robert watched her, warned by her father that she might flirt when she was joyous with the spirit of the holiday.

Ah, my lady had decided where to throw her glances. On the opposite side of the room was a dais, guarded by a carved rail, a place of honor. Here under the low roof with his head raised by the dais into wood smoke hanging among the ceiling beams was a lord and his henchmen at a long table that groaned under food. This lord faced Robert. He was grossly fat, red-faced, and sweating so hard his bright green houppelande was marked with it. A jeweled collar was about his neck, and his hands glittered when they moved. His henchmen shouted from one end of the table to the other, but the lord himself was quiet, with his lip curled up in a sneer. Recognition fluttered in Robert.

"Who is he?" he asked my lady. "The fat one in green."

"Him! That's Edward, Duke of York, four times pardoned for trying to murder King Henry."

York! Picture him younger, thinner, and in Wales. Picture him an old enemy, the first that Robert had made. He recognized him now.

". . . four times that he was caught," Constance amended. "God knows how many other plots he spun and blamed on others. Yet the king pardons him each time."

"Henry is a gentle king," Dame Margaret pronounced.

"Let the fat duke beware," Constance said. "He's not loved in London."

"Nor was he loved in Wales," Robert said.

"You know him, then?"

"It was long ago," Robert said. "I was a child when he came to the castle, at Christmas."

"And?"

Robert shrugged. "He went away again."

Wales. The gaunt stone castle. A huge ox roasting in the great hall, for the kitchens were overwhelmed. The children gathered before it, staring, except for Robert, who stood by the countess. Another woman stood by.

"The duke is coming through the gate with his retinue, my lady," she had said.

"Which duke?" the countess asked.

"Edward of York, my lady, who is cousin to the king."

For then Henry the Fourth was ruling on his usurped throne, and this King Henry was the Prince of Wales.

"Which king?" the countess asked, to be scornful, for many thought poor King Richard was not dead but hiding and might come back for his stolen throne.

Robert asked if this was the Duke Edward who fought so well.

"His courage is good," the countess said. "It's his character that's bad."

Edward of York passed Christmas with them. He was in his thirties, losing his warrior's hard body. He was a short man turning gross, his face marked by disappointments. He was an ambitious, intelligent man always crossed by his own treachery and with no hope of posterity, for he could not get sons. It was said he could be amusing when he chose, but at their castle he chose only to drink himself sodden. It was also said the sight of Count Llewellyn's six sons had soured the royal duke's temper, when he could not manage even one. It was certain that he acted like a wounded boar.

At New Year, according to the custom, the children drew water from a new well and went among the feasting company, dipping dried rosemary sprigs in the water and sprinkling the guests for good luck and all blessings in the New Year, while they piped out high-voiced songs.

It happened that Robert reached to sprinkle the Duke of York. The cold drops hit the duke's hot face and startled and angered him both, for he flung back his chair and staggered up, then flung his goblet at Robert as if he were some kitchen knave.

"Have it back!" Robert exclaimed and flung his vessel of water.

The duke seized a knife.

"If you strike me," Robert said, "I'll kill you for it when I'm grown!"

The count had meanwhile come running, grabbed Robert and thrust him back.

"Now there's a spirited boy," he said, "and if he's displeased you, I'll punish him, but none of it was meant for harm."

"Another of your sons?" the duke had asked.

"That one, no," the count said. "Now, Your Grace, I've a new horse that you'd like. The ground is hard, true, but there's a wolf in a thicket near the castle. Let's hunt and leave the castle to women!"

He'd laughed and clapped the duke on the back and jostled him until he was talked into hunting as drunk as he was, and his mind put on other than Robert. But the count turned as he supported York from the hall, and nodded. He'd approved.

The countess said, as the men swayed out, "Rob, you were right. I give you good counsel. Always be bold. Break before you bend. It becomes you."

After that York ignored Robert, whether by reason of forgetting or for fear of his host's anger, no one knew—but Count Llewellyn had invited guests and held them for ransom before, and now he showed favor to Robert. When he hunted, he took Robert. And as soon as the boy was fourteen, he had him as his squire, following into battle. He had been all for his thick-bodied sons and found he could not trust them. The youngest were stupid, and the two eldest craved his lands and title. He turned to Robert and from that moment, Robert had to plot for his life; for Rhys and Gryffyd were greedy lest they lose one penny of what they might squeeze from their father.

Yet with all their avarice and grasping at power, they could not come nigh this Duke of York. Four attempts on his liege lord's life, and four times forgiven.

He was aware again of Constance, smiling prettily at a young man in white and gold, whispering to the Duke behind his hand.

"And that one?" Robert said.

"God knows," Constance said. She leaned closer. "Pick a quarrel with him, Robin."

"Why?"

"That I may see you fight. A little, little quarrel will do." She measured with her thumb and forefinger how small it might be and please her still.

"Leave off," Robert said.

She grinned like a street urchin. "Welshman, your temper rises. Look how the oak leaves flutter as the storm begins!"

She poked at the embroidered oak leaves, rising and falling as he breathed. He could have kissed her, the pretty bit of impudence, but instead he scowled. He must remember York and wonder if York remembered him, for they said the duke was vindictive and always paid old scores. But remember York, with Constance by him? She was dressed in fine array, her hair in two braids and each thrust into a cylindrical gold mesh caul on either side of her face before her ears, with the open ends up and down. The mesh of the cauls was set with jewels at each crossing of the strands, and a gold fillet bound them, crossing her forehead low. She wore a mesh net, jeweled also, over her back hair, and over that a tiny transparent veil that had been stiff at the beginning but now had gone limp. Her gown was scarlet sendal, cut too low, but her father did not object to this, it seemed, as long as her arms were decently covered.

"He has a crooked nose," Constance said, "and his eyes are set too close. They say only natural sons have eyes so close. Do you suppose he knows his father? Ask him, Robin."

"I'll not provoke a fight for your amusement," he told her.

She moved away from him, affronted, and brushed her forearm fretfully across her forehead.

"Landlord!" she called. "Landlord! Open a window, or I'll roast!"

"Let it be," Robert advised her. "He needs the shutters closed to keep noise in and the watch out. This is well past legal hours and he's chancing it."

But she was not to be denied her open shutter, for the slim knight in white and gold had risen and slithered around duke, henchmen, chairs and all, with sword hilt catching and clattering as he came. He flung open the shutters on a window to the back court while the host watched, appalled. The dandy bowed to Constance. She inclined her head. The dandy returned to his seat. York had missed nothing. His eyes watched from their folds of fat.

"Robert?" she cooed.

He looked down. She was worshiping him with her eyes, which added to his turmoil. He tried to ignore her and watch the duke, but her perfume was warm and surrounded him.

"There!" she exclaimed, triumphant. "You're sweating! I told you the room was too hot!"

The Duke of York said something to the dandy, who nodded and kicked back his chair and stood. The room went tense. Well, it had come, and it pleased Robert well enough. A fight took energy and he had much to spare now. He pushed Constance aside and stood also.

The last man ceased talking in the middle of a sentence. By the fireplace, Wat's shouting crew was silent, and Walter got up and slipped out the back. Robert flicked a look of approval to Wat, who'd thought of having the horses ready to run.

The white-and-gold dandy pledged his cup to Constance and drank, an open insult.

"Mistress," Robert said, "it's time for you to go."

"Oh, nay!" she said. "Not I! I'll not miss this too."

"You will not be here," he said, "when the battle starts, nor when the watch comes to allay it." He caught her by the wrist.

Wat jumped to his feet, alert.

Constance jerked back against Robert's hold and began a tug of war. Then the white-and-gold man was beside them.

"The lady does not like you," he said haughtily.

"Get to your drinking," Robert told him, loud in the silent room. "That is your business, and none of this."

"I'll escort the lady home," the dandy said.

Robert said, "Dame Margaret!"

Dame Margaret roused herself with a shake. "Fighting?" she inquired, startled.

"I will not go," Constance said and flung herself on her stool.

"The lady is pleased to stay," the dandy said.

"The lady is pleased to do as she is told," Robert replied.

The dandy drew his sword with a sibilant hiss of steel. And Robert drew his. The folly bells jingled as he shoved a stool aside with a kick. Benches scraped and trestles banged as they were flung into corners and out of the way. The two opponents circled warily.

"Lords! Sirs! Lordings!" the landlord wailed. "Not in my tavern, as you are gentlemen! Your Grace!" He turned appealing to the duke. "Ah, lords!"

Robert yelled "Lancaster!"

The duke's man shouted "York!"

And Robert lunged to press the fight. The dandy fended him off, and his face showed he knew already he was overmatched. Robert rushed him backwards.

A man shouted, "Ten nobles on the one in brown! Who'll back the man in white?"

Shouts began all around, and in the midst of it, abruptly, Robert struck home. A stain sprang out on the dandy's cote-hardie. He staggered back against a post with bloody froth seething at his lips.

"À moi!" he moaned, and blood ran over his chin and he fell. Three of his companions overleaped the rail.

"Shame," yelled someone.

Wat bawled in anger. A sailor yelled "Boarders!"

And the fight turned into a riot, with everyone engaged. The land-

73

lord lunged about, snatching torches from brackets and flinging them into the fireplace to darken the room. Planks crashed. Everything movable was flung.

Then came an ominous drumming; fists raining blows on a door. "The watch!" the landlord bawled, despairing, and wrung his hands in a corner.

The battle hesitated. Robert slashed his opponent hastily on the sword arm, leaped back and seized Constance down from the table where she'd stood, swinging a stool at any who ventured near. He flung her shrieking out the back window to Walter and leaped out too. Wat shoved Dame Margaret next, and the sailors covered retreat as long as they could, then popped out from the writhing room. Robert gave King-at-Arms a crack to send him headlong, and galloped wildly after. The watch pursued them screaming *Stop! Stop in the king's name!* But by then they were in Lombard Street, inextricably mixed with merrymakers, while the watch tried to halt other brawlers spewing from every window and door. And so they got safely away.

There were sore eyes and swollen lips and tender noses among them. A sailor had been knifed in the leg and swore all the way to the jouncing of his horse that gave him hurt. Robert discovered his linen paltock sleeve was dark with blood, but it was not his sword arm so it did not matter.

The sounds of strife behind them lessened. They walked their horses as soon as they dared, to call less attention to themselves and their disheveled state. Bonfires still flared in many places, but only the younger celebrants were now abroad, and the tables with good things had long since been taken back into the houses. Garlands lay underfoot. All the lights had vanished, though a red glow in the sky showed where some slum was burning down.

Wat said, with deep satisfaction, "That was a good riot."

"And well for us if we were not known," said Paul, who always thought on the dark side. "York would be a bitter enemy."

"The watch got him," Wat reported with glee. "I saw it. A man-at-arms at each elbow, dragging the fat duke away." He chuckled. "Think on it. Twelve knights tossed in one dungeon, gold spurs and all. And a duke! God be my witness, a genuine duke, in a genuine London jail!" He guffawed.

"You're drunk," Paul said.

"With joy!" Wat admitted. "I'd tell my children of this night, if I only knew their names!"

"It's well for you you're leaving London," Paul said with morose envy.

Now King-at-Arms grew impatient for his stall and thrust up between Robert and Wat. Constance saw the wet left arm.

"You're wounded!" she exclaimed.

"It has already ceased to bleed," he assured her.

"It was only that I never saw you fight," she said sadly. "I never meant all London to join in!"

He smiled, despite himself. He had fought well, killed his man, and no shame to him, and was it not after all natural for a maid to want to know what a man was made of?

"Think on what to tell your father," he advised her sternly.

"My father is abed by now, thanks be to St. Anne."

The sorry procession halted at the garden gate. Wat flung himself down, and cursed as he felt some obscure hurt. Then he straightened again and opened the gate with an iron key. Murdach whined welcome from his iron ring. Wat hushed him. The horses moved in quietly. Wat barred the gate and they moved toward the stable. Then all stopped, frozen.

For under the blowing torch by the lintel stood the merchant, with his arms crossed under his beard. The two sailors flung their reins to Paul and hastened off to *Jesu* at the quay. The stableboys rushed the horses into the stables at a trot.

Robert and Constance and Dame Margaret were left to face the merchant. Somewhere down the street a swinging sign complained of rising breeze. Wat came cautiously out of the stable to loose Murdach from his ring.

"Wat!"

The knave stopped abruptly.

"Was it a good fight?" the merchant inquired.

Wat turned with a grin. "Mother of God!" he exclaimed with a lilt. "What a bloodletting, and with the Duke of York, that traitor! The watch leaped on like terriers, but we got clean away!"

The merchant smiled.

Dame Margaret said, "He'll stand there the night, fighting it over, but as for me, I want my bed."

Whereupon she marched away. Constance and Robert followed, moving aside as Blaunchette burst out to go to her master. They went slowly down the three steps to the kitchen. The hearth fire burned still, and a kettle bubbled and steamed there. Constance took his arm to halt him where they were alone, and he winced.

"Ah," she said, "I had forgot your wound, and you were hurt but for my vanity."

"I'll cherish the scar," he told her.

"Let me wash it," she said.

"It will heal swiftly of itself."

"Your wound, perhaps, but never mine. I have known you only days, yet there's not time enough in the rest of my life to heal me from this party. See out the window. Light streaking the sky. Oh, God, already? The night's gone."

"And here's Blaunchette," Robert said. "Your father won't be far behind."

"The folly bells rang out the day we met," she said, "they told me that you would not stay. Following your lady to France. Go then, Robert Heartless. They named you well. I do not care how soon you leave!"

She stepped back disdainfully, then suddenly burst out weeping.

He longed to tell her of the countess, that there was no true love he pursued, but only war and loot in France that he might wear the gold spurs of a knight. But wherefore? She must marry another; let her do it thinking his heart was far away.

The merchant came in then. The two men looked at each other with compassion for her.

"Here now, tears are in vain," her father said to comfort her. "You'll learn to love the old man. He's kind and will be doting."

She let out a howl, and fled.

"Well, I'm sorry for her grief," the merchant said, "but I look to preserve her life."

Dame Margaret came bustling in. "What did you say to her? The girl's fit for Bedlam the way she's weeping."

"Sleep by her. Comfort her," the merchant said.

Dame Margaret said, "I loved when I was young. My father married me to another, and it was a good marriage, but I never forgot the first. His name was Robert, too, and he was gentry. He was killed in the lists at Smithfield, the day I turned sixteen." Abruptly she turned away.

"Come over to the fire," the merchant said to Robert. "I'll wash that wound before it festers. Here, I'll help you with the cote-hardie."

The merchant unfastened his points and peeled off the paltock and threw that bloody-sleeved garment in a corner. Then he took hot water from the kettle steaming over the fire and sloshed some in a basin, wrung out a cloth, and touched it to the wound.

"The gash is clean, and not too deep. Here's some balm we use for saddle galls on the horses. It's good for wounds as well." He smeared some on and Robert set his jaw against the sting. "This brings back my own youth," the merchant said. "Patching up after a brawl."

"I am sorry for it, and that Constance was involved."

"Think not of it," the merchant advised. "I'll send to the landlord for the bill and the damage, and add something for his memory to fail. A little high play on a feast night is only to be expected. I was no calm man myself. Lift the arm. I'll bind it. When do you think on leaving?"

"Now," Robert said.

"It's not daylight. The road is dangerous."

"It would be more dangerous for your house if I stayed. The Duke of York remembers me, I think, from another time. I'll go before he finds me here."

"I do not care who knows it," the merchant said.

"Wat's waking the men and saddling horses."

"Delay another day," the merchant urged. "If York's in jail, he'll stay there. He's hated in London."

"I go tonight."

"Without sleep?"

"I could not sleep. Therefore, let it be now."

"Holy St. Anne," the merchant burst out. "I could weep with Constance."

But he woke a kitchen boy and sent him to bring down Robert's belongings. Blaunchette came over from where she had lain watching and put her muzzle on Robert's knee, her eyes turned sorrowfully upward.

"She never did that for any but myself," the merchant said. "All the household dotes on you."

"I have been happy here," Robert said.

"And yet you go. Before God! I had thought honest men were fools before this time!"

But he helped Robert dress, for the arm was stiffening fast. Robert strapped on his sword and picked up his folly bells.

"The house will be silent now," the merchant said.

Robert jerked a single small bell free and put it on the table.

"That's for remembrance," he told him.

The door from the courtyard opened, and they turned to the sound. Wat Strongbow stood there.

"The horses are ready," he said.

Chapter 10

THE MERCHANT looked out the side windows at the rose bushes in the narrow garden. They had bloomed all June but were leaves and thorns in late July. His daughter came in then, having just returned.

"What did you do with yourself this morning?" he inquired.

"I went to mass with Allys at St. Olave's," she said.

"And then?"

"To mass at St. Paul's."

"And then?"

"To mass at St. Mary-le-Bow."

"Afterwards?"

She gestured. *Home.* "I got some news at least," she said. "The Duke of York's out of jail. He left for Southampton yesterday."

"What of it?" the merchant asked. "A brawl in a tavern is nothing to revenge, and besides, he provoked it."

"York spent most of a month in a dungeon."

"He's spent years of his life in dungeons," the merchant said. "A little more won't swell the tally."

"But honor's involved. He sent a man to King Henry, praying for release, and King Henry sent back word he would not intervene, that the king's justice is above all, even the king."

"York should have had more sense than to bother King Hal with a trifle."

"A trifle? If the army was not delayed, it would have sailed without him weeks ago."

"Robin's lost among thirty thousand, stuffed into Southampton," her father said. "He'll not come out deliberately to tease the duke. Now, when will I be fed?"

That sent her to the kitchen with something to occupy her time. Then the table was set and food was brought, but she only dabbled with hers. Well, in another century perhaps lovers might meet and marry, but not in this, nay, not in this. He sighed, and thought how to tell her he'd made arrangements for her marriage.

"This morning . . ." he began.

She looked at him, sad-eyed.

"What of this morning?" she asked.

He could not tell her now. "It's a fair morning," he said lamely.

"I'm glad Wat's by him," she said. "Wat would cut a duke's throat as fast as any man's." She picked up her goblet and she tinkled. There was Robin's gold bell around her neck on a chain.

It was not the day to tell her, but it was well that all was done and the marriage contract seen to while the girl and Allys rattled around from mass to mass. The two old men had sat back, father and bridegroom, and the lawyers argued obscurities, and a word out here and a word in there, signatures, seals, and copies to each party. John Taylor was almost sixty, but eager. He was in fair health, had an excellent disposition, and was at an age where a young girl was a wondrous thing. Constance would have her way with him, no doubt of that at all.

It was strange to see her so quiet.

At length she said, "It were a shame for the moths to devour all Arnulph's fine things."

He guessed at what she wanted. "Is there such a hurry? Robin's not worn out his own. But take them, take . . . two garments. Remember, they must go on the back of a horse."

She did not finish her food, but called her maids, and puddled the floor with color as she spread the things out there. Silk and velvet and wool. Ermine and sable and vair. She stood in the middle to choose.

It was painful to see them so. That tawny made for a wedding. And there . . . that violet and azure silk, in diamonds, that he never thought to see again, made for Arnulph's own wedding and never worn at all. As he looked at it Constance bent to pick it up, and held it for him to see.

"It will become him," was all he said.

"Do you like it as well as the scarlet?"

"Equally," he said.

The problems of lovers and their partings. He was grateful for Mistress Anne in her neat cottage on the edge of his hunting preserve, a reasonable ride from London. He could visit if he chose, or not if he chose. Anne was a woman grown, the daughter of his gamekeeper, and his companion since he was eighteen and home from sea with his first prize in tow. She was assiduous to his comfort, and had never objected to his wife, nor sought advancement when he was left a widower.

He felt suddenly maudlin about it. He'd ride out today. He'd bring a gift. It had been a long time since he'd taken care to choose a present.

Yes, he'd visit today and let business rest. Anne had a fund of tasty gossip got of her father at the local tavern, all the latest scandal. It might be he'd hear of the Duke of York. Of late he enjoyed this talk more and more. A quiet sitting by the fire in the winter, or under a tree in the fall. Well, he'd had a hot youth and all things cooled.

He watched his daughter and Mary standing together, heads bent over scarlet velvet, thinking how the stitches must be ripped. Then he heaved up to his feet.

"I'll ride out to see how the deer do on my preserve," he said. "I'll be late for supper."

"I'll wait to eat with you," Constance said.

"I'll be late," he warned her again.

"I'll wait till you come," she said.

He nodded and departed. He bought a topaz ring and a bolt of yellow silk. He stopped once more to get a cask of pickled lampreys, and tie it on behind his saddle. Then, encumbered with all this, and whistling one of Robin's tunes, he rode gaily out of London.

To come back at a gallop on a lathered horse, with no gifts, no songs, and no smile, but a grim look. He strode into the great hall, and Constance started up from her sewing.

"There's nothing ready," she said.

"I have no time for eating," he said. "Where's Paul?"

"Gone to Norwich."

"I know he's gone to Norwich. Is he back?"

She shook her head.

"I can't trust the others," he said. "I'll take Blaunchette."

The white hound wagged, understanding she'd travel the black streets this night.

"My lord father," Constance said, "what can Paul do that I cannot?"

"Fight in London's alleys," he said. "Plots! Plots!" He contained himself with an effort so his voice would not inform the house. "London's like France tonight. Where two men whisper together, murder's planned." He broke off and started for the door. "I only came for Paul and a fresh horse."

She ran after him and caught his arm.

"Let me know the danger, at least," she said. "I'll help in any way I can."

He looked down at her, a little thing. But if he could not trust her, he could not trust himself.

"Anne had grave news from her father," he said. "When I rode in, she was preparing to ride to me, though I had bid her never come to my house. When were you last to confession?"

"Months ago," she said. "Does it displease you?"

"I would it were years!" he said. "It was a week ago they seized him. No . . . no, don't turn faint . . . not Robin, but your confessor. The priest's already convicted of Lollardy. Stay away from St. Olave's, it's brimming with spies. Suspicion is on all nigh him, and he was your confessor. Still, it's been months, they may forget you. They cannot try all London, and a spy can only spy so far."

"Can our lawyer help him?"

"It's hopeless," the merchant said. "Besides, we have many priests in London and one can easily be spared, while I have a single child and cannot spare her."

"He was a good man and kind to me," she said. "Let me visit him, at least."

"Not in this world. I told you these were grave matters. He's hung and stiff on his rope."

Her mouth opened, but no sound came.

81

A shuffle of feet.

"Well?" the merchant roared.

A boy from the stable spoke in a frightened voice. "The black horse is saddled, Your Worship."

The merchant dismissed him impatiently.

"Must you go tonight?" Constance asked.

"I must. There are Lollards gathering, and uprising planned. I will not sleep till I learn the plot."

"Have they kept it from you?" she asked, surprised.

He nodded grimly. "They know I've done king's business and helped spin plots in France. They fear I'll try to warn him. I will! Ay, I will. If I can learn what they'll do!"

"Thank God, Robin's gone," she said fervently. "We'll not touch him with our danger. If the king is murdered . . ."

"Then Lollards are scapegoats," her father finished. "Stay in the house. Do not open doors. If we must run, there's *Jesu* at the quay."

She hastened beside him into the courtyard and stood by as he mounted. Blaunchette waited, eager for adventure, a vicious fighter for all her loveliness.

"Obey me, Constance," he said, down from his horse. "I care for nothing but you, and would not leave you now if it were not to preserve King Hal for England."

And again at the gate, as she unbolted it.

"Be mindful of what I say," he warned her. "Bolt the gate, turn Murdach loose, stay within the house, and do not open doors!"

She waited in the great hall before the fire, listening to the storm thundering outside and trying to stay her trembling. She perceived now in her fear that high courage in some people was merely a doing before a thinking. If she had thought, she would never have dared to go out. Yet she had gone. She was an impulsive coward who acted, and then wept. She shook with terror now for what she'd done.

Oh, but her father would be raging if any told him she had left the house. But she'd done it openly, as if there was nothing to hide, surely they would not think to mention this to him. And if Paul, returning from Norwich, had accepted her action as normal—at least in the beginning—why should any others think it strange? If they did not tell her father, then she would not tell him either, for all her fear and wish to unburden her conscience. Pray God Paul kept his babbling mouth shut! Should she have paid him? That was a mistake. She saw it now. By paying him to be quiet, she had admitted she was uneasy.

She moved even closer to the fire, and could not warm herself. She was frightened for what she'd done, but she could not regret it.

She waited, tormented, and arguing it all over and over until dawn. Only then did the merchant come home. She leaped to her feet and ran to him, to clasp as much of his bulk as she could.

He pushed her back. "I'm wet," he said. "I'm dripping."

"Your Worship," she said, half sobbing, "you're safe. I care for nothing else."

"Now, now," he said, embarrassed at showing tenderness.

She bethought herself of his business. "Did you discover anything?" she asked.

"Murder," he said. "Is Paul back yet?"

"Do not send him on your business," she begged.

"I cannot write the message that must go to Southampton, and I cannot go myself," he said. "I must stay in London to quell the uprising that will surely follow the spilling of royal blood."

"The less Paul knows, the safer for us all," she said. "Send me."

He looked at her piercingly. "Ay," he said without argument, as if both had known from the start it must be she.

"King-at-Arms can reach Southampton in three days," she said, "no matter how bad the roads."

He nodded, mouth set. "I'll give you sailors from *Jesu* for escort," he said, and strode out through the kitchen, while she ran to wake her aunt.

She was on her way by sunrise with her party. She dared not think too long. From horseback, she looked behind and saw the steeps and spires and roofs of London above the disreputable walls. The beacon was still alight on St. Mary-le-Bow. July the twenty-fifth. She must be in Southampton by the twenty-eighth and there were seventy miles or more to go on dangerous roads, with many delays, ahead.

She turned her face to the west, and rode as if she had been her father's son.

Chapter 11

AFTER the muster, Robert left Southampton and stayed at an inn beyond the walls. He hated the walled port. It was a stifling, stinking place jammed with soldiers, sailors, pages, pickpockets, harlots, and scornful lords thrusting scornful horses through the press. The army had been delayed too long. The beer grew daily weaker and the wenches more rapacious. The army had spent its pay while waiting and now slept in the streets, and robbed when it could.

Gossip said August the first was departure time, but there were other rumors, untraceable to any source, that said they would never go at all, so that Robert remembered vividly his dream of a betrayal.

The Duke of York was here now, strengthening the feeling of danger near the king. He had arrived the day before, on July the twenty-seventh. Four times York had been forgiven. Was he risking a fifth attempt? There had been much to excite suspicion. Little groups of nobles in crowded streets, whispering with sober faces. Little parties gathered in corners, conversing, departing in diverse directions. Everyone knew there was an evil gathering, but what it was and where it came from was obscure. Robert could do little; but he knew the merchant was powerful in London and had sworn to listen for a plot. Therefore, Robert haunted the chief road from London, to intercept any messenger who might be sent.

The shadows of a hot afternoon were across the road. Another day futilely gone, it seemed, until Robert saw a cloud of dust that turned to a yellow mist enveloping a party riding hard.

Robert said, squinting, "There's a gray horse in the forefront."

Wat watched. "King-at-Arms," he said. "He always goes with his head very high. There's Dame Margaret on the chestnut. The others ride like sailors. *Jesu* must be in from Calais."

They spurred forward to meet the others, and the parties met, joined, and milled in the road. King-at-Arms swung aside to a green meadow, and Robert cantered after him until the gray horse stopped,

84

apart from men and bushes alike. Robert felt the hair of his neck rise up when he saw her face.

"Your father?" he inquired instantly.

"Well," she said. "All the household is well, but London's sick. The Lollards are gathering to rise. Oldcastle's in rebellion."

"Rebellion?" He showed his disbelief. "Sir John's no rebel. He's convicted by the Church of Lollardy, but never by the king of treason. Besides, he's in Wales on the run."

"He's near London, like a falcon above her prey," Constance insisted. "He's in rebellion now. He's turned on the king at last."

"The fool! The king will crush him!"

"The king will be dead," she said, "and his three brothers."

"Holy Mary!" Robert said, and crossed himself. "How? When?"

"They're to die at one time. The Lollards have been stirred up to prevent London from sending aid to Henry's party after his death. In the end, we'll be blamed for it all."

"York's in it," Robert declared.

"For once he's clean," she said. "His name has never been mentioned."

"He grows cleverer as he grows fatter," Robert said. "He lets others take credit and blame alike, and counts his gains alone."

"It may be," she said, and Robert knew how grave things were when she refused contention.

"Who's in it?" he asked.

"Thomas Grey of Heton," she said.

"I've seen him, hanging about in the streets with others."

"And one the Earl of Cambridge?"

"Ay, York's brother."

"York is not in this," she insisted. "I do not like him and will not defend him, but they say he's not in this. Our information is good. There is one other in the plot, more dangerous even than York. Do you know who is thickest with Cambridge?"

"No," Robert said. "Never him. Not Lord Scrope. Name the Archangel, but not Henry's truest friend."

"Henry, Lord Scrope," she said, and named him.

"But the two Henrys are always together," Robert protested. "Lord Scrope is privy to the king's thoughts. I've seen them riding and laughing on this very road. They were boys together. Scrope's the last friend of his childhood, since Oldcastle ran for his life."

"If you will not believe it, how will the king?" she asked, despairing. "It's a man's life to warn him, and he'll not be believed. I know not what to do. My father will try to quell trouble in London and show that we Lollards are cat's-paws, Scrope's tools, to be destroyed when he has used us."

"How could Scrope betray him?" Robert asked.

"French gold," she said. "A million crowns of it, they say. A better price than ever Judas took for the body of our Lord."

He had dreamed it. The fist had closed on golden crowns, and the money had dripped down endlessly.

"How much time is left us?"

"Little enough," she said. "No sooner was my father privy to the plot than he set me galloping. King-at-Arms knows how we have ridden. They will rise tomorrow."

"Tomorrow!"

"And set the Earl of March on the throne as the rightful heir of Richard."

"As to that," Robert said grimly, "he may be rightful, but Henry is the king, anointed and crowned, no matter how his father seized the throne. The Earl of March is a gentle prince, no man for high place. He'd be ruled by Scrope."

"Exactly so," she said. "Lord Scrope, the king's friend, who would be king instead, though he must stand behind a throne. Lord Scrope, who's made a pretty plot and provided a scapegoat besides. He'll send Lollards to the stake for murders that he'll do."

"The king's in Portchester, fifteen miles away," Robert said. "Tell His Worship I have ridden to warn him. Wat!"

Wat rode over instantly.

"Will you ride with me this night?"

"To hell and back."

"Perhaps not back."

Wat grinned. "Then I'll shoot at devils and imps tomorrow, which is well. I'm tired of deer for targets."

"I go with you," Constance said.

"Nay, you'll return to London with the news."

"I have pigeons and a code to send," she said. "I'll ride with you."

"Your beast is tired," Robert said. "He'll delay us."

"King-at-Arms will run when your nag lies dead in the road. He's of purest Eastern blood and stoutest English heart. There's dust outside, I admit it, but only mettle within."

"The road's unsafe."

"There is you, and there is Wat. If the two together cannot keep a lady safe, then she were better dead, nor breed more of the coward race. I tell you I will come if I must follow like a dog, scenting your footsteps with my nose."

"There's no gainsaying my lady when she's determined," Wat advised.

So Robert turned his horse to the Portchester road. My lady shouted to her escort that they were to wait at the inn with John and Walter, and then, with King-at-Arms running high-headed and pulling as gallantly at his bit as if he were fresh from the stable, they went off with my lady between them. Stray soldiers wandered along their way and looked hard at a woman riding, but no one stopped them, and soon night drove casual travelers in. The moon climbed into a starry sky and flooded the earth. When the outline of Portchester Castle showed square against the moon-drenched sky, they halted.

"They'll never grant us entry," Constance said. "They'll bid us wait till morning."

"The king might still be abroad," Robert said. "It will be well to watch the road, for he must come by here to the gate. If he does not come all night, then he's inside and must ride out tomorrow."

"Scrope's in Southampton yet," Wat said. "I saw him there this morning bound for a day's hunting, though what a man hunts in July, God knows."

"A king," Robert said. "We'll lie in wait. I saw a place at the bend, before the castle comes in sight."

They went back and lunged their horses belly-deep through underbrush into the shadow of trees, while the moon lay over the open road, exposing all to them.

"God grant if he come, that we know him," Robert said. "I've had only glimpses from a distance."

"He sits very proud on a horse," Wat contributed.

"And rides a favorite white courser most often," Constance added.

"Then may he ride that white courser tonight, so we may know him, nor stop strangers who'll give battle for nothing and cause us to miss the king."

"I'll know the horse," Constance said. "As for the king—when you are close, look for a deep-cleft chin and a scar by the left eye, that he had of a wound at Shrewsbury. It almost killed him, but never taught him caution. Robin, be careful."

"I've stopped men from ambush before," Robert said.

The moon sailed on, and the shadow of the trees slanted across the road. Twice Wat went cautiously to look over the crest of a small rise. The third time he came back fast and crashed through the underbrush, breathing hard. "Two riders," he reported. "One on a white horse!"

"You stop the second rider," Robert said, "and I will halt the first."

"Jesu," Constance exclaimed, "I love a bold man, but this frightens me. I'll hold your folly bells, and shield, and here's my veil to cover your face. No, over the hair also, or it will gleam."

Wat covered his nose and jaw with a kerchief and pushed his leather brain cap lower over his eyes.

The sound of hoofbeats were audible now, the thudding of tired horses.

"They're topping the rise," Constance reported. "I know the horse! The man on the right is the king!"

Robert drew Henry's sword and arranged his long sleeve over the hilt, so it might not be remembered. He looked at the riders, to judge his distance. *Oh, God!* The second man was short and fat, and looked like the Duke of York!

Well, a man must take chances. He leaned a little forward, ready, and felt his horse gathering beneath him. He looked over to Wat. The riders came closer. And closer. And were almost opposite.

Chapter 12

KING HENRY strode up and down the narrow cell impatiently. There had been so much delay! Not even the coolness within the thick walls of the Abbey of the White Canons at Titchfield could lower the heat of his anger. *Would to God Harry Scrope was here!* There was much to be discussed, and it seemed no other man could get things done!

He thought fretfully of his last interview with the French ambassadors about the possible marriage. That plucked owl, that Catherine of France, that madman's daughter! His mobile face darkened. That damned French archbishop, standing before him, accusing him of never wanting the girl at all but only delay to prepare for war, saying he had no right to the French crown and as little to the English, that if truth were told they should treat with the heirs of Richard instead of a usurper's son.

And I lost my temper, he thought, despairing. He'd been goaded to it, but he was rueful now. He'd shouted that the lot of them should get back to France, and he'd follow soon enough. Soon? The delays he never counted on. Scrope was one man and could not be in two places at once.

The friends of his youth, how he missed them! Dozens of companions and no worries or fears when they were by him. But now, whispers of a plot again. Henry sighed wearily, and paced more slowly. There were always whispers, and each one must be traced. Well, Scrope could find if there was aught to the latest, he'd probably heard of it by now.

. . . *as long as they did not use poison.* He'd a horror of that now. They'd used it for the first attempt when he was . . . twelve? He remembered a smiling woman giving him sweets, beguiling him with laughter. He'd been a thin and dark-faced child, harshly treated by a father who thought to prepare him for a throne. The woman had been pretty. But he remembered mostly the burning. And the retching that followed. It was the retching that had saved him, but he'd been terrified of a beating for dirtying the floor.

He had never relished food since. Always before he put it in his mouth he thought, *Suppose it's poisoned?* And the affliction in his throat bothered him yet. Fifteen years. They had not killed him, but they'd made him remember the attempt.

Suddenly, he could not stay another night within these walls. He must ride on. The old restlessness seized him; wild energy that would not let him stop. He had a need, a drive, a necessity to hurry on. Always to bitter unfulfillment. He was twenty-seven years old and felt his life would be short, either by reason of illness or assassins. Within him was a wailing he could not assuage. *Let me live out my destiny!*

A crushing sense of doom swept over him. Make haste! Time passes! A minute's gone! Another! It was his private agony of desperation. He dared not sleep a full night, struggling to add more time to his small supply.

Scrope was the only one who knew of it. At least, he'd heard the words when Henry told it. King Henry did not think even Scrope understood this tearing, but at least he did not think it strange when they'd seem to settle at one place for the night, then suddenly depart for another. Scrope merely saddled a horse and rode with him.

He looked out the narrow window of the cell, attracted by sounds of laughing, and saw some of his men under a tree on a bench with winecups in their hands. *Despoilers!* he thought. Suckers of gold! Not even honest leeches, healing a man. He looked beyond them, over the walls to a road winding down to Portchester that often carried travelers from Southampton past. There were some riders on the road, though it was twilight. He could see three together, the middle seemed a woman on a gray horse. They'd better get in for the night, he thought, and turned impatiently from the window to pace again. It was too late to set out now. He'd have to spend the night.

Why had his father wanted to be king? For this sorry knowledge of a murderer always lurking, so that he, Henry, who'd been a brave soldier, always wanted a wall at his back, always faced doors and never turned to leave a man behind him? The old king had regretted his throne at the end, he thought. Old king? Forty-six, but riddled with disease, his face so disgusting with discharging pustules that he only ventured out after dark.

I'll die in Jerusalem, the old king always said, repeating the prophecy which foretold it. He had put off a crusade to the Holy Land continually to prolong his life. But he'd been seized with a fit at the shrine of St. Edward Confessor at Westminster. He'd been borne through the cloisters to the Abbot's lodgings, and laid on a pallet before a roaring fire in a room. And when Henry came galloping and asked where his father was, they'd said, why, *in Jerusalem,* for so the chamber was called. His father died there, in Jerusalem. He'd not cheated the prophets by delaying his crusade. They'd had their way.

A short reign and a turbulent; as the snow came and passed away.
Henry the Fifth had his prophet too.

He'd waited there between his father's pallet and the iron Lancastrian crown of England, brought in great haste to the dying king so it could not be stolen by a man with a better claim. At length the king's breathing seemed to cease. The doctors bent over him. Henry rose and looked down on the ravaged face. Then a doctor pulled a silk cloth up.

Henry moved to the table and picked up the iron crown. The fight to hold it was begun. He knew not what he felt.

Then a movement startled him. A doctor exclaimed. He turned. At the pallet a thin hand like a skeleton's thrust up blindly, and blindly tugged at the silk. The old king was yet alive! His face peered up. The eyes looked around. To his son. His eldest son and prince, holding his iron crown.

"What right have you to that," he asked in a whisper, "seeing I had none?"

So Henry held a murderer's crown in his hands, there in Jerusalem. It belonged by right to the Earl of March. But March would make no ruler, and England was sore beset. Nay, a Lancaster had taken the crown from a weak king, let a Lancaster hold it from another weakling. March could not deal with rebellion at home, with a divided Church and an England ridden with heresy, with a parliament beginning to feel its strength, and a middle class rising to power. March could not restore England's prestige. It would take a Lancaster. They had many faults, but not one of them was weakness.

Henry's hands clenched in Titchfield as they had clenched hard on the crown in London, two years before. His problems were still with him but thank God for Scrope. Scrope stood by. The last friend left of them all. The first was Hotspur. Dead twelve years. When the Percy family rebelled, there was little plotting. They rebelled with armies and banners for all to see. Hotspur had marched to rid himself of a tyrant, the tyrant King Henry IV had become. Forthwith he marched on Shrewsbury and bottled up the Prince of Wales. He rode up to the walls and demanded admittance, and Henry had stood on the walls and refused. Two friends, forced by politics into opposing camps. Then King Henry IV came to Shrewsbury, for it was his battle, after all. Hotspur withdrew to Berwick. The old king marched again;

no weakness in the Lancasters. On the evening of July 21st his men tramped through fields yellow with uncut corn, for harvest time was near. But the harvest was dead men.

Henry remembered himself being wounded early in the fight; an arrow he never saw, stuck suddenly into his face and the blood dripping off his chin; but he'd pulled out the arrow and fought on. He'd fought till the fight was won, and someone called him and pointed, and he stumbled over and it was Hotspur lying there, burly even in death; but strange to see him quiet. Hotspur had been given to laughter and shouting, to riot and song and dance. What was active was Hotspur. And Hotspur was dead. He was weak from his wound, bleeding still and growing dizzier; a sixteen-year-old with all hazy and growing hazier. He knew he would faint, but while he could he clutched at his father's arm and begged that Hotspur might have burial. The old king smoldered with anger, knowing his son preferred the rebel and had rather seen his father dead and Hotspur living.

"Have him!" he'd said to his son. "Bury him! You'll bury all your friends before you die!"

The promise had been given. Henry was sure of it, though he had been sickening so fast from loss of blood. But the promise had been given. After that, he fainted.

Much later, when he fought out from the delirium, he found the promise had been broken while he lay helpless to plead for his friend.

By the king's order the body of Hotspur was dug up, rubbed with salt, and placed sitting by a pillory, guarded by armed sentries, so all in Shrewsbury might see Hotspur Percy was dead, and no man dare say he'd escaped to the mountains, and later counterfeits appear, as the king was plagued with duplicates of murdered King Richard.

After that they cut off Hotspur's head and sent it to be fixed on the gates of York; and the body was quartered and a quarter sent to be hung in London and Bristol, Chester and Newcastle, so all would know throughout the realm that gallant Hotspur was truly dead. It was politics for the old king, but Hotspur had been Henry's friend since he was thirteen and sent to govern turbulent Wales.

He could not bear these walls about him! He'd ride on to Portchester and meet Scrope there tomorrow. He walked to the window. He did not like darkness, but if he stayed here now, too many men would rise up from their graves and torment him.

Those other riders he had glimpsed on the road had been pressing on. Was he better than his subjects? He'd ride also, but also not alone. *Edward,* he thought. *He's a traitor, but at least he does not fear me.* And they were related by blood. He called his Duke of York "cousin," though in truth York was cousin to the old king.

So it was the Duke of York who rode by him, foot-to-foot. Instead of bold Hotspur. Henry crossed himself suddenly as he thought again of Hotspur, aware that York looked sideways covertly. Henry knew what they all said: he should have gone to the Church, he was too pious, he prayed too much. But then, he had so many to pray for. All his friends were dead or rebels. Except for Scrope! Thank God for Scrope!

"Your prayers are finished, Hal?" York inquired as they rode.

He wanted to talk. Henry did not.

York waited, then amended his presumption.

"Sire," he said, in one of his flashing fluctuations from equality to humility, "I know that white horse is your favorite, but I beg you to return and change him. He shows too well in the dark."

"I said nay to the others before I left Titchfield, and I say nay to you now."

"But he shies at every shadow," York insisted.

He did not want to think on horses and their colors; he had greater matters on his mind. This plot, this faint whiff of treason that had come to the sharp noses of his spies—they had tried to scent it to the source and failed. There was a clever rogue behind it. Some said it was the Lollards. He should have listened to Scrope.

They'll murder you yet, Hal, Scrope had said, *if you do not destroy them. We need some burnings to discomfit them.*

Or raise them in rebellion, he'd replied, and tossed off Scrope's advice.

It could not be there were so many. True, the Church was splintered, and three popes quarreling. The matter must be set right, before the splinters turned to cracks and then to chasms. When he had time enough . . .

Time. God grant me time. I'll raise England to a power. I'll unite the Holy Church. I'll seize back the Holy Land from the infidel. If You but give me time.

York said, "Sire, there's an inn nearby." A pause. "The landlord has a handsome daughter."

"I'll ride on," Henry said curtly.

This angered him, this waving of wenches in his face as a cure for his darker moods. This made his plight more sore. The curse of his life was the desire of his body, and when he took the crown he'd made confession of this and vowed and promised he would govern both England and himself. It must be both or neither. If not himself, then he could not govern England. If he learned to control desire, he could learn to control himself, his temper, and this rebellious country, all three.

Yet it was hard for him. He was full-blooded. Not cool like his brother Tom, who was twenty-six, married to an older woman, contented with her and faithful besides to prove it. It was easy for Tom. But as for himself, he boiled and seethed and could scarce breathe for the troubling of his hot blood. They were right, who said Thomas would have made the better king. Or even John, the third of the four brothers. But never Humphrey, the youngest. Henry's face set. *Humphrey is like me,* he admitted to himself, *or what I will be if I do not control these moods and wild distempers.*

Yes, Tom would have made the better king, better than any man so driven by rage and lust and loneliness and wild ambition. But he'd chained the lusting. God knew he had. Two years and over. A man can learn contentment with continence, he insisted to himself. *If he must.*

Edward again, interrupting his thoughts with chatter. What had he said? A dangerous night with the moon showing all?

"It's a fair night," he replied.

"A fair night for thieves. The moonlight almost blinds me."

"Stay on the left hand," Henry said distinctly, as York sought to drop back and go around.

"My horse bears over," York said. "I thought it might displease you, or make your beast sheer off."

"I can hold a horse straight," Henry said.

"Your pardon, sire," Edward said.

When they had started, York had made to ride by the sword arm. Was it old habit to ride on the right, or new plot to block the swing of his sword? York was a sharp man and intelligent, despite a fat man's lethargic look. And bold, besides. York had never been a coward. He was quick to chance an opportunity; he'd been quick to come on this ride. Too quick? Here's a matter to think on! York was devious.

Like the matter of the book on hunting, a fair good book, written by York while imprisoned for treason and attempted royal murder, and dedicated to the king who'd sent him prisonward and given the leisure to write it. That were a deft matter. Deft and merry and impudent, too.

York said, "Sire, this road is unsafe."

If he protests, then he's laid no ambush, and therefore it is safest to go on. If I stop, there will be assassins at any inn York favors.

"I will ride to Portchester," he said.

The path was clear then. An honest robber was not to be feared. He was glad there was only York with him. One man can be watched, a few would outnumber him.

It was a good trip and a swift one; and as they approached a little crest in the road, Henry knew it was probably a safe one, for from the last rise of ground he glimpsed the square tower of the castle.

But suspicion was in him yet. York had ceased his dire predictions, and seemed content. Was it because they had reached journey's end? Or was it because he had lured his liege lord on with protests? York was clever enough for this. It could be, just over the hill, armed men waiting. . . .

Not in the castle. There were stout yeomen there. If there was to be murder, it would be lying between the top of the hill and the next clear sight of the castle. It would be waiting close enough to the castle for a traveler to feel safe; but too far from the castle to call help. It would be as God would have it.

From the top of the hill, as the path began to dip, the road seemed clear. Moonlight lay ahead of them like snow. Insects sang. Henry always listened for them; little heralds, warning if any stranger stole by to still their song. He rode on amid the cheerful sounds of tiny lives in the underbrush that went back into tall deep shadows and trees. Where an army could hide. The castle was out of sight now. He looked swift from side to side of the road.

Between here and the castle, if it was to be tonight.

God, God. If I had a man by me I could trust!

He thought fleetingly of spurring into a gallop; but this stallion shied at anything and would fling him to the ground for the huzz of an arrow. Keep on at this pace then, unsuspecting as it seemed, and hope that all was nervousness at darkness, nothing more.

But he'd campaigned long in Wales, among Welshmen born to rebellion and suckled on ambush, and he knew. This was the place for a trap.

He was afraid of it. But he'd not let York see he turned craven so close to the castle. He kept his head high and his body straight, and listened for the instant's warning he would have, the place where the insects did not sing.

Chapter 13

ROBERT spurred abruptly, and the startled horse shot out of the underbrush with a violent rush. The bay horse on the road reared with terror. The white horse neighed and shied violently away. The king was flung sideways, almost from the saddle, struggled to draw his sword while still off-balance, pulled it free; but Robert struck it from him.

"My lord and sovereign," he cried through the muffling scarf, "I come not to waylay but to warn."

"Edward!" the king shouted.

But York was down in the road, with Wat on horseback standing over him, bow drawn to his ear.

The king turned back. "Then give me this warning that needs an ambush to be brought."

"You are betrayed, sire," Robert said. "You are to be murdered on the morrow, and your brothers also. The plot and the moon are to the full at once."

"How did you find this plot?" the king asked scornfully.

"From a true friend, as I am yours."

"Does a true friend mask his face?"

"If he is a Lollard, sire, then he must."

Nothing less than the absolute, dangerous truth could convince this king.

"Well then, Lollard," the king said, "who's in this intrigue?"

"Forgive me, I will name your friends."

"I have few and will have fewer. Name them!"

"Thomas Grey of Heton."

The king waited still-faced for the next.

"The Earl of Cambridge."

King Henry looked back over his shoulder. "Edward," he called, "your brother has been named a traitor."

York did not reply, but stood in the road.

"Henry, Lord Scrope," Robert said.

The king's hand clenched on his saddlebow. But he waited.

"The Earl of March is in the plot, but not of it. They've frightened him to silence. Scrope plans to rule England in his name, and execute Lollards for the plot."

"And York? What of York? Will you give his name?"

"I have not heard it."

"Where does London stand?"

"The Lollards there are loyal. They will not rise."

"That's a mighty promise. Who are you to make it?"

"A king's man, no more."

"Prove it," the king challenged.

Robert dismounted on the instant, picked up the king's sword from the dust, and proffered it to Henry. The king seized it, seemed as if he would strike; then sheathed it quickly.

"Let me guard you to the castle, sire," Robert said.

"Nay, I'll ride on with Edward. You say he's not in this plot? Still, if I die tonight, or tomorrow, I charge you, kill my Duke of York."

"Sire, I will," Robert said. He mounted his horse and pulled back from where it blocked the way.

"My thanks is this," the king said, "that I did not unmask you when I had the chance."

And he spurred away with his duke.

Robert sheathed his sword thoughtfully and pulled the veil away from his face. Wat came to him, and the horses stood side by side.

"For a hothead, he was cold enough," Wat commented. "Not a purse or a jewel tossed us for our trouble. And we'll be troubled, I think. York watched you very close."

Robert shrugged. "There's nothing he can prove, no matter what he may suspect. Here's my lady!" he said quickly, to warn Wat to silence.

Constance came crashing out. "That were bravely done," she exulted. "You stood to him bold as the lion on your shield."

"My lion is sleeping," he said, as he took it and hung it by his saddle, "and I was no bolder than he. It was as well I sat a horse. My knees were jelly so close to the king."

"Liar," she accused him. "You rode up bold as a lion, discoursed like a scholar—"

"You never heard a word."

"Brought him his sword like a courtier, and stood like a hero when he held it naked out."

"And if he'd struck?"

"I'd have killed him!"

He turned his horse toward Southampton.

"You think not?" she demanded hotly. "I'd have ridden to him all tears and sworn I was stolen away, and the first time he turned his back, the Earl of March would have had his throne. I do not carry a dagger to cut bread. Robin . . . it might have been better if you were unmasked. The king was much impressed."

"Greatly," Wat said, with irony. "Greatly!"

She caught the mockery. "Robin, did York know you?"

"I don't think so," he said.

"But the king knows him," Wat said.

"Not by name," Robin said quickly, "only that I'm a Lollard. There was no other way to explain my manner of seeking him."

"God, if York remembers you by name . . . It was well you wore the scarf. Here, give it to me. Praise be to St. Anne, it does not bear my father's mark."

Whereupon she flung the fine, expensive thing into some bushes, a prize for a scavenging villager.

"Robin, I brought with me some clothes that belonged to my brother. We could not bear to waste them in the press. Bury that cote-hardie. Your horses go back to London with me, where they'll vanish out of England. I'll give you two of ours. And Robin, give me your Bible, also."

"No," he said.

"Let me sleep nights," she begged. "Give me the Bible."

"If it's a noose for a head, let the head be mine."

"My father can guard it for you."

"It goes with me. I have sworn to Heaven I will carry it."

They were at the crest of the hill, and here he swung his horse around to see what lay behind. All was clear on the road, but far off there were torches flickering and racing over the battlements of the castle, to congregate at one place. King Henry had reached his gates. Tonight he was safe. Tomorrow lay with him.

Robin turned his horse again and trotted down the hill with the others.

After a while my lady said, "My father knows the Duke of Burgundy well."

"The one who took gold to betray his own king?"

"All men take gold, or some other thing," she said, being a practical merchant's daughter. "Burgundy is a gallant Frenchman, and he likes bold fellows. He'd like you. Robin, would you join him in France?"

"And sit the war out in Burgundy? Nay, I'll go to France, but only . . ."

"To that woman?" she inquired, with jealousy.

"To King Henry's battle," he said.

They rode on in silence, and finally Constance sighed.

"Well, you are the king's man," she said, "and will follow him, but Robin, do not forget how thankless that king was tonight."

Chapter 14

SOMEWHERE *out in the graying dawn*, King Henry thought, as he leaned on the cold stone of the parapet, York silent beside him, *was the Welshman who had warned him*. A Welshman. The accent had been thick. There was no doubt of his origin. And it was a neat trap too. Trust a Welshman for that.

"Loyalty," he murmured, "in an unexpected place. A man who'd warn me at his own risk."

"Loyalty, sire?" York asked. "Say he had good reason of his own, rather. A Lollard would plot Scrope's downfall in any way."

"You defend a plot to murder me, Edward?"

"Nay, sire, nay," York exclaimed hastily. "I did but mean—"

"Your brother's in the plot, remember," Henry said. "I'll not forget."

"Let me send after this man," York urged. "A little torture—"

"He said you were not in the plot, and if he changed his tale, you'd die. You've betrayed me too often, cousin. I tire of it."

"I swear before God, I have been loyal since you took the crown!"

"Swearing comes too easy to you," Henry said. "Therefore learn truth, which is often halt and stubborn. Guard! No one is to leave this castle today without an order signed by me!" He turned back to the duke. "Dear Edward," he said, "I'll not have you send warnings swift after my orders for a council."

The guards looked covertly at York. One ventured a malicious grin to the other.

Edward was safe for the day now, Henry thought, and he must think of other business. A letter must be sent to the Mayor of London. *Beware of the Lollards,* he'd say, dictating tentatively in his head. *But do not act against them unless they rise.* There was softness his advisers would not like. But he'd say to them, um, he'd say, *It is not a time for pursuing Lollards.* He must have peace in England if he would war in France. Scrope would say that any time was a good one to pursue. . . .

He flung the name suddenly from his thoughts, as if it had been a stinging nettle. Scrope! Scrope! He almost cried out the name. He'd pulled tight within, as if a hand jerked at his guts.

It could be gross calumny. Send a guard after the Welshman and drag him back. Torture out the last vestige of his knowledge! Nay. The man had warned him. He could not return evil for good. Suddenly he turned and ran down the stone steps, so abruptly he left York behind, openmouthed.

The guards glanced significantly at one another and paced away from the duke. One lifted a shoulder slightly. Their eyes followed King Henry as he went hotfoot across the yard below.

"The chapel?" one hazarded to the other.

The second nodded. "To pray the morning through. He'll be a saint, I think."

"I'd rather be a man," the first one said, "but we'll both be only heads on halberds if we don't watch that traitor there."

They resumed their pacing so that one of them always faced the Duke of York.

Henry had thought to laugh and joke with Scrope this day, take time for gossip. Instead he sat sweating in July heat in Portchester Castle, on an oak chair for a throne, with all the nobles come from Southampton to sit in council. They stirred, mopped faces, looked worried. Scrope turned continually toward him, and Henry as carefully looked away.

He had prayed half the morning that Scrope was maligned. He had risen from his knees full of vengeance for those who'd tear his friend down. Then he had gone to his chamber to read the reports that had been waiting for two days. The plot still swirled in obscurity, his spies wrote; but it was more than a scent now; it was a stench. Cambridge had been seeing the Northumberland knight Sir Thomas Grey, a cousin of Hotspur, secretly.

Henry bargained with heaven as he sifted through more reports. Let not one name appear among the others. I'll sacrifice Hotspur's cousin and York's brother. Let me not find . . .

On Sunday, the 22nd July, read this report, *Thomas Grey of Heton arryved att Southampton and entered into comunycation with Lorde Scrope. Bothe then did communycate withe thee Earle of March.*

Grey and Cambridge, both with Scrope, and all with the Earl of March. Henry was ill with this betrayal, but his reasoning was clear. All in secret communication. Let it be done openly and he'd grant coincidence in meeting. But secretly—that's intrigue.

He could feel their greedy hands shaking the oak chair that now did him for a throne. When this council ended, would it be firm beneath him? He looked over the assemblage of his lords. They feared him now. Silence, heavy as the heat, thick as the humid air. All the faces turning blurry. The iron crown bore down hard on his head.

"I have heard rumors," he began. "Of a plot."

He stared straight at Lord Scrope, who paled. *Guilty,* Henry thought, and passed sentence.

"Look among yourselves, my lords," he invited.

Heads turned cautiously to inspect neighbors with uneasiness. Scrope did not move.

You, who were my friend for all my life.

"Thomas Grey of Heton," Henry called. "Let me look at you."

After a hesitation, a man rose defiantly. He was in his early thirties. Hotspur's cousin. But there was no resemblance. It would be easier, therefore.

"Richard, Earl of Cambridge. Let me look at you."

The earl rose unwillingly, glancing wildly toward York. They bore great resemblance. Two traitors in one family. As well York had no sons. That were too many snakes for one bosom.

"Henry, Lord Scrope," he said, forcing out these words.

Scrope stood immediately, and straight.

"How say you, my lords?"

This heat, this heavy crown; his heart burst with grief.

"Guilty, sire," said Hotspur's cousin, bold as the rest of his clan; admirable friends, honest enemies.

"Cambridge? No words? I'll speak for you then," Henry said. "Guilty."

Guilty indeed if he did not now protest his innocence. What proof there must be for the seeking. Yet one more traitor remained. He looked full at Scrope.

"Guilty, sire," Scrope said.

Henry held himself tight-reined. He'd been betrayed before.

"Sheriff," he said, "take these three in safe custody to the new tower beside the Godshousegate in Southampton."

A shuffling of feet as the sheriff's men herded them.

"Is there anything you'd say?" Henry asked.

Thomas Grey curled a lip. Cambridge sent more imploring looks to York for intercession. Only Scrope made answer.

"I would ask mercy, sire," he said, "for the sake of our long friendship."

It stung Henry like a whip, a goad, a spur. This man would provoke murder, and then be excused for friendship's sake?

"Mercy?" he inquired of him. "You ask too much, Harry. You presume. What is broken cannot be used. Would you ride a lame nag, wield a broken dagger, take a wanton to wife? Go to, Harry, do not ask good service of cracked friendship. I'll give you justice as I am king, but I'll not give you more!"

The three men were marched out.

Henry rose. "My lords, the council is ended."

He walked out quickly. The crown was a torment on his head. He reached his chamber, dismissed the pack of gentlemen running after him, slammed his own door, flung the crown from him to the bed and stood with clenched hands. It was a moment before he noticed his little spaniel at his feet, trying to climb up to his arms. He picked her up and held his cheek to her silky neck.

"Welshman, Welshman," he muttered to her long ear. "It were better to have taken my life than my friend."

On Friday, August 2nd, the Duke of York brought Henry the news at Portchester that the commission of twelve lords, sitting in the castle at Southampton, had examined the three accused men. No torture had been used, as Henry had sternly forbidden it. Yet the proceedings were short. Cambridge and Grey had admitted their guilt again and threw themselves on the king's mercy.

"Scrope?" Henry asked eagerly.

York hesitated.

"He sings a different tune," he finally said. "He says that he was privy to the plot, but not to carry it through. He wished only to learn it and tell you."

"A strange song he never sang to me. Tell him this plea is ill-advised, since I would have been dead before he denounced them. Besides, the Earl of March had sung that song, though I believe him. He's timid and afraid of Scrope. How did the verdict go?"

"Guilty, sire, all three. March's name . . . was not mentioned."

"It will not be," Henry said. "I will give him pardon."

York licked his lips.

"You hesitate too much," Henry told him.

"Sire, my brother and Lord Scrope . . ." He gulped again, by which Henry knew York had fought against this but given in to his brother's wish at last. ". . . claim trial by their peers as their right."

"Claim? By their right? Scrope thought of that, and pulled Cambridge after him. He thinks on delay and delay and delay again, until my temper cools and I forgive him. What a puny thing my temper is if it cools so quickly and I think, well, he tried to murder me, but we had a happy youth together. It would take months, and he has not that much time. Scrope thinks on days when it was long work to gather up peers scattered over England. Now all the dukes and earls and barons in my peerage wander the streets of Southampton, waiting to go to war. I'll bring them together in a day, and give Lord Scrope his trial!"

"Sire?" York whispered.

"Oh, begone."

York waited a moment, then backed away and closed the door.

Henry watched for him by a window, to see him come out below. He was weary, weary with praying through a long night. He warred within to his own hurt, tormented of body and soul. And they said he was weather-tempered; stormy or sunny by turns and only God knew how the weather did; a man could only bask when it was fair and run for shelter when it thundered.

York appeared below, and they brought his horse to him. Henry had a sudden feeling that York was sincere in this effort to help his brother. But he frowned at his own fancy. As well send a child to sleep with a hungry lion as let trust nestle with York. He turned from the window to send two messages: one to the sheriff at Southampton to assemble a jury within a week; the second to his brother Thomas of Clarence, to preside. By nightfall, the Duke of Clarence came walking in, frowning over a paper in his hand.

"Twenty nobles summoned for the jury," Thomas said, "and here's the Earl of March, eager to serve. Does the guilty try himself, Hal? March is high in this plot. They promised him the throne."

"They threatened him," Henry said.

"Behead him," Tom urged. "You'll never have a better chance. Behead him while you have good proof of treason. End a claim to your throne!"

"He meant no harm," Henry said. "It's his misfortune to be heir to a third son, while I am heir to a fourth. He wants no crown."

"Others want it for him."

"I know you give good counsel," Henry said, "but I will give good pardon."

"That's a fool's trick," Tom said. "He'll trouble you again."

"Then he will trouble me again," Henry said, flaring up, "but I will not execute an innocent man."

"Innocent?" Tom said. "He'd have seen you killed. If you think on sparing Scrope too, you'd better speak now. Left to myself, I'll see him beheaded. He's grown fat on the loot he's stolen from you, calling you his friend."

Henry scowled. Tom shrugged and walked out, untouched by executions or blood. They were right, the ones who said Tom should have had the crown. He had the stomach for it and slept well of nights. All living was a chess game to him, and death but a piece off the board that could not be played.

They looked much the same, the two oldest brothers; only a year apart in age. But there the likeness ended. Henry had all respect for his brother, but he had never loved Tom; and Tom had never loved him.

King Henry came to Southampton on August 5th, when the jury sat in Southampton Castle, but he kept aside in a distant chamber while Thomas, Duke of Clarence, acting and speaking in the king's name, pronounced the sentence. Death to all three; but the infamy of hanging was to be omitted, and Grey and Cambridge were to be spared the ignominy of being drawn through the streets in a cart. Henry made no mention of Scrope in these orders. And so, very soon, Lord Scrope would be hauled through the streets from the Watergate to the Barred Gate in a hurdle pulled by a bony nag; like any common cutpurse. The crowds surged in the streets, waiting for the fun. They'd fling many a clod at the bound man. Scrope was not liked. He'd squeezed too hard; taken too much from too many. The stones would be flying; and the catcalls would follow him to his death as the mob shoved, bloodthirsty, jostling the cart to the place of execution outside Southampton's walls.

Henry heard a step and swung round to the noise. Then he smiled wanly as he saw Bishop Courtenay, who had free passage to his presence.

"Were they shriven?" he asked.

The bishop nodded.

Now came the sounds of Scrope's progress through the streets; sounds that made Henry wince.

"I shall pardon March," he said. "Tom insists that it's a mistake."

"Blessed are the merciful," Bishop Courtenay said.

They walked to the window. The crowds had already vanished and their howling was diminished by increasing distance.

"The proclamation was already written," Henry said, "to be published after my murder. They styled me Henry of Lancaster, Usurper of England."

Here's a birthday gift above all, Henry thought bitterly. Three days hence he'd be twenty-eight; and have little joy of it with three men new-buried as proof he'd live to reach it.

"I'll change my will before I sail," Henry said. He had named Scrope in the old one.

The bishop only nodded.

Where was the Welshman now who'd brought the warning? Beyond the walls, standing by to see the executions, pleased as they bandaged Thomas Grey's eyes even now? Was he grinning as Grey knelt on bare ground; avid as the executioner gripped Grey's hair with one hand and swung the sword high with the other? How did he think as the sword slashed down with all the might of the executioner, who was undoubtedly well bribed by Grey's good friends for the last service they could do their lost companion, which was to see that the first cut be the last and save him an agony of hacking until he was finally dead.

You'll not go free, Welshman, he promised him, as his anger waxed with his agony. *I can find you.* Tall, well formed, moving with grace. Face and hair both covered. Was he redheaded then? A Welsh accent and he handled his sword like a Frenchman. The horse had a white foot. Nay, forget the horse, he'd be rid of it by now. Welsh, with French training. Tall. Hair of a diverse color. And a strangeness about that sword. He'd kept his sleeve upon the hilt. It had, therefore, an uncommon device. Something more about the sword teased Henry . . .

Bishop Courtenay put his hand on the king's shoulder and Henry started, then caught hold of himself, ashamed of jumping for a touch. Courtenay thought him a good man because he'd given Lancaster's huge revenues to Holy Church; but that was only a flourish with a pen, while he'd let a heretic soul escape on the Portchester Road. He felt a deep sense of guilt. He began to pace, breaking free from

Courtenay's soothing hand. Scrope dying, and the Lollard gone scot free? *Beware me for a friend, I make a safer enemy.*

Suddenly, a roll of drums that transfixed him where he stood. The drums stopped. And Thomas Grey of Heton was dead. They were dragging the body aside, flinging the dripping head into a basket and handing it up to a man on horseback, to post north with speed. The head would be fixed on a pike and displayed at Newcastle.

Henry resumed his restless pacing. It was endless, endless, waiting for the next.

A roll of drums.

York had begged for him, begged for his brother's life, that fat little traitor with the words breaking on his smooth tongue, and tears in the little pig's eyes.

The drummer stopped, and the Earl of Cambridge would never trouble him again.

Henry braced himself for the last roll of drums, bending his head and praying for the soul of his last friend from youth.

I gave you death, not for the plotting, for others have plotted and lived, but because you were my friend and betrayed me.

The drums rolled suddenly. There was a tearing agony in him.

"Harry!" he said, aloud. "Harry!"

Then all was still. Scrope's head was galloping to York, to be fixed on the Micklegate Bar, where Hotspur's head had been set so long ago.

Bishop Courtenay said softly, "Sire, I beg of you the bodies of Thomas Grey and Cambridge, that they may be given burial."

Henry nodded curtly. He was unable to speak. The bishop had not mentioned Scrope. He was afraid to ask for him, afraid even to speak his name. *Ask me,* Henry begged silently. *Command me!*

But the bishop bowed his head, and made to leave. On the threshold he paused and looked back.

Ask Scrope's body of me, Henry thought wildly.

"Sire," the bishop said, "I am not so sick that I cannot go to France with you."

Henry shook his head, deeply touched by any kindness, and found his voice. "The doctors have forbidden it," he said.

"I shall go nonetheless, sire," Courtenay said, and vanished.

A true priest, a good man, a confessor to whom not all was told.

The bishop would go to France and toss away his life to fill the place of a man just dead. Yet it was to Scrope the traitor that Henry had opened his heart and mind and soul, from whom he had withheld no secret; it was to Scrope he had confessed what he never told any priest, and given him wealth and greatness. Now Scrope's body lay beyond the wall, for dogs and ravens, and no man would touch it without Henry's consent. While Henry could not bear to speak his name.

Now came York, subdued.

"Sire," he said, "the bishop told me of your mercy."

The duke came closer. Henry moved away. The duke halted.

"Sire," he said, with his voice hardening, "I think I saw your Welshman of the Portchester road."

"Watching the execution?"

"At St. Julian's chapel, where I was."

"Doing what?"

York hesitated. "I think he was praying," he admitted at last.

Henry drew in a deep slow breath. *He had not watched the death. He had prayed for them instead. Welshman, you've preserved your own life a little longer, though York will have it yet, and revenge his brother.*

"Sire, shall I trip him up for you?"

"No," Henry said. "You have no proof."

"But I think—"

"I want proof. Can you show me such as is there?" he asked, gesturing to the table with the copy of the proclamation of March's ascension to the throne.

"Nay, sire, not yet. But if I bring you proof—"

"Then bring it, but do not trifle with guesses. And get out!"

York backed hurriedly. Was that fear? Fear? In York? *What expression is on my face that York backs so quickly away?* He was at the door.

"Edward! See that carrion Scrope is buried," Henry ordered harshly.

"Sire, I will," York said.

"And send my captains to me. I'll not stay another day in this port!"

"Sire, I will."

The guard in the corridor closed the door.

And Henry was left alone, to think of Scrope.

Chapter 15

OUT ON the dark water, small lights moved mysteriously, tossing, the lights on Henry's ships—some twelve hundred transports or more with their torches and flares, following twin lanterns hung on the admiral's vessel. A very congregation of lights around and above six thousand men-at-arms and twenty thousand archers.

Robert watched the glitterings from the rail of *Dover*, and listened to the sounds of the sea: the gurgling of water, the creak of wood—and the snores of sleeping archers on the deck behind him, rolling back and forth like lifeless bodies as the vessel dipped and rose.

It had been different when they started; that had been for such as looked to adventure: the craft dipping and bowing and finding their places in a din of trumpets and drums, the flutter of sails and the crack of spars, a wild gaiety of banners amid the crash of shields lashed along the rails of every ship, with the king's *Trinity Royal* magnificent with a passion painted on her sails and a crowned leopard, gilded all over, on her prow. They had started on Sunday afternoon, August 11, 1415, in full sunlight, with the tide and the wind fair for France.

Now they were ending their voyage, and all was reduced to little lights and the watery sounds of the sea. He crossed himself suddenly as he shivered and he knew, with a knowledge he could not form into words, that it was the vibrant prick of something-soon-to-happen.

Another disaster? They'd had one as they started. Three ships had burned to the water in a tangle of spars and fire and drowning men, billowing smoke to the heavens, while their neighbors dashed hastily away. But then, the swans they'd seen passing the Isle of Wight negated the first evil omen.

Suddenly Robert stiffened. He thought he saw . . .

The captain passed then, stumbling over sleeping men.

"Lean out a little further, squire," the captain said, "and I'll be short a man of my tally when we anchor."

Robert said, "Out there. That flicker there." He gestured past the torches to another point of light, a tiny flutter all but lost in darkness. "Could it be France?"

"You've seaman's eyes," the captain said. "I could wish them for my lookout. That's the beacon on a castilian tower. Kidcause, the Frenchmen call that spit of land."

"I see white," Robert said, while prickles rose on his skin.

"There's a chalk cliff there."

"And a harbor?"

"The mouth of the Seine."

"Then we're for Harfleur, as was rumored?"

"You, not I, God be praised," the captain said.

From above came a shout, as the man at the masthead cried the beacon fire at last. The captain shook his head and moved off down the pitching deck, muttering to himself about the men who called themselves sailors these days.

A little later, Robert smelled France, for the breeze was warm off-shore. Then all day long he watched as they drew nearer. Toward nightfall they anchored amid jostling vessels, and swearing captains who feared for their cables as smaller ships cut across them. Now men shouted from ship to ship, discovering friends. But when night came, they quieted, for they began to think more of home than of fighting here.

Wat came to stand by Robert, who had been studying the shore and piecing together what he could of France. A beach covered with large, sharp stones—good weapons for slinging and plenty to hand for a moment's stooping. Ditches dug all over the beach, with the tide flowing through. A horse could not be charged through that. It would be hand-to-hand fighting afoot then, over shifting shale and ditches, and after that, the earthworks that stood out in bold outline against the sky, higher than a man's head, with bastions atop like the wall of a castle, and only a few narrow passages cut at long intervals.

Holy St. David, the beach could be held forever!

Then without forethought, Robert began in his mind to hold the beach and defend it against disembarking troops. He was used to defensive action, that was the role they played in Wales. Offensive action hardly counted, they were always badly outnumbered. Occasionally he'd harry a force of English, without hope of victory but with great determination to be a nuisance, killing a sentry here and stealing a few horses there.

Wat said suddenly, "The rumor they're shouting is that a thousand men will go ashore in the morning to test the temper of the French." He spat overboard with scorn. "They'll not live to reach the bastions."

Robert resumed defending the beach against a thousand men; then suddenly caught himself up. He'd been planning his own death. He had grace enough to grin in the dark.

He found he was unlashing his shield from the rail. It smelled faintly of paint that refused to dry in the damp. He thought of the news he'd sailed on. His father was dead, had been dead a week or more. He thought again of the old man by the fire, all aches from old wounds and pains from old wars. Wat had got green paint from somewhere and obliterated the red chief and gold molets. Now his arms were those of the senior member of his house. His house, forsooth! There was but him!

". . . Fairfield?"

"Here," Wat called.

"So you did not fall overboard?" the captain inquired of Robert. "It's as well. I'm to put you over the side in the morning, before dawn. A man came under my bow with those orders. You're going ashore."

"With the thousand?" Robert asked.

"*Before* the thousand," the captain said. "Twenty men are to test the temper of the French . . . or so they say . . . before any others are risked."

"Who ordered it?" Robert asked.

"The messenger came from the admiral's ship, where the council was. He called you Robert Heartless, and said you came from Wales." The captain peered hard at Robert's face in the dim torchlight. Then he shrugged and walked away.

"York," Wat guessed.

It was likely. Robert looked at the dark, unlighted shore. Twenty men against those bastions? Well, there was but one way to go and that was forward. A man could only back into the river, and he'd never learned to swim.

He would never see Constance again. That was the burden of his regret.

"I have a message for my lady," Robert said. "I bid you take it if I fall."

"Take it where?" Wat inquired, astonished. "To hell? My lady is not there."

And so, he meant to go along. Robert turned again to the shore and put one arm on Wat's heavy shoulder. Wat stiffened; then slowly relaxed. He spat into the river with contentment.

"And scout to Harfleur," Robert said. "That will follow the other order, I think. I've never set foot in France before. If we get through those bastions at all, I'll be a very jewel among foreriders, if this is what they plan for us."

"I was in Harfleur once," Wat volunteered unexpectedly. "A killing in a tavern, and a witness, alas. I had to leave London. His Worship sent me over with a ship of his. They have a trade in cloth that's woven here. Then the witness died in another brawl, and I had leave to return."

"How does it lay?"

"London? Why, it's flat."

Robert jogged his shoulder, and Wat laughed, knowing he was meant to describe Harfleur.

"The Seine runs so," he said, and cut a line in the air with a forefinger, straight from left to right, "and the river Lezarde runs so in its valley." He cut the first line in half, up and down, and had an airy cross.

"Harfleur is so." He stabbed a finger at the cross and put the city on the northern shore of the Seine, above where the two lines touched.

"The Lezarde flows through the town, then?" Robert asked.

". . . and widens in one place to make a galley-close," Wat said. "That's an enclosed port inside the city for the anchoring of ships. You can see the masts above the walls from the outside."

"Strong walls?"

"Would God London had such walls! Below the town"—Wat traced south and east on his map—"all marshland."

"Then beyond these earthworks there are swamps?"

"And fever."

"How far to Harfleur from the Seine?"

"A mile at least," Wat said, "and two miles from here to the Lezarde."

Three miles through swamps in unknown territory in the dark, *if* they won through the bastions. Horses sinking to the belly in stinking mud.

Wat said with regret, "I washed myself all over last night, too, and the water was very cold."

"How many gates?" Robert asked.

"Three that I know. One north, one west, one east. I did not think on defense when I was here before," he said apologetically. Then he added a dot to the west of Harfleur on his unseen map. "Graville, the abbey and castle, among green hills."

They were silent again, surveying the dark shore. At length Wat stirred.

"I'll see to my bow and shafts," he said. "I'll need them soon, it seems."

He left Robert at the rail, thinking.

Who had known him well enough to recommend him—or was it to condemn him—with this foreriding to be done? York seemed most likely. If York had remembered the Welshman at the Pope's Head brawl, known his name and then identified another Welshman at Portchester. That was the danger, to be put in the two places; his name known from one meeting and his Lollardy from the other.

This Bible he carried was a firebrand to set off his own burning. Constance had argued with him again and again to the last to let her carry it off to London, but he'd stood firm against commands and kisses, soft words, angry shrieks, coaxings, tears and all. The Bible was part of his fate.

He leaned against the rail, looked at France and saw Wales. Wales, under snow. The winter he got his Bible. A winter raid, for Llewellyn ap Gryffyd thought any weather good for stealing. A bold raid too, in force and much loot seized.

He'd been fifteen, standing aside while others quarreled over division of the spoils. Women and horses. Robert had glanced timidly at a pretty girl but had no chance for her, and was wistfully relieved as well. He'd been afraid of strange women still, though they pursued him. It was another year before he let himself be caught, and still another before he turned hunter. He got his share of the loot at last; a choice between a captured Bible and a good stout nag. He'd taken the Bible. They had laughed and called him priest, reading so much he blushed when a maid looked over and tried to read him!

He had gone out to escape the rough teasing, for the count's six sons had no bridles on their tongues. As he put the Bible carefully in his saddlebags, standing in the trampled snow beside his horse, he looked over its rump and saw other horses on a distant hill. He'd raised a shout, and the count came out like an arrow, and turned sober when he counted them, and long-faced when he considered his position. They were in a valley like a bottle with a narrow neck and no bottom. Once the English got in the neck, they could harry him; for Llewellyn ap Gryffyd was loaded with loot, burdened with captured stock and captured women, tied to his spoils like a merchant to his goods, and the path before him all deep snow.

He'd turned casually to Robert when he had done counting.

"Hold the neck of this valley until dark," he said. "Take ten men. I give you your choice."

Robert remembered it yet. Picking the men from those who stood around. The best shots, as he could remember. Their horrified expressions as they considered him, a fifteen-year-old boy dressed in high fashion, the pet of the countess, given to speaking French, taught swordsmanship by a French master so he had a graceful pretty way they never understood, though he could cut other swordsmen to pieces between the flailings of their arms. But the ten longbowmen had stood with him while the unwieldy caravan with its overladen horses and wailing women forced its passage through the snow and left a broad hard trail behind them.

He was alone, with the English coming at him, and more snow falling. His first command and such grave necessity. How could he hold this valley? He could not, with ten men. He bit his lips, and then remembered a time when he'd feared to walk along an unlit hall when he knew Rhys was waiting for him there.

"If he beats you, then he beats you," the countess said, "but do not seek to avoid all hurt. If fear rules you, then you're a slave. Will you be your own man? Then rule yourself and your humors."

He hardened there in the snow. He'd be no man's slave, not even his own. He'd rule fear and be the master if it killed him. There was a harsh streak in his nature, despite his pretty manners. Now he perceived the stony part, and was glad. It was the wall to which he put his back that day, unseen by any man, though ten archers were beside him.

And so he'd defended the mouth of the valley, under intermittent attack. He would not venture out from cover, though the English teased him. Visibility was bad in the snow, so he moved his men behind rocks and sent arrows from every angle. There might have been a hundred men, and he would not come out to be counted or killed. The mouth of the pass was small and the English uninterested, except as he barred them from their pursuit. They split their forces finally; kept a little one before him to hold him in, and sent the greater around the flaring skirts of the mountains to chase the struggling caravan and catch them as they emerged from the foot. But they had to plunge through snow also, and they had lost hours facing Robert. They got a few stragglers, but the main band had broken into little segments and they could not pursue the bits forever in hostile country. Wales was no place to divide your forces too fine. Even a shepherd would bash in an Englishman's head.

So they had come back down the valley in anger, on the path broken by the count's going out. Robert saw them coming, and knew Llewellyn ap Gryffyd had escaped. There was no reason now for him to stay and be ground between the two parts. He had his men shoot into the snow above until it began to slide, and then to rumble, and finally turn to an avalanche that blocked the neck behind him. It left him facing English only. He waited until nightfall and bitter cold, and when he saw them gathered around fires he burst suddenly out of his hole and ran for it with the six men left alive. The English had pursued him and pressed him hard for honor's sake, but he knew the country and they did not.

He rode hard all the night, plunging through snow encrusted with ice, so that his horse was cut and bleeding by the time they reached the castle. Icicles hung from the animal's nostrils, and he had frost on his lashes and brows. Laboriously Robert swung one leg over the saddle and thudded down to the courtyard on feet that seemed to shatter as they struck. Out of the agony of pain, he noted an arrow sticking sideways from his saddlebags. For a moment it meant nothing. Then he realized slowly that the Bible had stopped the arrow. If it had not been there, the arrow had gone through to the horse. The beast would have been sore hit in the bowels and have failed him. Afoot in deep snow, they'd have taken him. The English were not gentle with captives, nor did they keep them long.

He loosened the girths and slung the saddlebag with its arrow over one shoulder. The groom took his bleeding horse. Robert stumbled into the castle. The countess leaped up instantly and dragged him to the fireplace, and shouted for hot wine.

He shivered as he sipped it and tried to warm himself, and he thought of the dead men he'd left behind at the neck of the valley, frozen corpses now. Yet the arrow meant to unhorse him had been stopped. If he had not chosen the Bible for his portion . . . It had been ordained, therefore, that he should live. He tried to think why, but then the count came striding in while he shivered by the fire, unable to control the shaking of his hands, so that the countess must hold the cup.

The count stopped before him, and his sons crowded behind him. Robert's teeth clattered against the cup and he pushed it away.

"Wounded?" the count asked.

Robert shook his head.

"Good," the count said. "Tomorrow I ride against David ap Davis, who moves in the snow and has horses better than mine. You go as my lieutenant."

"You promised this to me," Rhys said hotly.

"Then I take back the promise," the count said.

The count and his son eyed each other like animals; then Rhys strode swearing from the hall.

From then on, Robert always rode at the count's right hand, into traps and out of traps; except when he was sent ahead to scout, or left behind to cover retreats. Which meant he was often raiding, for Count Llewellyn ap Gryffyd was no man for sitting on his bottom in a castle when his neighbors possessed more than he. Inevitably, therefore, Robert became known.

Another thing resulted from the pursuit in the snow. The same night when his fingers could move again, he shut himself away and melted ink. A sacrifice was needed. He was a Lollard and a Christian, yet the Welsh blood still believed in omens, in witches, and propitiations. The dark gods of another generation still moved. He had felt their presence in the shadowed glens, he'd heard them on the high steeps of mountains, almost seen them in the circles of stones left from centuries before.

His Welsh blood demanded sacrifice. Yet he was a Christian. So he made a Christian sacrifice. The Bible had preserved him; his life continued because of it; therefore as much as he lived beyond this was given him beyond his measured due.

So, with infinite care and much labor, for he never was a scholar, he inscribed his name in the Bible, and gave his life at hazard.

Robert stirred at the rail of *Dover*, moving from revery to reality, from the bitter cold of memory to the hot August of fact. How a man is made up of his memories, he thought, amazed. He is but what he has been.

This task on the morrow, now. Morrow? He looked up at the stars. It was past midnight. It was today. He knelt and offered up his prayers, and after that lay back on the hard deck among the common archers, looked up to the sky, thought of Constance, and slept at last till the captain came to wake him. Whereupon he rose in the darkness before dawn, and picked up his shield.

Chapter 16

KING-AT-ARMS roused from his weary plodding when he saw the walls of London, and began to trot when he passed through Ludgate. By the time he reached Thames Street he'd have stormed at a gallop given leave, with thoughts of his stall to goad him.

He burst into his courtyard with a whinny that brought her father from the house like a charging bull, to pull her from the saddle and clutch her tight.

She kissed him quickly and wriggled free.

"Father," she said in a whisper, "the two horses, the white-foot bay and the chestnut with lop ears. . . ."

He knew them for the mounts ridden by Robert and Wat.

"Wallace!" he bellowed. "Those horses leaving this afternoon to be sold into Scotland . . . choose out the two stoutest for our keeping and put those worn nags in their place. The chestnut and the white-foot bay look the worst to me. Get rid of them."

And turning away as if it was but a matter of trading spent horses for better, he took Dame Margaret by the arm and led her into the house.

Constance sat down at the table with her father while he poured wine.

"I had expected you sooner," he said.

"The roads were rock hard," she said, "and your sailors so saddle sore they begged leave to walk. And I lingered in Southampton with Robin," she admitted at the last.

"Two pigeons came home," he said. "The first with the news that the goods had been delivered, and the second that our competitors were outbid and undone, but I know no more than that. My blue-check hen, my strongest flier, never came home at all."

"She was never sent," Constance replied slowly. "I gave her in a basket to the captain of a ship named *Dover*, with grain for the bird and gold for the man."

"And my bird will return . . . ?"

"When Robin lands in France."

He did not rant, as she thought he might, with his best bird still out of the cote. He only poured more wine, and the way he did it . . . She did not understand, but felt as if subtly their relationship was changing. He was not being the indulgent father, nor yet the master of the house. He poured her wine as he would for another like himself, a merchant home after hard travel on hard business.

"London was quiet," she said, "when I rode through."

"Never a stir on the surface," he said, "but swirling below. King Henry has written a letter to the Mayor, we know that much, but what he commanded we cannot find. Yet it cannot be for persecution and arrests, for nothing has happened. For the moment, then, the danger's averted."

"For the moment," she said wearily. It would rise again.

Her father said heavily, "You'll be wed the seventeenth day of September."

Her heart began to race. "So soon?"

"None too soon," he said.

She looked at him uneasily. He had a somber way suddenly.

"I sent Paul to sea," he announced.

And she knew, without asking, that Paul would never return.

"What did he tell you?" she asked.

"It is not what he told me, but what he babbled to others."

"What did he say in these babblings?"

"That you left the house the night I said you must not. He said that he returned from Norwich late, and before he jumped down from his horse, you told him to stay in the saddle."

"I never thought he'd talk," she said desperately. "He was a tale-bearer, but of trivial things, and Wat was not here to go!"

He did not flush ruddy with anger, or shout; nor did he grunt and glower as when he refused to speak at all.

"I could not carry him myself," she said at last in a small voice. She shuddered as she recalled the journey through black streets, with the horses' hooves bound with rags to muffle their sound. She would never forget the sight of the priest, barely seen, dangling below his gibbet, a black thing swung by rising wind. She still felt the dangerous balancing on a saddle, while King-at-Arms snorted. There was no one to hold his head and if he leaped she'd fall. She soothed him, telling him it was the wind he heard and nothing more, and hoped it *was* wind and not the sheriff, as she sawed at the rope with more haste than skill, terrified of the body that had once been a man, and never fearful in his lifetime.

At last the rope was almost severed.

"Paul! Paul! Catch him!"

Paul's horrified white face looking up, then vanishing as he'd leaped back and let the body hit the ground. Back through the dark streets, the priest like a log over the back of Paul's trembling horse. The storm rumbling ever closer.

They stopped at the first churchyard they passed, and buried him quickly in hallowed ground that his soul might rest. She tried to make the grave look old in the guarded light of a shielded lantern, and took up rosemary from another's place and planted it on his. Then they ran for home like hunted things, for her dress was soiled with dirt and would shout their crime if they were taken by the watch. Lightning lit their way.

"Did he tell of the burial?" she asked her father.

"He swears it was only to me. And they have not dug up the priest. I looked to see."

The first drops of rain, falling as they came breathless to their own gate. By then, she was afraid of what Paul might repeat.

"Paul," she had said, drenched by the rain, "it was a good thing to do."

"You did not tell me," he said, "that you meant to do it."

"If they take me for it," she said, "they'll take you too."

He did not answer.

"If you tattle this tale," she said, "you'll die of it!"

Lightning flashed, and she glimpsed him, standing sullen.

"Here," she said, "here. Some coins for a night in the tavern."

Her father spoke again and drew her back.

"I'll not reproach you," he said. "If you are of such a nature as to ride on my business to Southampton then I cannot but accept you're boldly made. I know he was your friend, but he was dead. It was a foolish thing to think he must lie in hallowed ground."

She thought that if she had not paid Paul but frightened him to silence, he might have held his tongue and saved himself.

Her father sighed. "I'm growing old and weary of harshness," he said. "Ten years ago and I'd have killed him myself, weighted his feet and dropped him in the river. But now, I could not do it. I liked Paul. He worked hard and honestly, and God gave him the tongue he used too much. I told my captain not to kill him, but leave him in some port where English ships never touched. He'll make his way. He was a clever rogue, and never feared hard work."

"I'll marry the old man," Constance said. "There will be no more fussing. I'll undo the danger I put over this household if I can. The old man can be managed, once he's married, and he'll be an ally if it comes to trouble."

Her father nodded. "I'll have your mother's jewels out," he said. "We'll put a bold face on it."

She ached for Robin with a need that could scarcely be borne; but she loved him beyond herself and her desires. She would see him safe before she saw herself happy. Keep him away from them and their enemies, or he'd be pulled down too.

But she would pray for him! She had already sent up such a clamor of prayers that the saints would not sleep with the tasks she had demanded of them in the way of his protection.

"Wear scarlet," her father said. "Have the dress made immediately."

"The azure with gold flowerets will do," she said. It was girlish and guileless and cut low in front; and she could not bring herself to troubling with a new dress for this wedding.

When the table was cleared she went out into the court and down the empty quay. She sat at the very end, with her feet above the flood. Night was coming again. How many nights before she was wed? She did not hate the old man; she felt almost pity for him. He sent small gifts often: food, a jewel, a bird, a pretty veil. He'd said more than once, obliquely, that he regretted his age and hoped she'd overlook it. A man made up in gifts for other weaknesses. Nevertheless, she need not fear she'd be childless.

She would learn to abide him. He had a great deal of business. She could insist on doing the traveling, saying it was too hard for him. If she was clever, she'd spend more time away than in his house.

She closed her eyes a moment. She loved Robin Fairfield so, the world was colorless without him; black and gray like rain.

She stared down into the dark water, relinquishing him forever, as the water flowed out to the sea. So silently, so swiftly, so contentedly, it flowed, after the great turmoil of waters boiling desperately against London Bridge with its nineteen arches set so close they formed a dam. The water was five feet higher on the yonder side and must rip and force its way through. But it grew quiet here. She must learn to be like the water. The time was past for weeping.

She heard a thin, sad sound. Turning, she saw the tie-dog at his iron ring, like a statue watching. A lonely, ugly brute of an animal, wearing his life away unloved.

She got up slowly and went to him. The rope was thick and he made it tighter with pulling. She put her knee against his chest and pressed him back a step. He watched her face, staring eerily, and did not see the rope had fallen to the ground. He was always loosed at night to guard the house, but it was yet day. This was too early for freedom and he did not understand.

"Come," she said, and walked away.

When she paused to glance around he was yet by the wall, watching with his yellow eyes.

"Come," she said distinctly. "Murdach, come."

His thick tail wagged tentatively, then he came at a lunging gallop, all delight, romping heavily about her, his body a half-circle, his ears back and his face wrinkled, his mouth all agape.

She sat again at the end of the quay. He peered over the edge, snuffed at the smells and listened for danger. Then he sat down at a little distance. In a moment, he moved closer, watching for a blow. Then closer still, when it did not come. Then he was beside her, warm and heavy. She put an arm about him, for that he was alive and she was lonely too. He leaned against her, and ran out his tongue and panted.

They sat so, watching the darkening sky, and pigeons wheeling into their cotes for safety. Her father came out. She heard his footsteps and pointed to a black dot that did not wheel. A dot that grew ever larger in the sky.

"That bird comes fast," her father said.

On it came, disdaining flocks around it, overflying slower birds. Then it began to drop. Its tail spread like a fan, the feet shot forward. The bird alighted on the stable, and waddled into her cote.

"My blue-checked hen," her father said. "Your Robin has landed in France."

Chapter 17

THERE was the heart-pounding excitement of the boat ride toward a French beach looming nearer, toward bastions that seemed to grow more huge and black, until the bow of the boat jerked and beached on pebbles. Robert leaped over the side and ran to the shore, sword drawn, full of fighting fervor that could ignore wounds and danger, and joy in them.

And then he stood on the beach like a fool, with others who had followed him on the run, splashing madly to battle as they thought. All stared at the bastions built beyond the tide. More men came running up from the river. They stood also, shuffling. Behind them men cursed at horses flung overboard to swim ashore, now being dragged out of the river. Shoes rang as the animals lunged and kicked up stones. More boats came, with torches sputtering sparks at their bows, lighting up the beach and making fair targets of Robert and the others, outlining them in a glow. The torches should have brought quarrels and darts and arrows, but only drew insects to swing in circles around each flare.

Wat said, puzzled, "I had better brought beer in my quiver for us, than arrows for them. Are they sunk in their own marshes?"

Someone shouted, "Here's the Duke of Clarence, landing now!"

Robert yelled, "Hold your tongue!"

If the French were waiting for the best target, they had him now.

"Stand over by the shore," Robert ordered some men. "Between the duke and the French."

They moved to do so, as the boat beached.

Then a man with a proud bearing, who must be Clarence and brother to the king, stepped out and waded ashore. He was taller than Henry but looked much like him otherwise, except he had a colder, graver face.

"Who gave that order I heard?" he asked.

"I did, Your Grace," Robert said.

"Who are you?"

"I'm called Robert Heartless, Your Grace."

Clarence looked him over coolly in the torchlight. His face was unsmiling, his tone distant. "You were Llewellyn ap Gryffyd's lieutenant," he stated flatly. "That's recommendation enough to me. I have need now of a fearless man."

He moved his hand in a half-circle to embrace the men upon the beach.

"All are Welshmen here. They're proud and wild and unaccountable, they say. I know little of archers or Welshmen, for I've followed the sea all my life—but if you're proud, I'll not command your loyalty, but ask it. Robert Heartless, will you follow me?"

Here was a choice place! Clarence as his lord! Yet Robert had hoped to stay near the king, and Clarence would prefer to stay away. The king was hot and Clarence was cold and they clashed if they stayed together.

"Give me an answer later," Clarence said. "I want no man who's not wholehearted. Meanwhile, there's the bastion, and it will not come to you. So do you go up to try it."

Someone brought a wet horse, and Robert mounted. Wat seized at another, and the men on the beach scattered for mounts for themselves.

"Picked men," Clarence said without change of tone as he watched them. "Picked from under the gallows before the rope was too tight on their necks."

They were a rough-looking mob, unshaven, with eyes that glittered. But every man had a longbow, and feathers that seemed to grow from a shoulder.

"Like to like, from what I've heard of you," the Duke of Clarence said. "Welshmen, here's your master, Robert Heartless of Wales."

"How far will you have me go, Your Grace?" Robert asked.

"As far as any ambitious man would."

"To Harfleur, then," Robert said, and raised his hand, touched his horse with his heels and rode up the beach with the villains after him, heading straight for the bastions, for there was no shrewder way.

No arrows came. Not then, or ever—even when they threaded through the narrow passages in the walls, expecting instant death—because there was no one there. Not a Frenchman in sight to defend his land. Once through, they smelled marsh, and then they were in the swamp, guided by the stars and Wat's remembrance.

And why, Robert thought, as they traveled single file in the boggy path, *were the bastions never defended?* As for him, the river would have run with blood before an enemy had even landed.

They moved on slowly, with Wat going first, bow ready, guiding his horse with his knees. Next came Robert, then the others, each directly behind the man ahead, for there was quicksand too. They moved in inches, it seemed, hemmed in with stinking, slimy vegetation, stagnant water, mud, dead things that rotted, and insects coming in hordes to dine on Englishmen.

They reached Harfleur at dawn, and hung back among some trees southwest of the city. They scratched insect bites as a glorious August morning began and the sky turned pink behind the city, outlining the sharp black masts of ships caught in the galley-close within as they tilted in the Lezarde's lazy current.

It was a lovely town, surrounded by a heart-shaped red brick wall with the apex pointed to the green wooded hills of Montivilliers to the north. For all their beauty, the walls were well fortified and surmounted by a multitude of towers, each with the leaden figure of a bird or animal atop it, painted in blue or gold. There was a gate toward the west. Robert could see it had a drawbridge and portcullis, and was protected besides by a barbican, or outer palisade, of tree trunks as high as the walls. These trunks had bark still on them, and were clamped together with iron bands into little rectangular forts filled with earth and pierced with narrow apertures. There were more of these barbicans along the length of the town, and each would have to be reduced before the walls could be reached. More than that, beyond the barbicans was a ditch flooded with water, shining like silver now. Mining the walls would be impossible, the tunnels would only flood. The ditches must be bridged then, under fire from the walls.

The Lezarde entered the town on the northwest. No doubt the watergate was well protected. As for the eastern side, he could not tell, but the south was a flooded swamp with two great towers at the exit of the river Lezarde, a chain across, and tree trunks driven into the riverbed to stop small craft.

Robert contemplated the strong fortress before him, and thought of the three accepted methods of conducting a siege against a powerful city. The first was to cut off or poison the water supply. But the Lezarde flowed through the town, impossible to divert, impossible to poison. The second method was starvation, now unlikely of success. The English army had been delayed so long in Southampton by intrigue that the French crops had been harvested. Therefore, but one course was left: costly and bloody assault.

With this unwelcome news, Robert returned to Clarence and made report. To the Duke himself, and not an underling. This both surprised and pleased him and added respect for Lord Thomas. After that Robert stood about on the beach that had never been defended. Clarence had not been wasting his time. The bastions were now guarded by English soldiers, and more soldiers were being rushed ashore. Small boats darted in the Seine, sails dropped and sails rose. There was shouting over all. Flats and lighters seized from the port of Leure were floating catapults ponderously ashore. The siege guns were of wonderful variety: sheltrons, mangonels, springalds, trepgets, robinets more kinds than Robert knew names. Some slung boulders and some shot shafts. There were guns here too that used gunpowder, that stank and made a fearful noise when they were fired, but they were hard to handle, heavy to shift, fired too short a range, and forever needed repair. Besides, they could shoot but once an hour, though they flung stones that weighed four hundred pounds. The siege would take forever with such sorry weapons. A good mangonel was simpler, and flung its stones as fast as they were loaded.

No one seemed to know what was going on. Clarence sat on a horse on the highest slope of the beach, overseeing all and watching the stores pile up in scattered hills, but the bowmen wandered around wondering when they would eat.

It took three days to get them all inland and camped on the western side of Harfleur, but at last they were bedded down. It was too hot for sleeping. A warm miasma from the swamp drifted among them. Insects sang and bit. The horses stamped and swished their tails. From Harfleur a church bell pealed and woke Robert suddenly in the night. He got up restlessly, and leaned against a tree to contemplate Graville to the west, where small watchfires burned on the hillside. The king and his lords slept there. No, the nobles were sleeping there, not the king. He was a nightwalker, that was well known to the host, but the reason was a matter for argument. Someone had contributed the titbit that spread to the entire army. Along with jewels and relics of saints, sacrificed for money for a war, King Hal had pawned the lying-in gear of the royal ladies when they gave birth, gold basins and such. True, there was little need of these things if the king kept on as he did, forswearing women. Where was an heir to come from? Ay, he walked, and they guessed why, angrily. There were better uses for the dark hours than walking. If he would not sleep, let him get a prince for England! All the host agreed.

What was the king doing now? Standing at a window in that abbey, Robert guessed, looking down on Harfleur in the starlight, on the rising church spire, the dark streets, the pointed masts of ships, and the red glow of a farmhouse burning somewhere to the east.

He would be thinking of the strategy of war, of the only decision he could make. Weaken the city and then assault it. The king was not sleeping among his lords in the sweet, cool air of Graville. Nay, he was walking up and down, counting the men he must lose at Harfleur.

That was a queer, wry thought. *The men who would die at Harfleur*. They were alive now, these men; some sleeping, some talking in the dark. They were alive and would be dead. Robert began to walk among them, moving slowly through the men who'd die at Harfleur's walls. He had never questioned his life before, or any man's life, or living or dying; nor how it touched others; but Constance had reached some dim part of him, made him think, and turned him homesick too, for London and the house on the river. He felt infinitely sad. Then he checked his aimless walking. A shadow, darting! Robert watched, alert. It passed before a campfire. Or was it a flicker of light?

With decision, he went swiftly toward it and it stopped, it froze, like a hunted thing pretending it is not there.

"I'll know your name," Robert said clearly.

Men turned around from the nearest campfire.

"You've eyes to see in the dark, Robert Heartless," some man's voice replied.

"Come from under that tree's shadow," Robert said.

"Nay, come under the tree," invited the voice.

It intrigued Robert, who liked a lively game. He advanced warily, but stopped out of range of a dagger or sword. The few who had looked up turned back to their own fires.

"You know my name?" Robert asked.

"I've heard your bells before," the other explained.

"Do you jest at them?"

"Nay! I would I was of such a nature, to wear bells to war. You wear a handsome sword. The king had one like it, they say."

The tones of this voice, like to Clarence, though not so cold.

"It is this very sword," Robert said.

"He could not have prized it, to give it away."

Soft tones, measured, tinged now with mockery.

"I am entrusted with it only," Robert said, "that it might fight still for its absent lord."

"You turn a sentence like a courtier!"

"I was much with women. I learned it of them, not at court."

"Do they weep for you now, gone to France?"

"Nay," Robert said. "They've forgot me in Wales."

"One then? A sweetheart?"

Robert hesitated. She'd been fond, but she was quicksilver, and they'd known each other but few days, when they were counted. And yet, he hoped she missed him.

"Yes," he said at last, and acknowledged a sweetheart left behind.

"I had a sweetheart too," the voice said lightly, "but she never loved me. She fled to a convent when I would marry, but never told me why."

Silence. How could that be answered?

"Hear them murmuring?" the voice asked. "Hear them, around the campfires? Men speak so soft at night." Then abruptly, "How old are you?"

"Nineteen," Robert said, "but five years of it were spent in border wars. I fought in Wales for Llewellyn ap Gryffyd, but I'll serve King Henry in France."

Robert could feel the silence shimmering.

"See the sky behind you!" the voice said.

Robert did not turn his back. "They're raiding out of the host," he said.

"Again?" The voice turned hard, and sounded more like Clarence now. "The king issued orders against this. He must be sterner. Do you think on a skrie also? You're wandering about at night as if you seek to learn the ground."

"I'll take my loot from a battlefield, not a farmer," Robert said. "As for wandering, I was raised in Wales. I like to know who else prowls in the darkness, and why."

The church bell tolled again in Harfleur.

"As to who and why," the voice said, "I'll not tell you. Adieu."

Robert let him go. There was no need to follow. It was King Henry moving through his army while the lords slept in Graville.

So the king knew of Robert Heartless? From the Welshmen in the army? From Clarence? There was no danger in it, so long as the name was not hitched to the confession on the Portchester road. It was not likely, however, that this calamity would come about. Robert was not given to long worry over short possibility. He turned back to his own campfire.

It was the Duke of York who'd be the danger. York could set Robert Heartless at the Pope's Head brawl, and again near Portchester Castle, to make one dangerous identity of two men. York had half known him by some small thing, though he'd been masked and muffled. Not the accent. There were thousands of Welshmen in this host, and they all talked the same. It would be another trick, or habit. Traitors were experts in such matters. Still, York could not prove whatever he might suspect, and besides, what interest could a duke have in a squire?

Robert walked into the circle of his own men and sat by his tree again, his backside firm against his saddlebags and the Bible in them. Here was the sword that laid its edge to his neck. It would be best to burn the Book or throw it into a swamp. But then, he'd have been dead in Wales at fifteen, if the Bible had not saved him then. Clearly it was Heaven's intent he have it. He'd keep his Bible. Yet it would then be well to avoid the short, fat, sharp-eyed Duke of York.

Well, when light came, he'd find Lord Thomas, Duke of Clarence, and say he'd ride with him. York would stick close to the king where the chance of royal favor was, but Clarence would get as far away as he could. Regretfully, Robert made his decision. He'd join with Clarence, and serve King Henry through his brother.

Chapter 18

AT GRAVILLE, they kept regal array. Tents were everywhere, of red and blue and stripes, set gaily under spreading trees near the gray stone abbey. Among this splendor wandered heralds and minstrels, chaplains, pages, pavilioners, watchmen, clerks, priests, purveyors of the spicery and buttery and napery, countless others, all to do with the royal comfort; though the king was seldom near to enjoy it. But here, on good green grass, in sweet air, in sunlight by day and good bright torchlight by night, walked the nobility of England.

And here sat the Duke of York behind a table, under a tall tree, with the early September sun trickling through the foliage to speckle the paper before him. He was writing another book. And making another plot.

York was an intelligent man, with a crook to his thinking, put there by ambition he could neither realize nor completely relinquish. He knew it was too late now to reach for more than he had. He knew he stood at a stone wall and hammered with bare fists. Yet, if a man persisted long enough, even a wall might weaken. Henry of England was a reader. He'd brought chests full of books to war. Such a man could surely be pleased with one that praised him and his war. So the Duke of York had begun another book to advance his fading hopes. What he had failed to gain with swords or poison, he might earn with a littler weapon. A pen.

He wrote in English, the vulgar tongue, for King Henry favored it and therefore in that language York made his book, though he could have used Latin or French with ease if he willed, for he was learned.

His jeweled fingers glittered as his pen moved in slow, fair curves and angles. The lords walking about did not see a desperate man, but a studious one.

He set down how Henry had landed in France on August 14th, and fallen on his knees at the moment of landing, imploring divine aid and protection in his effort to obtain justice. (*And must he be forever on his knees? Especially on those hard stones.*) King Henry had conferred knighthood on many of his followers. A good cheap way of being knighted, York thought, for he was parsimonious in many ways. Plenty of honor and no expense. (*But no knighthood for Robert Heartless, though he wore a sword with three gold ostrich feathers for a hilt, which Henry must have given him. Still, Henry's thinking was devious, and his new policy was to favor first one man, then the other. The Welshman must be watched; he might wiggle into favor.*)

On the 17th of August, King Henry came to Graville, and here it was arranged that commands would be split, as the city was, by the river flowing through. Henry would take the western side, and his brother Lord Thomas the east. (*And with the Lord Thomas, who liked separate command too well, went the Welshman Robert Heartless. He could not be in favor, if Henry let him go.*)

On the 19th of August, the Lord Thomas made the long circuitous trip around the southern morass, to get to his eastern command. The road had been utterly destroyed by the French, and the swamp turned to a sea by flooding. (*The Welshman led them through and was not dainty how he went, so it were swift. Many a horse slipped, and many a nobleman landed in mud to send up noble curses. Yet they said that*

Clarence was pleased for the speed, though they went dangerously in darkness, for the French Lord de Gaucourt had marched the day before into the unguarded eastern gate of Harfleur and reinforced the city while the English watched them from Graville. Henry had raged, and sworn at Clarence for not closing the trap around the city sooner. Clarence only said, without a smile, that it made more Frenchmen to hold for ransom later. Henry had not been amused. And Clarence had marched the same night.)

But of course, York thought, he could not write of that. He lifted his pen, pleased the brothers had quarreled, and looked across the downward slant of hill, past Harfleur and her ditches and river glinting in the sun, over the walls to the eastern side, where Clarence was. There was the best command. It was from there the final battle would probably be launched. It was there that heroes would be made. It was there that Robert Heartless drew first blood for England in this war. (*Had Henry let the Welshman go to earn a reputation there?*)

York clutched his pen hard and wrote on, scowling.

Since the 19th of August, Harfleur had been completely invested and cut off. All cover had been burned right up to the French barbicans, to discourage citizens from prowling into the English host at night. Harfleur lay now in a circle of blackened earth. At the outer perimeter of this burned ground were the stone-throwing guns for the siege, dragged into position under the darts of the crossbowmen on the walls. Traps of wood had been built over them to protect the gunners, and these squealed like butchered pigs when they were hoisted to spring the gun or fire the bombards. And the noise! The bombards boomed, the catapults squalled, men shouted; boulders hurtled into the sky and crashed down with a sound of thunder. Stone walls collapsed and bricks and mortar exploded in avalanches of wreckage. The boulders split on impact and splinters flew like knives. People screamed inside when they were hit.

But from Graville's hill, it was almost pretty. Oh, he'd hear a faint crash when a house was smashed, but chiefly the war was visual: puffs of dust and flying debris by day; and fire arrows at night, like falling stars exploding into conflagrations. There were constant fires, and by their glare the watchers in Graville could see black shadows, frantic as ants, each night. There was constant activity then, when the French dared retreat from their walls and leave only watchers there. Then they fell upon their impassable streets. They took the bricks, the fragments, they took the very stones flung in, and patched their city. Each day the walls crumbled, and each night they were rebuilt. Yet not so high or firm as before. The drama of the rising and falling walls of Harfleur continued like the tide, while the crossbowmen of France and the longbowmen of England kept the air alive with darts and quarrels and huzzing shafts.

And, York made rueful note, while Harfleur fought, some four thousand armed Frenchmen sat on the other side of the Seine and watched. They did not dare attack King Henry's larger army; and got no reinforcement from Rouen, where their own king was according to some rumor. So all they did was wait and send spies. They were no danger yet. But if King Henry's forces diminished . . . York did not write the last.

Nor did he tell of the wounded, everywhere now. The worst were sent home to save supplies. Their war was done, let them take their bellies to England. Such as could fight remained, limping around in bandages. The monks at Graville had a hospital, and the wounded archers grouped together and speculated on their wounds and the walls; if the one would heal in time for the destruction of the other. It was September now but the walls were still too high, and the French still fought too hard.

The war had settled into a routine of deadly monotony on strict rationing, for somehow ships left with wounded but did not return with food. There was little sport to be had to repay a man for going short. King Henry had made firm rules against raids out of the motley host. Looting would be punished by death. He'd hung a few to convince the rest.

Other appetites were curbed. Decent women must not be molested. Yet, to avoid hanging his entire army over this, King Henry permitted another kind of woman about, but not in his camp. They were gathered at three miles distant and warned if they came closer their left arm would be broken. A few came. None twice. Three miles away—a good long walk to cool hot blood, but many a man hiked it. Unless he was among the wounded. Bloodletting calmed them. But naturally, York did not write it.

Another burden had been added. A curious listlessness among the men. It was not the languid air of lazy men, nor the weariness of tired men, but rather the dreaded apathy of sickness. Archers stumbled about their duties flushed of face, insect-bit and feverish. Some blamed it on the smells. The cattle had all been killed and the entrails flung into the swamp to steam there in the heat of day until they stank. Some blamed it on spoiled provisions, but got no fresh. Supply ships did not come. Some blamed it on the mussels the bowmen gathered from the creeks. Some blamed it on the fog that drifted over the valley camps. Yet it made no difference what they ate or where they slept. King Henry gave away to the archers his own supplies, but still they sickened with the bloody flux that turned a man's bowels into thick red blood that poured out as from a gaping wound. Many men died of arrows, but more died of the flux. But of course, York did not write it.

. He had much to consider in his book. This would not please Henry, that would not please Clarence, and the other did not please *him*. He would not write the name of Robert Heartless, though it was known now in the host. Robert had been in that first skirmish when some Frenchmen trying to follow their Lord de Gaucourt into Harfleur had lacked his luck at finding an unguarded gate. They came one day after and ran head on into Robert Heartless. Clarence let the Welshman wander like a roving dog. He might be anywhere. He'd been where the French sought to slip through. It was only a skirmish, but it was first blood, and the Welshman's name had gone to Henry. One of the Welsh lords had seen to that.

Strange, how thick the Welsh blood ran. In the midst of twenty thousand they maintained aloof identity, and there was Robert Heartless, clad in scarlet, a rallying point for a treacherous race that longed for their wild heroes. They cared nothing for books or learning, but their heads went up like so many startled stags when they saw the Welshman's scarlet flash in glimpses between the trees.

For all his riding, Robert Heartless had breath at night to sing. You could hear it almost anywhere if you listened for it, and already too many did. He lent the only spark to dreary days of sickness and woundings. They talked of him, and called out greetings when he came. And when he thundered by, a sound and a shout in the night, men leaped to their feet by their fires and listened until he was gone.

At Graville, however, Robert Heartless was but the subdued tinkle of small gold bells, though they were heard too often, for he had almost daily contact with the king. Clarence sent him on personal matters. The Welshman came in a whirl of flying clods kicked up by horses. He stayed only long enough to give his messages—some written, too many verbal. York did not like the latter. It meant the king must see him then, while his men waited outside like a pack of bandogs, surly, vicious and unapproachable. They stared with open contempt at the luxury around them, and spat and commented in Welsh.

When Clarence's lieutenant came to Graville, York always watched and listened. Henry gave no sign of anything; but then, the day was past when he flung his favor to any who smiled at him. Yet he liked Welshmen, he liked gallantry, and he saw too much of Robert Heartless.

It kept York awake, untangling the tangled skeins of royal favor, and what man had it, or who might get it next. Henry openly favored only the Bishop of Norwich, Richard Courtenay, but that was old friendship and York did not fear old friends, but new ones. It was a climber who must be watched, a man emerging from anonymity. The time for him to climb was now. Henry was lonely, his war waxed desperate. He was a man who needed another to listen to his problems. Who? York set spies to watch the Welshman. Which was how he found that Robert Heartless went often on his own business to the beach in the Seine, and got letters sent via a certain ship named *Jesu.*

York usually stayed away from the lower lands. He feared the sickness there. Yet on September 10th, when he learned a ship had come and Robert Heartless would surely go down, for it was *Jesu* of London, he rode there himself.

Most of the fleet was gone, but a few ships rode at anchor, and one was unloading cargo into lighters. Piles of materials in canvas bales were already pyramided on the stony beach, and it was among these stacks that York made his way on foot to find the captain. For he'd had another thought. Sometimes the sea captains had a pretty taste in wine or food, and such good things could be bought. York wanted to add to his secret store, for his only pleasure was eating and he had a constant horror of depletion.

But this captain proved to be rough-faced, rough-voiced and rougher still of temper.

"Dainties?" he inquired, and looked York over from head to foot. "We carry only dainties for the French. Arrows. Arrows fletched with goose and swan and parchment. No more is on my ship."

York did not believe him. He had a crook in his nature, and thought all men like himself. So he lingered on the beach, well hidden by the cargo piles. He even made a little hole in a seam in one bundle in a stack, and poked a finger in. And promptly jerked it back bleeding. He swore, and put it tenderly in his mouth. Then with both hands he pulled the rent he'd made more open and peered in. Arrows, all pointed straight at him. He sucked on his finger again.

A crunch of footsteps and he swung half-round. Out from an alley between the high-piled bales came the captain followed by some clerk. The captain stopped in the middle of a sentence.

"Now, sir," he said, without respect, "is this knightly of you, to doubt a poor sailor's word?"

York pulled his punctured finger from his mouth and put it behind his back.

The clerk whined, ". . . but if you did not mark which was swan and which was goose and which was parchment, how can I check what was delivered?"

"What he sells," the captain said, "he delivers."

The clerk frowned, and saw the rent in the canvas. He poked his finger in. And snatched it out. He looked pitifully at the bloody thing, then glared at York as if it was his fault.

"Arrows," the captain pronounced, with delight at this misfortune, "sharp ones, too."

Then suddenly he went alert and bellowed, "You!" He strode a step down, out of sight. "Not that one, not that with the black crosses! That's not for you. Load the others and leave that on the beach!"

York heard a thud as something was flung angrily down. Someone swore. A horse snorted. Then grunting and heaving resumed.

"Well, then," the clerk said, resigned, "if we have not food enough, we'll have arrows enough. I'll check this as delivered. They're carrying it off as fast as it's landed, anyhow."

He walked off with the captain, pebbles rattling beneath their feet. York only moved as far as the edge of his shielding pyramid and saw the bale that caused the fuss, dropped away from the others and set alone. It was wrapped as if arrows were within, but marked on the side with black crosses. He'd watch, York decided, and see who took it. With determination he pulled down a bale and sat on it. The shafts inside felt like welts to his fat behind, but he waited. He had learned to wait in prison.

At length he heard more horses clattering up; too fast for the sumpterhorses that moved only at a walk. Then, exchange of greetings. He moved behind canvas piles, working his way cautiously, all sound hidden by the laden sumpterhorses that crunched along continually. He got close enough to hear the voices of the newly come. Welsh, flowing like a rushing tide, frothing and pulsing. *London*, he heard, and *arrows* and *my lady*.

He risked thrusting his head out and saw a rough, squat man with a brutish face, incongruously clean and well shaven for such a gutter-bred beast, bending over the package with the crosses. A knife flashed, the canvas was slit. The brutish man dug in with a hand and yelled, "Arrows, lads! Proper arrows, fletched with peacock, the best in all the world. I've poached deer with these!"

Instantly he was surrounded by archers, buried in them as they struggled and reached and grabbed. York knew them. The Welshman's ban-dog pack.

The brutish voice rose over the tumult. "No excuses for missing shots now, lads. The Frenchmen will be beautiful with these in their chests! Peacock! Peacock! Who'll have arrows with peacock?"

An arm waved up out of the millrace of bodies, and peacock arrows gleamed in the sun. Broken English spattered like a fountain. Typically Welsh, they were seizing every shaft they could, while taking the other side. They clutched the peacock and swore that swan was better! *Nay!* others bellowed. *Gray goose!* The loud archers' argument covered the beach as they pushed and shoved and tried to outshout each other. No more was to be learned here. The argument of goose and swan had begun with the first arrow and doubtless would continue to the last. York walked away from the uproar unheard, passing behind each pyramid and glancing down each alley. Suddenly he stopped dead and jumped back, to be hidden. If those damned ban-dogs would only cease their yelping so he could overhear! It was impossible. A few strides away the captain talked unheard, and handed a letter over.

A pair of hands came from behind a stack of bales. White paltock sleeve showed at a wrist. A flash of scarlet and ermine sleeve. The hands gave a letter with the left and took a letter with the right. The captain tucked his into his belt and patted, to indicate the infinite degree of safety—then strode away, glancing toward the incredible uproar of the quarreling archers.

Messages, York thought. A private line of communication. By whom? To whom? He could guess. To the merchant Chapelle via his captain. From? Who had access to that valuable thing, privacy and a swift-sailing courier? He had to know, a guess was not enough. York moved boldly now, the sound of his footsteps covered by the noise. He passed the alley and saw the man. Robert Heartless, reading as if he'd devour the message with the intense concentration of one who has no speed of recognition of written things. York was a little contemptuous. Robert Heartless sweated to snatch reluctant meanings and never saw an enemy poised near him, or turning in swift retreat.

So Robert Heartless, the Lollard of Portchester, was in communication with the merchant Chapelle in London. York smiled happily as he labored over the shale to the horse he'd left by the bastions. Lollardy and Chapelle, eh? What an intelligent man might do with such knowledge. What he might do!

York started immediately for Graville. It did not pay to linger here. The flux was rampant. And he had the Welshman now, his destruction was in these hands that held these reins.

But on the narrow swamp path, retracing his way to Graville, York wavered. He was not a simple man and he did not like a simple road. He'd never run a straight course in his life. So he played with another thought. Consider if it would be worth while to make an ally of the Welshman, who had rich friends in London, and the favor of Clarence, brother to the king. It must be remembered that a dead enemy was only carrion, and if he tore Robert down, he cleared a vacant place into which still another man might step.

Also, if Hal died without an heir, and Clarence was made king . . . This matter would take thinking.

If Robert Heartless must be destroyed, this Lollardy must be used now, or the opportunity lost—for if Clarence was king, the heretics would run free. On the other hand, if he was to be courted, he might be a dangerous ally, or else a very strong one. York thought, a little wistfully, of safety and how it might feel. He had never known it.

And besides, if he let this chance the Lollardy offered go, he could still bring the Welshman down. Robert Heartless was honest, and uncompromising to boot. When he made a step forward, he would not step back. He would not lie, and he would not learn that art. He was stubbornly honest. Such men could be ensnared.

York was feeling merciful when he rode into Graville, and went into his tent for some wine and sleep and plotting, which he did not get, for grave news awaited him. The Bishop of Norwich was stricken with the flux.

York crossed himself for his squire's benefit, but when he turned away he allowed himself a smile. The flux, so. It was killing strong men, and Courtenay had been sick when he came. If Courtenay died, and it was likely, there was the empty place ready immediately. Henry was lonely and a man who must talk to those he trusted. None around him who'd had careless favor counted. With Courtenay dead, this was the chance for York. Then his smile faded. Or the chance for the Welshman.

York looked out from his tent somberly at the small groups whispering under the trees. *Down the Welshman,* he thought, almost with regret. He could not afford such an ally. It had been but a tempting thought. The Welshman was too dangerous. He must be stopped and the time to stop him was now, with evidence in hand. If once Robert Heartless had the king's ear, it were too late. Therefore, *now.*

York put on darker garments as more seemly, for Henry always expected the worst when a friend was stricken. Then he walked through the camp planning what he must say. He would make it clear, delicately, that he had always been maligned, that he was a good man turned traitor because of his generation and not by wickedness inborn, a traitor by dictate of fate and not instinctive nature. With an honest chance he'd make an honest friend.

The years had taught him. There were too many between him and the throne. He was too old now for the insanity of wholesale murder, too old to grasp at a witchfire that tempted a man into a bog. He had learned, and he'd proved it. He'd kept out from the whirlpool of treason into which his brother Cambridge dropped and drowned. He had survived, and his hands had been clean throughout.

He liked this feel of righteousness and good conscience, with nothing to be concealed. His ambition was gone and this gave him ease. All he wanted now was a high place and security there. Well, he was turning honest, but he'd not forget that too much truth was bad for any man.

He was admitted to the king and found Henry sprawled in a chair, amid a crowd of silent nobles standing around with sullen faces.

"Hal," York said, for it seemed warm friendliness was a good approach among these cheerless men, "here's a sad thing I hear. Now don't fret, Hal. Send your bishop back to England. He'll recover there."

"Not there, or here, or anywhere," Hal said. He was sunk in gloom. He'd brood now, York thought. There was desperation in his face, and he picked with one hand at a report on a table by him.

It was then that York noticed Clarence, leaning by a window looking out. Clarence, here? He cared for no bishops. He only cared for war and how it went. There was something to do with the war.

"Sire," York said, "not more ill news on top of all?"

"We've a man captured, out of Harfleur, lowered from the walls," Henry said.

"So long as he was captured," York said, reminding of the good.

"He was the fourteenth lowered," Henry said. "So he told us. We have captured ten."

"Ah," said the Duke of York. Four men over the walls and through their lines, running for help to the King of France himself, ignoring Bouciquaut, still sitting on the other side of the Seine, leashed by royal order.

Harfleur was sick and like to die, but she was risking the dash to Rouen, and sending many in the hope one would get there. Therefore Harfleur would not die quickly. She would linger, hoping for succor from her king. She would fight with desperation, her back to her red brick walls. She would fight till the last brick was kicked loose. And then she would fight in her ravaged streets.

Her temper was clear. It might not take long, those dying gasps, but it would take long enough. Illness was the enemy in the English ranks, fighting Harfleur's battle; her strong ally. The host was cut in half. Most of their ships had gone home. Bouciquaut was ready beyond the Seine, and King Charles, if he came quickly now, could pin Henry with his back to that river and squeeze him in between.

York glanced at the king. Hal was looking out the open door toward a certain outbuilding used for a hospital. Courtenay would be there, York thought. He put his hand gently on Hal's shoulder.

"I'm sorry for it, Hal," he said, "truly sorry."

The king moved, to get from under the hand.

"My friends all die," he said. "I fear to make one of any man."

"I do not fear to be one, Hal," York said.

It were well said, he thought. The king had looked up a moment.

"He might recover, Hal," York said. And wished it in that moment. "I'll pray for him." For Hal was pious, and liked prayers.

"He's my friend," Henry said hopelessly. "That's his sentence."

"There are many others, sire, who are sick," someone said compassionately. "Sickness steals through the entire army."

"As," York said, "the Welshman Robert Heartless does, going everywhere."

Henry did not respond, as if he did not hear.

But by the window, the Duke of Clarence turned and stared with a cold look on his cold and narrow face.

The king's eyes were closed; his hands were clenched.

Outside a trumpet sounded; it was time to eat, and little enough they'd get. The king's eyes opened at the sound. "I cannot even get food for them," he said.

"Perhaps the Welshman could," York said, deliberately. "I've seen him on the beach, talking to the captains. He gets . . . packages."

"I wondered on how you spent your time," came Clarence's voice, like a whip. "Following my forerider, while others fight at the walls. But then, a man stays out of danger so, not fighting."

York stiffened with anger. He'd been no coward, ever.

Henry said, "Hold, York! I will not have you quarrel!"

Clarence said, "Sire, this is a traitor I cannot abide. If he comes to the eastern side while I am there, I tell you plain, he'll never come again to the west."

"My lord," York said, with misgivings that Clarence chose to interpret this publicly as an attack on him, "I was but suspicious that the forerider stayed strong while others starved. I sought to do your business and find food by following the Welshman."

Clarence said, "As to the first, he's used to an empty belly, and as for finding food, we could fatten the army on what you've hidden."

The king looked at York.

"I did keep some small portion aside," York admitted.

"Have it out," the king said, with the flash of eyes that showed he'd not be gainsaid in this.

"Sire . . . yes, yes," York said. His fine viands, flung to yeomen! God! Mussels from the creeks suited them. His wines, his dainties. "I but waited till they were needed before the battle." He ceased protesting. Henry had a way of growing angrier if excuses were offered too long.

"This captain on the beach," Henry said.

". . . brought a special package from London, marked differently—"

"Containing arrows," Clarence broke in roughly. "I'll swear to it, sire. If you take a traitor's word over mine, then let me retire to England. I have no place here."

This was plain talking; too plain; it was dangerous. Clarence was a bulwark before the Welshman, and did not care who knew it. And Clarence was next in line for the throne.

York protested he meant no harm but was zealous in service to the crown.

Clarence stared at him, icy. Clarence was not forgiving. It was a bad day's work. Next time he'd wait till Clarence was gone. York shivered a little. He could not get to the Welshman by open accusation. It must be done secretly and quickly. Particularly it must be quickly.

When the king again bade them cease wrangling, York looked abject. He begged Clarence's pardon if aught was taken wrong; he'd meant no harm, no harm to any. He even walked over and offered to kiss Clarence's cheek. But Clarence turned away.

Chapter 19

SATURDAY, the 14th of September, turned to a bitter dark night. Winter threatened outright and the chill drove all to cover who could go, and kept the rest by their campfires. Only sentries walked, and these Robert passed without difficulty, for all the host knew Clarence's man and that he rode everywhere, at any hour.

It was a long ride, away from the army, and only Wat with him. He had much time to remember how his men had looked when he left them, with stern warnings to stay there. No man was to take off on a scry. They shivered by their fires and seemed chilled and harmless, as a snake when it is cold, but there had been a conflagration—some farmer's house—and a little shouting in the forenoon. He hoped it would not stir them. He'd chance it. The cold would keep them pegged. And he wanted news of Constance. Therefore, he rode with Wat until they reached a gibbet set where two highways crossed, and here they halted. The empty gibbet squeaked in the rushing wind that soughed among the trees and bushes. The moon played at hide-and-seek with the clouds. It brightened and darkened, and brightened and darkened, as did his expectations.

"They'll never come," Wat predicted at last, after they dismounted to save the horses. "Their courage is in their moneybags."

"I know little enough about the breed," Robert said, "but I know this. A merchant will come to his market, though it be in fear of his life. The Frenchmen know His Worship will come if he said this. They'll keep the rendezvous."

They waited, shivering; and the Frenchmen delayed interminably. The moon went dark again; and stayed dark long.

"I hear bells," Wat declared in a hoarse whisper.

"I hear hooves," Robert replied.

They listened together, alert to any sound above the restless wind, the squeaking wood of the gibbet, and the sound of a stream gurgling near. The clouds thinned overhead, and a weak glow filtered through.

"Four horsemen," Wat whispered.

Four great bulks on the road, approaching warily, without torches.

"Ho! Travelers!" Robert called.

The four horses halted under the wooden gibbet.

Robert and Wat mounted instantly and approached with caution. Until in a sudden brilliant brightening of the moon that lasted but an instant they could discern the form of the merchant Chapelle on the great horse, his belly resting on the pommel of his saddle.

"Well met," the merchant said. "Are you just come?"

"Lately, Your Worship," Robert said.

Wat muttered at the politeness.

"And your trip?" Robert concluded.

"*Holy Mary* sailed like a saint, and I've seen no one since I landed," the merchant said. "Ah, here's the moon again. You're gaunted, if I see right."

"Clarence is no man for letting me sit idle," Robert said.

The merchant's body heaved with silent appreciation.

"You wanted war," he said, "and you have it."

"Here's a strange thing," Robert said. "I hear bells and not my own."

There was an embarrassed pause. "The bells are mine," the merchant said; then, half ashamed, "I laughed at yours, but envied you; yet my belly is too great for such a girdle. At last I thought on this . . . here's moonlight again, see, quickly . . . silver embroidery in a band about my shoulders and silver bells sewn in." The merchant's voice turned complacent. "The color of the gown is violet, which is not true in this light. The fur is fox, dyed violet. The sleeves are to the ground, and the fur will wear, but it's the thing . . . the thing. I can scarce bear to put another robe to my back. Well, we are not met to talk of fashion. What will the Frenchmen offer me?"

"Lace and cloth of gold and silver, I know. I talked with one man; with the others I had no time to linger. I gave your writ messages to some, and passed others onward to Dieppe."

"I hope they have some German hawks," the merchant said. "With unbroken feathers and a fierce eye."

"I do not know," Robert said.

"Whatever comes, it will be welcome. How will you have your share?"

"Share?" Robert said, surprised.

"No man works for nothing," the merchant said, very brisk. "I'll consider you in my prices. How must the profit be divided?"

Robert hesitated a moment.

"The archers sent back to London," he said, remembering the sick faces and bodies broken by illness. "Use my share to buy them comforts. A hospital is cheerless."

Wat made a disapproving sound.

"Hospital?" the merchant said. "Ah, the sick ones. What is that illness, Robin?"

"The flux," Robert said, surprised at being asked.

"God save us," the merchant said with horror. "No wonder the monks took the men off the ships at night. Flux! It would scare London out of its wits . . . and its breeches! How are you?"

"I did not like a saddle for two days," Robert admitted, "but when I was small I had the marsh sickness, and this is very like."

"Call it what you will, flux or marsh sickness," the merchant said, "it's ill news. It was given out the men had arrow wounds. We thought there was hard fighting. Sickness! Henry cannot fight with sick men."

"He must," Robert said. "If he loses this war, he's the son of a usurper and they'll howl for the Earl of March. I heard him say that himself, to his brother."

"How close is victory?" the merchant asked.

Robert was silent.

The merchant grunted.

"Well for us," Robert said, "that Burgundy was paid. He's well bought. He's kept Bouciquaut anchored. There are rumors an army is coming from Rouen, but I've seen no sign of it, though I scouted twenty miles in that direction. I say King Charles can't move his army to Harfleur, or Burgundy will skip behind him and take Paris. Charles would save a city and lose France."

"I would not want Burgundy behind my back," the merchant commented. "I doubt an army will come."

"If it does, we're lost, between Charles and Bouciquaut," Robert said.

"If it does, warn me," the merchant said. "They'll strike at Calais next, and I can use a warning to get my money out."

"I see torches," Wat announced.

"Torches!" The merchant snorted. "Are they afraid of the dark?

They should be more afraid of lights bringing men out of the host for a raid!"

The approaching horses halted in a body, as the moon slipped out and showed them six men below the gibbet. The terror of the others could be felt. But when Robert offered no hostility, they began a slow approach and cautious recognition, until both groups were only a little apart.

"By Jesu and Holy Mary," the merchant swore, declaring himself by the way his ships were called so strangers would think it an oath and not an identification, "here's a hearty welcome for one who's come to toss his gold away."

A man exclaimed shrilly in French, a recognition, and the two groups merged and a babble broke over them. The torches showed fear-ridden faces.

"A man must be cautious these days," said the shrill-voiced Frenchman, pulling at a sparse gray beard.

"A cautious man is a poor man, Pierre," the merchant said. "What makes you tread so wary?"

The little man jerked his beard. "Rotting crops," he said, "unending rain, rivers in flood, the blood taxed out of us for armies never raised, robbers swarming to seize what's left, and . . ." he caught a breath and looked fearfully around, ". . . spies everywhere."

"The wolf eats, the sheep runs," the merchant said succinctly.

"I'll deal with you, I'll deal with you," the little one said hastily. "I'd not have come unless I meant to. I cannot get you Eastern horses, as you want. They're stolen the moment a hoof hits France, but the other things . . . yes."

Then they surrounded the merchant, all still ahorse, for none of the Frenchmen dared dismount in case a shout was raised to run. But after a while fright was forgotten in anger. It seemed the merchant was inclined to drive a bargain. His were the ships, he reminded them, his the markets . . . his, Almighty God be witness . . . the risks. He must have something in return. A babble of French cut the darkness, with cries of *Robber* distinct; the faces under the torches contorted and looked to Heaven for help.

Behind them, the sky turned red toward Harfleur. Another fire within the city, Robert guessed; a bad one this time. Toward the end of the haggling, even the merchants noticed it. The French were silent for a little, all the faces turned that way.

Then, the little one called Pierre said, in an altered voice, ". . . all to be shipped from Dieppe."

"Agreed," the merchant said.

Details were settled, and at last the French with their dangerous lights rode off.

Robert moved his horse beside the merchant's. There was a question he had ached to ask. He waited a little, while the merchant talked of the profit to come. He saw His Worship would avoid what he wanted to hear. He cut across some talk of scarlet cloth, embroidered.

"Perchance," Robert said, "you can tell me of Mistress Constance."

The merchant hesitated.

"She's in London," he said at last.

The moon went dark, and the fire burned fiercely toward Harfleur, wavering red in the sky.

He had hoped . . . how he had hoped . . . that she would come.

"It's best left as it is," the merchant said, gently for him, as if he understood.

Robert could not forbear.

"Is she wed?" he asked, and held his breath till the answer came.

"Soon," the merchant answered reluctantly.

"When?"

"Must you have the day named? You'll suffer for it when it comes."

"Tell me, nonetheless."

"You're no man for avoiding trouble," the merchant said.

"The date?"

"Two days hence, September 17th."

Two days . . . ay. It was past midnight now. Two days.

"Nevertheless," the merchant said, "my house is always open to you, whenever you come to London."

Robert said nothing.

At length the merchant turned his horse.

"If it's aught to you," he said, the last thing, grudging, "she loves you, and she's wept!"

Then he galloped off, with his three varlets behind him. The moon peered at them hurrying on, and darkened as the sounds of hooves faded.

Wat indicated the burning in the sky.

"They're raiding," he said. "Pray not those Welshmen of yours."

Two days and she'd be wed. God, let the old man be good and kind.

Wat said, "We cannot stand all night."

Mechanically, Robert touched heels to his horse, and they both rode back to the burning. There were always fires in Harfleur by night, set by the flaming arrows, but this looked to be a fierce one. He rode a little faster, and came to the top of a high hill overlooking the eastern part. The fire was not within the walls; the city lay stark in a red glow, a small fire in her heart but a greater one without.

"They must have made a sally," Wat commented. "That's one of their barbicans burning."

Another barbican had been reduced. It was another step to the red brick walls. Harfleur had begun her dying. Robert's mouth thinned cruelly as his teeth set hard with scorn of bought men. He hated Burgundy now and pitied Harfleur, which was betrayed but did not know it and fought on in honesty. *God pity you*, he thought with bitterness, and knew it was treason to feel so, and did not care. He thought of the Lord de Gaucourt, who had ridden in the eastern gate and reinforced a city that was doomed. De Gaucourt, who had flung his heart to a cause that was lost. Yet Robert understood. He loved, too, but not a city. And his love was also doomed.

But he could not stand all the night, moody and sad, looking down on a fire-edged city, thinking of Burgundy's betrayal that was saving England now. So he rode down from the crest.

His men were where he had left them, a somber relief. He rode up out of darkness, unexpectedly; and there was a stranger among them, who stood up abruptly as he appeared. A few words more, and the stranger left hastily. Robert dismounted and stared after him.

"One of York's spies," Wat hazarded. "The duke watches close."

Robert turned to the men, shivering by the fire.

"Who was that?" he asked.

"He was passing, sir," the man replied, "and brought us news. Richard Courtenay's dying."

King Henry's friend; King Henry's bishop. This was a night of ill news for all.

"What was his name?" Robert persisted.

147

"He never told us, sir," the man said. "He spoke Welsh."

Robert turned to Wat, but Wat was already gone. He returned a little later and came to Robert, and bent to dig a knife into the ground to clean it.

"York's man?" Robert asked.

Wat nodded, and straightened. "That's the second one," he said, and sheathed his blade.

Chapter 20

THE BELLS began to toll after first light on the fifteenth of September. Robert heard them as he splashed puddled cold water on his face. It had rained toward morning. The hill was wet and slippery as he went to a clear space to overlook the valley toward Graville. A long procession snaked down from there, to vanish beyond the far walls of Harfleur, and reappeared again going toward the beach and remaining ships.

The bells tolled on from the abbey and were answered from the convent high on one of the hills behind him, unseen but present in the voice of its deep bell. King Henry had protected that convent; put guards there during the first violent weeks when his host swept the country bare of edibles and loot. Now the nuns tolled for his bishop newly dead. Robert crossed himself. They said he was a good man.

There was death of many kinds. The death of the body; and another, the slow death of a love that must wane because it could not wax. Soon she would be married . . . hours now . . . and there was nothing he could do. Or would do. He wanted protection for her; only let her be safe.

Wat came up beside him, clearing his throat.

"More burning?" he asked, seeing the dark smoke drifting upward.

"Fires in the city," Robert said. "The rain put them out."

"I wonder there's anything left to burn," Wat said, and spat.

There was much left to burn, Robert thought. He was tired and hungry and a little sick of the flux, but there was much left to burn.

He began to walk, up and down, because he must wait for orders and could not stand still. He understood, then, a little of King Henry's restlessness. Up and down, within the limits a man must set and other things set for him.

All men are prisoners, he thought. And was glad when Clarence summoned him.

"What's the tolling?" the duke asked.

"I think the bishop's dead," Robert replied. "He was dying last night, Your Grace."

They both thought of York at Henry's side, whispering, bowing, sublimely friendly and sublimely untrustworthy. Henry would be lonely now, and lonely men make mistakes if they try the sound of their thoughts upon another mind.

"I like you, Robin Fairfield," Clarence said unexpectedly. "I have troubled myself to show it."

That was obscure, Robert thought, and could not interpret the meaning.

"I do not mind your independence," Clarence said. "Such men can be trusted with vague orders . . . or none at all. Even if they kill other men's spies."

York must have been complaining, then. Had Clarence stood against York for him? It was even possible. Clarence was cold, but the coldness was of good steel. Robert noticed now the shadows in the duke's face, his dull eye, the ruddy skin gone gray. Pray God Clarence did not follow the bishop, with Harfleur unconquered and King Charles restless at their back, all hanging on Burgundy counting his gold.

"Robin," the duke said, "I am going to Graville, to my brother. I want you to ride round the city and tell me what passes within, and without, how all things are, the temper of the city and our host. And if I should be . . . sicker . . . when you get to Graville, report all you find to my brother."

Robert nodded, understanding. Clarence was considering urging Henry to assault the city now.

They did not get along, these brothers; but Clarence would be nigh him now, and not for favors he might pry out. Duty came high to Clarence. If Henry died without an heir, this would make a sturdy king.

"Now do I thank God," the duke said, "for a man that I can trust."

He put his head back wearily against the oaken chair and closed his eyes, thinking of what he must do.

Robert bowed, and left.

It was September 15th, but winter was coming faster than the battle. Robert watched his men saddling, pinch-faced and blue-skinned, with their breaths shooting forth like smoke from a dragon's nostrils. It would be a hard ride again. They mounted and began to file downhill slowly, the horses down-headed, picking carefully in the slippery, browning grass.

It would be a race between time and defeat. The barbicans of Harfleur were broken and marked by the fire of skirmishes fought over each little fort. The walls behind them were breached. Open places showed the destruction in the city. Harfleur was in desperate state, yet the English were as close to defeat. King Henry must make assault, if he would, before he was too weak to fight but while the city was yet too strong for his taking. It was a desperate balance.

Yet Robert did pity these people; and did not recoil now from thinking it, or calling it treason himself. They fought so hard, and hoped so desperately. They dared their lives to slip through at night to beg for the assistance they should have freely had. But their liege lord King Charles was not a man for chancing it; he would not leave his capital unguarded for terror of his Duke of Burgundy marching behind. Burgundy was popular, and a perpetual danger to the French crown while he sulked in his duchy, counting Henry's bribe.

Robert was wrathful that it was the price of Burgundy that would determine Harfleur's fate, and even his. Not gallantry, not truth, not fierce heart or tireless defense. He was all in a turmoil as he rode by the broken walls. His emotions were as stirred by thought as his bowels had been by the flux. There seemed a new man growing in him; a complex man and not a happy one. He viewed his enemy with compassion and his ally with hatred.

It was better in Wales. If he was not your friend he was your enemy. If he was your enemy, you killed him. All was simple. But to see your enemy and wish him your friend? God! That unmanned you, made you hesitant, turned a man to a coward in his heart, fearing to see the other's blood. He looked to the walls he would cross in assault, and dreaded the thought of the fight.

It was not new. He had looked down often in the long, dark, rainy nights and pondered uneasily on beginnings and endings and the crossing of paths and the relation of one human to another. It was robbing him of gaiety and careless laughter; making his happy gold bells a lie he wore before the world. He had thought to enjoy this war; he loved bold dash, he'd wanted men to leap up and shout as he galloped headlong by. He'd had a taste of it in Wales, and thought to gulp it here.

But joy had seeped away. He prayed for Harfleur instead. It was Christian, but not manly. It had made him the more restless, kept him prowling the forests and hills around. His genius was for action and he knew it. But the thinking stayed, like a new-won habit persisting past forgetting.

The bishop was dead. What would it do to King Henry? The thin ranks of his friends grew thinner, and vanished. If Clarence grew sicker, and it seemed he must, without rest or ease, who would dare wrestle with York in the silent pull for power that had now begun? If Henry's friendship was given, all favor went with it. He would not listen to councils. He listened to friends.

Constance would be married Tuesday. It overrode all his thoughts, stayed by him almost continually, and gave a burning and a sickness and a kind of death. He made his circuit of the walls with this, and his report. The next day, the 16th, he circled the walls again with the thought of *Constance* gripping harder. The merchant had been right. It were better to have never known the date. This made for an exact pain. He finished his circuit, and went back to his hill and thought, *By so much time is Constance nearer the hour.*

He smelled smoke. Flames. There were always flames. Since the assault was first considered they had bombarded the city constantly to give them no rest within. Flames did not startle him, but habit made him look for cause. Smoke mushroomed up and hid all in a thick concealing cloud. Then he saw flames licking. Outside the walls. That set him moving. He rode down for a closer look.

Did they still sally from their breached walls? Did they, the heroes, dare? Wind blew the smoke and then he saw them, silhouetted before the inferno of burning English bulwarks. Crossbowmen! French!

More coming, men-at-arms galloping from the smashed wall, with varlets rushing ahead to fling a hasty bridge across the ditch. The English archers, surprised below, stood against the sudden sally, raising bows with shaking sick arms against targets obscured by the smoke. Then, suddenly, the longbowmen were overrun. They broke up the hillside in retreat, pursued by crossbow quarrels. Englishmen were dropping everywhere.

Robert shouted, "*St. David!*" and charged downhill. His men gave a ragged shout; he heard hooves start behind him. He jerked his lance free of its leather bucket and lowered it; the narrow green pennon streamed straight. His horse drove ever faster on the slick footing— it must rush or fall.

He dashed through the retreating English; they yelled to see him and leaped out of his way. And they turned to fight again. For as his lance crashed into a mounted Frenchman's armored breast and broke, long English arrows huzzed past him to rattle on French armor and break on Harfleur's walls. He flung aside the broken lance butt, drew his sword and began to fight in a swirling whirlpool of action—men afoot and men horsed, men in wool and men in armor, determined and desperate men.

In the midst of the fighting and rearing, squealing horses and shouting came a long cry, and the sound of thunder. Robert risked one glance to see if he was surrounded. And saw fat York, half-armored, coming down in furious assault. York swept into the French like a hammer, and smashed them back. Now they were outnumbered.

York fought the same swirling battle, breaking the French in two. Then he left the smaller segment to Robert and took the larger for himself. He pushed them back, he gave them no time to retrieve their bridges. He galloped over, the first of all his men. The others jammed through after him, and turned their attack on a break in the walls through which the Frenchmen were fleeing.

York was trying to get into the city!

The fight turned violent there. Citizens swarmed out, children on the walls flung bricks. Still York tried to force in. Behind him the wrecked barbican flared into flame. The sky above was black with writhing smoke; lashed with the red tongue of fire. Beyond the breach, men-at-arms swarmed to repel the attack. York saw them, and that it was hopeless now. As suddenly as it began, it finished. York fell back.

His men scrambled with frightened horses over precarious footing. One horse broke through a board and fell into the ditch with a splash. The French leaped from their lost barbican and fled across the bridge after the English passed it, dropping torches as they went to fire the wood. The crossbowmen knelt and fired after the English horsemen.

York retreated hastily, galloping up the hill. Robert followed him and they paused finally, grimy and smeared with smoke.

Only the dead lay below, illumined by the burning French barbican and burning English bulwarks. York looked down, his armor touched with brilliant red where the fire reflected on silver. Robert saw how, ludicrously, the fat man had parsimoniously had his armor patched in a great curved plate over the belly, to accommodate his newer fat and make the armor last for still another war.

"That was well fought," York said abruptly.

Robert discerned something more behind the pig's face, redder than ever from exertion of fighting. He thought the duke was going to . . . give advice? York appeared to reconsider. His face went crafty. And he rode off suddenly with his men behind him, a fool's figure of a fighter bursting out of his saddle, his armor clanging loosely and no helm on his jowled red face.

The rain began again in earnest. The flaming stores were quenched. The barbican turned to blackened lumber and smoldered to leave a smell of burning, but the bulwarks burned for days. Nothing more marked high courage from a desperate city. The English bodies were taken up for burial. The French were left for the citizens to retrieve by night.

Robert pulled his mantle hood over his head, against the rain, and resumed his scouting toward Graville, pausing first to talk to this man and then to that, until he had made the circuit, returned to the battlefield, which now was empty, and paused a moment. It was the evening of the sixteenth day of September, and they huddled in their mantles against the cold and wet. He must go on to Graville now, to report to Clarence; but the place where he had watched so often held him for a moment. The horses must be rested and stood head down, while men threw anything they could find across the empty saddles, striving to keep them from wet. Robert closed his eyes a moment and listened to the sounds below. The drip and gurgle of rain, the swish of wet leaves, wild squalling in the city as wood was pushed to shore a teetering wall. Stone grated as it was hoisted. They took the boulders cast in all day and levered them into the open breaches.

He tried not to think of Constance and her wedding day tomorrow, while he listened to Harfleur struggling tonight to last till then.

Even in the rain, the fire-arrows arced over; but with the wet, no conflagrations were started, though the smell of burnt wood still overhung this place, together with the odor of damp earth. And blood.

It was then the messenger found him.

Wat came over, saying one sought him. Wat sounded doubtful but the man was at his shoulder and spoke up, a voice in the rainy dark.

"My lord," he said, "the duke of Clarence commands your presence, instantly."

Wearily Robert said, "Wat, get the men to horse. We ride to Graville."

"Wherefore, my lord?" the messenger asked. "Clarence is not there, but at the chapel toward the south and east."

"There? Tonight? He was in Graville this morning."

"He's back," the messenger said, and lowered his voice. "They quarreled," he explained.

Robert did not like this matter but the brothers did quarrel, it had happened before, and he had had just such orders from Clarence before. He did not want to leave here. He had a feeling that the French would sally again; gates meant nothing, with great stretches of wall through which they could sling their fighting men. And here they had the wrecked barbican for cover, and the memory of a fight that morning. The night was cold and rainy; it hindered fires and aided men creeping out in a surprise attack. Now that he thought on it, tonight there were not so many sounds of building. They were not patching this wall, but leaving a sally port.

He'd not take his men. Send a man? But if Clarence wanted him, the message must be verbal, and if so, he must go himself.

"Do you have a sign?" he inquired of the half-seen messenger.

"He does not beg you, squire," the other said. "You're commanded."

Robert grunted with dislike.

"Wat," he said, "stay behind and watch the wall."

"Let the others watch," Wat said.

"I want you here."

"My lady wants me there," Wat said.

There was no use to argue with him; and if there was to be trouble, or a trap, it would be well to have Wat near. But he did not like it, any of it. He thought of York again, who'd have guessed where he'd be by now. This had the smell of a trap, with enough truth to bait him in. York's touch, there. Simple, but sly. Almost, he disregarded the command. But Clarence had always worked so, casually, with some wry word that Welshmen only worked well with freedom. If the messenger had now tried to run off, Robert would not have gone. But the man waited calmly and offered to show the way. So Robert chose another, in case of ropes stretched across a path to bring down a galloping horse. The man did not protest, but followed. Yet not so close as Wat, who rode with his knees. His hands were occupied with an ax in one and a knife in the other. The rain was bad for his longbow.

Chapter 21

YORK watched the king pacing.

"So they're still eager to fight?" Hal asked.

"Like the fiends of hell," York said. "Even the children on the walls."

Hal stopped his pacing.

"How was it that you rode on the eastern side?" he asked.

York was taken aback, but smoothed it over.

"Clarence is sick," he said, "I thought it well to oversee—"

"Clarence will oversee your death," King Hal said bluntly, "if you poach again on his preserves. He'll set his Welshman on you!"

Then the king paced again, thinking no doubt of an army wrecked with sickness, and Frenchmen still hot to fight.

That headlong attack, York thought. It had fired even York, to see the Welshman, one moment sitting quietly ahorse, the next flying down the hill with his lance before him and his pack of ban-dogs yapping after, and defeated men turning to fight again.

To have that wild flame inside! To nurture careless bravery, tossed into a fight like a trifle. Never to count the cost or care for the shortening of a life. Never to think, *I might die!* God, the boy was his enemy but he did admire him then.

He could be caught in errors of judgment. York was glad of that. He'd seen one at the walls; that headlong leap to battle, when it would have been better to wait; to draw them out, cut them off, and destroy them away from their walls. An error of judgment, or training? Count Llewellyn had always been a chance-taker, greedy for a horse or bit of gold; the boy had been trained in his wild fashion—see a sword and draw on the instant!

And he'd almost corrected the Welshman, told him the error. Almost that gallantry had tricked him into giving good advice. The Welshman had halted beside him, dirty and breathless; and even in the heat of battle, his face had been blank; without emotion. What was behind the mask? A fox, or a fool? Or a man growing apace in hostile times? How he had been schooled to keep his thoughts away, to give no hint to any of what was in his mind! Almost, York had told the Welshman, *you should have held back a little longer.* But the blank face startled him in so young a man. Thank God, he had not spoken! The Welshman would have listened.

Henry paced on. York watched him covertly, thinking again of the vacant place by his side. Who now would have Henry's favor and trust? His *golden* trust. York's fat fingers twitched and his embedded rings all glittered.

The Welshman would have made a good ally. Gallantry was worth something. It fired men and brought them running; those who lacked courage came to borrow it. He would have made a leader. York thought now in the past tense, as if the Welshman was dead. He could afford regret for a fallen enemy. The Welshman was as good as gone right now. York sighed. It was as well he'd taken steps, called his confidential spy the moment his armor was off, and set the matter afoot. Yet this was one plot he could not enjoy. He was getting too old, mayhap. For the rest, let Henry condemn Robert Heartless. He'd but think it the evil fate that always pursued him and caused him to be the instrument of destruction to those he'd rather favor. It would be a fine twist of plot. Robert Heartless hung by Henry's order. How long had it been now? Hours. He'd ridden back to Graville, set his spies off sniffing instantly . . . It must be almost time. He must listen for sounds of excitement outside.

Henry paced, and thought. It could go on for hours. Henry would worry at whatever decision he'd made, drive it here and there, and see if it stood off the dogs of weakness.

York walked to the table and poured wine, and held it out to Henry as he passed. Henry gave him one look and swung around to face him sharply, then stepped backwards two steps and sat down. York's glance faltered and fell. Hal would take nothing from him. Four times convicted of attempted murder. Henry still remembered the poison, sixteen years ago.

York sipped at the cup himself, and felt cold for all his fat and his woolen gown. He knew surely, in that moment, what he had refused to admit before. Henry would never trust him, and nothing could change that now. Vengeance burned in him suddenly, brightly, till his hands trembled and wine slopped over and ran down his chin. He wiped it hastily. *If it is not I,* he vowed, *it will be no one. If you will not have me, I will see you stand alone all the rest of your life.*

A growing tumult outside caught at his agitated attention. He had meant to listen sharper. He finished his wine at a gulp. Henry half turned in his chair and looked out the nearby window. York came up and they both looked out, among the tents and torches that flung wild shadows dancing, like a witches' holiday. Men were grouped together in excitement, standing on a high point where the trees had been cleared away to afford a view of Harfleur when the king wished to overlook the site.

"Smiling, York?" the king said coldly.

"Why, Hal," York said, "I am guessing the city is suing for surrender, and I have prayed for your success."

"I never trust you any time," Henry said, still icy, "and even less when you smile."

Then he turned and hastened out toward the nobles, only waiting at the door, to herd York out before him, contrary to all etiquette. But he'd not have him in back, York thought resentfully, and stopped when he'd reached the group. Now the king edged around them. No man followed him; a man could lose much if he startled the king by approaching from behind. So King Henry stood alone, his shoulders against a tree, looking toward Harfleur with the torches lighting one side of his face and body.

Below, the campfires of the host stretched in small lights all around the walls, ending at the black swamp in the south. Within the walls of Harfleur were several conflagrations waving redly, and the fire arrows arced continually like moving yellow darts. But this was common stuff, seen every night. It was the uncommon sight that made York put his hand before his mouth to hide his smirk.

There was a tall hill on the eastern side, a bald hill, with a convent on the top. They'd heard the bells often enough, banging away for any reason, but it was silent now. It was a burst of flame; like a gigantic beacon, a burning mountain. While York watched, a fierce flame bolted high into the sky; surrounding flames flared. Something had collapsed. The sky was alight!

York looked covertly to Henry. He was standing still, pegged to the spot almost, shocked. His face could not be seen, only a glimpse of an ear and a jaw, but the jaw was working. King Henry was swearing in fury; he was a madman now, in a rage such as only the Lancaster line could engender, like an insanity. It was a raid out of the host, against his command, a slap to his royal face. And Henry being pious, a burning convent was like spitting on his crown.

York sidled closer to the king, being careful to be a little before and seen, to add a dart to enrage him more if he could. Henry turned a black look on him, and jerked his head straight to stare intensely at the calamity across the valley.

"There will be help on the way, Hal," York said. "I had wounded in the sally out of the city, and left my men on the east till all could travel. They'd not let this tragedy occur without going to their aid!"

"I'll have the life of every man concerned in this," Henry said, harshly. "I'll have their lives!"

"My men will catch them," York assured him. "Sire, they know I am obedient to your commands and diligent that they be carried out. They will investigate a skrie."

"If they be not the cause of it!" Henry shouted, and turned on him.

"Sire, no!" York said. This was too close to the truth; he must turn the king aside from these thoughts! Give him something else to attack. "Nay, never. I have only pity for those poor nuns. God help them, with men who've had no women . . ." He crossed himself.

That hit the king. His eyes closed as if he'd shut away the world and its awful sights; and swung away to hide his face, his arm bent a little and fist closed as if he'd strike across the valley.

Someone called, "There's a man galloping," and pointed to a swift-moving torch stretching long, high above the ground, borne by a mounted man hurrying toward Graville. All watched eagerly. Few cared about the convent, but the diversion meant much. Here was something more lively than sickness, more interesting than defeat. If the king would bleed for helpless women, let him. As for them, give them news! The galloper circled below and began the ascent; the sound of hooves came to them, slowing as the horse labored on the climb. Henry turned and hastened to intercept the rider as he swung through a thicket out of sight, burst through tents, and leaped to the ground before them, gasping. He flung the torch to some lackey. His horse ran a few yards and stood, heaving and dripping sweat.

The man looked about, frantic; saw York and ran to him. York gestured to the king, standing with his back to a stone wall of an abbey building.

The rider dropped to his knees, white-faced, terrorized now by royalty.

"Were the raiders captured?" Henry demanded.

"Sire . . . yes!" The boy scrambled on his knees, to face the king more direct, and struggled for breath. There was blood on his face.

"Are the nuns safe?"

The boy spread his hands helplessly.

"One . . . one, sire . . . I think . . . was dead. The others . . ."
He did not know.

"Who did this?"

The boy's head was down, his chin on his chest.

"Must it be dragged out of you?" the king demanded, and took a step toward him.

The boy flung up a hand, as if expecting a kick.

"Robert Heartless," he said, "sire, Robert Heartless and his men!"

York's hands clutched convulsively; but he guarded his face, and luckily, for Henry with his chin out, and fury in his face, searched the crowd around and behind the boy until he found him. York was frightened then, and he had never feared the king.

"Sire," he said, controlling his voice, that it did not tremble, "he was trained by Count Llewellyn."

What else can be expected? he had asked. He had damned the Welshman, but with a kind of plea. York was pleased with his reply, but the king was not. Henry looked vicious, and turned back to the kneeling messenger, badgering him for information the boy did not have.

York slid away the moment the king's eyes were off him. It would be better if he had no more to say; he could be tripped up. He was too guilty and now he felt his guilt. He found a vantage point by the shadowed wall of a building. From there he could look through the nobles, past the messenger's back and see Henry's face. It had gone cold, though he still questioned the boy. Henry was in an icy fury; he was most dangerous so. In these bitter moods, men died. They lost their heads when hot Henry turned to ice. He forgave after a hot rage, as if in shame. But in cold rage, his mind was working and he meant all he said. Condemned so, a man died. York felt himself tremble. He moved again. Now he could see Henry full-length standing against the wall, the frightened messenger, and the nobles crowded together avoiding any appearance of getting behind the king, despite the wall; and beyond all, the flames eating higher into the sky, outlining them, and the trees on either side in black silhouette to frame it. A pretty picture, York thought—red flame and dark sky and torches and the glitter of cloth of gold on the king.

He almost missed one noble detaching himself surreptitiously from the group, to slip away. Almost, but not quite. He saw the man as he vanished behind a tent.

A few moments later Thomas, Duke of Clarence, came, holding to the arm of the man who dared tell him his forerider had been named most foully to the king. Would Clarence dare the royal wrath? Clarence knew Henry dangerous. York watched eagerly, to see the brothers embroiled again. If Clarence spoke out now . . .

Clarence was too wise for this. He was walking away slowly, aided, through the trees. York worried. He had wanted them together. Either Clarence would agree with Henry and damn the Welshman; or Clarence would speak for his man and infuriate the king. Now, did Clarence not see his brother? He must. He was using the crowd of nobles to hide himself from King Henry; he went past and in the other direction, through trees, toward the road the messenger had used to come; the one that circled sideways up the hill, passing through the thicket just below the tents.

Here was a thing to think on. Did Clarence plan a rescue? York followed instantly, his gown catching on outstretched dry fingers of branches that had already shed their leaves. His feet crunched the dry leaves underfoot, but the sound was hidden in the babble of voices now raised all over the camp. York followed down the road, into the thicket rising on either side, black. In the darkness Clarence stopped and sat on a stone, with the other man standing by him.

Clarence valued his forerider if he troubled himself to rise from a sickbed and wait to talk with him before he came bound before the king. It was not a rescue. It was that Clarence meant to speak to him. And what Clarence said, and Robert answered, York would hear. He walked down the road openly the rest of the way, and seemed to peer at the sitting man in faint starlight.

"Can I aid you, sir?" he began, and then seemed to recognize the other. "Why, Tom," he said reproachfully, "out in this night air! The physicians will reproach you. How are they to cure you if—"

"Stop your tongue," Tom said in a hard voice, "or I'll stop it for you."

Anger flashed through York, to be treated like some lackey. It almost strangled him for a moment. He had his touch of the family temper. But not their blind folly with it. He considered, and held his tongue. Tom might yet reach the throne.

Now came the sound of many hooves approaching. Then a glimpse of lights, torches carried on horseback, flitting between trees as the road curved and moved upward to them. A babble of voices. Around the bend. Now horses appeared, three abreast, filling the road, and many behind. York's men.

Clarence stood up, though he swayed a little for it.

Almost, for revenge, York gestured his men to ride past without stopping, but bethought himself again—there was only Henry between Clarence and the crown. So he said nothing, did nothing. The men halted of themselves, seeing the Duke of Clarence stand in the road before them, blocking it.

Robert Heartless was between the two leading men, his arms bound down tight to his sides. The encircling ropes showed dark across the velvet of his cote-hardie, and his ermine-lined sleeves were blurry-white against the horse. His blond hair gleamed in the torchlight from either side. His face was utterly impassive and he was looking over Clarence's head. *At me*, York thought, with a little flare of horror. It was promised revenge without a muscle moving. York's mouth twisted, and he heard gold bells jingle as the Welshman's horse moved a step forward, to be halted by a hand on his bridle as a guard leaned to stop him.

Clarence spoke, and only then did the Welshman drop that bright stare.

"They say there's a nun dead," Clarence announced. "It's nothing to me, one woman more or less, but the king's pious, Robin. He'll hang a man for rape, and God knows what he'll do for a death. A convent, Robin! Blessed Mary, why did you have to raid a convent?"

"You do not know me well, Lord Thomas," the Welshman said. Clarence stared at him hard.

"You have a nimble tongue," Clarence said. "Use it. I'll not lose such a forerider for a trifle. I'll back you in aught you say."

The bright stare had been on York again, but dropped away to Clarence. Suddenly the Welshman smiled.

"Lord Thomas," he said, "I'll not forget your words."

York signaled urgently to his captain, who shouted, and the cavalcade made to ride on. Clarence was forced to back away with his man aiding him, but he only waited till they passed and then followed them, and York came after, last of all.

He did feel alone. He must always stand alone. He had never had an ally without paying, and who could trust these? Of all men, he should know. He'd been paid and bolted agreements too often. Bitterly, he was glad Clarence would lose his man. What York had not, let no other man possess!

Back through the lawns and tents, to the side of the building where the king still stood like a stag turned at bay. York came last of all, and thrust a way through the silent watching crowd. Robert Heartless was off his horse and standing before the king, his arms still bound.

"So here's the honest man," the king was saying bitterly. "Off on a skrie."

"Sire," Robert Heartless said, "I have obeyed your laws."

York cursed silently that he could not see his face.

"There's a girl dead," the king said, "a maid who never harmed any, but said her prayers for all."

"As I have prayed for her, sire," the Welshman said unexpectedly.

Henry fought off his engulfing rage. York could see how bitter the battle was, and delighted as Henry got himself under control.

"Why did you raid the convent?" he demanded.

"I never did," Robert said. "Sire, will you hear me?"

"I have always given justice," the king said, "and you will have it now."

His eyes were deadly. The sentence was in them.

"I was called," Robert said, speaking clearly, "by one who swore he came from the Lord Thomas. I did return to the chapel. My Lord Thomas was not there but at Graville, as I had last seen him. The messenger thought to flee, but I tied him well, that he be still alive to testify to this. The plot stank of some mischief. I was raised in Wales and know such when I see it."

Damn him, York thought, flinging Wales in the king's face. And securing a witness in the midst of war and confusion. He signaled to one of his men and went a little apart, giving hurried whispered instruction. *Send and find, and kill him. I want no witness against me.*

"By this ruse," the Welshman was saying, meanwhile, "my men were left alone on guard, for I could not risk a sally from Harfleur. Twice the French have used the breach there as a sally port. Yet I did not judge the plot aright. I thought the plotters wanted me but it was my men, for while I was gone, someone knew they were alone and suborned them, and set them raiding for women and wine and gold."

"Wild wolves, left leaderless," came Clarence's voice, "by someone's plotting. Hal, does the tune ring to the same notes as before?"

York bit his lip to keep from defending himself, and saw his man go off to find a horse and depart for the eastern side and the damning witness.

"Yet," King Henry was saying, "your men did this."

"Sire, they are simple archers," Robert said, "deceived by one who was not simple, nor an archer."

"I've heard of your tongue," the king said, but he was growing cool, not cold. "You're defending them most nobly. You must. For remember this, as I do—you were also taken prisoner there!"

"Sire," Robert said, "I do not defend myself of stupidity, for of that I am guilty, leaving the men. Yet as soon as I saw how things lay, I rode back. They were gone. I saw the sky afire, and guessed much. I rode toward the fire, hard as my horse could go. I heard screaming and shouting. I saw horses galloping, and thought a maid was carried away and dashed toward her. And then this guard did seize me. I do not know what men I chased, though I might guess they were mine, seeing them now. This is the exact truth. Let it speak for me, as I will not any longer."

He stood a little stiffer. God! thought York, proud innocence, and how it showed!

"Who seized this man by the convent?" the king demanded.

One of the guards stepped forward with an uneasy look over his shoulder to York, for which the latter cursed him heartily but silently.

"I took him, sire," the guard said humbly, then added, "I and four others," when the Welshman turned that bright blank stare at him.

"Was he bloody, or burned?"

"Sire, no," the guard admitted.

"His clothing not even scorched?"

"Sire, not that . . . I see." The guard looked, and away.

"Did he *smell* of fire, then?"

"Sire . . . no," the guard admitted.

"Did you see him at the convent before you entered?"

The guard hesitated. "Galloping in the road, sire," he finally answered, obviously falling in with truth as the safest way, "with a sword out, following the others."

"Chasing them!" Clarence's voice cut in.

Silence. Then the guard nodded. It was possible.

The waving red in the sky had lessened and died; and given way to brilliant pink streaks shot with gold. The night was almost gone; and, York reflected, completely lost . . . unless he could retrieve it, somehow.

The king stood silent. He seemed only weary. His rage had seeped away.

"You are lucky or innocent, Robert Heartless," he said. "I will hang any man I can prove was at the convent, yet I cannot hold any guilty if I have no witness."

"Search him, sire," York said, suddenly moved to daring. "You may find your reason on his person or in his saddlebags."

The king swung toward him.

"You have too much interest in this," he said. "I'll have nothing of your advice. Cut those bonds!"

One of his lackeys stepped forward with a dagger, and cut the Welshman's ropes. But there had been a flicker, a faint . . . something, on the Welshman's face and York had seen it, for he had watched him and not the by-play. It was gone before York could intercept the meaning; yet there had been something . . . or was it imagined, merely a shadow cast by a wavering torch? No, it had been there. York was sure of it. A search, the mention of a search had touched him. He keeps something, York thought, he'd not have known. I'll find it! He felt hope spring up, triumphantly. But he turned away. He'd not alarm his quarry and send it running. Let it lie and think it lay safe.

Clarence said bitingly above the lively murmurs of excited lords, "Sire, give me leave, if any more of York's men cross the Lezarde, to exterminate them."

"I need every man," King Henry said, yet he glanced to York. "Keep your men on the west, York. I'll not warn you again."

He made as if to leave, but his attention was caught and he stopped still, and every eye followed his.

Robert Heartless stood, with the sky behind him, rubbing his arms down their length with the opposite hands to ease the bite of the bonds that had cut into them. His men were in a rough half-circle before him. They stared at their feet, or uneasily at each other, but dared not look at him. They were hangdog and scared. The Welshman had been trained by Llewellyn ap Gryffyd, not known for gentleness, and there was that name of Heartless too.

"I am thinking," Robert said gently, rubbing one wrist steadily, "of a girl dead this night. Who should suffer? The innocent dead or the living guilty? Here's a question."

They shuffled their feet.

"Wat?" the Welshman asked, and a nasty squat brute stepped up beside him. "You know the habits of these men and their possessions better than I."

This Wat stared at his master, not understanding yet but striving to, like a dog interpreting a tone.

"Find me one man," Robert Heartless pronounced, "possessing what is not his."

Wat almost leaped at them. They stood in their uneven half-circular group, stiff with fear, as the sun rose on September 17th, and the one called Wat ran thick fingers and heavy hands over their bodies.

The Duke of York moved closer, to miss nothing, and drew a bright glance from the Welshman. It halted him. He had not thought Robert Heartless saw anything but this search. Then Wat exclaimed, and pulled out a rosary from a leather jacket and held it up, sparkling in young sunlight.

"This is never his!" he exclaimed, like a hound sounding a trail just struck.

"My mother gave it to me," the other said quickly.

"She died the year she bore you. You told me that yourself."

"She left it for me," the man insisted, white-faced.

"Silver?" Wat asked, astonished. "For such as you?"

"Are the links strong?" Robert Heartless asked.

The brute named Wat pulled them in his hands to show it.

"Then no more talk," Robert Heartless said. "You know the penalty for stealing from a church."

Wat stared into his face. A handsome face, that did not relax. The sentence had been passed. Wat's ugly visage turned more ugly as he understood. He pulled the rosary long between his two hands with one swift gesture and swung round on the guilty man with another. The thief moved a step backwards, but never had another chance to run. Wat came with a leap and a kick. The rosary was over the guilty man's neck as his legs were kicked from under.

He hit the ground with a crash. Wat was atop, shoulders hunched. The man choked and gagged and thrashed in upflying leaves, but could not free himself. The leaves soared more wildly, but Wat's weight bore him down and the beads about his throat cut off his breath. He shuddered and ceased fighting. A moment, another moment. All stared, transfixed. Wat straightened, still astride him. Carefully he drew the silver-beaded rosary from beneath the dead neck and rose with it dangling from a hand, swinging and glittering.

"Remember this," Robert Heartless said, never having moved at all. "When I give an order, I will be obeyed."

There was a sudden movement. All heads jerked. The king was striding away, head down. With a start, the other lords trailed after him, not too close to his back. Except for the Duke of York, who stayed.

With black hatred that York concealed from long experience he said carefully, "It is well to deal in justice when the king is by to see. Some men rise quickly so."

Robert Heartless did not even look at him, but stood with his hands by his sides. It infuriated York to be ignored.

"Did you know," York inquired, "that you have a trick of standing with your feet apart when you feel stress?"

And so he told him, though he had not meant to. London, Harfleur, and the Portchester road. *Lollard, I know you, by this sign.*

Robert Heartless seemed to take no meaning, to hear no menace. But York was sure now he was quick to understanding, though his handsome face never betrayed what might be in his mind.

"Hal loves justice," York said. "He enforces all his laws."

Last year he made strict laws against the Lollards. You'll burn at the stake for your belief. For you have a fault—when you step forward, you never step back. Lollard you are, and Lollard you will remain, nor recant for even a king.

York knew the Welshman understood. He sought to pierce the silence and find fear. There was nothing. He could not stand here longer, staring up at a taller man. He cut a sorry figure so, and knew it. Therefore, York cursed under his breath and walked away, and knew he'd been defeated in this encounter. Yet he never accepted final defeat. He was still alive to prove this. So when he thought he could not be seen, he turned again. The Welshman was looking down at his feet, set apart, ready to leap to action. With great care, he moved one foot beside the other. Then he half gestured, and one came running with his horse, carefully skirting the body of the strangled man.

The Welshman mounted, seeming not to see it lying there. His men mounted also, subdued, nor shouting in Welsh as they usually did. They rode away, turning horses around the body, not looking at it. But being Welshmen, though they left him without a glance, they took his horse. It galloped riderless beside one of the other men, held firmly by the reins.

There was left then only the dead man, a few lackeys staring at him with interest, and a little dust, just settling.

Impelled by some instinct, York looked up at the abbey window above. There were lamps burning late in one room, and outlined by them was Henry, King of England, standing by the window and looking down the curving road.

Had he noticed, York wondered nervously, the scratched face of one of the guards? Or the burnt sleeve on another? Ah, well, what if he did so? They had been at the convent, clearly. They had to go, to capture the culprits. If Hal mentioned it, it could be explained.

Then York drooped wearily himself. Hal would not ask. Hal kept his counsel, and told no man what was in him. He'd burst his heart soon, with the burden therein!

God, York thought, if Clarence got the throne! This were an evil night for him!

Chapter 22

ROBERT tried desperately to sleep, to loose himself from his thoughts; but he could not. This was Constance's wedding night, and he'd rather be tortured than think of it. He lay on the pile of dry leaves, with his mantle around him, twisting and turning and listening to the pounding of rain outside and the snoring of his men in heaps on the dirt floor of the building, like puppies in piles. Across the big room, the horses stamped with the cold. *Blessed Mary! Let me sleep and have oblivion!*

There would be assault tomorrow. The king had ordered it. He tried to think of that, but it could not hold his thoughts. Constance came again, and yet again, and how it was with her this moment.

Finally he sat up shivering, and swore impatiently, and got stiffly up and went to the doorless opening and looked out. The rain came down like a river, obliterating everything. No fires burned in Harfleur. The city below was hidden. Suddenly he banged a fist into the stone wall, and felt the pain of it flood through him.

And then a stealthy movement.

"Wat?" he demanded.

"Ay," said the other hoarsely. The voice was at his shoulder.

"I'm going out. Stay with these knaves."

"They'll lie here," Wat said. "They have no liking for rain."

"I'm going to the walls," Robert said.

"I'll saddle two horses," Wat said, and his voice trailed off in darkness. Horses moved protestingly; a saddle hit a back. Wat cursed at the horse. Then the sound of another saddle, and then horses backed out of a picket line. Robert did not order Wat to stay behind. He wanted to be alone in this; and yet Wat's presence gave him comfort too. It was a night for souls in hell and suited him. The rain beat hard on mud and turf and horse and man and city alike. A few pale squares of light in the distance marked the windows of the building where Clarence lay. Robert guided himself by those windows floating, as it seemed, in the deluge, until he was by the place where he always stood to oversee the city. There was nothing but darkness below, as if Harfleur were drowned in a deep pool.

"Did you dream?" Wat asked.

It had been a dream, a short one in a fit of dozing. He dreamed a stag came out of its forest and walked toward him. A stag hunted weary, with its tongue out and sides heaving. Then he had awakened. He had thought instantly of Constance. But a stag?

Wat said, "Torches! Below. Waving. They must be in the shelter of the city gate. They'd be drenched out, else."

Robert saw them, fitful arcs, like a signal. He started down, his horse skidding on the muddy incline. When they were on the flat earth nearer the city, he could see men, disembodied; heads and shoulders in the light of torches burning under the tunneled gate of Harfleur, where it was dry but windy. The flames leaped and crouched, and leaped and crouched, and made long bright lines as they swung in signal from one side to the other.

Robert approached warily, along the side of the lost barbican for cover from arrows and shelter from rain, and yelled across the ditch. The torches halted swinging, grouped together, and moved nearer the rain. They appeared to lean forward to look out. Then, faintly, came an answering hail.

Robert yelled in French, "What will you, Frenchmen?"

Back came a bull-voiced answer: "We would talk to your king."

"I will take you to the Duke of Clarence," Robert offered in a shout.

"Only the king!" bull-voice roared back.

The torches in the tunnel turned to four fat fires, as four men held several at a time; silhouettes lined up in the gate before them.

"Do you mean to surrender?" Robert yelled, again in their tongue.

"We will only talk to the king!" they shouted.

"Will you wait?" he yelled.

"Yes," shouted bull-voice.

Robert jerked his horse around so sharp it went to its knees in the mud, then scrambled up and galloped hard for the hill.

The Lord Thomas would not stay behind. He was out of his bed and dressed in a hurry, shaking with fever, and out into the storm. The torches under Harfleur's eastern gate had dwindled to one small flame at the portal. Clarence stayed back, out of range of any trap that might have been neatly set, and Robert rode toward the barbican. Here he found the burgesses of Harfleur all in a body, swept by rain, on the lee side of the burned tree trunks, holding horses miserable and wet. They had one torch here also, held almost flat to the barbican, preserving its precarious life. The others were strewn flameless on the ground.

In the dim flickering, Robert loomed over them with a few archers behind him.

"Sirs," he said, when they backed to the barbican as if they had been pinned there by shafts, "I am not so fearsome as I look. I have been much in the swamps and am dirty and wet. Now I have command to take you to the king."

With no further ado, they mounted. The rain snatched at the last torch, and it died.

"Follow head to tail, sirs," Robert called. "I'll guide you safely then."

They filed up, stumbling and slipping, to where the Duke of Clarence waited among the rest of the wild Welshmen. Robert did not identify him. The duke did not speak to any but fell in beside Robert's horse, and they slid on through the misery of torrential rain.

Once Clarence said, "You've cat's eyes, Robin," which was a puzzle, for Robert had never seen a cat, though he'd heard them described. He guessed it was meant as a compliment.

"I have been over the trails much," he answered.

A little later the rain left off, and though they were drenched and dripping and uncomfortable beyond recall, at least the night was not so noisy. The Frenchmen talked a little; the hooves squelched in the mud; a horse snorted.

They dismounted in the shadow of the abbey. Some stars had come out cautiously, and with them a cold wind that swayed bare branches and set them clicking. Men were bringing torches out, to burn at doors. Fires were being lit within the silken tents of frozen nobles. Sentries came from corners and challenged the procession. Clarence pushed the hood of his mantle back, and when they saw the king's brother, guards backed in a hurry to let the riders pass. They dismounted in wet grass, under trees that shook huge drops upon them when the wind hit.

Clarence went inside. Robert waited with the others. He rubbed his cold hands. *Constance.*

Next a man came, and they were welcomed into the stone hall, where a fireplace roared. The wet burgesses clung together despite the sight of warmth. They looked hostile, unappeased. *Surrender?* Robert thought. There was little in those angry faces.

A servant came and handed wine around. Clarence went to the fire, shivering. He could scarce hold the cup to his teeth; the edge of it clattered and he put it away. The burgesses did not drink.

They waited for the king. This was deliberate, Robert was sure, for Henry kept owl's hours, and with assault planned, he would have been awake and pacing. Now he was waiting in another room, thinking God knew what; but keeping the burgesses uneasy, breathing swiftly . . . waiting. That meant, then, that he was in a proud mood, and high-handed, with his nerves.

A door opened. With no fuss, King Henry stepped within the room and bowed his head stiffly when all made obeisance.

"Tom," he said, "put on dry clothes."

Clarence said, "I am well enough as I am."

"I said to put on dry clothes, Tom!"

Clarence tightened with anger.

"Sire," he said, with bitter sarcasm, "I hasten to obey!"

Then he walked slowly toward the door.

King Henry made as if to walk after him, then saw the Frenchmen staring and checked himself.

Robin turned to go after Clarence.

Clarence shook his head. "Stay here, Robin," he said.

The diminutive seemed to echo through the huge room; King Henry turned and stared. Then he gestured to a long wooden table.

"Gentlemen of Harfleur," he said. "Sit down. Drink wine. Warm yourselves."

They protested politely. They did not want to sit. They did not want wine. There was this task of theirs, a matter to be stated. Even as they spoke, Robert could see they were against it.

"Then choose your spokesman," Henry said. "We'll waste no more time with courtesy!" He snapped that out. "Do you want peace?"

"Sire," said a tall slim white-haired man, in a dark blue velvet gown that still dripped upon the floor, "that is to be determined."

"I take no meaning from that," King Henry said. "You want peace or you want war. Which?"

"Peace with honor, or war without it, sire," the old man said.

"Surrender now," the king said. "I'll give you no conditions."

"We have no authority to surrender now," the old man said stubbornly. Evidently he expected to die, and evidently he was prepared to. There were only old men in the group of burgesses.

"Then in the name of God," Henry exploded, "why did you drag me from my bed?"

"To talk of surrender, sire," the old man said proudly. "Perhaps."

"Perhaps?" Henry's temper burned, nurtured by worry and no sleep, and probably no eating besides.

"On October 6th perhaps," the old man muttered. "Sire."

"Ah? You wish to wait and see if King Charles comes?"

The old man said, "He is our king."

"He will not come," Henry said bluntly. He was sure now. King Charles could not fly; and he could not save a city to be invaded on the morrow.

"Then give us a week. If it be so, we will surrender the city, if you give us surcease now."

"And if I do not?"

"Then you must fight for every step you take, sire!"

The man was old and thin and wet to the bone; his hair hung in white strings; and yet he was all dignity. His head shook tremulously, with a tremor he could not control for the strain; and his old gnarled hands were clenched in his sleeves. King Henry turned away and slumped into a chair. The Frenchmen stood and dripped and whispered together behind their old, veined hands. At last Clarence came, looked around, and guessed the situation.

"Gentlemen. Burgesses," he said. "Come, let's sit and talk. But wine first." He signaled a servant and sat down himself.

Robert moved to stand behind his chair, and saw with amazement that the Duke of York was opposite. Somehow the fat man had heard and come. The Frenchmen moved to sit, slowly and watchfully, but they drank the wine when it was served.

Looking down, Robert saw Clarence shivering. He gripped the arms of his chair to control it. He sat there, straight and cold so it seemed, but now Robert knew him better. He was coldheaded, but not coldhearted. He had learned to dominate the family temper. He had learned to strangle the fury of flaring emotion. It had taken lightness and youth and gaiety out of him, and made him stern. He was a year younger than King Henry, who was now twenty-eight, yet Clarence might have been forty and full of the patience acquired with years. He was the calmest man at the table.

The battle was in words, between a king who was weary to death with work and sleeplessness and worry, the while he flared with the temper that kept him alive, and the stubborn burgesses of Harfleur, defeated in battle but not in heart. They would die, they signified, before they surrendered, unless they had their week of grace.

Clarence put calm words to all, reminding the Frenchmen of the fate of assaulted cities, and King Henry in more hidden phrases that hinted of the condition of his blasted army.

Robert could admire him, yet his heart was with Henry who took this so ill and peevish. Robert hated defeat too, worse each time he'd been forced to turn and run in Wales. The countess had raised him so. She could be ruthless, and she'd taught him some of that. They said that a man was, in the end, as the woman who raised him. If timid, he'd learned it from her. If ungenerous, that came from childhood. If bold, he'd had it of the woman too.

Who had raised Henry? Never his mother. Wat had known and told Robert of every twist in the pattern about the throne, for London followed everything that concerned the king. Henry was an ill-born child, before his time and like to die and little any cared then, he was so puny, and no prince yet. His sire had not even bothered to be in the castle at his birth, and his mother did not care much for him. Ah well, she'd been married at twelve and delivered of a still-born son the same year, so that her parents took her back and would not let her husband have her again until she was full fifteen, whereupon she slipped a child and then bore Henry quickly thereafter, but he'd lived.

Robert's eye rested on the Lord Thomas before him, the second son, robust in health when he had health, which was not now. His face was flushed. Robert did not like the look of him. His cup was empty and one hand held it. Robert reached over for it. Clarence glanced to see who it was, and let the cup go. Robert filled it from a larger vessel and brought it again. Clarence sipped at it, and went on talking.

Robert was aware of King Henry's attention. Of what significance was a cup of wine? Blessed Saints, did the king think of poison? York was watching too with a piercing stare.

The talk went on, the same argument. The burgesses would surrender if given a week of grace. Henry would not accept surrender except immediately. Clarence sipped his wine as his voice grew hoarser and he coughed desperately, still seeking to bring agreement.

And after Clarence, Robert thought, came the third brother, John of Bedford, in less than a year—nine months, some said. Last of the brothers was Lord Humphrey. Two girls followed, one already dead in childbed, and the other in some distant country. The mother died of the last girl at twenty-four, worn with births and miscarriages. Henry had been eight then and grieved for her, though he'd hardly known her. Who had raised him? Not his mother. A nurse then. A nurse who'd given him his way, as some did with their nurselings. A delicate child expected to die before he grew, and a handsome one who could wheedle. She'd not tried to curb his temper but had given him all his way, for that he was sickly and like to die in childhood.

Robert thought ruefully of the beatings he'd got. The countess had sworn it was all for his good, but did not go lighter for that. It was the Welsh half of him, she said, that was hot and needed chaining. A Welshman was like to a madman for recklessness when he was roused. Therefore, she said, the Welsh blood must be tamed before it led him to destruction. It was the Welsh half she was teaching, she told him solemnly. She did not beat the Saxon.

So Henry's nurse had raised an obscure boy who suddenly was heir to a throne when his father seized it. Had she regretted then that she had not beaten him more and taught him to hold that temper?

It was like to lose him Harfleur now.

"My lord brother," Clarence cut in, "what matter if it be this week or the next, so you have the city?"

"Matter enough," King Henry said.

York pushed over a cup of wine. Henry's hand flashed like his eyes, and swept the cup off the table to splash wine all over the floor.

"Do not give me wine or any other thing," Henry said, with much danger in his tone.

York paled.

Clarence said, "You'd be better for a little wine, Hal. Robin, will you play servant here?"

Robert walked around and took a fresh cup from a pile upon a chest, and looked into it by the light from the fire to see there were no strange powders within. He poured some wine. He brought it over, stood by the king, drank of it himself, and set the tasted cup down and moved back to his duke.

Clarence said, "Good. For God's sake, drink it, Hal," and turned back to arguing with the burgesses.

They all knew the city was still too strong for taking without destroying Henry's army too. And there was the Frenchman Bouciquaut sitting across the river with four thousand men. He might sit till Doomsday. Or he might attack from the rear when Henry assaulted the city. Neither side knew, but both were stubborn. However, the burgesses were merchants too. A sacking was preferable to utter destruction. Give them something to save and they would. But they'd burn their cloth before they gave it away and they'd destroy their city before they gave it over, if they had no assurance a better bargain could be made. They still hoped for help from King Charles. In a week, they insisted, if their king did not come he would never come, and they would bow to Henry. They were adamant and there was nothing to be gained from refusing them. King Henry's hand crept over to the cup of wine. He took it in both hands and stared within. Finally he put it to his mouth and seemed to taste and looked again. Then he drank it all and closed his eyes, as if he waited for a thunderbolt and did not care if it came.

Clarence said, "Hal? How do you say?"

The king set down the cup, his hand lying limp by it. He was as drained. If he lost this army, there was no other at home, and England lay open to attack.

"Have your week," he said. "I give you your week. But the surrender, when after many days it comes, will be without condition."

The burgesses looked at one another, then rose and went aside to whisper. Henry brooded, staring at the table top, immovable. York squirmed and watched the burgesses. Clarence shivered in his chair. Robert looked down on him. The wetting would finish Lord Thomas. It was a bad night's work, no matter how it ended. A bad night for them all. He thought of Constance again, suddenly, and pain flooded him like the first pangs of a wound.

The burgesses trooped back. The oldest man stepped forward.

"Sire," he said unhappily, "we agree."

Robert guided them back again. The wind was sharply cold and the stars were colder. They rode through the trees and saw the valley of the Lezarde before them, the river, the dark town with a fire raging in her heart, and fire arrows flashing over. A few moments after they went down the hill a galloper thundered up behind them and they drew aside quickly to let him pass. They knew his message. Stop the arrows, a truce had been made. The city would be surrendered soon, and thrown on Henry's mercy.

Constance, he thought. But he rode blank-faced, even in the darkness. The countess had taught him to keep his wounds and hurts to himself.

The week passed. The English lay around the city, and King Charles did not come. The four thousand French began to move at last, but away from the smell of defeat, circling to join their lord in Rouen. Harfleur had struggled, gallantly and miserably, prolonging her death agonies until it had seemed she would drag the enemy down into her grave. Harfleur had struggled, but she was stricken, starving and diseased, beleaguered and unaided. Her liege lord never came. Therefore on Sunday, September 22, 1415, she surrendered without condition, and King Henry won his toss of dice with fate.

Chapter 23

AT THE hour appointed, King Henry ascended to the top of the western hill overlooking Harfleur. He was dressed in regal robes, wore a crown, and went right royally into an open-faced silk pavilion of blue patterns on white ground which had been erected there, turned in his gleaming cloth of gold and sat upon a throne raised on a dais, all covered in scarlet cloth with a cloth-of-gold canopy above it. All the peers and persons of rank, in gorgeous array, assembled around him. Sir Gilbert Umfraville stood beside him, with the royal battle helmet, surmounted by a jeweled crown, borne on a halberd staff aloft, proclaiming the majesty of England now enthroned.

The king sat stiffly, all hint of indecision, anger or loneliness wiped from his face. There were men behind his throne, a thing that upset him usually, but now he did not seem to notice. He looked stern and he looked royal.

Even the Duke of York was impressed as he edged imperceptibly through the throng of peers, closer to the throne, though it was reluctant admiration. York was no man for ceremony, being cynical and despising show except for its value in intimidation. Although he liked plenty of rings on his fingers, and enjoyed the flash of a gem when he wrote.

There would be much to write about today. From the pavilion down the slope to the western gate, a passage was formed by English soldiery on either side of an open lane. They moved and muttered, a hum came from them, a clinking and a clanking. Banners waved over them, armor glittered. It was sunny now, and the day turned hot, miserable for men in armor. York stole a glance to the king, smothered in robes. He was sweating.

York wiped his own forehead. He was glad to be in the shade of the pavilion after the procession. And now, he thought wearily, he must bear up his own bulk on his small feet until Henry at last had done with ceremony. Henry did all with ceremony when he did not know those he would be with. He kept them at arm's length so, awed them, and honored the customs of a day that was passing swiftly. Henry was twice born out of his time, York thought, once from his mother's womb and once into the wrong century. Henry was a knightly man, full of ideas of honor and courtly behavior. Not even a parliament full of thieving merchants could convince him this time was over.

Lord Thomas was less romantic. He faced an era he might or might not like. If Henry died, and Lord Thomas the king . . . *Nay, think not on that!* York told himself hastily. The stout Lord Thomas was not so stout this day, York thought with satisfaction. He was standing to one side of the throne, and slightly toward it, white-faced, black-smudged under the eyes, very ill and miserable, hardly able to stand on his feet for this surrendering of a city. He was in black and gold, which made him look the sicker.

His forerider was behind him, at his elbow. Robert the Welshman, in blue and violet silk, of a height with Clarence; but blue-eyed and blond, as the other was black-eyed and brown-haired. Clarence swayed a little, and the Welshman had his elbow and steadied him. Jealousy swept over York suddenly, and flushed his face. The ice-cold Lord Thomas with his cutting tongue had loyalty, and why? He gave nothing. York sent gifts as rewards for any services, while Thomas pinched pennies, for he had a wife who would not see money flung about. York spoke with guile and kindness; Thomas could flay a man with words. Yet he had loyalty and York had none.

It galled York hard, like a spurred nag. He was forty-two; the flush of youth was gone and its carelessness. Now he wanted friends, but had none. He burned with resentment, hatred of the Welshman and hatred of Clarence too. With satisfaction, he realized he was not the only one to notice a man without even the gold spurs of a knight among nobility. Henry glanced over, stealthily. Clarence's face was turned half-away from the throne, whispering over his shoulder to Robert Heartless. The Welshman was nodding, but his blue eyes were on the crowd, flickering over it restlessly even while his attention was for the whisper.

Outside a roar drew all attention. York looked down the open aisle formed by the bodies of the soldiers. There was a stirring, far down, heard rather than seen over a bulge of ground. He could see the top of gates drawn back. The roar increased, slowly, slowly. They were coming up the hill. They came in sight at last. There were forty of them at least, York thought, and closed his eyes in anguish. The surrender would be endless, and his feet hurt him already. They were escorted by . . . York gripped his teeth together . . . archers first, one with a lance, and on that a narrow green pennon. The Welshman's men. That was Clarence's doing. They were rough-clad, rough-looking, scratching and spitting as they marched. One had a skin of wine by the neck and swung it. They were like a pack of boarhounds lounging in a great hall waiting for their master to call them for a bloody hunt. They paid no attention to the Frenchmen in their midst, and there seemed to be more of them than York remembered. The Welshman must have been busily gathering the remnants of dead men's retinues. One here, two there, gathering and gathering a harvest of dirty followers. The personal popularity of Robert Heartless was spreading. *That* must be pointed out to the king, York thought. Here was a man thick with Clarence, who had followers who would follow to the death. Dirty and scrawny and itchy as flea-ridden hounds, but all with the glistening, shimmering beauty of peacock feathers massed in a quiver showing over every man's shoulder. Fearful marksmen, deadly . . . the Welshman's hounds. A hungry pack, but they obeyed him. They had seen one of their number strangled before their eyes for disobedience, as a hound might be casually beaten. They obeyed him still. A little fear, a little indulgence, a joke or two, a hero to worship, and the thick Welsh speech. What does it take to hold a man to loyalty?

York heaved a sigh. They might have chosen better-appearing men to escort the Frenchmen, but none, he admitted to himself, to keep the Frenchmen safer from a sudden spurt of some soldiers out of the English ranks for late revenge of the death of a comrade.

The Frenchmen were before the pavilion now in a group, isolated, sweating in the hot September sun. That one, thought York, would be Sir Lionel de Braquemont, the governor of Harfleur, come to give up the keys to the city; and that, in the hair shirt like a penitent, would be the noble Lord de Gaucourt, who had so dangerously reinforced the city just before it was invested, galloping madly into a siege and defeat. He was gaunt, his feet and ankles bare and dusty. And was he in a hair shirt to show his penitence for fighting King Henry? Or was it penitence for letting them surrender the city over his wishes? A pretty question.

Behind these two were a mass of other men. York dismissed them from his mind, except as he must stand on his swelling feet until they individually sued for mercy. They stood at the entrance of the tent, waiting for permission to come further. The guards waited too, looking at Henry. As for the Welshman's ban-dogs, they spat and passed the wineskin around, but stayed between the Frenchmen's backs and the host of English soldiery that had closed the lane and cut off retreat. The Frenchmen were tightly wedged. Every eye was on them except York's, who looked to Henry, and Henry who looked to his brother Clarence, sagging. The Welshman had him tight by both arms, holding him up.

King Henry said, "Tom," and gestured to his dais.

Clarence did not even look up. He was white and sweating, and he shivered besides. It was the Welshman who acted on the motion from the king. He heaved Clarence forward the little distance through the lords. All of them helped, suddenly, and set him on the dais. Clarence put his face in his hands, and the Welshman knelt on one knee beside him with genuine concern on his usually blank face. He asked some question in a whisper. Clarence shook his head. *No. No.* All under King Henry's eyes while a city waited to surrender.

He was handsome, York thought with envy. There he knelt with all in his favor, tall and blond, dressed in azure and violet silk, the cote-hardie in diamonds with some bit of gold embroidery in the center of each violet patch, and lustrous dark mink lining his sleeves and trimming the rest. He looked less like a plain Lollard than any York could imagine. Silken garments, a king's sword, a great seal on his thumb and incongruously, a cheap silver collar with a dagger slung from it behind his back. He must know that all eyes were on him and the stricken duke, but he looked only to Clarence.

The French stood outside throughout this play by the throne, their faces wan and nervous. The burgesses were frightened and showed it. The soldiers hid it, except for a twitch here and a lip bitten there. This king could destroy them, they were thinking. They had surrendered without condition, and this was on their minds as Henry kept them waiting to sue for mercy.

He let them wait longer. He leaned over from his throne, and spoke to Clarence. Clarence replied impatiently and gestured. He wanted nothing, except that this be done and over. Henry seemed taken aback, to be cut off so. His dark eyes flashed. He glared at some noble, and the noble signaled, and the Frenchmen were finally allowed to approach. They walked up to the throne, unarmed. Yet even then, advancing to surrender, some eyes went sliding down to Clarence and the man who knelt by him. The dagger behind the Welshman's neck made York's fingers itch. He would like to seize it. . . .

Sir Lionel de Braquemont knelt before the king and offered the keys of the city. Henry scowled, a bad sign, and snapped his fingers at his Earl Marshal, a wordless order to receive them. He'd not touch their keys. The Frenchman turned white, but handed over the keys to the Earl Marshal and sued for mercy in the name of Harfleur.

There was a pause. Henry glanced down at his brother, leaning against the very throne.

Then, in a cold, hard voice, Henry spoke formally. He promised, notwithstanding their refusal to surrender when he wished, that he would not withhold his mercy from the citizens. (He'd been balked and forced to wait by merchants, York thought. *He* would give little for Henry's mercy now.)

Sir Lionel apparently thought the same, but got to his feet and backed down a lane that opened behind him, through the Frenchmen, toward the back, where he stood.

The military commander, the Lord de Gaucourt, dressed in his hair shirt of penitence, advanced hesitantly. He did not want this; he did not. He would not bow to a foreign prince. It was in his face. His eyes swept over the crowd behind the king, to Clarence, and stopped. Suddenly there was the ghost of a wan smile on his face. Then he stiffened and came with a firm step, as though heartened by some sympathy. He knelt with a harsh, unconquered movement.

Someone had smiled at him, York guessed. Not the king. Not Clarence, whose head was in his hands. It must have been the Welshman, used to the side of the defeated, chased desperately in Wales. Henry's whole face set, though York could see only his profile. He'd noticed the byplay.

De Gaucourt was on his knees before Henry, speaking very low. The nobles were stirring nervously, whispering around the throne that Clarence's man had dared so much. They had seen the thing, or guessed it too. De Gaucourt's voice was lost, the whispers grew so loud.

Something could be made of this, York thought. Clarence was next in line for the throne and known to have favored the beheading of the Earl of March, thus disposing of that claim, and he'd been angry when the earl escaped. Here was a duke bidding for power. Or it could be made to seem so. He already controlled the navy. Now, if he could control the Welsh archers through Robert Heartless . . .

York thrilled again to intrigue. But nay, he must side with the angels. He must stand by the king. Yet, what a chance for Clarence! If the Lord Thomas had favored him at all, York would have urged rebellion on him. A quick murder of mercurial Henry. . . . His mind dwelt on it with pleasure. If only Lord Thomas had liked him!

The ceremony dragged on endlessly. Clarence was very ill, but struggling to last throughout. The king was alarmed, that was certain. He kept turning to look down. The Frenchmen came and knelt, one after another, pleading without finish. Why it could not be all at once and be done, York did not see. But Henry had wanted it all formal and regal, and now he had no joy of it, that was sure. He hated crowds, and had tortured himself when he ordered this. He had slid down in his throne and lost his majesty. He was moody and worried and upset, and showed it. And one after another, the men from Harfleur knelt and pleaded for their city at length.

It would be sacked, of course. Not tonight. The formal entry into the city first, tomorrow, but tomorrow night, after the king had seen the rubble, *then* it would be thrown to the army, and outside the sounds of the soldiery was the growling of dogs, waiting for their bone.

Meanwhile, the burgesses pleaded for their wealth. They offered ransom for themselves, their wives, and children. Henry nodded, time after time. The soldiery knew some were getting away, but there would be plenty of loot left for them. A night and a day in the city, unchecked. They growled.

And yet another Frenchman came forward and knelt, to save himself and some of his money and his family.

York sweated and shifted on his feet and wished he were in bed.

And then, quite suddenly, Clarence collapsed. He almost pitched to the ground from the dais, except the Welshman had him firmly.

The king's head jerked around. The Welshman looked up and said something, lost in the excited babble of the lords. The king nodded. The Welshman stood up, then bent and heaved Clarence up over one shoulder and made his way out, carrying him. Almost, Henry followed. Then recollected, and sat down again, watching after until the Welshman was gone.

After that, King Henry struggled through impatiently, agreeing to each plea, shutting off burgesses who became long-winded with gratitude.

When it was over at last, he stood up and made a short, sharp speech inviting the Frenchmen to a feast, formally, and the moment he'd done, he flung off his mantle, dropped his crown atop it, slipped out between hastily recoiling nobles, and called for his horse. It was trotted up on the instant. He was in the saddle before it stopped, and galloped for Graville as if outriding death.

York bellowed for his horse, and followed.

The Welshman's men were hanging around outside the building used as a hospital, some very drunk and noisy. A dangerous crew, they'd attack anything if given leave. (It must be pointed out to Henry when the time was right.)

York got inside without trouble, but in the hall he was stopped.

"I'm York," he said indignantly.

The Welsh bowman with peacock glittering at one shoulder stared at him with insolence and made a sign. *He did not speak English,* or so he wished it to appear.

York sought to push him aside. The Welshman's eyes opened wide with battle, and his hand slapped to an ax at his hip. York would not back, but he could not proceed. The devil would chop his head open, obviously. So he stayed where he was.

The door opened, and he looked through. Clarence was on a pallet, with a monk kneeling by him, giving him something to drink. The Welshman stood to one side, watching, with a brute-faced archer behind him, both armed in the presence of the king, Holy Saints. Henry was standing at the foot of the pallet, anxious. The door closed after the monk who had gone in. And York waited like a lackey outside.

At length Henry came out, saw York, and hesitated.

"I'll ride into the city, sire," York offered. "If you would stay by Clarence."

"Lord Thomas is riding into the city," the king said.

"So sick?" York asked, incredulous.

"I cannot, and he says he will. Clarence swears he'll be well by tomorrow."

Cannot, York thought. There's a bad conscience; Henry was hit by the victory so dearly bought. He would not see the damage he had done. Here's a conqueror who cannot look upon his work. A tender conscience was a handicap to any man.

They walked together a little way.

"And Robert Heartless?" York asked.

The king looked to him sharply. "With Clarence, of course," he said.

"That will be very well," York said, as if approving. "He can protect a royal duke from random shots. His men are diligent to his command. They'd attack the King of France if he but gestured them to it."

The king said nothing, and shortly after turned away to other of his men, but York knew he had taken the meaning. Any who'd leap at the King of France would go for England as well.

Well, thought York, contented, let *that* simmer in his mind.

Chapter 24

THEY ENTERED the city by the western gate. The walls were down on either side, and it were easier to pass there; but this was a procession of victory, so the gates were opened and they went through, out of the sun to a tunnel, hooves echoing, and out again into the sun and Harfleur.

There was scarcely a house left whole by the outer perimeter just within the walls. The horses lurched and slipped over wreckage. The street was so choked with rubble it was almost impossible to ride two abreast, so foot archers were sent ahead to watch for deadfalls and the like prepared by citizens yet unconquered, for one of the towers was fighting still, refusing to accept defeat. The archers scrambled like goats, but gave most of their attention to marking the prey they would pursue when the town was given over for sacking. They whistled and shouted at likely women, and any female was likely to them.

The French stood back in shadows and ruins, accepting the inevitable fate of captured cities. They would be given up to the soldiers for a night and a day. Their faces showed exhaustion rather than hatred, apathy rather than resistance. The children ventured nearest: dirty-faced, runny-nosed, pitifully thin and coughing, with skimpy bandages over old wounds. The splinters from the catapulted stones had found their targets in these little ones. Robert tightened with distaste at this warring against children. Yet this would be his life, till a shaft from an arrow or a lance found him on some battlefield. The wounded children stared at him. He felt their eyes. Once he looked back and smiled, in pity. They shrank away, all in a row, as if pulled from behind. A girl of sixteen or so, with one hand gone and a bloody rag where it had been, stood her ground and cursed him. He did not smile again.

He bethought himself, guiltily, of the Lollard priests teaching the evil of war; that this was mischief concocted by kings, and not from God, and woe to the man who followed after warfare. He abhorred all this around him, and yet he knew he would fight again. He was the child of his age, and his age was war. But, he thought, if this town was London and that girl had been Constance, God pity her.

The circuit of the town was made, or as much as they could travel in through the streets. Then the Lord Thomas went out again, through the eastern gate in its broken walls, protecting nothing, only a symbol now of an entering victorious army. But Robert rode to the duke and begged that he might stay a little, and the duke said, *Ay, but not too long.*

So Robert waited in an alley floored by broken bricks and let the procession pass him, and when they had gone, he turned, with his men, and made his way to the church of St. Martin.

The stone steeple stood yet, a miracle to sturdiness and the will of God, but part of the building was damaged. Robert dismounted and gave over the reins to Wat, and signified all were to remain behind. Wat countenanced this, because the doors were gone and all could see within. It was bright there, for a stone had crashed through the roof, and a shaft of sunlight glared down upon the boulder and illuminated the inner parts.

Robert walked in, around the great boulder, skirting other stones from the roof itself, and parts of broken saints glittering with gold. He picked his way to an altar, mindful of the Lollard teaching. He must not kneel to any image.

Yet he would pray for these people he had seen huddled in doorways and lurking behind wreckage. He would pray that they might not be tossed to the army as a fox is tossed to hounds.

Constance was on his mind now, and had been through all the march. He knelt on the stone floor in the wrecked church, his sword scabbard ringing. He professed Lollardy, believing much but not all. He could not cleave to every letter of any man's teachings, but believed he would get from the Scriptures all he needed of God, for the Bible had saved his life that he might read it and profit. He would bargain with heaven, but how could he ask so great a boon as a city's life and honor when he had nothing to offer in return? The Lollard teaching was that gold and silver was sinful in a church, but he must give something. He had nothing, neither land nor money, yet he must promise something, or why should heaven hear him, else?

He had done the merchant's business in this war, and thought now in terms of give and take. If I ask this, I will give that. . . .

He owned nothing but himself. He could offer prayers, but already heaven had them. If he could rebuild this church . . . impossible! A man must offer what he has, not vague possibilities in the future dependent on solid benefits received first.

So he prayed, his lips moving without sound, for surcease for the city and for the children. And if this come about . . .

He hesitated, drew a deep breath, and promised what he had. He promised himself, and that he would never marry any maid. Let him die before this vow was broken. He crossed himself, hurriedly. Then he rose to leave, and turning almost fell over a man kneeling behind him. He had heard someone come in, but was deep in desperation and knew Wat would not let an enemy pass. He'd paid no attention, and as little now.

"Your pardon, sir," he said perfunctorily. And then, "Sire! I had not known you."

Whereupon he dropped to one knee among the fragments of broken saints and bits of gilded ceiling.

King Henry rose, so near the shaft of sunlight his gold houppelande blazed with light from shoulder to ankle, like a smashed saint made suddenly whole again.

"Get up," the king said. "Get up."

He appeared to forget Robert, though the folly bells jingled as he moved. This was not the regal king of the surrender, nor the angry one of midnight dealings; but a pensive king, who seemed to dream. He turned his head only, measuring the destruction emblazoned here by the sun.

"Out of all the host," he said unexpectedly, "only two came to give thanks for this victory. What did you pray?"

"Mercy, sire," Robert said. "Mercy for the city."

The king said, "Then your prayer is quickly answered, Robert Heartless. Harfleur will not be sacked. I have commanded this."

But captured cities had always been given to the armies that took them. No commander dared risk the temper of troops balked of their historic prize. Nay, here was a man who dared! Robert glimpsed the stormy will and black anger they credited to this man and more. He saw a fierce devotion to justice. And even admiration for the desperate battle Harfleur had made. It wiped out the balked petulance shown in Graville. Henry would and could enforce his decree. Harfleur was spared.

And Robert's vow accepted.

"My brother Clarence is returning to England," the king said. "He is too sick to stay. You may return with him as he wishes, or if you will, remain with me. But think on it. Think. A winter campaign in a hostile land with the remnant of an army. My council advises against it, but I will go forward. I want none but volunteers who have reasoned to the end."

And the end could be death.

"I'll follow you, sire," Robert said.

"I thought you were Clarence's man."

"I signed the Indenture to follow you," Robert said.

"A legal point," the king said.

"A loyalty," Robert said.

The king stared at him, hard. Then seemed to lose interest and looked around dreamily at the broken images, the hole in the roof where the sun poured through, the boulders that had done the damage. Robert felt very calm. There was not the heart-pounding emotion of signing the Indenture, nor the fierce joy of sailing for France.

The king said, "There remain to me but six thousand men to fight all France." He touched the white scar by his eye, and did not seem to know he did it. "I must fight. I cannot sail home, broken. My victory is no victory, until I march through France. With my six thousand men . . ." he smiled, "and one."

And in that was the Lancaster charm.

God, Robert thought, he would follow this man anywhere, and knew not why. Not for his moods or angers, or for the commanding presence he could assume. For compassion, perhaps, and admiration and a boy's worship that had lived on in a man, and more . . . more. He knew not!

The king jerked around suddenly with the decisive way that startled men so often and strode off. The gold houppelande swung. Robert saw with a shock that the king was barefoot!

It held him poised, that a king would come in penance. Then the moment broke and Robert rushed after him. The king clambered over rocks in the choked street with his dirty, scraped bare feet. Robert followed, leading his horse, walking humbly behind the king. His men trailed behind, speechless, awed, without understanding, but leading their horses, since the king went afoot.

The silent people of Harfleur watched from their ruins, all the way to the gate, where the anxious royal retinue was waiting in terror lest anything befall the king; but never daring to disobey his command to stay. They surrounded him, and brought water to wash his feet, and put on his shoes.

The king spoke once. He turned to Robert.

"Go find my cousin of York," he said. "He begged you for his service if you stayed. Now you are his man."

It was not to be understood. Was loyalty rewarded so? Robert had not expected material things, but to be flung to the Duke of York, that traitor, hated by all? What was in the king's mind when he did this? It had not been an idle thing. Robert remembered the look in Henry's face. There had been a meaning and a purpose; but what it was, was hidden.

Robert sat alone on the slope of the hill on the western side of

Harfleur, below Graville, thinking and watching late wildflowers blow in the wind. He scouted yet, for York now, and the threads that bound him to the merchant's daughter were loosened more. Walter and John had been sent home sick. Of the three, only Wat remained. Also there was his vow. And for the end of it, he knew he would not return from this campaign. He had scouted far, and seen the footprints in the muddy roads, the marks of marching men, the evidence of gathering hordes. The French host was answering their king at last.

He thought of one hundred and fifty miles of hostile forest to the final goal of Calais, the English port embedded in the body of France. That was King Henry's plan: to march through France to Calais, and sail home from there head high, having shown to all that England feared no foreign king. Robert doubted they would ever reach it.

And so he had written a letter. He said only he would try to stop at Dieppe if this were possible. Perchance, he thought longingly, she would reply. Surely her husband would not grudge a letter in her hand? He wrote at the last that King Henry had challenged the Dauphin to single combat to settle the issues of the war, and given him eight days to answer. After that, they'd march.

Having done with this, he took out the silver comb Constance had coveted and wrapped it within, and sealed all with the seal of the sleeping lion. Then he had sent it by John, returning to the merchant's house on Thames Street. If the wind had been fair, Constance might have it now. Let her construe it as she would.

He knew too late he loved her. For no less would he have parted with the comb. Now he would go on to death, if not on the battlefield then by the plotting of York. It did not matter to him. He had ridden so much, slept so little and eaten so seldom that all things were alike. When a man was tired enough, it was like old age. It dulled the edge of reason and desire, and nothing cut.

He thought of the countess who had raised him. He had hoped he might see her once again, but it would not be so. They were marching to the north, along the channel, not near her brother's castle at all. It was probably as well. She'd had high hopes of him. *When they speak of you,* she'd said when they parted company, *let them tell me heroes are still made.* He'd fallen short. Oh, God, he had fallen short.

He sat all the afternoon watching the wildflowers blow, with nothing to guard and nothing to watch. It was the last day before they left. The Dauphin had not replied to King Henry's challenge, and the war would be pursued.

When he slept that night, the final one at Graville, he dreamed of a golden lion sleeping in a forest. It seemed someone essayed to wake him, but the beast would not, and slept on while danger moved nearer. The dream was in surrounding darkness, with the form of the dormant lion gleaming with an unearthly golden aura. All around were sibilant whisperings, yet the lion would not wake. Robert knew he dreamed, and that it was his mother sending warning. And yet the lion slept. It seemed a moment after that Wat was squatting by him, shaking him by a shoulder. The morning was cold, but he woke in a sweat.

Wat said, secretively, "You cried out."

"I was dreaming," Robert said, and sat up.

Wat waited. He respected the wonders Welsh blood saw. Then it was on his face, as he understood. The prophecy was of evil, coming soon. He rubbed his hand across his mouth. Then he shrugged and went out of the building in which they had slept, to see to the horses. He would follow still, like Murdach, having found a master.

Robert glanced out the door, left open. The sky was gray, the stars were gone. There was the heavy wetness of more rain in the air. He stood up, shivering, and went outside to hold his hands over the crackling warmth of the campfire. His men were already roused, and talked low. Robert began to struggle with his points and four men started up to help him, but Wat was beside him first.

All watched furtively from fires nearby, from doors, from tents, from under trees, from the moment he stepped into sight. The entire camp knew what his orders were. The Duke of York commanded the van and with it, Robert Fairfield. And the command was this. That Robert ride ahead, scouting before the army stepping off into the unknown.

Men watched him still as he ate his meager breakfast, mounted his horse, and rode forward. They watched him as men do when they think to say, a little later, "Why, I saw him ride by this morning. Dead, you say? Before God, it does not seem that this could be. I saw him ride by this dawn. He passed so near, I could have touched him."

Robert rode with one hand guiding his horse among the trees and tents, the other resting idly on his thigh. They could take little with them, and that was food. All else must be abandoned. So he had chosen the warmest garment Constance had packed from her brother's things. He rode dressed in scarlet velvet and wool from head to toe, with ermine lining his sleeves and mantle.

Yet he felt incomplete. He missed the insignificant, delicate, constant tinkle of the folly bells he had always worn since he won them in a tournament at Chester. In deep forest they would be folly bells indeed, betraying him to enemies. Therefore, he had put them in a cloth and packed them behind the saddle with his Bible, to silence their senseless joy. It seemed to him he had put away all youth and laughter. His face was stern, therefore; forbidding.

He got another name from a man who spoke it carelessly, seeing him pass that morning. It was no fond Blue-Eyed Rob, nor yet an angry Robert Heartless. But it stuck and spread, though he never heard it. They called him Robert the Lion.

Chapter 25

ON SUNDAY, October 6, 1415, they departed from Harfleur early in the morning, under driving rain. There was not a man of all the army but knew it was reckless adventure, and the decision of the king against the advice of his council. For this desperate venture, King Henry had six thousand men. They had been campaigned hard, this ragged host. It showed in harness out of joint, in torn jackets, hollow eyes and hungry faces. It was a dwindling wreck of an army insufficiently supplied, but it had one thing. The sick and faint-hearted were gone. There were left only those who had chosen to stay, a hard core of veterans, a pack of lean and starving wolves, deadly in battle, joined in purpose, and willing to die for their king.

They began to die that morning in the rain, as they passed within half a mile of Montivilliers. Robert sent back report of men running on the castle walls and banners waved. When his galloper returned in the afternoon, it was with news of a French sally on the van, and of bloodletting in the muddy fields before the enemy dashed headlong back to their walls when King Henry came up with the main body.

"If each castle we pass draw its prick of blood," Wat remarked, wiping rain from his face, "we'll be bloodless when we reach Calais." He reconsidered his remark as they rode on, and corrected it. "*If* we reach Calais."

They had eight days, and eight days' supplies, but they were not gone one when Robert knew they could not make it. The roads were bad, when there were roads; and they marched through country made for ambush. Thick forests surrounded them, every river was in flood, every bridge was set under bowshot of a castle, and every castle was hostile. They were delayed by flood and mud and hunger and constant stinging attack by small parties that hit and ran away. Men died. They were left where they lay. Men were captured. They were abandoned. There was no time to bury dead men or parley for captives. Henry's battle was with time and against starvation. Hungry men marched slowly, but the fields were stripped and the harvests out of reach in castles. Red rags fluttering from bushes to show defiance were the only crop left for the English to pick. They pushed on doggedly.

On Friday, October 11th, with six days gone of their small allotment of time, they came before Arques. *Six miles*, Robert thought, *from Dieppe*. The castle rose high upon a hill, dominating the land around, and the bridge over the river was blocked with timber and under fire of the fortress. There was no time to fight through. Therefore, King Henry's herald rode up to the walls and shouted that if passage was not granted instantly, the open town at the foot of the castle would be put to the torch, the woods destroyed, and the new springing winter wheat laid waste. The captain of Arques knew the value of delaying the English, yet if the town was destroyed and the peasants driven off, the castle itself would starve. It was every man for himself, and no help to be expected from King Charles, who had sat in Rouen and let Harfleur die. Grudgingly the captain of the castle let them pass.

After that, the army turned to march along near the sea; but Robert was sent into Dieppe to see if ships bearing food were near. It was his first stroke of luck, and an omen. He was sure there would be a letter for him, and so he hurried on. The land went upward toward the cliffs that faced the channel, but he stayed along the river on the lower ground. The nearer he came, the faster his heart beat. A letter, a letter! It was madness to hope for it, but a man must hope to live. They rode into the straggle of houses that declared the town.

The tower of St. Jacques rose over all, as they halted in a street and inquired of a citizen where the merchant Dumont might live. Robert spoke with asperity, as if he might be come to collect a debt. He was the only one who spoke, for his French was very fair, and all that could be determined from it was that he might be of another district in France; never that he came from Wales. His men stayed closemouthed. He had warned them on Welsh clacking, and promised a beating for English. There was no need to bring neighbors' wrath on Dumont by proclaiming he dealt with England. His heart clamored to go immediately there, but first, the king's business.

The inner harbor was formed of the mouth of the Arques River, so hardly crossed by the army six miles back. There were no ships there. He rode toward the outer harbor with covert glances following him, though no man stopped him. Robert was dressed like a lord, and his men looked rough. It was a bad century for seeking trouble. No one interfered.

From the pebbled beach under the towering cliffs they had a clear view of the outer bay. It was empty but for a single ship; and Robert was despairing. There would be no supplies for the army. The conspiracy that had kept food from them at Harfleur continued. Some merchants were taking the money, if it was not stolen before it reached them, and did not ship the goods. They thought then, that Henry would never leave France to investigate and punish.

"That ship," he said, indicating the lonely vessel. "Could she be English?"

"As English as London," Wat said. "That's *Holy Mary*."

Robert's hands tightened on the reins. A letter for him, surely!

He turned back for the merchant Dumont's instantly, his men all piling after him at a gallop and the Frenchmen staring at the noisy, speechless cavalcade. Someone called after them once, but none answered; Robert because he would not, Wat because he was ordered not, and the others because they could not, having no French.

At the fine house of Dumont, Robert dismounted, leaving Wat to keep the men silent and in order. He knocked at the door. A wench came, her eyes popped when she saw armed men. She slammed the door and fled. Next the master of the house came, all alarm, and since he had seen Robert only once and then in darkness, Robert had to step inside and recall his memory. The little man pulled nervously at his sparse gray beard.

"Surely you remember," Robert said. "It was a dark night, and there was a gibbet at the crossroads, and none of you dismounted."

The Frenchman jerked at his beard.

"I saw *Holy Mary* in the outer harbor," Robert said, having no time to seesaw back and forth with words. "Is the merchant here?"

The Frenchman jerked his beard again, till Robert longed to jerk it for him; then at last he backed to a door and pushed it open, as if about to weep.

"Sir," he called, "sir," to one within.

Robert saw, over his head, a table revealed in sunlight, all spread with glittering coins, and behind it, starting up as the door moved, the merchant Chapelle, jingling with silver bells at the shoulders of his violet gown.

"Robin!" he exclaimed, and came around the table with his hands outstretched in greeting. "Here's a lucky meeting."

Robert glanced at the Frenchman, who was looking pitifully and anxiously at the coins strewn over the table.

"Now," the merchant said good-humoredly, "we'll not make off with them, Pierre."

The Frenchman looked piteously at them again, and then to the table, but withdrew and closed the door behind him.

"I had hoped to make rendezvous with you," Chapelle said. "I waited a day and would have waited another, with the English army so close."

"Constance had my letter?" Robert asked.

"Your letter and more, the silver comb. I do not know if it were well done or not. She wept. Let us talk of other things. Did you come to Dieppe to look at the harbor?"

"I came to find ships, and supplies for the army," Robert said.

"You cannot be short of food. I saw warehouses full in London."

"We did not see it in Harfleur."

"It was bought and delivered to the warehouses. I saw it."

"We never got it."

The merchant looked stormy. "Someone took a profit," he said. "Have you food on *Holy Mary?*"

"No. We're deep in merchandise, loaded by night. She'll sail like a slut going home. Dumont's getting this money out of the country too. He thinks King Charles will fight. Burgundy's restless. There's something afoot. I hope the king's spies are alert, I cannot find out how it goes, but when merchants part with their money to send it from the country . . ." He shook his head. "How is the army?"

"High in courage."

"But not high in flesh, if you seek food. The Frenchmen expect the army, and they'll hide everything. You'll get nothing as you march."

"We'll march empty then," Robert said.

The merchant smiled grimly. "They breed men in Wales, if nothing else," he said.

"Did Walter and John get home?" Robert asked, to turn the talk again toward London.

"Back to that!" the merchant said. "Yes, and glad to be home. They do nothing but eat and sleep and brag how they took Harfleur."

There was a pause. The merchant would not say it.

So Robert did. "Is Constance well?"

"Yes," the merchant said. He reached down and flicked a coin.

"And . . . wed?"

"Ay," the merchant said.

Robert's heart contracted. "Happily?" he asked.

"I cannot say," the merchant said. "She does not speak of it, either this way or that, but the old man dotes on her. He let her come with me on *Holy Mary*."

Robert stiffened.

"Not that he knew she hoped for a meeting with a Welshman," the merchant said bluntly. "She's on some business for him. She persuaded him he must make his life easier, and she will do the traveling. He bade us hurry back, but Constance bade me wait till Doomsday, if you might come."

Robert was silent. So close . . . so close!

"I'll bring supplies on my next trip, if you can wait four days," the merchant said. "Three if the weather holds. The wind prevails southwest."

"We cannot wait," Robert said.

"You'll not have food enough to last until Calais," the merchant said.

"I've been hungry in Wales," Robert said.

The merchant stared straight at him. "Who's to know if you vanish?" he inquired softly. "Let them starve if they will in French forests with French armies all about. It's a fool's trick. Return to England with me."

"If you sent a man on your business," Robert asked quietly, "and he never returned, but went another path for that your way was dangerous, what would you demand of him?"

"His life," Chapelle said promptly. "I'll urge you no more. I do not say the same for Constance."

"Will I see her, then?"

"Do you think I could drag her back to England, else? Robin, do you love her?"

Robert nodded.

"Then I'll permit the meeting," the merchant said, "though it's hardly wise. Robin, don't play the knave. She's married, and must stay so."

"I know it," Robert said.

The merchant's face was bleak. "I've had no joy of this," he admitted. "I do not know if I did well. It torments me of nights, if she is happy. He's a good man, but good men sometimes lack courage in bad times—" He broke off abruptly.

It was evident that London was dangerous, and the merchant wary. Was the old man the bulwark Chapelle had hoped? He must be, for his own sake, now that he was married to the girl.

"And how is it with you in London?" Robert asked.

"How is it with you in France?" the merchant countered.

"You have friends," Robert said.

The merchant nodded slowly. "I would they were more and higher," he said. "A man can plan too much for safety, and find it eludes him. But it was for my daughter only! I ask nothing for myself." He looked at Robert. "I would, by Holy St. Anne, that I had considered you and pleased my daughter! Yet I did plan safety for her!"

"I would have schemed so, in your place," Robert said.

The merchant looked at him, as a man looks at something lost.

"How does Clarence in London?" Robert asked.

"Sick," the merchant said. "I pray for his swift recovery, if no other does. The Lollard laws will be bad if they're enforced, and Clarence would oppose that. If the old man proves craven, should these hard times come," he emphasized, "there is ever a fast ship behind the house. If I must flee, I will take my daughter to Italy, and will you follow us?"

"I will fight in the streets of London," Robert said, "but will not walk those of Italy. No man will push me from my country, though he wears a crown and names himself the king of it!"

"Beware your tongue, Robin," the merchant said. "You're the stuff of rebels!"

"There are few I give my confidence," Robert said.

"I am honored by it," the merchant said.

"If I get back to London," Robert said, "it may be I can help you. The Duke of Clarence knows me."

The merchant nodded. "Powerful friends," he said. "If you have those, Robin, you have better than money. Power! Well . . . I must return to London to see what my enemies plot. You've watched the harbor long enough through that window. Constance is not on the ship, but on the western cliff. She likes to overlook the water."

He found her near the edge, sitting on a low flat rock, clutching her knees and skirts. She faced the sea, and her long black hair was whipping from the back of her head over her right shoulder. When she turned her head, she freed her face of it with a hand and smiled at him.

"I knew it was you," she said, "when I heard a stone fall."

He sat beside her, and she leaned her head wearily on his chest. He put his arm about her, but hesitantly. She was another man's wife. The old man sat between them, and made Robert awkward.

"Are you well?" he asked, bending his head down to talk against the wind. Her hair hit him in the face, and she struggled one-handed with it, and pinioned it at last.

"Well enough," she said. "Robin, you're thin."

He dropped his eyes. "I thought of you," he said, "often."

The wind blew fiercely, eddied, dropped suddenly and left them in a calm.

"Look how my hair has blown about," she said. She moved a little back from him and made a play at taking a silver comb from a pocket and dressing her hair like a preening bird. All useless, for the wind blew again. She dropped her hand. "Robin? You meant to send it? You do not regret parting from it?"

"I meant to send it. I do not regret it."

"Ah, then, you've declared your love."

"My love is worth nothing," he said somberly.

"It's all the world to me," she said.

"How does your old man?" he asked harshly.

She pushed her hair back with the hand that held the comb. "Robin," she said, "you look half a bandit."

"I'm dirty from swamps and rivers," he said, "but I was shaved this morning for the letter I hoped you'd send."

"You seem different," she said.

"And you."

"How?" she asked.

"More quiet," he said. He burned with jealousy of the old man, and yet he wished her happiness of him. He was thrusting a dagger into his own body with his own hands. "Are you happy?"

"Robin," she said, "you never meant to send the comb. It's the other maid you love."

"There never was another maid," he said, and told her, "but an old loyalty I put aside when I sent this comb." He took the hand that held it in both of his. She wore on a chain about her neck the single gold bell he had left behind. He looked away.

"Robin, never lie to me," she said.

"I do not lie."

"Robin, have things gone very ill?"

He shrugged.

"Will you return to London when the war's done?" she asked. So she did not know how desperate this venture was? Nor London either, probably.

"Nay, nay," she begged, "don't smile on me as on a child that asks for what it may not have. You'll not regret returning. I swear it, Robin. You'll have your way if you but promise."

"If I were killed . . ." he began.

"Do not talk so," she commanded.

". . . would you have my ghost come wandering into your courtyard?"

"I would," she declared hotly, like the girl she'd been in London.

"Knock on my window, Robin, or howl if you cannot knock. I'll come out and sit with your shade till I die and we may go together. Robin, promise you will return, alive or dead!"

"Ask for no promise," he told her gently. For he could neither make nor keep it. He could not stay away from her were he in London, and soon or late the scandal would start and drag her down and he loved her too much for this.

"Promise," she said fiercely.

He had a vow, and she a husband. To have a love in holes and corners, that were not for Constance. For him, well enough, but not for her. He would not have her brought down, then left to face all while he sailed again for a war.

"Promise," she insisted.

At that moment, her father bellowed from below the cliff. They saw him backing on the pebbled beach to where a boat was in the surf.

"We must go down," Robert said.

"If you'll not come to me," she said fiercely, "then I must come to you. Robin, I'll persuade my . . . I will find business in Calais, and go to my father's countinghouse there every day until you come."

"Here's a dangerous place," he said, and helped her down the rock.

"Robin, listen! I'll wait for you in Calais! My husband will never . . ."

"Do not stumble here," he said. "Give me your hand."

"Robin!"

"Not in London," he said, "nor in Calais."

She stopped and looked up at him.

"Don't you love me?" she asked, like a child.

"Yes," he said, and urged her down the path.

"Then I'll wait for you in Calais," she said, insisting. "I care for nothing else."

She pulled at his arm, but he said nothing. He helped her down, and with his arm about her waist walked her unwilling to the beach and the small boat grating there on the pebbles, with sailors to their knees in water holding her. The merchant saw them coming and flung two bags clashing into the boat, hauled his violet gown high out of the wet and showed his hairy legs as he climbed in.

Robert handed weeping Constance after him. She had her silver comb clutched tight in both hands, so she teetered where she stood. Her father caught at her gown to save her falling overboard.

"Robin!" she called. "I'll wait for you in Calais. Robin, remember! I'm as constant as my name!"

The boat was shoved clear and the last of the sailors leaped in. Her father shook his head violently at Robert.

She called out again, her voice thinning with distance and almost obliterated by the wind.

"I'll wait for you in Calais. Robin, remember, *I'll wait!*"

He raised a hand in farewell that must be for always.

A grating of pebbles made him turn. Wat was there with the horses.

So they rode away again through the town, like bedraggled foxes from a henhouse where no hens had been.

Chapter 26

FAIR WEATHER was their hope, and they got driving rain. Speed was their necessity and they got flood and forest and frozen roads that turned to deep mud when the sun emerged at last. Food was their most desperate need, but villagers fled, strong castles closed their gates, and only the weakest manors could be forced to deliver the meager supplies they did obtain.

But they were struggling on to a goal now. The Somme. There was a famous ford over the river Somme, good even in floodtime, and it was here their own King Edward III forced passage before the battle of Crécy. It was called The White Spot because it was easily located from the west by keeping a patch of chalk cliff in sight. It was possible for twelve men to cross abreast at each of two ebb tides. The name and history reached to them, declaring omen. Once past this ford, they felt, all else would go well. *Once across the Somme . . .*

On October 12th, they had almost reached the river. Robert stopped short by order only six miles from the ford. He camped, impatiently, anxious to go forward, and sent Wat back with news of his whereabouts and private orders to listen to any rumors. Early in the morning, while the day was still in darkness, Wat came riding with the news that the rumors were too many to be counted, but he was sure of one thing. A prisoner had been captured and questioned by the Duke of York.

"They squeezed him dry," Wat said, "and got only sour juice. He says the ford is heavily guarded, and ten thousand men are waiting to shoot us back into the water."

"A squeezed man spurts more lies than truth," Robert said. "Are the horses saddled? We'll look for this host."

They must find how the tide stood, and when it ebbed. He wanted to move as soon as he could see the road.

"The horses are ready," said one of the men.

"Too late for your plans," Wat remarked, peering into the dawning light as some riders approached in the deceptive gray. "Here's fat York himself."

"I cannot recognize him," Robert said.

"Nor can I," Wat agreed, "but that's his horse."

In a matter of horses, Wat was exact, so impatiently Robert waited until the duke pulled up and looked down to him standing by the road.

"Turn aside," the duke said abruptly; "follow the Somme inland into the body of France."

"We're but six miles from the ford, Your Grace," Robert reminded him. "It will take little time to see if it's guarded or clear."

"If you will not obey," the duke said, "there are others who will."

It was beyond the authority of York to make the decision to go forward into battle if an army waited for them to fall into a trap, but it was also beyond his authority to retreat from it. Therefore these orders were from the king, and definite, or York would not be here to assure them. It reminded Robert they were the inferior force now, and at severe disadvantage. King Henry would not risk his men at a ford.

"As you go," York was saying, "cling to the river. Look where we may cross to good advantage. Send to me the moment you see a place. Be alert in this!"

As if he were some lackey who needed to be watched.

"Your Grace," Robert said, "if this is the king's will, I obey him." *Not you, traitor!*

York flushed dangerously.

Robert snapped his fingers, and his horse was brought on the run. He mounted and galloped off without looking back. His Welshmen followed as he turned away from The White Spot. It did not matter to any of them if they forded or did not ford. That was a matter for Robert Heartless and what he made of it was not their affair. Therefore they were easy in their minds, if troubled by gnawings in their bellies, but Robert was all turmoil within, for every step they took away from their destination of Calais doubled the journey back again, and this with an army in such condition that they could scarcely march as far as they must. Yet the king said, farther!

Robert signaled, and his Welshmen spread through the trees like hunting dogs, yelling comment and obscenity to each other as another day began. It was Sunday, October 13th, the day they had meant to be in Calais.

Yet now, he realized, he was turned toward the countess and where she stayed. Was he meant to see her again? Almost, he hoped so. But if he did, it would be at terrible cost to the army, forced to march so far inland by the gathering host of the French. He wanted to see her, but he searched diligently for the ford whereby they could cross and stop short of her brother's castle. The river barred them, running deep and in flood. Everywhere passage was possible, the French had been before them. Causeways through treacherous swamps were broken up so they could not even reach a feasible ford. Where they could approach the river, the bridges had been burned and the water was swollen and impossible to chance. And always on the other side, when they could look, was a large French force that moved as they moved, marching parallel, to prevent a desperate crossing even at flood.

The French had found a policy at last, safe for them and deadly for Henry. It had turned to a war of attrition, and the French began their fight. The English made forced marches to gain the chance they must find to cross the Somme. The French made forced marches to prevent it. In the end, if the English survived starvation, they could be forced to march all the way to the headwaters of the Somme to die there, exhausted and outnumbered, in futile battle for nothing.

The only answer to sudden intelligent resistance that Robert could find was that the Duke of Burgundy had gone to his king. If he could reach the countess he could be sure, for her brother was a partisan of this duke, who was Henry's friend and took his gold to be so; but now was probably King Charles' henchman and took his gold to be so. It must be that the threat to Paris was gone, and Burgundy where he could be watched. King Charles could fight then, and he would.

Robert thought of Constance, waiting in Calais, growing more distant with every step. It was the answer to her problem at least, if not the one she'd choose, for it was not likely now that any of this army would ever leave France, but would stay, buried in her.

The river wound on endlessly, and the army weakened each day. Also, each day they drew nearer to the castle where the countess was. On October 16th they passed Boves, and reached a plain. From there Robert pushed his exhausted horse on to the great stone building he could see, hoping it was where she dwelt.

The courtyard was thick with a beguiling scent, and full of casks of wine just delivered. One had burst in handling and ran like blood over the gray flagging. The Welshmen sniffed audibly as their horses splashed the red stuff up.

Robert dismounted and flung his reins to an underling who came running.

"Is the lord of the castle about?" he asked.

The man stared, with fright. "He's . . . hunting, sir," he managed to say.

Hunting Englishmen, Robert thought grimly, but it confirmed his guess. Burgundy had gone to his king, and called his henchmen in.

"But I think the lady of the castle will give you greeting, sir," the knave added hastily. "See, there, up at that window. See, my lady is waving. You are to come in, she means."

Robert looked up and saw a tiny figure waving the end of a veil. His heart began to pound, but it might not be she, so he forced himself to walk with all dignity into the castle, up a long flight of stairs, to halt in a blasting draft in the hall above. Another stairway, entombed in a wall. He went up with his hand to his sword, although he encountered no one, for all the servants had run into the court to see the strangers and no fighting men appeared to be around.

Now a long dark corridor, with one torch blowing fitfully in the gale that swept it. Far down, Robert saw a slight figure outlined against the open door of a sunlit chamber. Warily, he moved toward it.

And suddenly, stopped. The next instant he shouted, and the echoes rolled as he rushed down like a charging lion to seize up the lady there, fling her backward into the room and swing her wildly in a circle while she shrieked that her bones would not countenance such play. Whereupon, with great tenderness, he set her upon her feet and knelt and kissed her hand like a gallant. Her ladies twittered in the background nervously, and drew her attention. They were watching Robert with wide eyes.

"So," she said to him, in Welsh and with asperity, "it begins again! Do not encourage the silly wenches!"

"Wenches? Where? I see no one, madam, but you."

She laughed and snipped his chin with a finger.

"I'll have them out, all the same," she said and ordered them from the room, in French. They left lingeringly. "The men are gone from the castle," the countess said to him in Welsh, "so do not preen yourself too much on the sensation you cause here. There's none to compete against you but old, fat fools. Now, let me look at you to see what makes them stare."

She stepped back to survey him as he stood.

"Where's my jesting boy? Where's my Blue-Eyed Rob? He's gone. Here's a fighting man with a week's beard, in scarlet and ermine and a great deal of dirt." Her attention shifted suddenly. "What's that knave glaring from the door?"

Robert glanced back. Wat Strongbow stood squinting against the sunlight like the mastiff Murdach when he saw what displeased him.

"That's my lieutenant," Robert said in Welsh, which Wat could not interpret. "Set to guard me that I do not stray too far after lovely women. See how he knew your presence?"

"Rascal!" she said, and laughed. "I do not blame them for playing your fool. If I were a pretty maid, I'd be tempted."

Wat came pussy-foot closer, until he could see at last that the lady's hair was graying and her skin fine wrinkles. His belligerence vanished. He ducked his head, embarrassed at last.

"He's a wild man," the countess declared, smiling pleasantly at Wat while she chattered on in Welsh, "and those savages in my courtyard are no better. From the sounds they're guzzling my wine. Set to watch you?" She came back suddenly to what Robert had remarked of Wat. "Still, you were born to be hunted by women, Rob." She began to walk around him critically, gave him a crack on the backside and came full round in front of him again. "And whiskered and dirty, you are yet the handsomest I've ever seen."

"Your sons were handsomer, madam," he said.

Her mouth thinned with dislike. "There was only enough of me in them to take the boar's look off their faces. For the rest they were their father. He's dead," she said, offhand. "I had the news lately."

Robert did not condole with her widowhood. For her, it was all clear gain. Nevertheless, the count had been a fighting man and taught him much.

"How did he die?" he asked.

"As he lived, like a boar wounded and thrashing in a thicket, enraged at all the world. He raved, they said. He talked of you when he lay dying. Rob, if we'd been there, we could have seized most of his wealth for ourselves." She sighed. "Well, we were not there, and he might have lived forever if we'd stayed. His sons scarce waited his burial before they fought over the spoils. Rhys hunted Gryffyd over a cliff. It's for the best I'm here, after all. My brother's wife is lately dead in childbed, but he had three heirs, all healthy, and will not marry again. He's tired of high-bred women. It took three wives to get three sons. Now peasant wenches are his taste, so I am ruler here. I'll give you good welcome, Rob. I'll strip this castle bare." She refused to acknowledge that they would never meet again. "It will be like the old days," she said, "and we'll spend new days in remembering."

"I'll be gone by tomorrow," he said.

Her face went bleak and seemed to thin and age.

"My brother is not in the castle," she said. "Burgundy's gone over to King Charles."

"And so he is unbought," Robert said.

There was a hubbub in the courtyard, voices raised above the shouts that had come up all through their talking.

"And if you must march to the headwaters," she inquired, "and fight where the Somme rises?"

"Then we must fight," he said. He walked over to the window. "The vanguard's coming. The king will not be far behind. Here's pretty news to greet his coming. The lord of the castle gone, and Burgundy's betrayed him. Although he must have guessed the last. Have you food enough for this visitation coming?"

"I ordered oxen killed the moment I had news the army was approaching," she said. "The meat will be tough but better than . . . what have you been eating? Not much by the gaunted look on you."

He bowed elegantly. "Walnuts shaken from the trees, and water from the Somme when we came near it," he said. "Madam, the bounty of France."

"I'll see how the food progresses," she said abruptly, and went to the door to shout imperiously at some woman in the hall.

A little lady for all her great voice, he thought; a handful of bones like a bird, shriveling with age. He remembered her as taller, more robust. But she was tiny, and looked transparent. Yet it was this woman who had defended the Welsh castle twice and sent the besiegers wounded away.

She turned, and caught his look.

"If I die tomorrow," she said, "I'll not care, for having seen you once again. I swear by all the saints, you're handsomer than before! You have a look of command. It agrees with you. I would trust you, had I never seen you before. And as a woman speaking . . . the blue eyes! Rob, you could be a dumb thing, and . . ." She sighed.

"You ever had a way," he said, "of praising what was yours; tapestries, and horses, and hawks and dogs and jewelry and silk and . . . me."

She laughed and came to him, and put her arm around his waist companionably.

"A handsome man is a delight," she said, "but a vain one is a curse. It's as well I beat you often when you were small enough." She looked up at the height of him, and laughed. "I could not do it now."

Noise in the courtyard again.

"This king of yours," she said, and sobered suddenly, "I heard he hung a man for stealing a pyx from a church, and marched his starving army past."

"He's pious enough for all three popes," Robert agreed.

"Do you still carry your Bible?" she asked.

"Madam, I do," he said.

"Leave it with me," she said, "and take it up another day."

"Madam," he said, "we both know I will never come this way again."

She made as if to coax, then sighed.

"The knave that stared from the door," she said, loosing him and going to the window to watch the coming of the king, "you said he was set to watch you. A lady, then. Blonde?"

"As dark as you are, madam."

"Were," she corrected regretfully. "Blue-eyed?"

"Brown and bright as your own."

"A sweet, gentle maid?"

"A leopard's whelp."

"You've hunted out another such as I was once."

"She hunted me," he said.

"I am not so jealous of her then," the countess said, "if she is spirited. It's the soft, pretty maids I hated when they mooned after you."

"This maid is jealous of you, my lady," Robert said.

"You spoke well of me to her? You did not tell my age? That's as well. Let her think there's another who'd have you instantly if she dared to look at another man. She'll cherish you more. Rob, do you have my keepsake, the silver comb set with stones?"

He hesitated.

"She got it of you! Do not think on excuses! It's plain enough she's overwhelmed me, which would happen soon or late. They ever looked after you, and I admit to jealousy. I slapped many a pretty face and sent it back to its parents."

Another hullabaloo in the courtyard, and trumpets.

"I will never marry her," he said deliberately, "or any other. I have sworn a vow."

The countess' delicate face flushed. "Is your loyalty then to another?"

She thought it herself. Let her think it, for that were kindness, and he had a tender heart. He inclined his head.

It seemed she grew younger with the color in her face, and the sudden brightness of tears in her eyes.

Trumpets sounded again.

"God!" she said, startled to recall. "I had forgot the king! I must go down and welcome him. Rob, we'll speak about this later."

He bowed, and she was gone.

King Henry sat at the high table, in the place of honor, and the countess was beside him. With the highhandedness of a woman who rules a household utterly, and has lived long enough to scorn conventions, she passed over dukes and earls and set Robert on her other side.

"For, sire," she said as the king glanced at Robert, "he is my foster son, and dearer to me than my children."

The king did not seem inclined to protest, or even notice. It seemed he barely heard. He was prepared to brood, thinking over what lay ahead, a march to doom. The company waited on his mood. The Duke of York sat, red-faced, toying with a dagger lying on the linen cloth, glowering, and casting side glances from his pale-lashed eyes.

"It's a dull enough evening I'll offer you, sire," the countess said to the unresponsive king. "There's nothing in this castle save one minstrel fit for baying with dogs."

"All the others are gone with Burgundy, no doubt," the Duke of York suggested.

The countess ignored him.

"It's not like the old days in Wales, sire," she said. "There was a lively time. Do you know Wales well, sire?"

Henry roused himself, unsmiling. "Wales? I was born there."

"And ruled there and fought there," the Duke of York contributed.

"I saw you once, sire," the countess said, "when you were marching. You were little more than a boy, riding by with Hotspur."

The king's head came up when she mentioned that name.

"I do not know Wales well," the king said, suddenly answering her first question, "nor any Welshman. Being born gave me no understanding, ruling lifted me too high, and fighting only made me enemies."

"Well," she said, as if agreeing, but only in part, "they are a contentious race. Wave a sword by a Welshman's grave, and he'll rise and fight for the sake of battle."

"I say amen to that," the king said.

"Our castle was ever in an uproar, sire," she said, "with fighting. And with Rob's pranks and brawls. One dark of the moon"—she leaned closer, and caught his flickering attention and kept it—"not a glimmer of light anywhere and I have gray hairs to prove my fright . . . this great knave sitting sedate as a bishop beside me dragged a tun up the stone stairs, the great stairs, and with much labor he and his companions would have grudged to honester work, they filled it with huge stones. Then, while the castle slept, they rolled the tun down the stairs, where it rumbled like thunder, burst like a thunderclap and sent rocks bounding over the hall like an avalanche! All leaped from their beds shrieking, and the men ran out with swords, thinking the castle was taken and nothing left but to sell their lives for the dearest price. Assaulted? There was nothing to fight but rocks. Rob had taken to his heels. We heard him and the others laughing, but they did not venture back for two days' time. I tell you, it was lively then. The weak died of fright. Rob has a gentle nature, but he was always fighting, somehow. Sire, do you speak Welsh?"

Henry nodded, and brightened a little more when she switched to that speech, saying she'd talked Welsh so long her native French was makeshift now.

"There was another night," she said in Welsh, which had York frowning, "when we were supping and the count, God forgive him his many sins"—here she paused to cross herself—"flung a bone over his shoulder, and two dogs seized it at once and contended. Gryffyd owned the one dog and so flung a bowl at the other. Rob leaped up and swore the second dog had all right to vie for the prize. The next instant he and Gryffyd were at swordspoints, the table was flung over, both dogs ran yelping, and our food was all over the floor. My Rob will have justice, if only for a dog. God be my witness, his word once given is never broken."

Unfortunately, she had come back to French for the last two things she said, and York pounced on them.

"What a paragon is this!" he exclaimed. "Not your son, madam? What then?"

"My foster son," she said as if she had not understood a subtler meaning thrust in, "and more to me than all six sons of my body. How are your boys, sir, for you must have some by now?"

That were a thrust in return, and it wounded sore.

"I am lucky to possess none," the duke said harshly, "for who knows how boys turn out?"

York was drinking fast and deep and she remembered from a certain Christmas how he could turn nasty for this. She did not answer, though she longed to, and looked around for diversion.

"Ho, minstrel! I see you. Drag him out, Armand! Drag him out, I say. He's lurking behind that arras. I saw it move!"

The minstrel was seized and shoved roughly into the space between the tables, which were set in the form of a U. He unslung a rebec from his shoulder with shaking hands and began to sing, more ready to dodge than produce melody.

The king fingered the scar under his eye.

My lady began to talk again, confidentially to him, under cover of the singing. Robert listened, to separate her voice from the babble all around, and was filled with horror. She was talking about the lists at Chester.

"Rob always fought with the weapons of war, leaving blunt lances for the cowards."

Holy Mary, this was a tender subject. The countess was fast raising memories best left to sleep in the king, if indeed they slept, for Henry was known to be tenacious in recall. He seldom fought in the lists, being light of body. Sir John Oldcastle had been the royal champion, fighting in his place, as he was big and heavy and hard to knock from the saddle . . . for all but a king. For now Sir John was a heretic and in rebellion. And the countess talked of tournaments!

". . . cannot remember now who his opponent was, but he rode a fine black horse with a flashing silver chamfron-and-pike on its face. The lances shattered fairly, but the black horse in passing thrust its pike into the nostrils of Rob's nag, which reared and flung him down. The other squire, I do not remember his name but he was some lord's cub, claimed Rob's horse and weapons as the victor's right."

"He had no right," the king said, interested. "It was the horse that struck the blow and a foul one besides."

"It was so decreed," the countess said, "and that they must break another lance. You could scarce hear the heralds for the uproar. Rob borrowed a fresh horse, and overthrew the other," the countess said. "He broke his neck. They cheated Rob, for they did not give over the armor or the horse, yet he won as prize a girdle of gold folly bells." She paused as if recalling something. "Where are your bells, Rob?" She jerked the table linen aside, to be sure they were not on him. "You let no man laugh them off?"

"I took them off, madam," he said, gravely, "so they'd not betray me in deep forest."

She let the linen drop. "I will never forget how you overthrew . . . what was his name?"

"I don't remember," he said.

"Ah, well, he's buried now. Let his bones lie quiet, the ill-bred knave. And that minstrel will lie quiet too, soon enough." She glared at the man. His voice cracked. The countess swore. Without a word, the minstrel turned and fled, pursued with joy by several large and noisy dogs.

When the uproar died down, the countess turned to Robert.

"We have but one night," she said. "Bring back the old days, Rob, when you had us laughing."

Robert glanced at the king, who nodded.

Then Robert stood up and called Wat and they conferred briefly, and said they must have a large strong dog and a skirt. Someone caught a boarhound, eager for diversion; and the countess jerked table linen loose and flung it to Wat, who wrapped it around like a skirt and simpered coyly with his ugly visage.

Whereupon they made a drama for the company, improvising as they went, acting in the rectangle within the tables, while Robert intermittently declaimed verses of a French poem learned long ago.

Wat was a fair, shy maiden coming from a convent to her home, riding the boarhound for a horse. Robert halted this maiden, and then ensued a conversation as he asked her where he might find a bed for the night, whereupon Robert switched to Welsh, which Wat did not speak, and the confusion of languages soon broke down into wildest ribaldry, with Wat answering stoutly in French questions he did not understand. It was merry enough interpreting the gestures, for Wat was a clownish master at double meanings and innocent faces, but when a watcher understood both languages, the tears ran down his face. The king's head was thrown back, and he was laughing. The boarhound barked and turned unmanageable. Wat was flung down to the rushes on the floor with his skirt to his shoulders, where he shrieked in high falsetto.

Robert helped the lady to array herself, the lady was affronted, the play grew wilder. Wat appealed to some sweet knight to save his virtue which were lost if help was not prompt to come. A young earl still in his teens leaped the table and came to rescue the fair maiden. The affair broke into mock sword play and mightly slashings in the air with imaginary weapons, while the dogs leaped and barked, and tripped both swordsmen so the earl fell flat on Wat, who lay howling on his belly hiding his head with his skirt.

The countess called for more wine and demanded that Robert sing, and the king commanded he sing the Welsh songs, and he did. The lackeys rolled in casks of wine from the courtyard and stood them on the board, and the king drank and ate and laughed, and forgot for a little while. Yet when dawn came, it was the king who discovered it.

The countess had been saying that her Rob had but one fault, a stubbornness born in him that made him cling to any cause he undertook and always keep any vow he made to the exact letter of each word, when the king looked up. A narrow window was outlined by brightening sky behind it. Others followed his glance until the company grew quiet, remembering what lay before them.

The king said softly, "Madam, we all thank you for this hospitality."

"I would it might last forever," she said.

"Nothing lasts forever," he replied, "neither love, nor loyalty, nor life."

Then the Duke of York, who was learned in books and betrayal alike, rose in his place and held up his cup to the sun. He spoke in Latin. Robert did not drink with the others, for he'd pledge to nothing he did not understand.

Hurriedly the countess whispered the translation. *We who are about to die*, he'd said, *salute you.*

The company put down their cups with a clatter. But Robert raised his and drank it to the king.

Chapter 27

THEY MARCHED ON, across open chalky country now, toward the headwaters of the Somme, still balked by swamps or floods or French from the crossing that meant their life, until at last they came to a place where the river bent and bulged toward the French. King Henry saw the small advantage tossed to them by fate and instantly left the river, to make a forced march straight across the inner part of the curve, cutting the distance to where the Somme straightened again and brought both armies together. The French had to follow the long outer perimeter on the opposite bank, and they fell behind. Henry stole a day's march so.

This was their last chance; the time of their decision. Robert rode into the town of Nesle, hardened with this knowledge. It was life or death, as they crossed the river or not. He rode down a street lined with silent, sullen French, recalling the march through Harfleur. But behind these French were no ruins, but houses with red rags fluttering defiance at every door. He halted in the square and sent his archers galloping, herding citizens to him like sheep, snapping and barking sharp commands.

He sat haughtily ahorse the while, stony cold, as he had seen dreaded Llewellyn ap Gryffyd when he was thinking on ravaging a man's lands. Robert's blue eyes seemed piercing in the shadows of exhaustion; his curved mouth was straight. He seemed an icy man, and felt as cold as a dead one; as if all was happening outside, and he but a watcher from some window. The citizens gathered closer, his archers on the edges holding them so they could not disperse if they would. Robert thought incongruously of his last talk with the countess the morning he'd left her castle. She'd walked with him to his horse in the damp, cold courtyard as she had so often in Wales when he rode out raiding with the count. Neither spoke openly of the battle surely coming, but it lay on them like an all-pervading mist.

"I'm old," she'd said wearily as they halted by his horse, "and you a fighting man. There are not many years before us. Do not waste your allotment as I wasted mine, in hatreds and regret. Go back to your lady."

He did not reply. He had made a vow he could not break.

"Rob, Rob, do you think I fought for the castle twice to preserve stone walls? I would have fled and let them go, but the castle sheltered you, my Blue-Eyed Rob, ever running and busy, finding wonders in the flight of birds, the sound of wind, the way the mosses grew. I defended the castle and learned courage and more. I learned it is possible to do great things for devotion, to do wonders, to do the impossible."

"I have learned it also, madam," he said. He had sent Constance back to her husband.

"Cross the river, Rob."

"If God wills it," he said.

"Rob, I think of you when you were little, watching a bug crawl on the floor. You smiled just so to watch him struggle at a wide place, and took him up on a straw and helped him over when he could not span the crack. I think heaven will remember you did not stamp on him. Rob, cross the river. I will not see you dead in France."

"Madam," he said, "do not distress yourself."

He mounted his horse. She put her hands to the reins to delay him yet a moment.

"Rob, this vow you've made never to marry. If this is for me, I release you. I'd keep your love and let your duty go, as any woman would. Rob, you are the only son I truly had, and the mother of a son is fierce as a she-bear and as partisan. Rob, find a crossing, if it must be over the bodies of my countrymen!"

"I still remember your advice," he said, "and always will. *Break before you bend*, you told me. I'll not disgrace my training, no matter how it falls."

Nor would he! Neither that teaching which she gave to him, nor that from the count who, though he was wild, was never craven, nor left anything he began undone. He looked around among the townspeople of Nesle, and they watched him with hatred and fear. He saw it, and his mouth twisted cruelly in Llewellyn ap Gryffyd's natural way.

"There's a ford near here," he stated. "Is it guarded?"

The red rags tied to every door flapped defiance in the wind. Robert's blue eyes narrowed.

"You've heard of King Henry's mercy," he said. "You think on being spared? Then know this, I am not the king, nor like him. I am Robert Heartless and his mercy is not mine. He would give pity, but I'll give burnt houses, wasted fields, slaughtered cattle and raped women!"

The few women in the crowd tried to vanish behind their men.

"You think we are marching to our death? It may be. But there will be none of you left alive to rejoice."

"Ohhhh, he's blackhearted," Wat's voice said happily from the sidelines. His voice carried to all, though he seemed to speak to a petty merchant he had pinned to a door with his horse. "Handsome as an angel, but then, the devil was an angel once!"

Robert sat silent and implacable on his overridden horse. If there was pity in him, it never showed; if tenderness, it was not to be surmised. The red rags fluttered, but he was in their city with armed men, and all their lives they'd bowed to overbearing lords.

"My lord," one ventured, "if we showed you the ford, would you give us your knightly word that you would leave us?"

"Debate it," Robert invited, "among yourselves. Be all of one mind. Think on it. I'll burn a house or two to warm myself the while. This air is chill."

Wat reached over and seized a torch from a house bracket and looked around, as if for a place to light it and begin the work of destruction.

The spokesman said quickly, "I'll lead you to the ford."

"Then I will give my promise," Robert said.

Wat slammed the torch back in the iron holder with disgust, but turned cheerful again.

"Now, sweeting," he said in his hoarse French, "do not look so longing after your husband. If my lord delays returning with him, we'll dally together, eh?"

The spokesman turned white. The crowd shifted uneasily. They knew how fighting men behaved without a leader.

"Long faces?" Wat asked, with all concern. "Consider your good fortune! If it be not English lords, then it will be French lords, and that's the poor man's choice. Be merry, you have saved yourself. I think you have. Of course, I've a nature that's all impulse, and if my lord's away too long, I'll not be curbed!"

The Frenchman said with dignity past his fear, "I'll show you the ford for your promise, but spare my people, sir."

"I am not a word-breaker," Robert said. "I keep all vows."

Then he picked up his horse reins when the man moved ahead, and followed him down the street and out the gate. The people watched from alleys and windows and dark places, and if the English army was not an hour behind, he knew he'd have felt the sting of crossbow quarrels in his back.

The Frenchman ran, and Robert roused his weary horse to a trot. They hurried on toward the river, so he knew the man led him true; yet he was still suspicious. It had been too easy a victory, despite his harsh-appearing action. It had been too easy.

They came to a clutter of houses, and Robert smelled the familiar rotting vegetation of a swamp. They went down a rough road, and the Frenchman halted and pointed. Robert's heart leaped up, and then crashed down. A vast swamp, with two causeways to the river; but both the passages were destroyed. The very stones of the causeways were scattered and sunk in the quicksands, and only their beginnings marked the place where they had been.

"The ford?" Robert asked.

"Past the swamp," the Frenchman said, with anxiety and triumph contending in his face.

"What town is on the other side?" Robert asked, as if he did not see this blockade.

"St. Quentin, my lord." The Frenchman was fearful again. He glanced back, frightened, toward Nesle.

"Who guards the other banks?"

"The men of St. Quentin."

"Who else?"

"No other, my lord." The man stood profiled, edging sideways back yet not daring to return alone.

Robert ignored his pleading glance and stared over the noisome slime and mud. They could not cross on the little rubble left on firmer areas that marked the way the causeways had run; nor could they force this swamp. Yet beyond were two fords, and only the men of St. Quentin to guard them.

He swung his horse around and, still-faced, went spurring back with the news.

The vanguard galloped up with snapping banners and flashing lanceheads, but King Henry was a hundred yards ahead. The king lunged past Robert and dashed precipitately out on the broken causeway until a wide gap halted him. From there he surveyed the treachery of mud, and the forested heights beckoning from the other side of the river. He picked his way carefully back, his horse slipping badly on the broken footing, while the vanguard winced, fearing for their king.

He looked at York.

"These houses standing by," he said. "Fling them into the breaches.

Cast down anything that will bear weight. I will cross here in the morning."

That was all he said.

The people in the scraggling village shrieked as soldiers jerked off doors, dragged out furniture, lifted stone hearth-pieces and dragged down beams. Women fled with their children. Townsmen seized oxen from disintegrating stables and turned them loose, bellowing, to save them from the hungry soldiers, who had no time to grasp at food with their very lives at stake. Through a scramble of inhabitants, lowing animals and barking dogs, the soldiers dragged lumber to the causeways, flung wheels, carts, logs, firewood, stones, anything. As the town was broken up the nearer breaches filled, and men ventured out farther on the unsteady footing to jam logs down to the stone base under the mud, and lengthen the broken road. Night came. They worked by torchlight. The village vanished and they cut trees. As the stars paled with the approach of yet another dawn, there was a thin causeway of rubble where a single file of men could lead horses precariously to the ford.

The king turned to Robert Heartless.

"Take two hundred archers," he said, "get to the other bank, and hold it."

And so Robert Heartless was the first to teeter over the dangerous footing to the river. He was the first to slide his frightened horse down a muddy bank and the first to gasp at immersement in the icy, swollen river. His horse was in to the withers, fighting the strong flood that almost overwhelmed him, struggling hard to keep hooves to the muddy bottom. Some smaller nags were carried off and scattered downstream; but most came slipping and sliding across with Robert. When he counted on the other side, he'd lost only three men, and he rallied the rest in gray morning and led them to high ground, and set his men to fight off any attempt to dislodge him. Wat came back from a quick circling to report French scouts watching them. Robert attended instantly. There were some twenty horsemen, misty in the morning light that filtered through the treetops. They were standing together in a clearing with tall trees all around. They made no move of hostility but conferred together excitedly with horse heads turned carefully away from the English, the better to flee.

"The stout men of St. Quentin," Robert said, with scorn.

"Finally out of bed," Wat agreed, "and behold! Englishmen, on the wrong side of the Somme. Who can they blame?"

Suddenly, one of the Frenchmen saw Robert and Wat watching. He shouted with alarm, and the next instant they'd galloped off.

"There's the alarm raised," Robert said calmly, for if it was not one Frenchman it would have been another. Two hundred cursing archers were not to be hidden here, nor did he wish to hide them, but only to make them look like a host. "Wat, down to the river. Tell them we'll have Frenchmen at our throats at any time."

King Henry ordered the van over, freezing wet and full of curses for French rivers. By an hour after midday they were in full crossing, and after dark that night they still came through the swollen waters, wading up to their necks afoot, and over the saddle if mounted. Some lighter horses were swept away, and more men lost by drowning. But they came, with torches high overhead, spitting sparks down into black and swirling water, while the French held back and allowed it.

The wet men told how the king stood by one makeshift causeway entrance, and the Duke of York by the other, seeing all kept order and moved in turn. There was no confusion. Robert thought of a king and a traitor working together, while he waited to repel the French attack that never came. When he turned his head a little, he could see two thin lines of lights moving across nothing, dipping into gleaming water, and rising up on the bank to converge and enter the forest as one glittering line.

The French never came, but the English did, half-drowned and sputtering. By midnight it was finished and the ragged army settled for the remainder of the night, huddled about fires to keep from freezing, while bowmen almost wept over their damp bows.

The Duke of York came early in the morning, on horseback and in armor save for his helm, which meant the nobles expected action at any time, for no man wore armor if it could be avoided.

"Here comes His Grace," Wat said, looking past where Robert stood by a watchfire, "with his belly patch. A pinchpurse, to patch old armor instead of buying new. I hope it chafes him raw!"

But he looked pious as the duke stopped by their fire, glancing down from the height of his saddle.

"The king was pleased with you," he announced, the only reference he ever made to the fact that Robert had aided in the crossing. "We saved eight days' march by crossing here."

Robert looked up at the patch of sky between the trees, estimating when it would be light, and Wat moved behind him to help him lace his points.

"The archers he gave you will return to the vanguard," the duke said.

Wat pulled hard on each point, so that Robert's damp hose might be tight and without hint of wrinkle in drying, to show off fine legs if it be only to squirrels and conies.

York commanding the vanguard in a position of trust, Robert thought bleakly.

"The horses?" he asked over his shoulder, casually.

"Saddled just now," Wat replied.

York called out the two hundred archers must wait here till the vanguard came and then join that. They looked sullen. Robert's Welshmen clumped together, as if about to make a stand.

York turned back to contemplation of the lacing of the hose.

"I'll set you a puzzle," he said. "Can you guess your orders today?"

"To avoid the battle, Your Grace, which our weakness now invites."

The duke did not seem pleased, but nodded. The situation was clear enough to all, even an archer of dim wit. The hunters had become the hunted. Some said the French had sent heralds threatening battle, but King Henry sent them away, saying he would march straight on to Calais.

"Find the French," York said, "before they find us. They are behind us, we hope, or will be when we march straight away from the river. But if they are not . . . It should come easy to you, after Wales, and running when more than two men stood together."

Robert looked straight at him then. "I've seen the backs of Englishmen, Your Grace," he said.

York set his jaw.

Robert spun on his heel. His horse was by him, held ready, and he mounted. His Welsh archers mounted too, and they crashed in underbrush moving into a group. Robert led them off through the trees toward the rutted forest road where the French had been.

And York was suddenly with them again, pushing past archers and swinging in toward Robert.

"If you mean to ride with us, Your Grace," Robert said coldly, "a duke of England is a prime target for ransom, and I have few men to protect you."

"Say my family has a failing for rashness," the duke said.

They rode on in silence, which pleased Robert well enough, for constant vigilance was his task and the expectation of sudden attack from any quarter kept his nerves taut and his belly aching as he sought to see French before French saw him. Once in a halt to rest the horses he chanced to lean back, with his hand on his saddlebags, touching the Bible within, as was his habit. York glanced over and away. There was no reason to suppose he'd seen the gesture, but he was ferret-eyed. The habit must be broken, Robert thought. It did not please him that this was added to his tense watching.

The army plodded on, trying to struggle ahead of the French. Then a mile beyond Péronne, Robert called "Ho!" and dropped from the saddle to study some marks at a crossroad. The record was plain in trampled dust and hoofmarks, bruised grass, broken branches, and a dropped crossbow bolt. The French army was not behind as they hoped, nor even to one side, as might be possible. The French army had swung aside and marched hard, and now was between them and Calais.

Wat spat angrily at the crossbow bolt from his horse. The duke crossed himself slowly, and Robert ordered a galloper back with word, glad that he had time enough for warning without a blasting of horns to warn the French as well. He moved on then, boldly, expecting the French to come like a storm. But there was only dust and bitter cold and the knowledge of a great host passing. The tension grew greater with every stride of their horses. The archers had closed in behind, silently.

York said abruptly, "I am forty-two years old and have no son. I will leave nothing behind but a legend of treachery."

Robert watched, eyes narrowed against the wind. Everything moved on this raw, gusty day: trees and dust, and bushes. And, strangely, York's tongue.

"My title goes to my nephew," York said, and added, a little later, after thinking on it: "I never liked him."

The footprints were gone from the road now. The rising wind slapped them away in puffs. If they had come a little later, with the road smoothed where it crossed, would they have known by the bruised grass and the dropped crossbow bolt? Or would they have passed on, thinking of a herd of cattle, or decided the bolt was lost by some poacher?

"Even now," the duke said, "you think I ride with you to desert the faster if the French come, to make a separate bargain and save my life."

Robert did not gainsay him. What possessed the man? Did he feel death's touch with the icy wind? The trees bent as if a sea gale swept them, and the sound of rushing was all about. It was not a pretty moment, expecting a flash of darts from behind those trees. Did York make some kind of halt confession?

"Would you like to return to the vanguard, Your Grace?" Robert inquired. "I'll send back what men I can spare."

The duke said, "I'm called traitor, not coward."

Robert turned to watch a height.

"Men call me traitor," the duke said, as if he could not leave the subject, "because I always hesitated. That was my true fault. I looked back and forward and sideways and waited too long before I moved for what I wanted, even in treason. I changed direction like a hunted hare, tormented alike by ambition and conscience. I have a conscience. It's undone me. The king is another such, though he acts boldly. It's afterwards he thinks on it, and worries if it were well done. Therefore he's king and I'm a traitor."

They rode a long time before the duke spoke again, like a man impelled against his will by the shortening of any time in which to talk.

"Have you considered," he said, "that the king has never favored you? Have you considered another man would pay for loyalty?"

York was fat with more than flesh, Robert thought. He was swollen with intrigue. Brother to Cambridge, beheaded for treason. The duke was no better than the earl, except he had outlived him. Now death faced him and he was tormented. He had a conscience, he had spoken truly there. But wherefore had it waited so long to appear?

"You could advance," the duke said, riding close. "Your path upward would be shorter if I preferred you to the king. We could help each other then."

"I do not love gold," Robert said, "or traitors."

The duke pulled his horse away.

"You've a blunt tongue when it suits you," he said, "but I'll overlook it once. The young are merciless judges and must learn kindness from the cruelty of the years."

"Let no man misunderstand me, Your Grace," Robert said. "I speak what I think, and never trust my enemies."

"Then I am yours," the duke said, "from this time on."

No word passed between them until they camped for the night. The duke signified, shortly, that he would rest with the foreriders. Robert did not question this. The man was no coward, and he almost regretted how he'd spoken in the day; but then the traitor would have pestered him with honey in words, tempting him to taste of treason, which was all York offered any man.

He dismissed the matter and slept and dreamed of Constance passionately, an odd gift from heaven after a bitter day.

Chapter 28

ON OCTOBER 23rd, still without French attack, Robert and his men pushed on to secure passage over the river Canche, while the main body halted on the safer side for the night. He expected trouble but found only gently moving reeds in a swirl of dark current, and quiet deep forest beyond.

It was not sensible that the Frenchmen avoid battle so long, or continually throw advantage away. It exasperated Robert. He beat the forest for broken branches, lost gear, cropped grass, anything. He found nothing to indicate an army had passed, and so moved on, slipping along the narrow forest trail single file, with the duke just behind like a tail to his horse.

They camped that night in deep, brooding forest overhung with drifting mists. They lit a small, cautious fire, and hunched over it in turn. The flames beat feebly on their drawn faces, and chill beat at their unprotected backs. So must it be, Robert thought somberly, when a man was in his tomb. Thick, dark, damp and silent, ever silent, so a man could think on his sins. The Duke of York evidently thought on his. He sat like a condemned man and nibbled at cold bread.

A high wind came wailing in the trees. The mists billowed. The men looked continually over their shoulders, filled with apprehension, and talked in whispers. The whispers were sibilant in the darkness and beckoned Robert's attention. He frowned. And then it came to him: *this was the place of his dream!*

He felt a stirring within, a cold creeping, ready to see apparitions and hear warnings from beyond the grave. His Welsh blood waited for wonders, for beckoning ghosts, while he breathed fast, and faster, in a mystic fear. Yet the countess had taught him reason and denied the power of witches and wizards and calls from deep darkness not of this earth. He pushed aside foreboding and strove to maintain judicious balance in this eerie place. The confidence of his men depended on his calmness. They were Welsh, and doubly felt this knowledge of strange spirits. Their eyes moved continually as they whispered together of horrid things.

Then a sudden shout sent them all leaping up and scrambling for weapons. Robert lunged toward the sentry giving warning, and faced three horsemen emerging from white mist. He got one good look and dropped to his knee with his sword still naked in his hand.

The Duke of York expelled his breath, and sheathed his weapon.

"Now, Hal," he called, in a voice with a tremor, "you've overridden your lodgings this night. You must turn back."

For answer, the king flung him a glance and dismounted. His page followed suit and seized his horse, and after a moment the third man did the same.

"Your lodging, sire," the duke persisted, turning formal, "is on the hill and out of danger."

"I'll not turn my back to my enemy for any reason," the king said. "I'll sleep here tonight."

Before God! Robert thought, with horror and admiration, *he's as daring as they name him!* Then he bethought how many men he had, to guard the king of England, and swallowed and beckoned Wat.

"Every man does guard duty," he said, "out in the forest, a ring of sentries about the king."

"They're afraid of the forest," Wat said. "They say the ghosts are abroad."

"They'll be more afraid of me," Robert said grimly. "A ghost may pass them by in mercy, but I will not!"

King Henry turned his head a trifle, as if he wondered at the murmur, but made no inquiry. The duke began to help him off with his armor.

When Robert came through the glade from inspecting his sentry posts, King Henry sat by the fire on red-and-gold horse bardings, eating the meager fare they had to offer, stale bread and walnuts. He seemed content to pick at this. The bowmen nearest watched him furtively, nervous of royalty on one side and ghosts on the other. Silence was thick, except for the snap of the fire and the soughing of the wind like souls crying out.

All Robert could think of now was Frenchmen leaping from the forest and finding the king of England by a watchfire with a handful of men to defend him. The French were near. He knew it. The ominous feel of their closeness would not be shaken off. There was in him the same chilling intensity of the dream at Graville. The lion was sleeping and could not wake to the true danger. Robert walked continually around the glade with his uneasiness, circling the camp while he crawled with this walking with peril for companion. Once he crossed directly through the clearing. The fire was hardly more than a glow. The two men who had accompanied the king were asleep. The king also, lying on his stomach on the gaudy horse bardings, his arms under his head, his sleeping face to the dying fire. Only two men were awake: Wat, sitting crosslegged in half a drowse at a distance, and the Duke of York with his pig's eyes bright, pulling a corner of the barding higher over the king.

He looked up as Robert halted by them.

"Nay," he said, "I do not think on slaying him, though it were the best chance I ever had. He has not slept like this since . . ." A fat, jeweled hand waved listlessly. "He is ever sleepless at night, yet for your guarding, he is content and sleeps. Is your name Percy, like Hotspur? How should he be such a hero, when he fears the hours of night?"

"It may be he knows his friends walk then, Your Grace, and carry weapons," Robert answered softly.

The duke flushed.

"He was wounded at Shrewsbury," York said, "and called for his childhood nurse! Sixteen, and he must have his nurse to comfort him!"

"And she rode into a battlefield, therefore," Robert said, "making nothing of peril to answer him."

"She was well rewarded," the duke retorted. "He was scarcely crowned when he gave her an annuity. Johanna Waryn's a rich woman now, all for a little wound of his face."

"That almost killed him," Robert finished. His blue eyes glinted. "I took an arrow in the chest, and never rested till I got back to my lady and she put salves on it and made much of me, and I was seventeen."

The duke stood up. "I might have befriended you," he said, "but we are enemies. You have the king's sword and think you have his favor besides, since he sleeps while you stand by to guard him. I say he trusts no one."

"I am not a dog," Robert said, "to wag for golden scraps from a royal table."

The duke clenched his fists, and his face flushed redder. Yet he was so versed in treachery, his voice stayed soft though he raged.

"Stay a while," he invited. "Let us talk now of Lollards and their fate when they're discovered."

"My mother was Welsh," Robert said. "They are dark and vengeful women, and they give their natures to their sons."

"You dare to threaten me! You dare this!" He almost trembled with rage, but his voice was a whisper still. "There was a lion in the Tower menagerie. When it was young, it was pretty and mewed; but when it grew, it was dangerous and roared. So they killed it."

"It is the nature of lions to turn fierce when they're baited," Robert said. "If he be caged, then he may be killed, but if he be free, Your Grace, let the hunter beware."

The fire snapped, and sparks flew up as wood fell.

Robert glanced to Wat to be sure he was awake, then turned and went into the forest again to hearten his guards in their places, for ghosts and witches scratched all about and it was a measure of their courage that they stayed among these supernatural things. And in this weird, dripping wood full of sighings and movings and swaying mist, it seemed as if his mother strove to talk with him, as if he had mistaken her warning, as if her concern was for her child and never kings and nations. Once he shivered violently as she reached from darkness and touched him. Yet what was to be feared from her?

He was full uneasy and moved on, and would not go back to the clearing again. Then, somewhere in the endless pit of night, Wat came out and whistled.

"Wat?" Robert asked, starting.

"The same," came the hoarse familiar voice. "Stand still, sir, but talk and I'll find you in this blackness."

"Did you leave the duke alone with the king?"

"He's asleep and snoring. You can hear him from here. You should be sleeping also." Wat's disembodied voice spoke from behind a tree.

"Not while the king is by the fire," Robert said, feeling Wat's presence beside him.

"The king will need you more tomorrow," Wat said.

"So you feel it too?"

"They're near," Wat agreed. "If a Frenchman kills me, I've cheated the hangman."

"Go to the devil," Robert said.

"I will, undoubtedly," Wat agreed, "but do you go to sleep. I'll keep these guards from tumbling witches for want of better fare."

"He hasn't snored," Robert said suddenly, missing the sound.

"Turned on his side," Wat suggested.

"Or turned on the king."

Robert hastened back to the clearing and stood at the edge for a moment. The king had turned his face away from the fire, no more. His two companions slept, sprawled out. The duke was by the fire on his back. Robert walked closer and stared down on him, suspicious. The duke breathed softly, and did not move. Robert flung a few sticks of wood on the fire and it blazed up again, to warm the king against this ground chill.

Robert looked longingly at his saddlebags and blanket and wished he could lie down, but he was now so tired that if he stretched out he would not wake for thunder or clarion horns. He dared not risk it. He picked up the blanket and flung it about him and sat well away from the fire, so that the warmth would not beguile him to sleep, with his back set firmly against a tree and the clearing before him. He drowsed.

The wind was rising still. The mists tried to linger among the trees, but the wind swooped on them and tore them and set the rags to flying madly like dancing ghosts. A shrieking began in the treetops, as of women suddenly bereaved. Robert was reminded sharply of a certain raid, when he brought back the bodies of their slain tied to horses, and the Welshwomen ran out to lift the heads of the corpses to find husband, or brother, or son. Their wails had been like screeching metal. . . . So the wind wailed now. From his exhaustion, Robert listened with closed eyes, and heard the message clearly. It was his mother, it seemed, and she howled in the treetops for *revenge*, as if he had not taken her warning, and it was now too late for more than this.

Yet the night was without incident, and in the morning a detachment from the van came thundering up to find and protect the king, and Robert moved out quickly with his archers to seek the Frenchmen he'd sensed all the wild and wind-tossed night. He found them. Quickly. Where the forest broke into fields on the banks of the Ternoise River.

There on the opposite bank the smoke of a thousand fires rose whipping into the sky. A thousand banners fluttered. And Robert saw how it must have been. The armies had marched parallel down two separate valleys. The scouts along the sides had never met. For three days at least they had been marching down the valleys side by side, drums and trumpets silent, to the rendezvous now made.

Wat said, "I did not know there were so many in all the world! London's smaller than this camp!"

"Stay here and watch," Robert said. "Let no man be seen. I'll bring this news myself."

He galloped madly back, leaping from his horse as he burst into the clearing. The king, half armored, jerked around. The duke dropped what he held in his hands.

"The French?" the king inquired calmly.

"There are three miles and a river between the armies," Robert said.

The king moved again, his unfastened armor clanking loosely.

"It's the will of God," he said, wearily.

The king's companions resumed fastening his armor, hastily now. A page rushed the royal warhorse forward. His red bardings fluttered like scarlet wings, and the embroidered golden leopards of England glittered in sunlight that pierced the trees in long pale shafts. The horse wore a silver chamfron-and-pike on his face, and two long tassels dangling at his mouth.

"Change my saddle to the dark nag," the king said, indicating Robert's worn-out horse where it had stopped.

"It's no better than a sumpterhorse, and half starved besides," the Duke of York protested. The king turned his head to him. "Sire," the duke stammered, "it's lived on grass and leaves . . ."

"The more reason the forerider should have Bay Cornwall," the king said, "for he's had grain while lesser horses went without. Robert Heartless, put your saddle on my horse, and I'll use yours till I can get another charger for myself."

Robert murmured, "Sire," and loosened his saddle and cast it over Bay Cornwall, scarlet bardings and all. He tightened the girth, and from habit, patted his saddlebags. He stiffened, and hesitated for a fraction of a moment. Wat had saddled his nag this morning. Wat would not have noticed, but there was a bulky object missing from the meager possessions kept in the saddlebags. An oblong. A Bible. With a name inscribed. Who had been in the clearing? The king, the duke, the royal companions. Wat had come into the forest once. Had there been opportunity to seize the Bible then? The duke might have observed the habit of . . . The other men scarce knew the forerider, and would never suspect heresy. It was the king or the duke. It was York.

York said, "How long does it take a man to change a saddle?"

Robert knew well enough what he meant.

"I do but acquaint myself with this charger, Your Grace," he said, very smoothly, "for there are some who will never change masters."

The king looked between the two of them very quickly.

Robert swung up to the saddle.

"And then," York said, "there are others who must change masters, whether they will or no."

Robert spurred the charger and it dashed away, strong and full of fire, a Spanish horse trained for fighting, a prince's ransom on four hooves, wrapped in scarlet and gold.

At the river the men stared at the horse, and Wat reported the French had left, moving quickly for such a host, so that some commander was efficient among them. A few of the tall conical tents had been left behind, standing among the trees, abandoned to the speed of their going.

Robert forded the river openly, tempting arrows to see if they would fly at him; but the French had vanished as they had been spirits, leaving behind but the litter of camping men and the dead bones of wood that had made fires.

With the scarlet bardings of Bay Cornwall dripping river water, Robert began to trail them.

"The battle's too close for the fat one," Wat commented once, after turning to see if York would appear at all. "He hangs back with the king now."

"And with my Bible," Robert said. "He got it last night when we talked in the forest. Nay, do not look so, it's not your fault but mine for touching it and teaching him I had it with me."

"A duke dies as fast as any man," Wat said, his face like an animal's mask, "when an arrow flies false in battle. Or should he die now?"

"If there's damage, he's done it," Robert said, "and open murder will not help me, but hang you. I think he'll hold it for a threat, instead. Is that bush moving?"

"Wind, no more," Wat said. "Tonight I'll rob that duke."

"He'll sleep with the vanguard, well ringed with sentries," Robert said, "and never venture near me till he's decided how to use it. The French must be werewolves to vanish in a morning."

"A fat man can vanish as easily," Wat said.

"The king needs his commanders now," Robert said, "and York's a good one. I've heard of his campaigns in Wales. Let it be. I'll set it right myself, if time be left us for it."

He rode on grimly. It was true enough he should have left the Bible, nor been stubborn to refuse for that he was forced against his will for his life's sake. God was in heaven, and not in a book. Well, a man learns all things too late. The Bible was gone and his name was writ in it. He had only contempt for his own risk even now, but he feared a finger pointing beyond him back to London. It could be said that Constance made a heretic of him, and this used against the merchant; and would her old man stand firm against such calumnies? The old are timorous.

And if the duke said, *Betray the king, or see the merchant's maid die at the stake for heresy?*

The duke did not sleep by them that night, as Robert predicted. A lion was a danger to the hunter until his cage be ready.

Chapter 29

THEY WERE in hilly country now, and Robert mistrusted this with the French so close. When yet another steep rose up, he galloped to peer cautiously over the crest. And found the French a second time! They swarmed below like bees, all but crawling on each other. A great buzzing rose from them as they settled on plowed land, but the beating of his heart was louder now, and faster. They were not marching or moving below, except to stand together, and fight. He seized his lower lip with his teeth, and suddenly his belly contracted hard and he went weak and sweating.

He knew it to be fear, rank, coward's fear; the kind he'd spat for, noticed in other men. All his life he had lived in the shadow of death, but always in Wales there had been a valley to flee down, a mountain to clamber up, a way to hit and a place to run. All his life he had lived by the strategy that had governed Wales. *Never fight a pitched battle.* Now it was before him, and he was trembling and cold, with panic rising fast. He fought it back. It was stand and fight; there was no place to hide, and no way to retreat, and if they did, what was Harfleur but walls to bottle them up for starvation? Nay, it was not for him. His death was waiting below, and his hands shook with the knowledge. Death came to all, but not leering and pointing the place, the inescapable place. There, by that thicket? There, by that wall? Where will you lie, young sir? Choose it now. The bitter pain ate his belly until he could have cried out.

But a man is as he's raised, and as the blood put in him. *Fear's a chained dog*, he thought, *set to cry alarum, as he should.*

He had sworn he'd take a short life, if only it be a merry sort. He thought of twenty years, the last five those of grace, since he should have died in Wales.

His hand hurt grievously. The pain came through the blinding fear. He had reached up and grasped a tree branch overhead. With an effort, he unclenched his fingers. He would not wipe the sweat of his face, to call attention to his plight. Wat was on the other side of the tree. At least his weakness had not been seen. He was Robert Heartless yet.

Slowly the griping in his belly went, slowly. His shoulders sagged down into place from where he'd held them hunched against the blows of fear. He shrugged them, and found the fear had left a gift. His exhaustion had dropped away, and was replaced by lightness and clear thought.

He set his hand on the pommel of his saddle lightly, and looked down to where death waited; and saw not his grave, but a battlefield.

Three villages, northwest, northeast and another south of both, nearest to Robert's hill. Within that triangle lay the fate of England. He smiled a little, gently, and turned and galloped down. He pulled his horse up before York, blocking his path.

"Your Grace," he said with a fixed smile, all gaiety, "a full fifty thousand Frenchmen lie beyond that hill."

The duke raised his hand. Row on row behind him the van marched to a halt. The duke stared at Robert's bright look.

"French?" he asked, as if he could not believe they had caught up at last. "Marching ahead of us, you say?"

"Nay, Your Grace," Robert said. "Camped across the road."

The duke wiped his forehead of new-sprung sweat, forgetting his mailed hand, and left a bleeding scratch.

"I'll send to the king," he murmured, and after that they waited.

Robert's fine horse, which had been the king's, fidgeted at delay, and pawed the ground.

"So, gently, sir," he admonished it. "There will be action soon, and well if you know French. Your next master will speak it for his native tongue."

A muscle jumped in York's jaw, and shook the fat.

"Mayhap he'll read his Bible to you," Robert added cheerfully. "If they be writ in French."

York's head turned sharply. The shaft had hit. For if they all died, of what use was the fatal evidence that York had stolen? There was no time to seek for heretics. Robert felt release. Excitement rose now. He could not wait for the battle. Let it begin! Let it begin!

"How many did you say?" York inquired again.

"Fifty thousand, never less, and maybe more," Robert said.

The duke sat heavily on his horse, his mouth open and sagging. Little puffs of steam shot into the cold air and vanished before his face.

Now the king came, with a party of nobles, galloping by. Robert turned and followed after them. Under the trees, the king surveyed the field below. Robert watched to see him blench, though he'd not spit for cowardice again. He'd learned it came to every man. But the king's face did not change.

"There's a pride of French," he commented at last, and turned to his lords and ordered battle formation.

The command was passed down. The yells grew fainter.

"I would we had ten thousand more English archers," some noble said.

"You speak like a fool, Sir Walter," the king replied candidly. "It is God's will that only these be with me."

His face was open, he moved more light, and it seemed King Henry was relieved that the search was over and the dodging done. His nobles did not all seem as happy, however, and muttered to one another as they rode down the hill again.

The king went to a level stretch of land where winter wheat was growing, and stopped in the midst of it on his white horse, facing the army. He stood in the saddle, to be better seen. And had all their attention.

"Bowmen of England!" he shouted, "I bid you remember Crécy and Poitiers!"

The words rolled back, on other men's tongues, till it reached the last in the ranks.

"I bid you remember the many times England has plundered France and sailed home fat!"

The sound rolled back, like an ebbing tide. Henry's face was bold, his manner commanding. Here was no weakling king, but a warrior.

"I bid you think on your wives, and mothers, and children!"

The words were passed.

Henry had none to think on, neither wife, nor sweetheart, nor mother, nor daughter.

"You will win back to them!" he shouted passionately.

Then he stood as tall as he could in the saddle, armored except for his helm, leaning his weight on the pommel.

"In this fight," he shouted, for all to hear and note his vow, "I mean to win or die! England shall never pay ransom for me!"

And so he cast his life into the balance. If his yeomen must die, so must he. He took his stand there in the winter wheat on the side of his poor men. Let his nobles ransom themselves if the battle went ill. He would die with the archers of England!

All that long, gray afternoon Robert kept watch at the crest of the hill, borne high on emotion and determined to follow his king, living or dying. He cared nothing for the battlefield below and looked on it contemptuously. He discerned the banners of Constable d'Albret, commanding the French host, and of Marshal Bouciquaut, of the dukes of Bourbon and Orléans, those mortal enemies united strangely here, and many others who'd contend for command and raise confusion; but nowhere among the multitude of banners could he find the royal arms, the leavening in the mass below. Neither the king nor the dauphin appeared to be with his army, and mad or dying as they were, this was their place.

In the English army some wept, some kneeled with priests, some laughed, some gambled, some brooded silently in the bitter freezing wind that whipped them all, but none deserted. This was the measure of Henry the Fifth, by the Grace of God, King of England, that men who could gain nothing but lose all would stand and die for him.

"They're dispersing," Wat said, breaking Robert's thoughts.

Could the French be such fools as to rest for the night and not engage the weary English immediately? What a patchwork of command they had, to let the chance slip away. Now it seemed to Robert this army was a huge, inert body without a head.

"Campfires," Wat said, with mild surprise.

"And rain again," Robert said, and pulled his mantle hood over his head.

"Then we'll fight in mud," Wat said with anger. "Cannot a man die but in a pig's trough? I hope the rain will leak into the fat duke's armor if he is not already in the French camp buying free."

"He never went down this hill," Robert said positively. "There, more campfires. They'll not fight tonight."

He was almost disappointed; keyed for battle, willing an end to this indecision. Then he crossed himself quickly, for he was wishing his life away the faster. There was no hope for them, six thousand against fifty thousand; starvelings against well-fed troops; an invader against men on their own land. Yet he was eager to engage. King Henry would be among them, and not safely in the rear.

"Go down," he said to Wat, "and tell them the French are settling for the night."

Wat returned with the order that the English host must ride to the southernmost village below, and Robert moved down accordingly, following a white road that gleamed in a soft blur underfoot to guide them. The vanguard spread out to become the right flank of the English army as it formed before the village called Maisoncelles, in the open, almost within touch of the French left. In the pouring rain, Wat stood by Robert, peering to the brightly lit tents of the adversary.

"I make it four flight-shots," he said.

"I make it too close," Robert said. "They'll disturb our sleep."

The men behind him laughed grimly and stared too, to where the enemy made holiday. Their lines roared with shouting to servants and hailing of friends. There were sheltered fires everywhere to show that they had warmth. And the French horses neighed continually as they were led to and fro in a shadow play before the fires to keep them from standing in cold, driving rain.

"Take shelter all," Robert said. "There are the woods and fields to bed in. Sleep where you will, but keep your face to the enemy."

There was some coarse jesting as to what could be expected if a man turned his back to the Frenchmen, and then they cast about for shelter in the hedgerows. Robert placed his shield across two low branches of a leafless tree, and in this dank shelter he squatted down with Wat and ate the last rations that remained. They would fight empty on the morrow. The men wandered about continually in the mud, trying this shelter and that; and in the midst of black peril Robert heard snatches of the interminable archers' argument on which was best, the feather of goose or swan . . . or peacock, when it could be had?

What did a man remember, the night before he died?

The rain dripped steadily, and made him think of the Thames and its lapping. The memory came to him of a night the household sat up late for the sweetness of the summer air. The merchant and his greyhound rested on the steps listening to the lapping Thames, and watching the moon on the water. Robert and Constance had wandered out on the quay, holding hands, with London all around them. The flaring beacon was lit on the tower of St. Mary-le-Bow, guiding in late travelers, the wonder of London Bridge arched over the river, with its disproportionate arches, the chapel and stores upon it borne over the flood along with the heads of traitors on pikes. The bulk of Westminster Palace loomed across the river, and the wood noted for its highwaymen, and the river again in the sweep of the half-circle, and then the great White Tower surrounded by light, for the king's ships were built there by torchlight and sunlight. Hammering resounded continually, like London pulsing with life. A night wind wound around them; and the Thames was aglitter with the insubstantial silver treasure of the moon. Constance played a little on her rebec, a haunting air.

"Your cheeks are wet," Robert accused her, seeing the gleam on her face.

"Here's weeping for happiness," she said, "at meeting you."

"Your eyes will turn red," he warned her.

She put her rebec by, and wiped her eyes with the hem of her gown. "Here's vanity," she said, "to be clear-eyed for you."

"Red-eyed or not," he said, "there's none in London to compare with you."

"Here's insanity," she said, "to love you and know you will not stay."

Then her father came walking heavily down the quay.

"I hear no more music," he said, "and am come to find why, though I know well enough. That's kissing enough for any maid when she's betrothed to another. Inside, all. The night grows damp. The air's unhealthy. The wind's shifting and bringing a smell from a slaughter-house. Besides, it's unlucky to sit in moonlight."

"Why?" Constance had to know, still clinging to Robert's hand.

"When you kiss a man by moonlight, the moon grows jealous and sends madness."

"Oh, God," Constance said, "let's run for the house."

But she walked, and looked up at the moon before they entered.

"Hide your face, Madam Moon," she declared. "I'll kiss him again before I sleep and be sent to Bedlam in the morning!"

Her father swung his arm and whacked her bottom so hard she shot into the kitchen with a shriek.

"My bottom," Wat said distinctly, recalling Robert to France and reality, "is as wet as if I sat in a river. I do not mind cold or rain or hunger, but I like my behind warm and dry. It's tender."

"You surely kept it tenderly in London," Robert said. "Whenever I looked you had it resting in the kitchen."

Wat said dreamily, "Remember the pigeons in peppery custard, all wrapped in buttery crust? You never ate them, for that the doves were all your friends. We used to wait for yours to come back to the kitchen untouched."

"I wish I had such a pie now," Robert said.

"And the fruttures, the fig fruttures in a batter with spices," Wat breathed gustily. "We got the figs of the Gallies who lived in the block past the custom house. The best figs."

Robert recalled the cook flinging dough upon a flat pan to make small flat round cakes of a morning, all full of crushed figs. They were served with honey. Robert had considered them too sweet and pushed them aside. Blaunchette had filled herself to bursting with the fig fruttures he had fed her. Now he regretted every one.

And this, he thought with bitter humor, was the answer to his question. What did a man think of the night before a battle, his last night on the earth? Not of great deeds, or mighty things. He thought of his love, the place that could be home, and food.

And the things that he regretted. The walk with Constance by the Tower of London after mass, to watch the keeper of the zoo there bring out the famous white bear.

"We cannot have you leaving," Constance said, "without a sight of our white bear."

They watched as he was led shambling out by a rope tied about his neck. The keeper got in the boat and the bear leaped into the water and swam behind with his white coat awash. In the middle of the river the keeper leaned on the oars and the bear dove and fished, sporting in the water before the gaping crowd gathered to see.

"Is it not a fine thing?" Constance asked. "The bear gets his exercise, is happy and will live long therefore, yet costs nothing to feed. Would we were all so carefree as this bear."

"I had rather be dead," he'd answered.

"Wherefore?"

"Why," he'd said, "he wears a rope and goes not by his own devising, but his keeper's. I will wear no tether and have no keeper and answer no will but my own."

Well, he thought wearily, perhaps it was best I said it. She will remember it of me, and be content with her present estate. But he regretted every word. He'd wear her tether now. Too late.

Rain fell without ceasing. Robert huddled against the cold, and could not warm himself.

Wat coughed, not as before, from the affliction in his chest, but warningly, as a man about to broach a question he felt he should not ask. Robert waited, staring at the bright tents of the French, listening to their gaiety with morose resentment. Wat shifted slightly in their mean shelter under the upturned shield and coughed again.

"There is one thing," he began, and halted, and then burst out like the spurt in the storm that soaked them anew and almost hid the other camp, "one thing that I would know . . . I never dared ask before, but . . . you have a scar on the back of your neck . . . the back . . ."

"I got it running," Robert said, to add a touch of mischief in their misery, ". . . but not fast enough."

He felt the suspended disbelief and relented, for Wat was one who needed perfection in idols, as he saw perfection—an image of bravery, with naught else a thing to matter.

"From a quinten," Robert finished.

"Ah," Wat said with relief, almost shouting above the storm, "I never considered *that.*"

And so he was secure again, his hero unmarred. *And I,* Robert thought, *what do I seek?* When he was young, he held to legends and fixed his imagination on the brilliant and gay Prince Hal; but now he was older and had met King Hal, and found him different, flawed like a gem, with an uneven temperament hiding the brilliance of a striving soul that battled with his too-hot nature. Yet he triumphed often, the man victorious over the animal. That was something. That he strove. And more to be admired, perhaps, than easy victory.

Wat cleared his throat. He wanted the story, clearly.

"They set up a quinten," Robert said, "on a flat field outside the castle."

He saw it again, a tall pole like a maypole, with a crosspiece like a paddle set edgewise to spin around at the top a little above the head of a mounted man. The broad end was the mark at which to ride full tilt with a lance. A man who missed was a laughingstock; but a man who hit must ride for his life, for a bag of sand was hung at the handle and lunged around with the spinning of the paddle, to take a man at the back of the neck.

"My horse stumbled," Robert said, "the sandbag knocked me to the ground and split open the back of my head at the same time. I was senseless for half a day and in bed for a week with a headache."

He rubbed the back of his neck reflectively. It was wet like the rest of him, but his fingers slipped on the smooth scar tissue. And what was life but a riding at a quinten? He who lost, vanished. He who hit took the consequences of success, an unseen hurtling danger coming from behind.

He blinked, and yawned. He was numb with cold and wet and exhaustion. What he would give for the warm bed in which he'd healed from the quinten. *That* had been good, and he'd cursed it when he had it. A pity he'd not live longer than another day; he had learned much, and all of it . . . wasted. . . . His head dropped forward, and he thought of a hot flame, a warm, hot . . .

He woke with a start to Wat's rough shaking. *Sleeping before a battle*, he thought fuzzily.

"The French?" he asked, and shook his head to wake himself.

"A herald," Wat said, "sent for you. The king commands your presence."

"The king!"

"Maybe he wants his horse back," Wat suggested irreverently.

Robert peered up at the drenched herald, and behind him a man with a lantern, showing the muddy ground and two pairs of legs by its light.

The Bible, he thought clearly. York could not let his revenge go. He chose the last moment. Why?

Chapter 30

THE KING, in this peasant's hut? It shocked Robert just to see the miserable building with a dripping tree overhanging it, and mud chopped by horse hooves all around. The guard pulled the door open and instantly acrid smoke escaped from the hovel, blinding Robert for a moment. Then he saw, squinting against it, that a fire was burning in the center of the dirt-floored room, with nobles crowding around, setting shadows tall against the wall behind.

"Out!" the king said, over their murmurs. "Out!"

The lords turned, and milled, and filed out sulkily, glancing at Robert standing in the light of the herald's lantern, seeing his knees more clearly than his face, except for York, the short fat man coming last of all, and lingeringly, looking vengeful.

The guard gestured and Robert stepped inside, head high. There was no softness in him now. The door closed behind him. The smoke swirled and settled, and then flowed upward thickly toward the ceiling hole, spreading out at the roof and clinging there when it could not all force through.

Robert made obeisance, and was gestured to his feet.

The king paced back and forth, stopping now and then to stare at Robert openly before moving on again. At length he paused with decision. He had made up his mind. Robert braced himself.

"My brother Clarence," the king said unexpectedly, "said you could be trusted."

He stared at Robert for an answer, but got none.

"Yet my cousin of York," the king said, "thinks you cannot, though God witnesseth *he* knows little enough of loyalty."

The king stepped closer, peering sharply at Robert's impassive face.

"I have never trusted men who do not show their feelings, perhaps because mine will not be concealed. What's in you? I'll put a question fairly, and give me fair answer in return. How far would you obey me?"

"As far as you'd command me, sire," Robert said.

"Others have sworn so, and betrayed me in the very breath of swearing."

"If you want words," Robert said, stiff-necked, "I'll give them. I swear it, by St. Anne, by St. Catherine, by the Holy—"

The king held up his hand, and showed his anger.

"I've had enough of swearing," he said, "and your tone betrays contempt." The king paced, biting his lips, then turned and faced Robert squarely. "Will you be loyal to me till morning?"

"I will be loyal so long as I live."

"Till morning, then," the king said. "That's the span of your life. You saw the multitude of the French? What will you say to that?"

"The night is passing swiftly, the battle's in the morning, and an old man is a pitiful thing."

"Would you go among those French tonight, alone?"

"I will go where you command me, sire," Robert said.

The king stared hard at him.

"Once," he said, "another man did these things for me."

Scrope, Robert thought.

"I trusted him. I . . ."

He paced, memories aroused he obviously would not remember. The last friend of his boyhood, dying under the headsman's sword for treason. King Henry swung around almost savagely. "Say I am proud, and the truth's out. It goes ill with me to beg!"

Robert waited, impassive.

The king reached into a sleeve impatiently and snatched out a parchment hidden there.

"None of my nobles know of this," he said. His eyes were bright as with a fever. "This is blank, with my seal attached. Make a treaty with the French. I'll come to terms if they let me pass."

He flung the parchment at Robert like a stone, meant to cut and wound not the receiver but the thrower. Robert put it in his cote-hardie.

"Agree I will return Harfleur," he said. "Agree I will pay damages. Agree I will leave France. Get me in return passage to Calais. I'll save my bowmen if I may. I have led them here for my ambition, and this is my deadly sin."

"My gift is with a sword, sire," Robert said. "I have never been an envoy and am but a squire, which they may resent."

"I know how to reward a man," the king said with an edge of harshness, like a man being forced to give an earldom by necessity.

"I'm no bought man," Robert said. His Welsh blood rose and pounded in his ears.

"Hot blood?" the king inquired, startled. "From cold Wales?" He smiled unexpectedly, and then he nodded. "Clarence swore you could be trusted, and commended you when I had my back to a wall. He's a judge of men. He's surer than I, who pick friends who betray me. Let us see if he's always right. Let us see if you return, and not bargain with the Frenchmen for yourself and stay with them."

"If I do not come back," Robert said, "it will be because I'm dead."

"Then get to your dying," the king said, "and do not trouble me more."

York was standing by with some others around a fire. He came swiftly toward Robert when he saw him emerge.

He still has the Bible, Robert thought. *He still hopes for a bargain. Or waits for higher stakes.*

"Wherefore did he send for you," the duke demanded, "out of all the army?"

Robert snapped his fingers to a horsegroom, and the man ran to bring Bay Cornwall in his soaked red drapes.

"Wherefore did he send for you?" the duke asked again, from between his teeth.

"Your Grace," Robert said, mounting his horse and gesturing the horsegroom out of hearing, "ask the king for his reasons."

"Beware Henry's secrets," the duke said. "Men have a way of dying with them."

"Your Grace," Robert said, "do not threaten a man this night. We'll all be dead by morning!"

And contemptuously he reined his horse about and rode toward the fires of France, with a fire in him also, that King Henry who was a proud man should swallow his pride and sue for passage to save his common men, these archers in hedgerows all about. As for the king, he'd rather die, he was that fierce proud, but for these miserable creatures huddling under trees. . . . What king before him had treasured archers? None but loved their men in armor, with long pedigree and short loyalty. Yet under each of these bushes, in each muddy wet freezing bowman struggling to keep his longbow dry though he were drenched, in each of these was a little flame of loyalty. It was dark and muddy, but in himself Robert could see the little flames alight all through the fields, bright enough to illumine the pages of history. *Historians, say we died with honor,* he admonished them as Bay Cornwall slipped and slid like a ship in wild weather toward the lines of France.

He made no attempt to hide his passage over the plowed field deep in mud and stones; and at the first campfire of the French he halted haughtily and seemed once more the lord who had cowed Nesle.

"I will talk with the Constable d'Albret," he said, no more.

He was wet and muddy, but he rode a Spanish warhorse with gold leopards on its filthy bardings, there was ermine on his sleeves, and his sword hilt gleamed out gold. The men there gestured backwards into the moving multitude of shouting men, for after all, he was alone. He saw that on their faces; and rode deeper into the mass, under the steady roaring of their noise, until it seemed all France surrounded him and he was buried and drowning in Frenchmen, forcing his way among them in thick mud, among leaping pages and slipping men trying to hurry with wine and food, and horses led up and down to warm them. Every man was busy at work or pleasure, and none took notice of Robert despite the golden leopards of England, until he asked for the constable again.

Then a great tent was pointed out to him, where it was pitched in the midst of the host. It was high and conical and the banner over it hung limp in the downpour, but a fire was lit within so that the tent glowed like a giant lantern. Robert dismounted by it, gave Bay Cornwall to some passer-by and bade him lead the animal, identified himself haughtily to the guards as the envoy of England, and demanded to see the constable.

The guards were stupefied, but it *was* a Spanish horse, and it *was* a gold-hilted sword, and his French was aristocratic. The chief of the guards vanished doubtfully inside the tent and became another shadow on its running sides. Robert waited in the rain that washed over his face. Over the gurgling of the downpour came the sounds of laughter from inside, interspersed with curses at the vagaries of fortune. They were dicing for the nobles of England who would be taken prisoner on the morrow. A roar of excitement as some important lord was won. They clamored with guesses at the ransom he'd bring.

Robert's eyes drifted about the camp, or as much as he could see between the bright tents and leaping campfires—shielded under blackened wooden roofs on four poles—by which the men sought to warm the camp and dry themselves.

Then his eyes came to a high-sided wagon with two wheels, all painted scarlet. On the sides, crudely sketched, were golden leopards, in a parody of Bay Cornwall's drapes except the beasts were crowned upon the wagon. It was plain enough. When they captured the king, they intended to ride him through Paris in this cart. Robert's mouth twisted, and he thought how Henry's face had been when he sat on the white horse in the field of springing winter wheat. The cart would never be used.

Then the tent flap was flung back, and his attention came there. The guard gestured and Robert stepped inside, to stand before a crowd of French nobility in sable and ermine and cloth of gold, all staring with interest. The air was close and warm with the smell of unwashed humanity and wine. Some were old men, some were young, but all were flushed with drinking. There was plenty of straw underfoot to keep their boots from the mud, plenty of wine inside to keep them heated, and a stout tent overhead to keep them dry.

Since none spoke, Robert did.

"I would see the Constable d'Albret," he said.

A man in cloth of gold flung down some dice and faced him.

"We have no desire to treat with England," he said contemptuously. "When we tried, the Usurper of England laughed in our face. Now we shall spit in his."

"My liege lord may yet be bought off," Robert said, with uncompromising stiffness. If they expected compliments, they'd get none of him.

"We buy no one off," the constable said. "We are determined on this fight."

"Hear him at least, my lord," someone said, and was hushed by a glare from d'Albret.

"My liege lord is willing to leave France," Robert said.

A roar of laughter greeted this, and the constable waited impatiently until it subsided.

"He will leave France indeed," the constable said, ". . . after he pays his ransom."

". . . and return Harfleur," Robert said as if the other had not spoken.

"We shall take that back when your army is crushed."

"My lord Constable," began the interrupting voice urgently.

The constable ignored it.

"There is an English garrison there," Robert reminded him, "and the citizens have all sworn fealty to King Henry."

"We'll wait outside till the garrison starves. As for the citizens, they'll swear again, to King Charles."

"My liege lord," Robert said, "is a merciful man, and would avoid bloodshed."

"His bloodshed."

"Therefore," Robert continued stonily, "he sends this message. Leave him in peace, and he will go in peace. Yet he will go to Calais, if it must be over your host."

"What? A cornered mouse offers to make terms with the cat?"

"My lord Constable," began the insistent voice again.

D'Albret turned angrily. "I command here," he said. "Never forget it!"

"I would have audience with the King of France," Robert said quickly. It did not suit his purpose to have them brawl and settle the matter now. Let it rankle overnight and grow.

"He is not here," the constable said, annoyed.

"I ask audience with the Dauphin."

"He is not here."

"My lord Constable," the contending commander said, mocking, "this envoy is getting information of you cheaply!"

The constable's eyes narrowed and he looked peevish, both at advice and playing a fool.

"Get you gone, envoy," he said, "and be glad we do not hang you."

"Say your prayers, Englishman," called a young and drunken voice.

Robert turned at the tent flap. "Do not neglect yours," he advised. "Our king is with us, and every man will die before he leaves his sovereign. Can any of you say this?"

A couple of the drunker lords laughed, but the older of the men looked sober. Robert swung round in the straw underfoot and stepped out into the deep mud.

No attempt was made to stop him as he rode back through the vast throng in the dark hours of the night; yet when he approached the line of English huddled half frozen under ice-caked branches that clicked in the constant wind, he was obliged to identify himself repeatedly.

He dismounted, empty of hope in the failure of his mission, before the peasant hut, and had to walk through archers standing all about in the rain. Their leather jackets were black and shining with wet in the light of torches they carried. He could hear their teeth chatter in the bitter cold. The horses they held were half drowned and stood hopelessly, tails to the wind.

The guard at the door let him pass into the smoky hut after one look to see who he was. A blast of air announced him, and a puff of smoke escaped.

King Henry looked up from where he sat on a stool by the fire, a book in both his hands. The door closed, the smoke swirled and Robert knelt in the midst of it, and then rose as quickly.

"I am no envoy, sire," he stated bluntly, to the questioning look. "I will not dissemble. I can but say I will this or will not that, and defend my opinion. So it is when I bear another man's word. They would not treat with me."

Unexpectedly, Henry smiled and stood, and put the book gently on the stool, back up but open to his place.

"It is the will of heaven," Henry said, and his face was clear and bold and untroubled. "I will go forward with clear conscience. Fling the parchment to the fire."

Robert did so, and they watched it burn in silence. Then the king began his incessant pacing, and questioned Robert on details of the French encampment and all that had passed.

"Jesu!" Henry exclaimed once. "You have forgot nothing. The mud's deep, and your stallion could only fight his way, pitching up and down? That will hamper them. I'll dismount my archers and let them skip around mired Frenchmen on armed horses. Now, their command's divided. Who questioned the constable? Describe him."

Robert did, and Henry chuckled; then walked the length of the room and turned to show he had no joy of anything. His face was suddenly tense again, wracked with nerves and exhaustion, sleepless-ness, hunger, premonitions, as if he saw the end of a reign but barely begun.

. . . as the snow at his coronation, full of fury and quickly gone . . .

Back and forth he went, from a pallet in one corner to a pile of silver armor in the other. Robert's eye studied the mail. Atop all was the royal fighting helmet, encircled with a crown of gold adorned with many gems and one great ruby, the ruby of the Black Prince, who had never lived to be a king. The French would send all their weight against the man who wore that crown and ruby.

"Sire," Robert said, "if you would give me leave to wear your helm tomorrow—"

"And be killed in my place? I'll wear my own crown, I've been troubled enough for the right. I have another plan for you, since it seems you can be trusted. Outside are two hundred archers, the same you took over the Somme at Nesle. Your own knaves are coming in from the hedges. Take all this night to the woods at Tramecourt, where the French must pass you when they march. Hold there during the battle. When we are overwhelmed, force through the fringe of their rear guard and get you to Calais, and warn the garrison, for the French may think to seize it back from England in the chaos after this battle."

Calais, and Constance waiting there. He could not keep the thought away, but he could deny it.

"Send another to the woods, sire," Robert asked, "and let me fight with you."

"I do not ask you, Robert Heartless," the king said, turning harsh. "I command you! Can you occupy the woods in secret?"

"The French offend heaven with their rioting," Robert said. "They would not hear a troop marched through."

"You have a cheated look," the king said, "and this you do not trouble to hide, though I know you could if you so desired. How can you be disappointed? I'm sending you back to your sweetheart! Think on her. You spoke of her at Harfleur!"

Ay, think on her, never to be seen again, or met. Her marriage and his vow, two barriers that could not break.

"I cannot enforce this command," Henry said, in a different tone, "for I'll be dead. I'll ask then, prettily, as you swore you would be loyal. I counsel you, as you love England, to warn them in Calais."

He did not want to go, to hide in the trees like a coward; but he went. Thunder rolled as he led his archers to the Tramecourt woods, to crouch there through the night.

Chapter 31

THE FREEZING RAIN stopped at daybreak of Friday, October 25, 1415, the feast of Sts. Crispin and Crispinian. They were numb with cold after a bitter night, but with the coming of light, Robert climbed an ice-encrusted tree to watch the French host form.

There was an advance guard of ten thousand chivalry in full sight, all with lances cut short to bear against men on foot, for they had seen Henry's dismounted men. The gaudy flaunting banners over them hid all behind in the confusion of moving horses and unwieldy armored men, until many of the banners were suddenly furled at once and sent from the field, which meant an order had been given to get some out of the way.

Now the second formation was revealed as the flags and pennons were thinned. It was stretched across from wood to wood where the French occupied the field. The line was full thirty men deep, jammed together and shifting with great difficulty. Behind that was a rearguard, and even farther back, riderless horses with men at their head chafing for the battle to be over so they might hunt escaping English. These would be Robert's pursuers as he broke through to Calais, but he barely glanced at them.

The thing that interested him most was that King Henry's move down into the valley had forced the French to form where he wished, in the narrowest space, with the woods on either side hampering them so he could not be flanked. There would be hot fighting in the constriction. And, he thought, as hot to escape it. The French were crushed together. He looked down to his men on the ground.

"Ho, Wat! Pass up two bowstrings."

Wat came climbing with them and helped Robert tie the long flowing sleeves tight to his forearms so they would not interfere in hand-to-hand fighting. The knaves below looked up and watched, and stamped the ground, and beat their arms about their bodies to warm them.

The tying done, Wat squirmed around to view the enemy himself.

"Crossbows!" he said, and spat contemptuously, so that one of the men below must move very hastily aside. "Wedged in behind the knights. They'll never fire from there! Thank God, Hal knows how to use an archer, and puts his in front with room to bend a bow!"

Wordlessly, Robert indicated a heavily armored squadron of horse on the wing of the French vanguard. Wat grunted, as he realized their deadly duty. There would be a like squadron on the other wing. At a signal they'd charge in great diagonal rushes to trample the English bowmen and drive them back.

Against this, Hal had set his archers in six herses, triangular arrangements with the point to the enemy, to present a broad face for volleying flights of arrows in every direction. Behind them was the pitifully thin second line of two thousand English men-at-arms on horseback. Behind that only carts loaded with arrows.

It was in his archers that King Henry would trust, and with them he would fight. They were nobodies, these archers, nameless and bannerless, clad in old-fashioned leather jackets and old-fashioned hose like long stockings, separate from their drawers. Many had rolled these hose below their knees for freedom of action. Some had removed them altogether, despite the cold, and stood barefoot and blue-legged in mud. All wore leather brain caps with crossbands of iron to strengthen them. All had sharp wooden stakes, pointed at each end. One point would be thrust as an anchor in the ground, and the other point would jut forward to receive a charge of horsemen. This was their only defense. For their mission was offense. Each man had his longbow and bristled with arrows in hands, quiver, and stuck in belt. The shafts were ash, a cloth-yard long, barbed with iron or steel and fletched with goose or swan or parchment. They were nobodies, these archers of England, until they bent their six-foot bows. Then an oyster shell was a fair mark, to be hit as far as it could be seen. Four thousand of them stood on the field, to their ankles in mud, arguing over their arrows, flexing their hands, pulling their bows tentatively, testing with a wet finger to see how the wind was and turning to squint at the sun.

It was now past nine in the morning and the armies had been eying each other for three hours. The Frenchmen grew hungry now and Robert saw them eating, and even feeding horses in the front ranks.

Once Wat said, "Look!" wistfully and pointed, and Robert looked in time to see a Frenchman throw some crusts carelessly down in the mud.

"We'll fight the faster for being the lighter," Robert said, with an attempt at humor.

Wat snorted and they waited still, astride limbs of the tree, until at last the English lines stirred. They gave this their attention. It was old Sir Thomas Erpingham marshaling the line.

"It seems we must begin," Wat said.

"King Henry cannot wait too long," Robert said. "Time is with the French and against us. Hungry men fight well until they grow weak, and then they cannot fight at all."

There were the sounds of drums and trumpets in the English ranks. Three whoops carried a battle cry clear and high over the noise of the instruments. *St. George! St. George!* ST. GEORGE! The hair stood up on Robert's neck to hear it, and his breath came faster. The drums and trumpets went silent, suddenly.

The line of English knelt, the armored men beside their horses, and the archers in formation. All crossed themselves, and each bent to kiss the sodden ground and take up a pinch of mud to his mouth, signifying he was dust and would return to it. In a haze of rising battle fervor, Robert crossed himself and bent to kiss the rough bark of the icy tree.

When he straightened he looked for the king, and saw across the field a fluttering blue-and-silver banner which must be King Henry's, although from this distance he could not discern the chained antelope depicted on it. Some men moved aside and there, afoot among his archers, was the king. He had worn all his identification, royally and dangerously. His surcoat was brilliant with the quartered red-and-blue arms of England and France, with golden leopards and lilies. The jeweled crown glittered on his bascinet. And while Robert watched, the mailed, helmed, crowned figure raised a silver hand.

Robert did not need to hear.

Forward the banners! was the order.

Outnumbered, starving, trapped, King Henry seized the initiative and began the attack, when he would and where he'd chosen. Trumpets and drums clamored. The few banners the English possessed tilted forward. The archers in their herses strode out. Robert's hands clenched on the tree, and he heard the battle cry again. *St. George!*

The wing squadrons of the French countermoved. Robert swore helplessly in Welsh as armored men on heavy horses bore down on archers afoot. At four hundred yards the first arrows rattled futilely on French armor. At three hundred, the French were inclining their armored bodies forward clumsily, to keep arrows from their visor slits. At two hundred yards, horses were going down with arrows buried to the feathers, and knights pitched from saddles with shafts protruding from face-slits. At a hundred yards, the arrows shadowed the field. Incredible flights cut down the horsemen and broke them. A fraction drove in to the target. Horses struck the sharp stakes and reared back screaming, transfixed and dying, pinning riders as they fell and panicking all. The remnants of the squadrons turned and fled, slipping in the hoof-chopped mud, scrambling over dead, horses and men.

For the momentary check, the French had no answer. Their crossbowmen were jammed behind their vanguard. Some commander tried to get them forward, but it was too late. A few managed to squeeze through the press of armored men sitting ahorse leg pressed to leg, but they could not match the rapid fire of the longbowmen and were driven in.

Whereupon the English archers resumed the steady, hopeless attack, walking forward and volleying as they came.

The Frenchmen deigned at last to consider them dangerous. From somewhere a command was given. The mobbed banners of the tremendous vanguard tilted forward, and ponderously the heavy line swept into an answering attack. Almost all the great men were in these ranks, and the commanders. *Montjoye!* they shouted, and *Au feu!, Au bruit!* and *Passavant!*

Back came the cry, *St. George!*

French knights were falling with English swan and goose protruding from their helmets, but they did not drop fast enough. They were too many. On they came, with dead men charging too, held upright in the crowding.

The two lines hit in midfield, the staggering shock of armored horsemen against foot archers. The longbowmen recoiled and fell back. Ten feet lost, twenty feet . . . the rout was starting. Wat cursed steadily, and Robert set his jaw to hurting. The smell of blood swept to him, and the screams of dying men above the clatter of battle.

The battle was lost, here.

Then abruptly the lances of the English center countercharged through their own retreating archers. Robert glimpsed the whipping banner of York in the forefront, and saw York on his great horse charging at the head. A second crash, of armored lines. The lighter gave way, and the English were flung back. But their bowmen had turned again behind the armored men to pour another hail of arrows over the heads of their horsemen to help them stand and hold. They re-formed hurriedly, surged forward again, and the two lines locked in battle in the mud.

All of the English were now heavily engaged. But the second French line, thirty men deep, stretched out from wood to wood, only watched, waiting for word to attack after the entire English army exhausted itself on their van. The great line stood, immovable and invincible, watching with contempt. That changed, gradually, to disbelief. For the French van was in deep trouble, and this against mere bowmen and a handful of men-at-arms. The French main battle would be needed and quickly.

Robert saw it from his tree. When the main line of the French rolled down to rescue their van, they would pass the wood of Tramecourt, and Robert's path would open to Calais.

Robert called down for Bay Cornwall, and the charger was brought under the tree. His sodden royal bardings had been ripped off so the drapes would not obstruct his legs. He was a Spanish horse and trained to battle. He would fight viciously himself, rearing and striking with stiffened forelegs, killing anything in his path, and there would be much to kill before him, Robert thought, as he glanced at the rear-guard of the French and the pursuers behind that. He looked back to the battle to estimate his chances and guess at his timing. The hail of arrows had lessened. Archers were running out of arrows, tossing useless bows aside and snatching up swords, mauls, billhooks, axes, anything, from the littered field, to hack into the dense writhing of French nobility and slithering, slipping horses mired to their hocks. The desperate mobile ferocity of the English was telling. Robert glimpsed the royal standard. Henry of England was fighting afoot, with his archers.

The field was muddy, bloody chaos. French horses were down kicking or dead, with dead men heaped and piled against them, damming fights into pools and whirlpools. English archers were leaping on these piles of dead, banging grotesquely on the bascinets of passing mounted Frenchmen with their mauls and billhooks, so the field rang with the clangor. The French dared wait no longer. They had held back too long already. The commanders agreed at last, their hands forced by the desperate situation of their bogged vanguard.

Robert sat in the tree helplessly, and watched from afar.

The main battle moved. Men, close-pressed like a wall of steel, rolled down inexorably upon the battered, panting English. The long-bowmen stood where they were in any order, while they caught their breath, wiped bloody hands on buttocks and bellies, and gripped whatever weapons they had retrieved from the fallen. Steadily the French battle marched, their armor clashing. They were clearing the wood, passing Robert, opening his path. It was time to go, time for horsemen detached for just such swift duty. . . .

On the field, the broken French vanguard recoiled back into the new French attack, but without passage to move through to the rear. The men in the main battle came on, stirrup to stirrup, legs locked in the intolerable press of too many men in too small a space. The vanguard suddenly saw they were trapped, caught between the lines, and turned desperate for their lives, fighting their way, clawing into their own main battle. And the main battle swept their own men before them, flinging them back panic-stricken to the ravenous English.

A moment of panic, Robert thought. One moment of panic now! Yet he must go and leave them.

"Bows!" he called down.

The Welshmen pressed forward as he dropped from his tree and seized Bay Cornwall. Their eyes were wild. They'd heard the cries and clangor. They were leashed mad dogs, hearing others fighting. *Snap the leash*, Robert thought, *and they'd be wolves*.

He could not see the battle now, but only listen. Battle cries were few; men needed breath to fight. The battle was trembling, hovering out there. He led his men toward it. Then from the edge of the wood, atop Bay Cornwall, Robert saw a sudden spurt from the English ranks, some men-at-arms surging desperately into the French, prying them off a stand of surrounded archers Robert could not see. It was York's banner, lunging in. And it was York, driving off Frenchmen to give the archers respite. Robert's blood turned hot and wild, and he remembered Harfleur, when York had come to his aid.

Now York, who had no son, was fighting with no man to aid him. Robert saw a Frenchman with a battle-ax jam into the English ranks fearlessly. The ax swung up . . .

"York!" Robert yelled.

. . . and the ax swung down. York's horse lunged aside, too late, and the fat duke took the blow on his helm and was cleft to the chin. Robert saw red flood over the silver armor. The horse leaped again, convulsively, and the Duke of York crashed dead from his saddle.

Robert sat, stiff in his, and marked the man who used the ax. *Alençon*, by the banner that snapped on his lancehead. The French Duke of Alençon.

"Alençon," Robert said.

Wat looked over to see if it meant an order.

Robert was watching Alençon. The duke was thrusting through the mob, his henchmen forcing passage for him, and every man singleminded. Men with a goal. Toward the banner of the Trinity and St. George. Toward the blue and silver with a chained antelope upon it. Toward England! The Frenchmen were hunting the king!

Damn Calais! Send it to hell with the wild yeomen dying here! Let Clarence look to his own crown, if Henry lost his today!

His eyes were brightly blue and shining. When he spoke, he spoke in Welsh. He had forgotten English.

"Knees," he said.

Half his Welshmen leaped down from their horses, and the half of these went to one knee. The others stood behind, and the horsemen stayed in the rear.

"Bows!" he called out. He flung up his hand, they drew their bows to their ears; then he dropped his hand and the arrows rose like a cloud, continuously, one in the hand as one left the bow. The rear of the French battle crushed inwards suddenly as wounded horses leaped away from hurts. Arrows swept over and reached farther in. Another instant and there was confusion. A shout rose from the French that they were attacked from the rear. Some struggled to turn and face the challenge in their hopelessly crushed ranks. In that moment Robert charged, and the archers like screaming madmen behind him, roused so hot they'd do any deed. They rammed into the mass, then abandoned their wedged horses and ran over the rumps of live horses like mad dancers, behind armored Frenchmen who could not turn.

A cry of despair enveloped the battlefield and spread alarm. Incredibly the mass of armored men were panicking, smashed from the front with the ferocity of desperate men who had nothing left to lose, confused by their own vanguard still clawing into them, with no communication, no orders, jammed together so they could see nothing, and a sudden attack from the rear.

Robert leaped Bay Cornwall to stacked bodies to see over the struggle and waving banners tossing in all directions. The Spanish stallion balanced on the shifting mass fearlessly, golden gauds and bangles flashing, tassels tossing, ornaments aswirl. Then the sliding pyramid of bodies disintegrated under his weight, and Bay Cornwall leaped heavily for firmer footing.

Robert heard *"Criaunt! Criaunt!"*

A Frenchman struggling to stay upright before him tried to surrender. Robert shoved past. Bay Cornwall reared and snapped his iron-shod hooves at a Frenchman who vanished, trodden down. In the moment aloft Robert glimpsed Henry standing, bestriding a man who was down and fighting off assault to save him. And close . . . too close to Henry . . . the flashing banner of Alençon and his men, hewing a way to the king.

"Rally the bows!" Robert shouted.

Wat guessed at the Welsh and screamed in gutter English, trying to call in the archers. Those who heard came, crowding afoot behind Bay Cornwall as the stallion crashed viciously through the mass, rearing and lunging with forelegs stiff. Blood splashed red over his legs and chest and fouled his golden ornaments, but he was crushing a path like a battering ram.

He reared. Robert saw Henry alone, his opponent dispatched. Bay Cornwall reared again. Robert glimpsed the king, who had turned to peer through the slit of his bascinet. Down and up into the air again, and Robert saw the Duke of Alençon, lanceless now and axless, draw his sword and charge the king from behind.

Robert shouted uselessly over the din. Bay Cornwall screamed in answer to the shout and lunged a last time, and broke through the press to an empty place in the battle. Robert lowered his lance and charged. Too late! Alençon was leaning over the king. His sword swept down. A clanging blow. A bright fragment flew into the sun and Henry of England was down on the body of the man he had defended to his ruin.

Bay Cornwall thundered through the mud and over bodies. Alençon saw the charge and tried to dodge away. Too late for him, as for the king. Robert's lance shattered as it hit, and with the broken point and fluttering green ribbon in him, Alençon hit the ground. Bay Cornwall trod him under and smashed into the knot of his henchmen. In an instant Robert was in a swirling sword fight with them all. In another instant Welshmen were racing in afoot among the mounted French, thrusting horses in the belly to bring them down, dragging Frenchmen off, stabbing through chinks of armor. The bowmen were feral, insane, red-eyed and howling. They could not be withstood. The encounter was done. Robert turned back instantly to the king. Henry was on his knees, a man at each arm dragged him up. His bodyguard had reached him at last, and one pulled off the dented helmet.

Robert halted Bay Cornwall, dismounted and ran toward the king, with foam-mouthed Welshmen leaping after him, and the red-smeared Bay Cornwall following like a pet with a mighty blowing of his nostrils.

King Henry was on his feet as Robert reached him, staggering but refusing vehemently to retire from the field. Someone was showing him the royal bascinet, exhibiting the blow he had received. A great dent was in it, and a *fleuron* had been struck from the encircling crown. Men helped the king aside, to remove the wounded man he still protected. Robert saw it was the king's youngest and dangerous brother, treacherous Humphrey of Gloucester, dripping blood. He remembered how he would have leaped to York's aid if he could have done so, and York his mortal enemy. In battle, then, all men were alike. A curious thing. He felt weak and dizzy and icily cold, and looked down to clear his head, closing his eyes tight. He opened them to see a brightness in the mud, and picked it up and rubbed it clean with his fingers. A fleur-de-lis of gold with pearls and a balas winking like a gobbet of blood. It had been struck from Henry's crown. He came forward, still dizzy, to kneel and offer the floweret. King Henry looked at him and scowled.

"Still in the field?" he inquired. "I thought you halfway to Calais. Was it the wound that held you?"

Wound? What wound? Dumbly Robert followed the king's glance, and saw his scarlet cote-hardie ripped so flesh and linen showed, and the cloth stained darker than it had been. He touched the place, wondering was the blood his? He smeared his fingers and frowned on them.

"I had not felt it, sire," he said honestly. "I hold my shield too high, and got it so. It's a fault in style, they say."

"You chose to disobey?"

"Sire," Robert said, with a wry face, "I am no man for taking messages."

The king pointed down. Robert bent his head obediently to look, still kneeling in the mud, still dazed from the sharp wound he did not feel. A cold, wet sword hit him on the neck. He started half up with a wild thought of summary beheading. The sword bounced to his shoulder and held, and Robert halted as he was, and heard the words that dubbed him. He rose, disbelieving, muddy and bloody and dirty, Sir Robert Fairfield, knight.

"Now see to the field, that the enemy does not form in force," the king said harshly. "This time, obey me! I'll not knight you for a second disobedience. I'll behead you!"

Then he turned aside abruptly, to give orders for harrying the French. Sir Robert Fairfield, knight, turned to look at the field. The second line of the enemy had fallen back into their third line, panicking all. The great host had taken to its heels and was dispersing in all directions.

For a moment he stood, suspended still in the daze, as if this all was dreamed. Then he shook his head hard. The wound was nothing. The king was sore hit and still fighting. He could do no less. He held up a hand, and they brought Bay Cornwall. Then he rode out on the field.

Chapter 32

SOME of the archers were dead, many were lost, a good portion were looting, but those who heard Wat's rallying shout snatched the nearest riderless horses and rode quickly after Robert as he looked for any who thought to re-form. There was death and confusion, and isolated battles still raged inside fences of dead men and debris, but the battle scene was now mainly of looters searching industriously. Robert called out to some, as he passed, that they must seek for the body of the Duke of York, killed hereabouts.

"Let the worms have him," Wat advised.

"He was a brave man," Robert said, "who learned loyalty late and died of it. He pressed the fight when it was hopeless and flung his life away."

Wat shrugged. "I am a better hater than you," he said.

"He loved the king," Robert said, "though he betrayed him."

"Did he betray you too," Wat asked, "before he died? Where's your Bible?"

"He'd not carry it into battle. I'll search his quarters, if I get near them."

"I was trained young in that game," Wat said. "If it's there I'll find it. Here's a cart with linen in it. Let me bind that wound before you're drained."

It was true enough the wound had begun to make him tremble, and the pain of it now was obvious. Robert glanced hastily around the field. There were no concerted stands that he saw; no possible heroes bringing hope to lost men, raising even wounded in a last-ditch rally, the last fitful starts of a lost battle, as a body twitched when life departed. So he dismounted. Wat pulled the undertunic away from the bloody place, while the other men leaned on their pommels and watched.

"Deep?" Robert inquired. It felt now as if it went right through his body.

"Only to the ribs," Wat said, "but it's long and it's bleeding hard."

"I've learned to cure a fault with this," Robert said. "I'll carry my shield lower. Cut the points. I have no time to linger."

And when it was done, and his hose laced to his ripped paltock with ends of points, he mounted again and surveyed the field. There was motion toward them, and it caught his attention. He leaned a little sideways to ease the wound.

"Wat, there . . . a stir upon the road. Seven men, I make it."

"Seven," Wat agreed.

"French, if they come from that direction. They're in haste. They've left half their harness behind. The last one has no shield, and the leader no surcoat or banner."

"But a drawn sword," Wat said.

Masses of leaderless French still wandered upon the battlefield, eager to make a stand. Give them a leader . . .

Robert spurred Bay Cornwall across the field to intercept the stranger knights, grimacing at the pain.

"I make that cry Brabant," he called across to Wat.

"Brabant!" Wat yelled back across some abandoned carts that split them, and agreed.

If Brabant, Robert thought, then brother to the Duke of Burgundy, whose uneasy friendship must be preserved lest he attack in revenge.

He set the spurs in Bay Cornwall again to rescue Brabant before he died, for English archers heard the Frenchman shouting, saw his eagerness to rally, and ran from all directions to seize him. Robert rushed down, but there were carts and bodies and sharp dropped weapons everywhere to avoid, and Brabant was far away . . . dismounting? Robert could hardly believe it. He had dismounted. He had seized up a fallen trumpet. A trumpet? He was ripping loose the long blazon, stuck a dagger through it, put it over his head for a surcoat—a thing to identify him to all—and flung another trumpet blazon to a following knight to fix on a lance as a banner.

He intended to rally the French!

But his delay was fatal. The English archers caught him and his men, and even as Robert snatched Bay Cornwall up, a knife had flashed. He jammed his horse into the confusion and found Brabant in the center on his back in the mud. They had jerked off his helm and cut his throat. Blood was spurting over his armor.

"Fools!" Robert said. This was political disaster! "You've slaughtered Anthony of Brabant and his brother will dog us to Calais. Remember this, when you die of it!"

The killers stared stupidly up at him, eyes glazed with fatigue and battle-madness. They blinked, swaying with exhaustion. One wiped bloody hands slowly up and down his leather jacket, his mouth open, slack. And Robert saw they were little better than mad. His own fatigue and weakness overcame him a moment; they blurred before his eyes. Wat rode beside him promptly. The blur cleared. Robert turned to the Frenchmen, still on their horses but disarmed. They had taken off their helms, and he could see their weary faces.

In their tongue he asked if this was truly Anthony of Brabant.

They answered wearily that it was. Brabant had left his retinue behind to gallop to the battle. They had tried to tell these animals who he was.

The longbowmen muttered angrily about the gibberish these foreigners talked, and who could understand it.

Robert said, "He died, my lords, because they did not know him. The trumpet blazon he took for a surcoat confused them. They would have held him for ransom had they known him. I am most sorry."

A Frenchman held up a hand, limp with fatigue. It was war and the fortunes of war, but the Duke of Burgundy would make trouble if not assured it was an accident, all misadventure.

"I will send to the king," Robert said. "As you are gentlemen all, you will explain to my sovereign how this thing happened."

The nobleman nodded gravely.

"Your name?" he asked.

Robert hesitated.

"Sir Robert Fairfield," Wat said in his guttural French.

And so because he was a knight, the Frenchmen surrendered formally to Robert.

By now the archers realized what they had done, and despite their weariness began lively recriminations against each other for the wanton destruction of thousands of marks in ransom. They could all have been rich men! Who had the knife? Who—

Robert ordered the babble silent.

"Now," he said, "take these gentlemen safe to the king, nor think on killing them to cover your grievous fault."

"For," Wat added cheerfully, "if these gentlemen get not safely to the king, there will be Englishmen on the lists of slain no Frenchman ever killed. Every face among you is here." He tapped his head. "Plain enough, lads? Plain English, and no gibberish?"

The archers looked uneasily at one another and muttered, and at last trudged off with the captives disarmed in their midst, picking their way around carts and bodies. The young duke, dead in his armor, was flung stiffly over his own warhorse, bleeding like a hung carcass, with an archer walking on each side to steady the body of the man they'd killed.

It seemed as if all was over at last, when Wat called alarum from a little way off and Robert turned to see a galloper hurrying to him, slewing a light nag desperately around obstacles.

"We are . . . at—tacked!" the messenger screamed the moment he was in earshot. "The king's . . . orders . . . rear!" He pointed, jerked his horse sharply around and tore off in another direction.

Hastily now, Robert raced back on a horse that galloped heavily and shook him hard until he could guide himself by an uproar, the clash of arms and shouting. He ripped into it through a small thicket and burst headlong into a fight. Frenchmen fled on his appearance, bolting like rabbits before the wolf.

"Hold!" Robert shouted. "No man follows! I'll have his life!"

They jerked their horses to sliding halts. He meant to be obeyed and all his archers knew it. But they came round, wide-eyed. Robert Heartless refusing pursuit? And Robert knew then he was no longer a Welsh border fighter. That Robert would have forgotten all in joy of chasing a running enemy. This Robert stood instead, in the middle of carnage, and let them go. There was looted baggage strewn around. A few priests were venturing out of bushes where they had fled when the royal baggage was attacked.

Wat said, "Peasants with scythes," indicating the slashed bodies of the English guards. "Mayhap a man-at-arms to lead them."

"Mayhap an army of men-at-arms to lead them," Robert said, "and entice us into a trap. The king can eat without silver spoons, but needs every archer to win through to Calais."

It was more than a silver spoon or two. Crown jewels were gone. Let them go. Today his archers were his jewels.

"Take the priests up behind the saddles," he said.

When it was done he rode back to the king, before Henry thought all France was lunging from behind. He liked neither men nor armies at his back. Let them come from the front, and he was unafraid.

Thus Robert did what he never thought he could so. He rode away from a fight, because it was the wiser course.

The battlefield meant nothing, nor the dead men in strange attitudes, half sunk in mud where they were trampled, for that was battle; but when he had nearly reached the king he saw . . . *murder!* Murder all around. He pulled up his horse with a jerk that flung him forward and made him gasp and breathe quickly against the pain in his side.

This was not death in battle but wanton murder underfoot, a meadow of murder, the bodies of unarmed, unarmored French captives, men cut down without a chance at defense. Throats were cut, heads were smashed, and not a weapon near them. Men were paunched, and their bloody guts hung out while the fingers of tied hands still twitched.

"What bloody work is this?" Robert demanded of the nearest Englishman. "Who murdered bound men?"

The noble looked up from contemplation of a dead man, and sheathed his bloody sword.

"It's the king's own order," he said.

"Tell me no lies," Robert said deeply shocked.

The nobleman's mouth twisted with hatred. "The greatest men in France lie here," he said. *"Kill them,* he commanded, and when we refused, he ordered archers up to do it. And so we performed the deed." With one foot he touched the body of a youth. "With his ransom," he said bitterly, "I could have built a castle."

Someone muttered in loud anger.

"It's *Sir* Robert Fairfield," said a mocking voice. "Are you proud of your knighting now, dubbed by Harry Cut-Throat?"

"Who spoke?" Robert asked.

"He's as bloody as his king," a man yelled.

Another voice, steadier, a responsible man, no killer. "Would God Clarence had the throne," it said. "This king's frenzied! We'll be next, I tell you. We must defend ourselves!"

"Who spoke?" Robert repeated, and turned with difficulty.

No man answered. They stared at him with insolence, a new man

on his way up, a king's pet, dubbed after disobedience. He'd get nothing of them, he thought. It might have been any of twenty stirring
up rebellion, and a fool's work to force the issue now. King Henry
had brewed revolt, if this was his work, but Robert could not believe
it. He was hot tempered, and he fell into rages, but . . . full two
hundred bodies? Robert heard a priest praying softly from behind for
the souls sent brutally from this world.

He never ordered it, Robert insisted to himself. He had sworn loyalty to a just king, and he'd hold to it. But if this was Henry's command, what then? Could he be loyal to a murderer of helpless men?

The king's banners blew out in wind that rose in gusts as Robert
approached, still-faced. The chained antelope fluttered on the silver-
and-blue field with red roses scattered over it. King Henry stood below his standard, still in armor but without his dented helm. He
looked at Robert as he drew rein and dismounted. The priest behind
one of the archers prayed on, joined now by others, so there was a
soft chorus as Robert went to the king and knelt.

"Have they set you to running so soon?" Henry asked. His face was
cruel.

"It was the French who ran, sire," Robert said. "A snarl of peasants
over baggage. No more."

"Peasants!" Henry swung around in a rage, and glared at his nobles.
"There were no cowards in the French ranks today," he said, "but I
think there were some in mine!"

None of the nobles attempted to answer the grave insult. They
stared sullenly at the ground. A single drop of rain splashed on the
king's taut face like a tear. He looked upward briefly at the rain that
commenced anew, but did not attempt to shield his head or face
from it.

"We'll stand a while and wait," he said sharply. "The French may
come again. God knows they want to fight, but have no leaders they
can trust."

"Nor we," came a whisper from nowhere.

If Henry heard it, he made no sign.

So all stood silent, the nobles in cold armor, while the rain came
pounding down and washed the murdered men clean of their blood.
Out on the battlefield the bowmen searched industriously among the
dead. Their flickering torches, ill-burning in the wet, dipped and rose

in a slow dance as the holders bent and stood. Once Robert looked for Wat, and did not see him.

"Looting?" he asked one of the other of his men.

The man shook his head. "He said to tell you if you asked, that he went back to Maisoncelles to find what was forgotten."

The Bible. Wat had remembered the Bible. He waited, watching the looters, and the men bringing in English wounded as they searched among the dead. He thought with pity of the French wounded, left to crawl into thickets, if they had the strength, for protection against the night now coming and robbery from their countrymen.

Wat returned, his face dark with anger. He shook his head. The Bible had not been there. In death, then, York would prolong his hold. Where was it hid? It was a danger still.

Robert looked to his men lolling in their saddles, spitting and talking wearily and looking with longing at the looters. He gestured to Wat, who grinned evilly, then turned and spoke to the others. They let out a brief yell and dismounted in a hurry, galvanized out of exhaustion, and ran out on the battlefield to loot their share.

The king had turned at the sound, and looked away again, to stand by his banner, straight in his heavy armor, impassive, his eyes following the Welsh archers scattering eagerly over the field.

Wat was quick and he'd dragged his horse after him by the reins, and in a little time of industrious work, turning over bodies and stripping them, he gathered a handsome set of armor for Robert, which he brought back with delight and dumped at his feet with a crash, together with gold spurs off a dead count's heels, and a splendid bascinet of silver set with a wreath of gold roses and a coronet above it. The noblemen nearby glared as Wat ripped off muddy mantling with a flourish to show the prize beneath.

"As fine as any man could wear," he said, displaying it high above his head, then polishing it with a muddy sleeve and setting it with the rest. And off he went for more looting, this time with an empty quiver to fill.

Robert looked at the armor at his feet. Once it had been all his goal. It meant little now, though he had thanked Wat. In this battle the armored men had died, and the quick unarmored archers fared the best of all.

He contemplated Wat, happily rooting over the battlefield for small, valuable prizes, stuffing his quiver with jewels from stiff dead fingers and gold chains off dead necks as he flung bodies about like beef carcasses.

Men came back and forth constantly to the king with reports, their torches sputtering more in heavier rain. The Duke of Gloucester, they said, was sore struck in the bowels, but was thought to be better. The English dead had been piled into great barns. The torch was set. The king turned stiffly in his armor. Flames licked the darkening sky even as the message was given. Robert watched the distant pyres of stout yeomen who'd died for England. King Henry's mouth twitched nervously, and his mailed hands turned to fists. Fifteen hundred Englishmen were marked by the thick black smoke of their burning. Robert put his hand up to the saddle. His knees were shaking, and he needed the support of his horse.

The rain increased. More messages came. The bodies of the Duke of York and the young Earl of Suffolk had been quartered and were boiling in two great caldrons so the flesh could be parted from the bones, and these carried back to London for comfort to the widows.

Robert thought of York, pieces of flesh boiling like the meat of an animal. Even now the man had power over him. He could reach from his caldron, in the matter of the stolen Bible. Yet Robert crossed himself and prayed for him. He remembered the charge to save the archers. Every man had a quality worthy before God and this must be remembered. Every man. All that was left of York was a few bones, and an unfinished book he had meant to write.

Men came with food from the French camp, and captured wine. Henry refused all, but Robert was glad to drink wine to ease his side, which had now turned to steady pain.

At last King Henry called for silence, and raised his hand.

"It's over," he said, and looked among his sullen nobles. "I thank you all for your aid this day. By the Grace of God, we have humbled a great host with a little band."

Someone muttered covertly, "It's not God this king should thank. His ally was another, and he's sent two hundred souls to hell as ransom for this victory."

"Well may he glance over his shoulder for the assassin behind," said another soft voice. "One day he will see the killer there."

Robert only turned his head. There were six men grouped together. He would remember them.

Now the king sent for Montjoye, the French king-at-arms, who had been captured late and escaped the murdering. The French herald came walking fearfully among the dead Frenchmen.

King Henry pointed to the outlines of a proud castle in the distance, hazy in the rainy twilight just before full dark.

"What castle is that?" he asked.

"Agincourt, sire," the Frenchman made answer.

"Then," King Henry said wearily, "let this be called the Battle of Agincourt forever."

Chapter 33

AS FULL DARK came, they found Maisoncelles by the red light of burning barns. Groups of murmuring men stood about in the rain before the king's hut. They fell silent as they saw Henry approaching. He paused a moment, arrogant, to look them over, then seemed to thrust through as they recoiled to make a path.

At the door of the hut he paused again, looking among them. Every man was uneasy, for the king's mood was chancy now. Two hundred dead Frenchmen proved that he was dangerous. A man could lose his head tonight if he crossed his dreaded sovereign.

"Sir Robert!" the king called, as Robert turned to move off painfully. "I did not say you were to go! Or do you prefer to crawl off like the other curs?"

Robert dismounted for answer.

The king entered the hut, leaving the door open behind. Robert followed, and Wat was at his shoulder, scuttling uninvited behind. The king stared coldly at the archer. The guards waited, poised, for a command. But the king turned away without speaking, and Wat sneered and kicked the door shut in their faces. The king unbuckled his sword and flung it clattering into a corner.

"Help me out of this armor," he ordered.

Robert did so, while the king moved with impatience till the task was done. King Henry unwound the strips of blanket that had protected his legs from the metal and flung them aside with the leathern jacket worn under his armor. He rubbed his wrists where the steel had chafed him. Rain had leaked through the joints and left wet streaks upon him, but for all that he looked right royal in this commanding mood, even in dark blue woolen hose and white linen undertunic. The golden leopards on his high collar glittered as he came to the fire and held his hands above it. Robert noted his hands were shaking. The king's face was very white, and the haze of dark beard on his jaw made him seem the paler. Suddenly he dropped to a stool and ducked his head into his hands. His shoulders hunched and he shivered violently. *How could this man be a murderer? Yet he had given the order. No other man would dare to slaughter prisoners.*

Robert picked up some wood. The king raised his head, instantly suspicious at any movement. He watched sharply as more fuel was flung on the fire. The flames blazed up and cast out heat. Smoke eddied upward.

"You feel that wound," the king said abruptly. "You do not use your left arm. Hit in the chest?"

"Nay, sire," Robert said warily, "across the ribs only."

"It were better in the chest," the king said, with an angry mouth and angry eyes. "There'd be one heretic the less."

Robert brushed his hand against his thigh to get the wood-dirt from it. Now he knew where the Bible was.

"What's in you?" the king demanded. "I do not trust men who never show their feelings."

"It was York accused me, sire?" Robert asked.

"He gave me your Bible, if that is what you seek to find," the king said. "I had it last night, before I ever called for you."

"And yet, sire," Robert asked gently, "you sent me to the French camp?"

The king's mouth was thin. "I sent you unsuspecting," he said, "and you returned."

"I went, suspecting," Robert said, "and I returned."

The king smiled, but cruelly. This was not the gay Prince Hal of legend, nor yet the gallant king all London loved.

"And nothing, nothing on that handsome face," the king said. "I marvel at it, Rob. You're carved of stone."

Rob! He'd said *Rob*. He'd learned it of the countess, but he'd used it, the diminutive of childhood. Only two persons had ever called Robert so. The countess, and the king. *Rob!* It caught him by the throat.

"I did not need York's betrayal," the king was saying. "I knew you from Portchester. The moon was full that night. It showed me a masked man with his sleeve over the hilt of his sword. *Wherefore?* I thought. This must be a wondrous strange hilt to need concealment. I looked to the blade therefore. Do you think I would not remember at last the marks I put on it myself?" The king got up suddenly and fetched a leather bundle from a corner. "This is proof," he said, "not words spoken by a dead man who cannot testify."

"I have not denied it, sire," Robert said.

"You make me think of Oldcastle now," the king said in a fury. "He would not break. I begged him to recant. I—"

Suddenly he flung the Bible. It struck Robert in the chest and made him grunt, but his right arm came snapped up of itself and caught the package to him.

"The score is settled," the king said. "Your Bible for the warning at Portchester. That's justice. Your life for mine. But if a man come to me a second time, saying, Here's a knight who's a heretic . . ."

He eyed Robert from head to foot. "Here's a ragged Welshman," he said, "all tatters. Do you dare appear before me dressed so? Get out, I'm a king, not a clown, to have such beggars about me!"

The man was exhausted, Robert thought as he stood together with Wat in the rain outside. He'd flung insult, but he'd had some reason. It was in his eyes.

Wat said, "If you stand here so, your wound will turn to ice."

The king had compared him to Oldcastle, the name no one dared speak.

He said to Wat, "Tell me of Oldcastle."

"Here?" Wat asked, astonished. "In the rain?"

"Tell me of Oldcastle, the things before he ran for his life, the things I do not know."

"Why, he was King Henry's friend when he was a penniless prince and out of favor with his father. Oldcastle was dearer than Scrope, even in disgrace, for Scrope betrayed in secret for money, while Oldcastle was forthright and seized for his fervent belief. Oldcastle was a Lollard, and when they summoned him about a book he owned that had been seized, he rode away from King Henry to his castle. They say King Henry never forgot that Oldcastle left without permission nor trusted to royal protection."

"But Oldcastle betrayed him."

"No," Wat said, "not till the very end, when he was forced. When he left the king he closed the gates of his castle against a bishop, but when Henry sent to take him for trial for heresy, Oldcastle came. He would not rebel against the crown, and it was his life at stake, remember. He was Lollard and he was convicted, for he would not back a step in his belief. They flung him in the Tower with a death sentence, but he broke from it and fled to Wales. Some say the king ordered the guard relaxed, but it's only rumor. What's true is then Oldcastle rebelled, though it came to nothing, and the king's pursued him since."

"But he escaped the Tower."

"Oh, yes," Wat said, "he escaped. Little good it did him. He's an outlaw now."

And if that rumor was true, and Henry had ordered the guards to be lax that a man might escape from the Tower? Then the king was one who never left off friendship. And Oldcastle had returned rebellion.

Powerful friends, Chapelle had said. That was the only security. Constance would be safe. There was nothing else he wanted; neither gold nor power. Safety for Constance.

"Where can I get a whole garment?" he asked abruptly. "Quickly."

Wat thought a moment. "There were some things in York's hut when I searched it," he said. "They're never his, but he saved everything worth money, and the hut's unguarded too since the duke's dead. Over here." He led Robert in the mud and they went inside into the pitch darkness. "Ah," he said, with satisfaction, "not stolen yet. I feel the fur and gold embroidery." He brought something and thrust it at Robert in the dark.

Robert felt soft fur and orphrey work and velvet, but could not guess the color. He dressed in he knew not what, wincing for his wound.

"The points tight?" Wat asked, helping.

"Tight," Robert said. He'd not pamper a gash on his ribs.

Outside again, nothing had changed. The nobles huddled about, intrigue thick and no one to be trusted. So it had been at Southampton.

"I'll rouse the men," Wat said. "We can move in the dark and none will know we're gone . . . until we're gone."

Like Oldcastle, skulking off. *No, I'll trust him once.*

"You're not returning?" Wat asked, guessing with sudden horror.

"I'll go alone," Robert said.

"No," Wat said. "I was born to hang. You saw how the Frenchmen could not kill me. And," he reminded, "you saw how the king killed the prisoners!"

But he was returning, nonetheless. Why? Why, really? For that he was a knight and the king his lord? No, the time was past for knightly gallantry, a new age stretched and yawned and sneered at the old age and its ways. Did he go back to gamble for high stakes—his life against preferment? It was a dangerous game some men liked to play. Nay, not that. He would not give his loyalty for gain, or he'd have gone with the Duke of York.

What then? What then?

It was the Welsh blood betraying him with emotion, great risk for a little thing.

Rob, the king had called him. *Rob*.

And for this he was going back.

The guard stared pop-eyed at sight of them, then opened the door as if these might have been instructions. Robert walked in. The king looked up from where he sat by the fire with a blanket around his shoulders. He stood up slowly, letting the blanket drop to the floor. Then suddenly he threw back his head and laughed.

Robert had expected anger, or contempt. Even arrest. But laughter! He looked down hastily at his clothes, but they were fine. Black velvet covered with tiny rampant lions in gold. Ermine lined the sleeves and finished the neck and hem. Black hose matched the cote-hardie and displayed an elegant circle of golden lions chasing each other about the left calf.

"Here is a jest," the king said, "as good as York's, who dedicated to me a book he wrote in the prison to which I sent him. Now, this is the boldest wretch in camp! You dare come here with your Bible under your arm, my sword at your side, and my brother Clarence's clothes upon your back?"

Wat said, "Oh, God!" imploring heaven.

The king nudged a stool at the fire with one foot, and Robert sat. His points strained with sitting so low and jerked the bandage against the wound with pressure from his undertunic. Carefully, he turned his wounded side to the fire, and thought of his father and how the old man had clung to warmth complaining of ancient wounds.

The rain hissed on the fire, spattering in from the smoke hole, and beat hard on the thatch above. Wat effaced himself in a corner, and it seemed the king and Robert were alone.

"How do my gallant nobles in the rain?" the king inquired.

"Like sheep," Robert said, "huddling together, with not a ram among them."

Henry nodded. "My cousin of York is dead," he said.

"He died gallantly for England, and for you."

"You defend him?" the king asked, astonished.

"Too late. I think he meant to be true hereafter. I regret now some things I said."

"You're forgiving," the king said. "That's dangerous. Beware of it. And yet he did protest to me, many times these last months, that he had been loyal since I took the crown. I have no proof he lied. Of course, I never trusted him, but it may be that . . . I might have."

"He changed his heart," Robert said, "but he could not change his reputation."

The king crossed himself slowly. "He was a merry man, always with a jest to make me laugh. They wondered why I kept him near me. I say, if it is my fate to be always betrayed, then give me merry traitors."

"I am no longer merry," Robert said, "and I never was a traitor."

"You're a heretic," the king said bluntly, "that's the beginning of betrayal."

"Heretics died for you today," Robert said.

But the king was not listening. He was staring straight ahead at the smoke writhing over the fire.

"There were two hundred of them," he was saying, with his eyes haunted by what he saw in the smoke, "the best fighting men in France, captives, disarmed and bound. The cry came we were attacked in force at the rear, then that Brabant was attacking from the front. I was engaged on two sides. I ordered them dead."

Something tight in Robert eased. Even so. There was no evil in this king, despite his temper and his ambition.

"Then came archers with dead Brabant, and the other was only a skirmish. Two hundred souls are cursing me from purgatory. I will never be free of them." His fists clenched. He saw them out there, bodies in the rain, abandoned to the French peasants creeping down to pick among the dead.

"If it were a full attack," Robert said, "and those men had seized weapons, we were lost and England too. Do not forget England."

"I have said that to myself, over and over endlessly," the king said, "while I stood out there, and while I sit here." He watched Robert's face closely. "In my place, would you have ordered them dead?"

"God forgive me," Robert said, "yes."

"With never a chance to say their prayers?"

"Let them settle that with heaven," Robert said grimly.

The king studied him over the licking flames and haze of smoke between them.

"You had a gentle, sweet look once," he said, "a boy's face, full of laughter, amused at little things . . . singing, joking, joyous. I liked to see you wandering at Harfleur, playing at war, meeting merchants in the middle of the night to deal in yards of lace and bolts of velvet. Are you surprised I know this? My spies told me. It were a little price for the service that you rendered. Clarence trusted you. You could have stolen half Harfleur and he'd have looked the other way and sworn to me you were by him when it vanished. To trust a man! God! To trust a man!"

The king put his head in his hands. When he looked up again, he was smiling wryly.

"I used to linger near your campfire, out of sight, to hear you sing the Welsh songs. My nurse used to sing them to me. Sometimes at night I'd hear your folly bells go jingling, and they'd say nearby, *That's Robert Heartless, with his gold bells.* Clarence used to say it was the sound of safety to him—York would never put a knife in his back while Robert Heartless was by. Heartless? Robert Heartless. Have they named you right? I think so. If you had a heart, you've lost it, Rob. You had a boy's face then and merry eyes; but the boy is gone and the bonnie eyes are blank and cold. There's none crueler than blue eyes when they will not laugh. The best steel's blue. It cuts the sharper. I say you might do anything, were you determined. Rob, you were such a boy as I would have liked about my court to bring us gaiety. Now you are such a man as I would send alone to hold a castle in rebellious territory."

Robert watched the flames, and thought of Constance and her safety. Yet he would not beguile friendship from the king. He was too proud for stooping.

"Outside," the king said softly, like a conspirator, "they whisper against me. My own earls hate me for this . . . this killing today, yet not for the souls sent unshriven from this world. I could forgive such hatred. They think only on the ransom lost to them. They will do anything for money. Even Scrope. Even Scrope." He sounded disbelieving.

"I trusted him with my life, made him rich, and richer, and still he grew greedier as he grew older, and friendship was less than French gold. Yet I miss him. God, how I miss him! We used to talk of nights. I did not watch my tongue or hide my feelings. I said what I pleased, and it was good to be honest. Did you see him die?"

"Nay, sire, but I heard he made good ending."

The king put his face in his hands.

"For every noble who is not loyal," Robert said quietly, "I will raise up a thousand common men who are, and this for love of you alone."

The king took away his hands and raised his head.

"And you?"

"The judgment is yours, sire," Robert said.

The king studied him a moment.

"You have the clearest eyes I ever saw on any man. They urge me to believe you. But then, Oldcastle had such honest eyes, and I trusted him and got rebellion. Hotspur's eyes outshone the angels, and he rose against me. Nay, I will not trust such eyes again." He jumped to his feet and began to pace.

And Robert thought, with deep compassion, he would be lonely and troubled until he died.

The king turned. There was hard distrust in his face.

"York's dead," he announced. "He tried to murder me, four times. I loved him well but never trusted him."

He walked hence and back again.

"There was Hotspur, my good companion, like another boy with me when I was thirteen and sent to hold North Wales. He was slain at Shrewsbury, my enemy. I would have slain the man who killed him had I known his name."

He paced and returned.

"There was Oldcastle, a gallant knight. We raised devilment together. But he's a heretic, condemned and in rebellion. God give speed to his heretic heels for the good times we had once."

"They said," Robert ventured, "you ordered the guard relaxed the night he escaped from the Tower."

Henry did not seem to hear, but paced several times before he stopped.

"He could recant," Henry said abruptly. "I'd take him back. I'd forgive all. I've been betrayed before. But he will not recant, and I know you would not recant, and who can trust a Lollard?"

Robert watched the bright flames steadily.

"How soon will you sell me?" Henry demanded. "Tonight? My nobles would rise if they had a leader, and there's something in you that makes men follow." The king moved closer. "They named a man you met in the night," he said. "They named the merchant Chapelle, and he has enemies. They talk of Lollardy. His daughter is your true love, they say. She's a heretic. If she is seized for it, how long can you be trusted?"

"Not the length of a breath," Robert said, and he was standing facing the king. "I'll kill any man who touches my lady."

"Ah, now we have the truth," the king said. "Where's the loyalty you protested?"

"Sire, you have it still," Robert said.

"What's your price for it?" the king asked, now contemptuous. "You're bold. You have ability. I pay high for merchandise I want, and I want a man I can depend upon. I was jealous of Clarence at Harfleur, and the careless way he'd say, *Don't jump, Hal. My Welshman's outside and he'll know what caused the sound.* I'll pay for the same confidence. Don't calculate. Give a good, round figure. You'll not come cheap."

"I'll take one thing," Robert said.

The king breathed gustily. "And that's my favor?"

"Nay. Your friendship."

Henry turned paler. "Don't ask it. Friends give me betrayal and I return death. Name me marks or crowns. Or a castle. Name a title. Name gold. Gold bought Scrope. It will buy any man, therefore."

"Sire," Robert said, "a dog will give protection and listen for noises in the night, and cost you nothing besides."

"My brother Clarence lies sick in England," the king said softly. "My brother Gloucester lies wounded in this camp. My brother Bedford who governs England is weak and they could overcome him. Look —your sword is by your side, and mine's in the corner behind you. We're alone. If I was dead tonight, Rob, the Earl of March would have the throne and he looks to another for advice. You'd have a kingdom to loot."

The hurt was plain in the king. He could not know it himself, but it showed in his eyes.

"I will not betray you," Robert said.

"All men do," the king said carelessly, as if it were a trifle of which he made nothing. "Soon or late. Scrope and Cambridge, York, Oldcastle, Hotspur . . . too many more to name. You're heretic."

"You had heretics for friends when you were prince, sire," Robert reminded him. If he could but sit! The wound was weakening him fast and his knees were trembling under him.

"When I was prince," the king said airily, "when I was prince I did as I pleased, but now I am king and please England. I'll make her queen of nations before I die. I'll rescue the Holy Land from the infidel, and I'll abolish heresy. These three things I vowed when I was crowned. But my family is not long lived. If I can have but one of three, which shall I choose? England or church? England or my immortal soul?"

God help him, Robert thought, here was a man torn to bits.

"I will not choose," the king said decisively. "I will live long enough. Unless I be murdered tonight."

"No man will murder you tonight," Robert said.

"What if the Lollards should plot against me? Who would you serve?"

"If they plot against you, I'll betray them."

"Why, you're only a traitor after all, like York, by nature variable, like straw running rootless before the gasp of any wind!"

"Yet if you persecute the Lollards for their belief," Robert went on doggedly, "then I will cleave to them, for so it says in my Bible here. I will give to the king that which is his, and to my God his own."

"A pretty speech," the king said, with his mouth wry as if he tasted that which was very sour, "and full of logic, but consider, you wear gold and silver and ermine and velvet, and if you are a good Lollard, you should not."

"I see no harm in this," Robert said, "let the others do as they will."

"So," the king concluded, "you hold yourself your own judge."

"Sire, yes."

The king appeared to consider the short reply, and all it meant.

"I had a stallion once," he said, "that would not stay in any pasture, but leaped fences. He was a fine thing to see on a moonlit night, running so free. But he broke his neck at last at a fence I had made higher to contain him."

York had talked so, obliquely; the family had a similar way of stalking around a subject, fencing. It was, Robert decided, best answered in silence, which he gave.

"And yet, he was my favorite," the king said. "I mourned him."

He swung into his pacing up and down, till he turned on Robert again like a man who'd cross swords.

"The men you've killed," he asked abruptly. "Do you see them when they're dead? At night, when you are in your chamber, do you hear them walking?"

"Nay, sire," Robert said. "I sleep."

"Scrope comes at night," the king confided, horrified, "with a bloodied face, and stands in corners. How can his face be bloody, when he has no head? I hear him. I hear him now, outside."

"The guards are walking in the rain," Robert said.

"I hear assassins everywhere," the king said.

"They'll not come nigh this night," Robert said. "I have a hundred archers out there, watching."

"Tell me," the king asked, with his head to one side, "do you think me a coward?"

Robert shook his head slowly. "A coward would have killed the Earl of March in Southampton," he said, "with good reason to be published. But you let him live, and kept the knife at your throat."

"He wasn't guilty," King Henry said, as if annoyed.

Then a great noise came, a crashing as of a forest falling, and the king spun toward it with his hand flashing to his swordless side.

"The burning barns," Robert said quietly. "The roofs are falling in."

Henry's face contorted, as he thought of his dead archers; fifteen hundred would never leave this field.

"How many Lollards among them?" he asked.

"Full half's a fair score," Robert said. "Heretics burning, sire, but for you."

The king gave him a look of anger.

"And of every two men walking in London," Robert said, "one's a Lollard. Consider a persecution. London would rise; if London, Wales where there are Lollards; if Wales, then Ireland where there are none; and Scotland scenting battle will catch fire and revolt."

"I put down one rebellion of Lollards," the king said grimly.

"They were not Lollards, but such rabble as surges to any civil discontent, and leaderless besides."

"But now there are leaders, you mean, in London. My father always used to say, when I was small, if we can reach London, we're safe. I was twelve, I think, one Christmastide when my uncle of York had been at his plotting. We rode in haste to London, and she sheltered us. London ever meant safety to me once. Now it's full of Lollards, and they give me a choice—my throne or my soul."

"They're Englishmen," Robert said, "and loyal."

"My spaniel is loyal," the king said bitterly. "One night she barked, and when I sought to quiet her, I saw a foot beneath an arras. There was a killer hid and she yapped at him. The guard came for her barking, else I'd not be here. Clarence would rule if she had not barked and warned me. He thinks you useful. He does not love Lollards, but he'd forgive one heretic if he were useful. He'd forgive the prince of hell! You'd make a sharp tool, Rob, and dangerous, for when such turn, the hand bleeds. How could I reward you to make you faithful to the death?"

Robert did not answer.

"I could have kept Scrope," the king said now. "I saw at the end he was slipping from me. I'd known him all his life. I knew every mood, how he moved, how he thought, what he would do in any situation. I knew when the friendship broke and he stayed only for power. I could have given him more gold, more than the French. I could have held him. Still, there is ever another to offer more! But I should have paid him, and held him a while . . . a man needs another. I should have flung him gold and kept him for a little time. I do not know you. How do you think? What do you want? Every man demands something. What do you want? I'll have my answer, Rob! I command it now, what do you want of me?"

"Friendship, sire," Robert said.

"Never ask it!" the king said passionately. "Nay . . . nay . . . I'll give even that. Recant, put aside this heresy, and you'll stand among my earls. I swear it!"

"I believe as I must," Robert said. Not one step backward. Like Oldcastle.

"Only God knows what's in you," the king said, "I cannot judge." He came closer, intense, and lowered his voice. The firelight was red on his pallid face. "You would have ordered them dead?" he asked, anxiously.

The murdered Frenchmen again; the man could not forget them.

"It was England or France," Robert said, "I know how I would choose and never let it trouble me again."

"But you would have ordered them dead?"

"Every man," Robert said.

The king stared into his face.

"I believe you," he said. "In this I believe you."

He sat down on the three-legged stool as if he could not stand any longer, and in the same moment, there came a tap on the door. The king's head snapped to attention.

Robert walked over. Two of his archers stood outside in the rain, grinning. The king's guards stood aside, alert and suspicious, with lanterns making pools of light in the mud.

"I have food, Sir Robert," one of the archers said smugly, delighting in the *Sir*. "We looted it from the Frenchmen. They had too much wine!"

"Not wine," Robert said. Wine would look like blood to a man squeamish after battle and nervous after dark. "Beer. That's beer? Roll the cask in."

The king watched, as if about to leap away. The archers carefully ignored him and got out as fast as they could, leaving drops of wet all over the dirt floor, and a wet cask inside the door, besides some food in a blanket. The door shut, and the archers' voices faded. The guards began their walking in the mud again.

Robert unrolled the blanket, and saw bread and cheese inside.

"Now you've turned lackey," the king jeered. "Knighting made a kitchen knave of you!"

But he watched as Robert knocked the cask open and filled some pewter mugs the archers had thought to throw in with the food. He left one beside the king without a word, kept one and extended the other. Wat scuttled out of a shadow to seize it. The king started perceptibly.

"I had forgot him!" he exclaimed.

"He can be trusted not to speak," Robert said.

Wat vanished back into his shadow, and turned to the sound of noisy swallowing and a smacking of thirsty lips. In the firelight, the king looked down at the mug beside him. Finally he picked it up and peered into it suspiciously, as if to see poison bubbling there, green and acrid and smoking.

Robert tossed his down, and needed it for steadying; the wound made him feverish and weak.

For his part the king suddenly drank and flung the mug in a corner, and rising in the same motion went to the pallet, where he dropped down crosslegged and reached over to pick up a harp that leaned against the wall.

"Where were you raised in Wales?" he asked.

"The castle of Llewellyn ap Gryffyd, sire," Robert answered.

"That bandit," the king said disdainfully, and plucked at the harpstrings. "I never thought integrity lived near him."

"Why, sire," Robert said, "that was his wife."

The king looked over quickly.

"Did she leave you to nurses?" he asked.

"A nurse might have had a lighter hand," Robert said.

"She wanted you to grow well-mannered," the king said seriously.

"She swore she'd cure my stubbornness," Robert replied.

"In that she failed," the king said. "Was it she who taught you the Welsh songs I heard you sing at Harfleur?"

"Welsh, and French," Robert admitted.

"I have enough of Frenchmen," the king said sharply, "but I'd hear the Welsh tongue now." He struck the harp so it resounded.

So in the gloomy cottage they sang, Robert and the king, in Welsh together. They grew thirsty and drank beer. It tasted better as they drank more, until at last Robert swore the bitter stuff was as good as ever at the Pope's Head in London, and then it was a step to the tale of the riot there; lively talk with a pall of sadness, since York was dead this day.

The king listened avidly. "Is there beer left?" He waved the mug at Wat, who was serving them. "Give me some of that bread. I was jailed once, when I was Prince of Wales. The sheriff said he cared not if I was king of the gypsies."

The king chuckled, eyes brighter with the drinking, and then with wit and charm and laughter, told tales of adventure when he was prince. He was winsome.

"You should have been one of us," he concluded, "but that you are too young; yet you'd have made another like—"

Suddenly he was sober-faced, and broke off to another subject.

"It was Wales I loved the best," he said, "and the fighting there. It took my fortune, for my father never sent money to pay the soldiers. Luckily, I had the revenues from Lancaster, and used them so. I got naught of Wales save poverty and scars as keepsakes." He fingered the scar below his eye. "Glendower was the great enemy then, a magician. He made spells, but he was practical too and sent assassins to help his spells. Before God, and this is true, we found one under my bed, and how he got in, no one ever found. A guard was bribed, no doubt. I wonder what he had of it, what price was offered and taken to let a murderer in. How much am I worth, do you suppose?"

His eyes were narrowed now.

Robert smiled. "I left a great heiress behind to follow you for two shillings a day."

The king laughed, bitterly. "Study law," he advised. "I'll make you my chief justice."

Then he put his harp aside and lay back on the pallet and talked up to the ceiling and writhing smoke of Hotspur and hunting in the mountains, and did not seem to notice he was talking Welsh.

At length, after a long silence, he said, "Rob?" and turned a little to see if he still sat by the fire.

"Sire?"

"Rob, this friendship, I cannot give it. There is none left to give. I have been betrayed too often."

Robert inclined his head, and the king turned back to his staring straight up. He began to talk again, very quietly in Welsh, of fighting in Wales and writing begging letters, that were never answered, to his father for the soldiers' pay. Finally he fell asleep as he was talking, with his harp beside him and his sword across the room.

Wat came softly from his corner, as if he was stalking a deer. He had a straw-filled pallet in his arms and set it tight against the door and lay down there with a grunt. Robert moved another pallet with his foot near to the fire, and sat upon it. His head drooped. He lay down, unwilling, curled up a little to ease his side. He closed his eyes but a moment. He feared to sleep. He forced his eyes open unwillingly. They closed despite him and the pain.

He dreamed of Constance; fair dreams and ill dreams. He thought she cried out to him from Calais. Then he was in battle; and out of it. He walked among murdered Frenchmen with horror and the dead hands reached up to him. All things mixed, then smoothed and darkened. He knew he dreamed, but he thought he wakened. He stood on a road leading nowhere, vanishing in darkness. He heard Constance calling to him, and he turned away. Then he turned back and saw her, very sharply and yet blurred, both at once; there was light between them. He heard himself call out, and he tried to go to her, but slowly, slowly, like walking against a strong tide; and she vanished.

The anguish woke him. For an instant he was all confusion. He was still walking in the dark place; but staring at a strange roof. He was very cold; he ached; his side was throbbing.

He sat up stiffly, favoring the hurt, and stared about him dazed. Rain had put out the fire and nothing was left but gray ashes. He was numb and blew on his hands, and saw light sky through the roof hole. Had he then slept all the night? Horrified, he moved stiffly around. Henry was sitting crosslegged on the pallet with his back against the wall surveying him.

"You talk in your sleep," he announced, "and that knave of yours snores like a bear."

Robert got up with difficulty and jabbed Wat in the ribs with a toe. Wat's snore choked off with a gurgle, and he sat up.

"Holy St. Anne," he groaned, "I'm one ache from nap to toe from fighting." He got to his feet.

The king stood also.

Wat kicked the straw sack aside and opened the door. Wet air rushed in. The guards turned to stare. Robert's archers under trees looked glad to see their master. The king picked up his mantle and walked over to survey the day.

"We'll have more rain," he remarked and secured the mantle around him.

He glanced at Robert impersonally and walked outside and away, a taggle of nobility coming quickly to walk beside him.

Wat said, "A royal memory is a short one."

And so, Robert thought, he'd lost. Well, he still had his head and must use it. The Welsh nature had played him false. Now let the Saxon judge. Where should he go? Not London and endanger Constance more with the disfavor he was in. Back to the countess, who'd welcome him? If he could not fight for England, he would not fight for France. Wales then, bare mountains, and a bandit's life. But he'd not start by looking like the rogue he'd be.

"I'll find a barber," he said, "and you see that all the men are fed and mounted. Get extra horses from the French camp if you can."

Wat nodded and went happily off, and Robert found his barber, and tilted his chin to the sky.

The Saxon nature had decided, but the Welsh was being perverse. It wanted to go to London, and it could not. But where was the Welsh cleverness that sent a man skidding swiftly around all obstacles the Saxon swore it could not climb? They said a true Welshman was never set aback.

He watched past the barber's earnest face for a flight of birds. But the birds were in the trees, avoiding flight. He thought of clouds to guide him, but all the sky was overcast. Of winds, to give direction, but all was still. There were no omens.

There was his vow spoken in St. Martin's and he must keep it, as he kept them all, to the very letter and exact word.

Ah! the Welsh blood said. *Ah!*

The barber cried out he must not start so!

He had sworn to marry no *maid*, and he had meant Constance, but she was married now. It was a loophole, a legality, a technical definition of a word, but a Welsh mind could fit through. He was joyous. The vow was at an end. The barber begged him not to jerk, else his throat were cut.

But her husband lived! He was quiet enough for the barber.

God, this thinking in exhaustion, when a mind could not examine all at once but leaped from part to part. He was out of favor with the king, and he was Lollard, and this was the basis of all. It was Wales, and only Wales, and he must run like Oldcastle.

The barber muttered, "It's done" with relief, showing he did not like these nervous customers.

"Ay," Robert said. "It's done."

He walked slowly back through the mud. The king was his sole answer and the king refused him.

So be it! So be it! his Saxon blood said, despising the mercurial Welsh that would hope in hopelessness. *If he'll have none of me, then I'll have none of him!*

He was passing a group of nobles drawing maps with a stick in the mud. The king was among them, watching the design.

Robert stiffened his back despite his wound and walked disdainfully past, and away to where Wat saddled Bay Cornwall.

"Take it off again," he said.

Wat stared, not understanding.

"Take off the saddle," he said distinctly, "and put it on some captured nag. This horse goes back to the king."

He's proud, King Henry thought, glancing furtively after the Welshman. *Be it a vice or a virtue, he's proud and stubborn and he'll never come to me again.*

One of his nobles spoke, louder than necessary, recalling his attention.

"No," he said, impatiently, "Sir Gilbert will command the main. I'll go with the van."

A disbelieving hesitation. Then three at once protested inadvisability, with unconquered French still ahead and some sixty or seventy miles to Calais. It sounded well enough, but the Welshman was out of sight and King Henry felt suddenly unsafe. Any of these nobles here would be glad to betray him for the sake of the ransom they'd lost with the killings. Clarence sick and Gloucester wounded, and who was to stand by him?

". . . feeling unwell, sire?"

"As well as any man after a hard fight," he said brusquely, and indicated the broken branch was to resume its tracing of a route in the mud.

He would not reign long, and he might leave a civil war behind him. He could weep for England, poor in all but courage, with rebellion on her borders and heresy in her heart. He would never reach the Holy Land. Time was too short to unite the Church. There was left, then, but one vow of the three he'd made. England.

They were badgering him now about what was permitted each man from the loot, for they were short of carts and horses to carry it away.

"Only armor," he said, "to replace what a man has lost, and such small things as can be carried on one's person. The carts are for the wounded. I want to reach Calais before Burgundy stamps on my tail."

Trust, he must have one man he could trust. All his friends were gone and he feared to make new ones. Conciliate the Lollards. That was the Welshman's price. It would be Oldcastle over again.

Henry said, "Let a list be made of the names of all men who died here today, that they may be remembered."

Half of them were Lollards. They had died as stoutly as the rest. For England.

Rob will go to Clarence, or Clarence will send for him. Clarence liked the sound of little bells. The sound of safety. Clarence had thought much of Robert Heartless, and yet Robert Heartless had left him without hesitation. *I'll follow you,* he'd said in St. Martin's church in Harfleur, and Clarence had sailed without him. He'd been promised nothing, given nothing, but the horse Bay Cornwall and that was of necessity. Bay Cornwall, seen again in battle, his scarlet drapes replaced by scarlet blood. The Welshman had started away from his dubbing. *Did he think I meant to kill him?*

How long could a man rule when he refused food for that it might be poisoned; went sleepless for that the guards might be bribed; kept his thoughts to himself till they burst his head because he dared not share them?

I talked too much last night. I said things I should not have spoken. And so had the Welshman, in his sleep, curled on his pallet by the fire, hugging his pain with both arms. *Constance,* he had said, over and over. And then he'd said one other name clearly. *Oldcastle.* That had brought back memories. *I trusted Oldcastle, but Oldcastle did not trust me. He bolted for his castle in the night and locked his gates, and I did not know he'd gone until they told me.*

A booted foot with a golden spur thrust out over the map of mud and crushed the marks. The nobles were taking their leave, to pull the remnants of the army together for the march.

Someone said, "Look!"

And King Henry looked.

It was the warhorse Bay Cornwall coming, led by the lout who'd snored all night. The horse wore his chamfron-and-pike, and his bridle of scarlet with leopards, but his back was naked. The lout led him to one of the nobles.

"Here," he said in his hoarse voice, insolence barely veiled. "Here, sir, is the king's property. Robert Heartless returns him."

Utter silence. The nobles looked stealthily at Henry.

Proud, he was proud. He'd fling back a gift if he could not revere the giver. Here was a man who kept nothing if his conscience would not let him. Here was a man who could not be bought!

The choice had been very clear to Henry last night if he would favor the Welshman or not. It was his immortal soul or England, and he'd thought on it all night. If he persecuted these heretics, his soul was safe; but the rebellion in London would shake the land. Was he first man or king? If man, his soul was his chief concern. If king, he must put his people first. There had been his choice. Man or king, which was he?

But the choice was gone now. He'd decided too late. Robert Heartless was proud. *He'll not come to me again, and I cannot go to him.*

Chapter 34

ROBERT HEARTLESS stood on the road holding a gray horse, with his men behind him, as the battle-weary English took formation, cursing at sore muscles, hiding small bits of loot in their clothes, and mourning comrades who'd died in the night.

Wat said, "And the first time I counted, there were eighty-five, but the second, eighty-seven. Shall I count again?"

"No," Robert said, "we'll call it eighty-six."

Wat nodded, relieved. "A proper band," he said. "Not so large we cannot scatter and disappear; yet not so small we cannot attack a manor house. Here comes the king. He's on Bay Cornwall."

The king rode by, bareheaded in the rain that fell straight to the earth, his nobles silent around him. He did not look their way.

Wat spat. "Well may he watch for enemies," he said, "he has a gift for making them."

Robert mounted his horse, and the others did the same. They waited again, with rain running down their faces. Robert contemplated the field of Agincourt. Wreckage, broken carts, arrows, bows, discarded lances, dead horses and dead men, and carrion birds rising gorged and flapping whenever they were disturbed, which was often, for the French peasants were gleaning still of the fruits of this black harvest, stripping French bodies. As they went they left behind the naked, gleaming whitely. Robert moved his left arm restlessly on the pommel of the saddle, trying to give his aching side ease. Death was for the losers. For the victors, he knew not. But the man who stepped backward never forged ahead.

The dukes of Orléans and Bourbon, Frenchmen who'd escaped the tragic fate of other prisoners, now rode past with their guard to join the van. The army was formed and ready to march.

There was one last duty left. Robert swung his gray horse around and out onto the battlefield and rode up to the head of the formation. His archers followed, shouting and glad to move. Eyes turned to their noise. The king swerved his horse around to face the din.

Robert pulled his gray horse up sharp and wheeled it sideways though it cost him a gritting of teeth for the wracking he'd got. His men piled into each other noisily, trying to stop as short.

Robert looked at the king directly. Let no man say he was one for skulking. He'd not go as Oldcastle had, in the night.

"Sire," he said, "I would have your permission to retire, and leave you."

"I gave you warning," the king said softly. "I gave you warning. My friends die young."

Then he looked around at his nobles and touched the scar at his eye.

"You had bells," he said, speaking distinctly now. "Are they lost that you do not wear them?"

"Sire, no. I have them."

"Then put them on," the king said, and that was blunt command.

Wat rode instantly to help him. Everyone waited amazed on this wild whim of the king. Wat lifted the bells out of their cloth behind the saddle, and they jingled merrily. They had no gift but laughter, and they tinkled in the midst of death.

The king watched without expression as Wat buckled the belt around Robert's waist. The gray horse pranced impatiently as the other animal pressed into him. Then Wat dropped back.

The gray horse curveted and the bells jingled again.

"Sire," Robert said, "I ask permission to leave you."

"I refuse it," King Henry said. "Ride at my back."

The nobles all caught in their breath sharply.

"So long as I hear your bells, Rob," the king said, "I will never look behind."

They marched, winding slowly through the field of Agincourt. With the vanguard went the king, riding between the captive dukes of Orléans and Bourbon, those mortal enemies. Behind the king was Robert Heartless with his murderous crew of archers.

Her husband was old, and old men are fragile. They did not live forever. If he must wait a little, nothing came easy on this earth and all must be hard-earned. He had lived long enough to discover it.

The peasant women watched the army go, and marked one man for his handsome face. A sodden black mantle fell loose from his shoulders over the rump of his horse, with the hood down on his shoulders so he might see in all directions. His face was tanned, with a wound-pallor beneath. His eyes were narrowed against the weather, and his mouth set hard. He carried himself strangely in the saddle, bent slightly forward and to the left.

His identity was plain to all with wit enough to read it. He wore gold spurs, so he was a knight. He carried a battered shield of a green tincture, with a golden lion thereon above the motto WAKE ME NO MAN. These were the arms of the Fairfields, carried with bloody honor at Crécy and Poitiers. And Agincourt.

This then, was Sir Robert Fairfield, knight, riding on to Calais and the lady waiting there.